# pretend for me

haircuts and heartthrobs
book one

**Swati M.H.**

Kismet Publishing

Copyright © 2024 by Swati M.H.

All rights reserved.

No part of this book may be reproduced in any form or by any electronic or mechanical means, including information storage and retrieval systems, without written permission from the author, except for the use of brief quotations in a book review.

This is a work of fiction. Names, characters, businesses, places, incidents, and events are either a product of the author's imagination or used fictitiously.

Cover: Cover Me Darling

Editing: Silvia's Reading Corner

# also by swati m.h.

**Elements of Rapture Series**

Adrift

**(Forbidden, single dad/nanny, grumpy/sunshine, age gap)**

Ascend

**(Marriage of Convenience, single-mom, friends to lovers romance)**

Ablaze

**(Brother's best friend, friends-to-lovers, one bed, firefighter romance)**

Abyss

**(Enemies to lovers, dad's best friend, workplace romance)**

**MomComs Series**

Mother Pucker

**(Hockey star, single mom, reverse age-gap, doctor/patient romcom)**

**Feel the Beat Series**

My Perfect Remix

**(Single-dad, friends-to lovers romance)**

My Beautiful Chaos

**(Fake-relationship, second chance romance)**

My Darling Neighbor

**(Enemies to lovers, surprise pregnancy romance)**

## **Fated Love Series**

Kismet in the Sky

**(Slightly forbidden, second chance, workplace romance)**

Surrender to the Stars

**(Enemies to lovers, hospital romance)**

# author's note

Content warning: This book is intended for mature audiences. It deals with themes related to parental death, saying goodbye to a parent, and cancer that may be triggering for some readers.

*To my brother.
I still can't believe you traded me your $20 for 4 quarters to go play a couple of dumb games in the arcade in 1994. No, you can't have your money back. I taught you a valuable lesson about scammers that day.*

# piper's rabbit sex playlist

**"Pony"** by Genuine
**"My Neck, My Back (Lick It)"** by Chia
**"Work From Home"** by Fifth Harmony, Ty Dolla $ign
**"How Many Licks?"** by HLil' Kim, Sisqo
**"Candy Shop"** by 50 Cent, Olivia
**"I'll Make Love To You"** by Boyz II Men
**"Peaches & Cream"** by 112
**"What's Your Fantasy"** by Ludacris, Shawnna
**"Doin' It"** by LL Cool J
**"Let's Get It On"** by Marvin Gaye

one
# piper
You're So Long and Thick

"You're wearing two different kinds of sneakers."

"Hmm?" I ask Nisha as I pluck a peppermint candy from the bowl at our cashier stand and pop it into my mouth. I quickly spit it out into my hand, giving the offensive thing a disdainful and betrayed look because I'd forgotten to take off the plastic.

My best friend gives me an unimpressed once-over.

After fifteen years, however, her once-overs no longer faze me like they did in high school.

I follow Nisha's gaze to my feet, noting that, indeed, I'm wearing my black Chucks on one foot and my white Dr. Scholl's slip-ons on the other.

"Huh," I state, blinking at a sloth's pace. My eyelids feel like they're weighted down with anchors. "Well, would you look at that! At least one foot got it right."

I'm talking about the foot concealed under my Dr. Scholl's shoe, of course, because as every salon stylist worth their weight in salt will tell you, blisters are like vaginas—they can't handle a little friction without making a mess. And standing some days for close to twelve hours meant I had little time for friction and messes in my footsies. My nether regions, however? I've always been more than amenable to friction and messes there.

My eyes climb back up to my upturned palm with the plastic-wrapped peppermint I'd spit out, as if seeing it for the first time. I unwrap it properly before popping it back into my mouth, hoping it'll wake me up. At the very least, it should stop my yawning epidemic. I heard somewhere peppermint is supposed to help wake you up.

"Or is it lines of coke?" Hmm. My brows furrow in contemplation. Perhaps it was the lines of coke I'd heard about. Not that I'm going to conduct a scientific experiment to compare or anything. At this point, I'm hoping the peppermint comes through for me.

"Lines of coke? What?" Nisha's stare stays on me, the little crease in between her shapely dark brows the only indication she's wondering if I've completely lost my marbles. "Are you feeling okay? You're acting weirder than usual."

I grin at her, seeing her through the slits my eyes are now peeking out of. "How do you always find new ways to flatter me, bestie?"

Shaking her head, her silky black hair swaying like she's starring in her own shampoo commercial, she taps the screen of her iPad with her stylus. "Anyway, we've got a packed day ahead. The Hammond party is coming in later this afternoon for Mark's pre-wedding treatments. Both Sarina and I have them covered."

"As if that's a hardship," I quip. "If Mark's best men look anything like Mark, I'd be happy to cover them for you."

Nisha continues, undeterred by my innuendo, "Mr. Rothschild should be in any minute, and since he refuses to work with any other stylist, I can get his regular service done in about forty-five minutes."

My two best friends, Nisha and her sister Sarina, work as full-time stylists at my San Jose-based luxury men's salon,

*Haircuts and Heartthrobs*. While the lease is under my name—courtesy of my famous hockey star brother, Rowan Parker—Nisha and Sarina are both partners in the business.

She scans her bright screen, brows lifting. "Oh, and aside from several of your regulars, you also have that new client." She eyes me warily, as if examining a suspiciously ripe avocado. "Dev Menon is coming in this morning at eight-thirty."

"Yup, yup." I nod, holding the back of my hand to my mouth, suppressing another yawn. Clearly, I should have gone with the cocaine instead. Kidding!

Nisha leans in, surveying me again. "Piper, are you on drugs?"

I snort at her unintended pun. "Nah, that stuff I said about the lines of coke was in reference to this peppermint."

My best friend pinches the bridge of her nose in annoyance, a sure sign I'm skating on thin ice. "Do you need to go home? Remember who Dev Menon is? A man richer than God Himself. In fact, I'm pretty sure the Big Guy asked him for a loan."

"Of course, I know who Dev Menon is." Kind of. I've seen him on the cover of business magazines and on a few sidelines of some gossip rags. In each one, he looked like a character from a classic film noir—tall, dark, and intriguing—with a gaze that could both charm and intimidate. "And I promise, no drugs in this system besides my regular baby blockers and multivitamins." I pause, remembering one more. "Oh, and migraine meds. I took some right as I felt one coming on this morning, but I'm A-OK now." I wave a thumb in front of her face with conviction.

She swats my hand. "Did you chase them down with tequila? I swear, you're acting like a malfunctioning robot."

"You and your compliments." I poke my best friend in the arm, making her frown deepen, before I bend to pet Vajayjay. She's decided to bid me a good morning, coiling around my

Chuck Taylor-adorned ankle. I direct an equally warm greeting back at her, wiggling the tips of my fingers under her jaw just the way she likes. "Who's the most beautiful pussy in the land?"

Vajayjay responds with a royal meow to her awarded title before letting me pick her up. She's one of our trio of resident hairless cats at the salon, and the one who's taken the most liking to me. The other two—Beaver and Snatch—have found their own favorite human in my best friends.

"Yes, you are," I coo, scratching her behind her ear before following Nisha down the corridor with my cat in tow. When my best friend turns to look at me over her shoulder with that same concerned look, I wave at her with another yawn. "I'm just a little sleepy, that's all."

"Sleepy?" Sarina pokes her head out of her room, her ringlets a stark contrast to that of her twin sister's sleek mane, despite their shared tan complexion. "You sleep at ten and wake up at seven. I'm pretty sure bears hibernate in shorter intervals." She scrolls her eyes down my torso, taking in my rainbow-colored cropped top and low-hanging ripped jeans, before landing at my feet. "And what's with the Coachella cosplay? Did you lose a bet with a hippie or something?"

My other best friend, Sarina Arora, ladies and gentlemen. A fierce single mom, and the reigning champion of brutal honesty, if Sarina has ever minced her words, it was only to season them with sarcasm and sass. She's also the only twenty-nine-year-old I know who prefers spicy mustard in an unhealthy sort of way. That, and the show, *Unsolved Mysteries*.

I roll my sleepy eyes. At least, I try to, but it's entirely possible I look like one of the zombies from *The Walking Dead*, having lost my pupils somewhere at the back of my head. "Oh, hush."

I suppose I don't look the part of a luxury salon owner on any given day, but I might be stretching even my own style limits today. And for the life of me, I can't figure out what my problem is. Why the hell am I so sleepy?

Sarina isn't wrong. I do tend to maintain a pretty regimented sleep schedule—at least on days that the *Oscar Mayer* brothers aren't tag-teaming me well into the night. But I try to keep those to a minimum of one night over the weekend. As much as I love my vagina getting pummeled by two beautiful men whose names I can't remember even six months after having met other parts of their bodies, a girl's gotta prioritize her beauty sleep the rest of the week.

*Omar and Miles?*
*Oden and Murphy?*

What are their names? I wonder for the next twenty minutes while I prepare my station, ensuring I have the tools and products I need for the day.

"Ugh, whatever," I muse, setting Vajayjay on the ground. It's not like it really matters if I remember their names. They're happy being dubbed Oscar and Mayer based on their rather, uh, endowed endowments, and I'm content not exchanging mundane small-talk, pretending we're interested in anything more than our physical attributes and prowess in bed.

It's the reason I give most men I sleep with names like Jimmy Dean and Bratwurst. Keeps things nice and uninvolved. Untangled.

Joshua, our receptionist and salon manager, waltzes into my room, offering his cheerful morning greeting, though it dims slightly as he assesses my outfit. He hands me a load of laundry I'd placed in the dryer last night.

While *Haircuts and Heartthrobs* is always booked out, the fall season tends to be our busiest, with Nisha, Sarina, and me in back-to-back appointments. We have other service providers at the salon, too, including two full-time massage therapists, a duo of manicurists, an esthetician, and an acupuncturist.

Despite our occasional conversation to expand our stylist team to accommodate the seasonal rush, we've managed a delicate balance with our current staff that none of us wants to shake up.

Vajayjay hangs out in her cat tree in my room while I fold the hair cutting capes and towels and set them in a cubby. Afterward, I scroll through the pictures Rowan sent me of him and Shayla with my six-month-old niece at Kai's first hockey game.

My little brother is a defenseman for the Boston Bolts and lives with his wife Shayla, her son from her previous marriage Kai, and their new daughter Kiara. And while my brother and I don't see each other often, given I'm in California and he's in Massachusetts, we talk almost every day.

Though currently, I'm a little peeved at him, too. It's not his fault per se, but since I have no one else to take my frustration out on, he's the lucky guy.

Earlier this summer, *Haircuts and Heartthrobs* was set to launch a new marketing campaign, with Rowan as our embodiment of refined masculinity and timeless elegance, given my brother is known for his off-ice style and fashion sense. But just recently, Mane Masters, a well-known men's grooming chain, secured sponsorship rights with the Boston Bolts, so Rowan had to drop out as the face of our salon to avoid a conflict of interest.

I'm mid-yawn, my eyes heavier than they were when I walked in, when there's a knock on my door. I tear my gaze away from my phone, thoughts still swirling with who could replace Rowan in the campaign, when I see Joshua standing beside another man.

A man who could put every other high-powered, high-browed, high-maintenance man who walks through this salon to shame.

A man who'd exude power and wealth, despite his richer-than-God billionaire status, for the mere fact that he's breathing at all.

A man so handsome, my nipples pearl inside my bra.

He regards me from head to toe, clearly noting my eclectic get up. *Yeah, I'm with you, buddy. I look like a hot mess.* Why he's not turning around to head for the hills right this second is anyone's guess.

"H-hi!" I stammer out a high-pitched greeting, sounding like a chipmunk with a helium addiction.

"Piper, this is Mr. Dev Menon—"

"Please, just Dev," Dev interrupts, cutting Joshua off mid-introductions, the deep tenor of his voice betraying his nonchalance.

The man is about as nonchalant as high-noon tea with the Queen.

"Very well. Dev, this is Piper. She'll be taking care of you today." Joshua gleams, waving over to me before leaving.

With some effort, I pick myself up from my seat near the shampoo bowl and find my hand encapsulated in his rather large, warm one. My heart races as my eyes connect with his.

"I'm Piper." I give his hand an overly enthusiastic shake and ignore the wave of goosebumps traveling up my arm.

"So we've established," Dev replies, a tiny smirk betraying his stony, well-manicured demeanor.

"Right. Well, just making sure you heard me loud and clear. Never know when a client is hard of hearing." My words tumble out like a runaway train. "Piper, not Peeper or Pipper. My brother sometimes calls me Pepper; he even has me saved in his contacts as such. But nope, I'm just plain old *Piper Parker*." I enunciate for his benefit, "Piper Parker picked a peck of preening peacocks."

Seriously, someone punch me.

Dev stares at me in half-concern and half-bewilderment while I laugh in *full* embarrassment. But clearly, my embarrassment doesn't outweigh my self-preservation because mortifyingly, I trudge on.

"My parents were going to name me Peter, you see." Dear God, please stop this verbal sewage. It's rare, but this is what happens whenever I get nervous. I babble on until someone—usually Nisha—slaps me upside the head like an old glitching TV. "You know, Peter Parker, like Spiderman?"

Dev blinks at me without so much as a word. He's not a talker, this one.

"You know, *'With great power comes great responsibility,'* and all that?" I continue, trying to explain Spiderman's curse. "But then I turned out to be a girl and—"

"Ms. Piper?" Dev finally interrupts me, releasing his hand from my never-ending handshake. "Could we get started, say, in this decade? I have an important board meeting in an hour."

"Yes! Yes, of course." I jump into action, waving him over to the salon chair. "Can I get you something to drink?"

He shakes his head before his sharp eyes sweep over my room, adorned with masculine decor and hues. An oversized TV dominates one wall, while shelves lined with vintage whiskey bottles and grooming products flank another. He also takes note of the cat tree in one corner but doesn't question it.

He settles himself in between me and the mirror, and I adjust his chair to the correct height, noting the thickness of his locks and the clear whites around his deep chestnut eyes. They're framed with a dark thicket of lashes that would make models weep.

And let's not even get started on his razor-edged jawline or the perfect amount of dark scruff over his tanned cheeks. And I'll definitely steer clear of his apparent rows of abdominal muscles and biceps that could crack walnuts. Focus on the haircut, Piper. Leave the ogling for later.

From my limited knowledge, Dev is the heir to his father's multi-billion-dollar tech business. His father is of Indian descent, his mother American. And while Dev was born and raised solely in the States, he's fluent in over seven languages.

Things you learn while *Entertainment Tonight* is blaring in the background as you beg your rabbits to breed...

I sweep my fingers into his hair, grazing my nails over his scalp, feeling Dev shift in his seat with a clearing of his throat. Our eyes connect in the mirror before he quickly averts his gaze. "God, you're so long and thick."

Eyes colliding again, my cheeks heat in mortification, but I swear the slightest flare erupts inside his molten browns.

It's my turn to clear my throat. "I mean, your hair is so full and wavy. A hair stylist's dream, really. Now, what are you thinking of doing today? A trim or going shorter?"

"Just a trim, please."

"Can do!" I say, just as my curious cat makes her way out to inspect our new client. I'm sure she's wondering the same thing I am: what is that delicious cologne he's wearing?

Dev follows Vajayjay through the mirror with mild discomfort. "Is that...? What is that?"

Before I can answer, and to my utter disbelief, Vajayjay hops into his lap. This abused feline, distrustful of all men— the same one we rescued with her siblings from a run-down trailer park after discovering the junkies living there were putting out cigarette butts on their flesh—actually decides to cozy up on a man's lap for the first time in the three years I've had her.

My jaw drops, and considering everything else that's spewed past my lips over the past few minutes, I really should have snapped it closed again.

But of course, I don't.

"She's my hairless pussy, Vajayjay. And it seems she's rather fond of you."

two
# piper

Feel Free To Work Your Fingers
In Her

D ev's hands hover apprehensively over my cat, inspecting her with the same cautious interest one might reserve for a slimy tapeworm peeking out of a pile of poop. "Does she bite?"

My lips curl into a smile. He's making this too easy. "My pussy or my cat? Because depending on which one you're asking about, it would be a different answer."

For reasons beyond my comprehension, watching this gorgeous and intimidating man nervously consider how to pet a cat is both charming and hilarious. Seeing this softer side of him, so far removed from the imposing and influential man who came in not too long ago, eases my nerves and makes me feel more comfortable around him.

"Your pus—" The slightest tint settles on Dev's cheeks, and I have to hold back my giggle. "Uh, this cat."

"Oh. Then no, she doesn't bite." I smile at the gray and pink feline now curled on Dev's lap before trying to suppress another yawn with the back of my hand. "Goodness, me! I don't know what's gotten into me today. I've been yawning all morning."

Dev tentatively strokes Vajayjay's back, his fingers

exploring her wrinkled skin. I remember that feeling—the first time I held her. Her flesh felt like oiled leather, and I remember thinking how beautiful she was. Unique and misunderstood.

Mom's always said the same about me.

Reaching for my phone, I adjust the lights and music to create a tranquil spa ambiance. Based on Dev's preferences in his online profile, he prefers a spa setting to watching sports, unlike most of my clients. Though, now I'm curious if he likes hockey. Because if he doesn't like hockey—especially my Bolts—this will never work.

Wait. *What* will never work? What is 'this' I'm even referring to?

Lord, I'm sleepy.

The lights dim just enough that I can still see what I need for his haircut before the sounds of a thunderstorm stream through the speakers.

Returning to my spot behind his chair, I place a hand on his shoulder. "Want me to move my Vajayjay off your lap?" I suppress another giggle at the way Dev visibly tenses under me. "I mean, I don't have to. She can stay there while I shampoo your hair and massage your shoulders." I press my lips together almost painfully before adding, "She's a big fan of massages herself. Feel free to work your fingers in her."

Dev's eyes flick to mine in the mirror, and I struggle to maintain an innocent facade.

"I was talking about my pussy . . . cat, that is."

The blush creeping into his cheeks is priceless, and while I should feel guilty about making him squirm, it's too fun to mess with him. I wish I could take a picture because I can firmly say I've never seen something more endearing in my life.

He's about to speak when Beaver and Snatch prowl into the room, stirring Vajayjay awake. She cranes her neck to give her siblings a warning glare, as if letting them know not to encroach on her territory.

To my utter shock, however—twice in the last fifteen minutes to be sure—the other two cats make their way, albeit hesitantly, toward Dev, circling his ankles.

*What the hell is going on?* Is this man a pussy whisperer of sorts? Does he emit a secret scent that lures felines? *Am I a feline?* Because I feel pretty damn lured in myself.

I'm transfixed by the scene unfolding before me: my three typically standoffish cats, who shy away from interacting with our regular customers, are willingly cozying up to this one as if he's their favorite brand of catnip. Beaver even rubs his neck along the leg of Dev's pants while he watches with unease and a hint of fascination. I'll give it to him, though, he doesn't move or wave them away.

As if laying a firm claim on her man, Vajayjay rises to her paws, arching her back and swatting in their direction with a hiss.

Beaver and Snatch finally get the hint, slinking away from Dev and making their way out of the room. A second later, Vajayjay jumps off Dev's lap and saunters out, giving him a lingering backward glance. I swear there are hearts in her eyes.

Mouth still agape, I stare at Dev. "I have never seen them act like that."

"How many of them do you have?" Dev asks.

"Just those three. The all-white one is Beaver; he's not the friendliest, but he adores Nisha. For some reason, Sarina and I haven't made his shortlist, though. And the overweight one with the brown-tipped ears is Snatch. She's all about Sarina."

I watch Dev's expression during my explanation, realizing he's likely regretting asking.

"Me and my best friends, Nisha and Sarina, rescued them about three years ago from a terrible situation. It was a whole ordeal with cops and fines. But then the three cats needed new homes, and since we suspected they were siblings, we didn't want to separate them. I was going to keep all three, but since Vajayjay and Beaver aren't fond of rabbits, we decided to keep them here. They've learned to stay out of trouble, and we make sure to lock away our tools at the end of the day." I shrug. "Now they're just a part of what makes this salon unique."

"Rabbits? Do you have actual rabbits or is that another euphemism for . . . something else?"

"Oh, you mean like my rabbit vibrator?" I ask, placing a cape casually over his shoulders and making him cough unnecessarily. "I do have one of those, too, but in this case, I mean real rabbits, named Natalie Nutbottom and Kevin. I'm trying to become a breeder, you see, but it hasn't been going well because, no matter what I try, they won't bang."

Dev blinks, probably wishing he never stepped foot into this salon. I don't blame him, because I'm in full-blown oversharing mode again, talking like an auctioneer on crack. It seems Mr. Unflappable in my salon chair knows how to make me feel all out of sorts.

"I see."

Trying to rein myself in—a task I've never been able to accomplish—I ask him to step over to the shampoo sink where he settles himself into the chair before resting his head in the curve of the basin.

I turn on the water, adjusting the temperature. "I'm still reeling from the way my cats took to you," I say, bemused with what I'd just seen. "Those cats don't like anyone. Hell, aside from Vajayjay, they can barely tolerate me!"

"I can't fathom why," he deadpans.

Ignoring his sarcasm, I press on, determined to crack the shell of my all-too-reserved client, who would be perfectly content not to speak for the duration of his service. "I see in your profile you were referred to the salon by my friend Hudson Case. How do you know Hudson?"

He steeples his hands over his abs, and I notice a multicolored temporary tattoo peeking from under his sleeve, a complete contrast to his polished attire. "We're friends."

I wait for him to expand, but Dev just closes his eyes, dismissing any further conversation.

Well, I'm nothing if not persistent. "Did you attend his and Kavi's wedding? She's so beautiful, isn't she? Big Daddy was such a grump before, you know? Well, he's still a grump, but—"

*"Big Daddy?"* Dev's brow lifts as he looks up at me.

I shrug. "Oh yeah, I've always called him Big Daddy. He hates it, but to be honest, it's better than what I call some of the other men in my life. Not that Hudson is *a man in my life* in that way. No sirree, we've never Netflix and chilled, if you know what I mean. I'm referring to the others who I, on weekly occasions, do the horizontal Mambo with. I can't ever seem to recall their names, but the two I hang out with often are Oscar and Mayer. Those aren't their legal names, of course. I mean, they could be; they're perfectly good names. But they don't strike me as an Oscar and Mayer. I had to break things off several months ago with the man I called Franklin, because, *frankly*," I snort, caught off-guard by my own wit, "he was a stage-five clinger. I mean, listen buddy, this was only supposed to be about sex and—"

"Piper?"

"Uh, yes?"

"Please continue the rest of the service in silence."

*Well, okay then*. I mean, I was just getting to the good part about how Franklin and I were arrested for indecent exposure but, *clearly* Mr. Reserved and Cocky isn't into stories that aren't actively making him bazillions.

Duly noted.

That's the last time I opened my mouth!

The warm water cascades over his scalp as I rake my fingers through his soft, wet hair, struggling to keep myself from imagining doing this outside of this salon, where he'd be more than just my client. Because those images—me with him in any other capacity—are utterly ridiculous. The man is only tolerating me because of his precarious position in my sink. And no, unfortunately, "my sink" isn't a euphemism for my vagina.

He wants me to be quiet and get my job done? Fine. That's what I'll do.

Though, I won't lie, it's fucking hard.

I work shampoo into his silky strands, watching Dev's shoulders sink deeper into the edge of the basin. My eyes fixate on the vein on the side of his neck, pulsing with every breath. His broad chest expands with each inhale, and I catch myself stealing glances of his plush lips.

Plush lips that have no business being on a man so pompous and distant.

Once his hair is rinsed and towel dried, I guide him back to the salon chair to massage his shoulders. The rumbling sounds of thunder and rain filter through the speakers, providing a soothing backdrop as I knead his tense muscles. They're like metal cables under my touch, but gradually yield as I work. My thumb finds a particularly tight knot in his upper back, and Dev moans, sending an unexpected zing down my spine.

Except it's not enough to keep another yawn from slipping past my lips. God, what is wrong with me? Here I am, hands on this gorgeous man, and I'm struggling to stay awake.

Minutes blur. I reach for my shears, and though I manage to trim his hair without slicing my fingers, my eyelids drag over my eyes, each blink akin to pulling up dead weight.

Usually, I have enough energy to light up a city, but I'm

dragging today. The soothing thunder and rain sounds aren't helping, and neither is my quiet and reserved client.

Could I be getting sick? I did wake up with that ocular migraine sign. Thankfully, I caught it in time with the meds I took, though.

I've never been a fan of the quiet, the silence, the hush. While some mistake it for peace and tranquility, I find it unsettling. Perhaps because it's in the quiet that my thoughts become deafeningly loud. Or perhaps I've always seen it as a harbinger of chaos and calamity.

A chaos and calamity I likely would have seen coming had I been feeling more like myself.

A chaos and calamity that would soon flip my life on its axis.

A chaos and calamity that would leave me reeling, unsure of my footing, for days to come.

With Dev now scrolling on his phone, I reach for my clippers as a distant thought filters through my mind—a fuzzy image of the side effects label on the new migraine pills. I'd just switched from my old prescription, since it always made me nauseous.

*Did it say it can cause severe drowsiness in some people?*

Am I "some people"?

Time slows as another yawn sneaks up on me just as I place the clippers—forgetting to adjust the guard—on the side of Dev's head, right above his ear. My hand slips, and in a blink, the clipper takes a detour so close to his skull, it would make a Marine proud.

At once, all the sleep vanishes from my eyes, which are now two giant saucers on my face.

"Oh my God!" I gasp, my hand finding my mouth for reasons other than to stifle a yawn. "Oh God, oh no!"

I watch in horror as Dev rises from his seat, much like King Kong from the depths of the ocean to wreak havoc on

Manhattan. Except, if King Kong also had a toothache and a bad haircut at the same time. Either way, I'd probably still take King Kong over this beast because maybe then I could be his Ann Sparrow—the only woman to calm the beast. But alas, I'm having the opposite effect, as Dev's livid and appalled glare finds me in the mirror.

I gingerly reach for his bicep. "Dev, I can fix—"

My words are swallowed by the roar that erupts from him, practically sending my ass to the floor. *"What the actual fuck?!"*

# three
## dev

### A New Brand of Crazy

I had plenty of chances to turn around and leave.
And I should have taken them.

First, when she greeted me wearing two different shoes and a rainbow-colored top that revealed more skin than Khloe Kardashian's PETA ad, her smile all too sweet, and her ass-length honey brown hair cascading over each shoulder like rivers of silk. She actually reminded me of the *My Little Pony* doll Deena used to play with. The one that looked like she was the result of a psychedelic experiment gone wrong.

And second, when those things resembling aliens prowled in looking like they were still pissed about their botched wax jobs, surrounding me like Area 51 escapees. I won't admit this out loud, but they were strangely cute. Weird as fuck, but cute.

And then third, when she started talking.

Oh God, the talking . . . It was like an incessant car alarm that has my ears ringing even now.

Who the hell gives their cats names like that, talks about breeding rabbits, and goes on about sexcapades with men named after sausage references? I could tell she wanted to prattle on, but Jesus Christ, a man can only take so much.

But what did I do instead of turning right the fuck around and walking out of this clown show? I stayed. Like someone caught in a fucked-up spell, I stayed.

Maybe it was her "girl next door" charm. Although, if she were my neighbor, I'd probably be banging on her door, telling her to shut the fuck up. Or maybe it was those sparkling green eyes, like gold-speckled marbles. Or hell, maybe it was her scent—a perfect contrast of tangy oranges and mischief.

The girl had trouble written all over her, but fuck if I wasn't trapped in her whirlwind of eccentricity. If only for curiosity's sake.

What the hell was I thinking coming here today? Today, of all days, when I am to represent the great Deepak Menon, also known as Dad, during our quarterly shareholders' meeting. The one he specifically said not to fuck up, because apparently, even after more than fifteen notches on my belt of successful acquisitions, Dad still doubts my capabilities.

That's good old Deepak for you, though. Blood may be thicker than water for most, but for him, it's another ingredient in his daily smoothies.

And now I look like a failed attempt at resurrecting nineties punk rock, all because I bought into Hudson's spiel about his overpriced stylist being God's gift to hair. Clearly, he and I have differing opinions on a good hairdresser. Was this all some sort of sick prank on his part? Maybe he referred me to this nutjob because he knew she'd fuck up my hair and he'd get the last laugh.

I should have known a place that looked like a dining establishment—what, with every surface made of wood, leather, or marble, its plush velvet seating, and opulent chandeliers—was probably better suited for waitstaff than stylists. Who the hell names their salon *Haircuts and Heartthrobs*, anyway? Is it a luxury men's salon or a romance flick?

This is a disaster.

I'm not one to lose my temper. Generally, I'm more of a 'walk away and let karma take its due' kind of guy, but between my stylist's endless babbling and the fact that she "slipped" while holding goddamn clippers to my head, I couldn't take it anymore.

I glare at my reflection in the mirror, my hands fisting at my sides. How the hell am I going to go into a fucking shareholders' meeting looking like this?

"Dev," the rainbow princess, who was a fucking human radio, jumping from one unnecessary conversation to the next only minutes ago, at least has the wherewithal to look remorseful. "Please, let me fix—"

"No," I snap, giving her a glare only my father could outdo. "You've done enough."

"What hap—" A woman with tan skin, inky black hair, and a sleeve of tattoos stops at the doorway of Piper's room to look in. Her eyes widen as they land on my hair. "Piper, what happened?!"

"I'll tell you what happened." I pull the cape from my neck. "Your stylist is an imbecile, with less talent than a preschooler! My hair looks like someone took a weed whacker to it!"

My eyes land on Piper, who flinches at my words, as if she's been physically struck and a pang of guilt pierces my chest. Maybe calling her an imbecile was harsher than I'd intended.

"Piper, how did this happen?" The woman in the doorway studies Piper with bewilderment before looking at me. "Mr. Menon, I can assure you we can fix your hair. Piper is one of our finest stylists."

Throwing the cape over the back of the chair, I cross the room in two long strides, causing the woman to step aside. "That won't be necessary. I think I've seen enough."

I'm storming down the corridor, my pace quickening with each step, when the echo of hurried footsteps resounds behind me. "D-Dev, please give me a moment to explain."

"Pretty sure there's little left for you to explain, Ms. Piper," I retort, my gaze fixed ahead, my cool tone unwavering. I continue toward the exit with unyielding resolve. "But you're welcome to, if you're eager to do so, in the presence of my lawyers."

Something burns inside my chest as those words leave my mouth, and I catch Piper's soft gasp trailing behind me. I'm not one to casually dispense threats or belittle someone for their mistakes, but the weight of my responsibilities—my dad's unattainable expectations, Mom's recent prognosis, and the turn my life has taken over the past couple of years—have pushed me to the brink. This haircut was just the last straw.

Just as I'm about to reach the door, Piper's hand clasps around my bicep and the jolt from her touch has me coming to a sudden halt.

Her shiny eyes lock with mine as she comes to stand in front of me. "I know it's no excuse, nor is it your problem, but I took a new migraine medication this morning, and I think it's made me extremely drowsy. None of this would have happened if I had figured it out sooner, and I apologize for that."

The anguish in her voice sends another pang of guilt through me.

"I understand how upset you are," she says, blinking back tears. "And if a lawsuit is what you'd like to proceed with, I can't stop you. But, please know, I didn't mean to mess up your hair or your day. It was a complete mistake, and I take full responsibility for it."

As I observe the sincerity emanating from her, some of my irritation ebbs. I shift on my feet, feeling both empathy and uncertainty wash over me. Uncertainty is a word I've never allowed in my vocabulary, my life, or my work, running the world's largest driverless transportation and grocery delivery service.

But here I am, completely at a loss in front of this woman who doesn't deserve my understanding or my empathy, given the state of my damn hair, but is somehow siphoning it out of me, anyway. *Goddammit*! What sort of mind games is she playing?!

And as much as I want to stay pissed, I remember the brutal migraines Mom used to deal with. The kind that would have her chained to her bed for days.

And now she's chained to her bed for another reason entirely . . .

When she notices I haven't responded, Piper continues to speak. Because, of course she does. Even humbled and remorseful, the woman can't seem to control her pretty mouth.

"But as you know, involving lawyers and doing all that paperwork can be so cumbersome," she continues, oozing faux concern. "Plus, these types of things have a way of making the news, and if the media gets a whiff of it, can you imagine the headlines? *Big Bad Billionaire Bullies Beauty Salon Over Bad Haircut. Remorseful Stylists Now Living on the Streets.*" She feigns a frown, followed by a sigh. "It would be a travesty all around, in my humble opinion."

My mouth drops open. Is she . . . is she threatening *me*? This tiny, five-foot-nil woman, who could be blown away in a bad windstorm. Did she just imply that she could manipulate the media against me?

My mind races as I try to comprehend the audacity of her words and her shift from being apologetic only minutes ago to daring and formidable now.

Jesus Christ, she's a new brand of crazy, and for reasons

beyond any explanation—given the way my dick just stirred inside my pants—her kind of crazy seems to intrigue me.

My brow lifts incredulously, not breaking our intense eye contact. "*A bad haircut?* You call making me look like I'm auditioning for a role in the *Addams Family*, a bad haircut?"

*"Love you!"*

I blink in confusion before my brows furrow at the way Piper jumps. What the hell? Did she just say . . . ? And why does her voice sound so weird all of a sudden?

*"Love you!"*

The words resound again somewhere off to my left, and I follow Piper's stunned gaze to where Vajayjay stares back at me with her jade-colored eyes. She's standing on a large button, in a row of buttons along one wall I hadn't noticed before.

Vajayjay pushes the button again and the same high-pitched nasally voice emits from it. *"Love you! Love you!"* She then saunters over to another button and the word, *"mine"*, rings from it.

Both Piper and I are standing there speechless as Vajayjay hits the *"mine"* button twice more while looking at Piper, as if trying to ensure she hears her. Then, with a nonchalant flick of her tail, she pads over to my feet, rubbing herself along the leg of my pants.

*What in the ever-loving-fuck is going on here?*

Piper's fingers rise to cover her lips, clearly suppressing another smile as she watches her cat. "Oh my God." She looks back up at me. "I think my cat has a crush on you. We've been teaching the cats to communicate with these buttons, and well, I think she's telling me to back off her man."

*Back off her man?*

Is this place a madhouse? Did I accidentally enter an insane asylum?

In my thirty-one years, I've never felt so out of my

element. Like I'm surrounded by people—*and cats*—from another galaxy.

As I start to leave—because all kidding aside, I need to get out of here before I start questioning my own sanity—Piper's hand lands over my forearm, sending another zing up my arm. "Listen. All I'm saying is, I messed up, but I can fix—"

"Can you magically regrow my damn hair?" I ask, louder than intended, but it makes Piper suck in her cheeks as she suppresses another grin. Any semblance of her previous teary remorse has completely vanished, only infuriating me further.

"Well, no, but I can make it so it doesn't look so . . ." she presses her lips together, "uneven."

Vajayjay continues her rubdown of my leg.

"I think you've displayed enough of your hair dressing prowess for one day. I'll get it fixed elsewhere where the stylists aren't asleep on the job."

Piper places her hand dramatically over her heart. "Ouch! Low blow, Mr. Menon."

I suppress my eyeroll and the almost-lift of the corners of my mouth. In fact, I don't think I've ever rolled my eyes at anyone in all the time I remember. And I certainly haven't almost smiled after they've fucked up my hair.

I reach for the door, turning to Piper once more. "I wish I could say see you next time, but clearly . . ." I don't finish the rest of the sentence since it doesn't need to be said.

"Dev, in all honesty," she says, looking sincere once more. "I feel terrible about what happened. Please, let me do something to make up for it. I'll do anything."

"Thanks, but I think I'll manage." I look at my watch before pulling the door open. "See you never, Ms. Piper."

And right as I'm leaving, I hear a loudly emitted, *"I miss you!"* in that same nasally tone.

Damn weird ass cat.

## four
# dev

### Five Schlongs Hen Party

HUDSON CASE

Got a full frontal of Dev's new haircut after the shareholders' meeting today.

[Image attachment: New Line of Chia Pets Available While Supplies Last]

DEAN MEYER

Dude. @Dev Menon, what the fuck happened to your hair? It looks like the before picture in a Rogaine commercial.

DARIAN MEYER

Jesus. Not trying to bust your balls, man, but the heavy metal ship might have sailed.

GARRETT MEYER

Oh, fuck! I'm totally using this for the face of the scarecrow I put in the front yard during Halloween!

HUDSON CASE

I was practically howling from laughter.

# Swati M.H.

**DEV MENON**

Assholes.

@Hudson Case, this was the work of your so-called incredible hairdresser. I fucking look like the love child of Chewbacca and a topiary!

**GARRETT MEYER**

[Ryan Gosling covering mouth laughing GIF]

**HUDSON CASE**

What? Piper is a top-notch stylist. It's why my hair always looks so good. Brings people to tears.

**DEAN MEYER**

Pretty sure it's your 'sunny' personality that brings people to tears.

**HUDSON CASE**

[middle finger emoji]

@Dev Menon, how bad did you piss her off?

**DEV MENON**

I didn't do shit. Not even when she prattled on about her crazy sex life like fucking Jabberjaw Joe.

**GARRETT MEYER**

Someone sounds jealous.

**DEAN MEYER**

I would be too if I was doing the right-handed prayer every night.

**DEV MENON**

And her hairless cat was into me.

HUDSON CASE

With that haircut, I don't doubt it.

DEAN MEYER

Dude! Have some respect for the fact that the rest of us are married and can't be talking about other women's hairless . . . kitties!

DARIAN MEYER

This conversation just got really weird, and I'm worried Rani is going to think we're talking about *hairless cats*.

DEV MENON

We *are* talking about hairless cats. Piper has a hairless cat that jumped into my lap and practically begged me to pet it.

DEAN MEYER

This sounds like the premise of a really bad porno.

[**Darian Meyer** has left the chat]
[**Dean Meyer** has added **Darian Meyer** to the chat]

GARRETT MEYER

@Dev Menon, are you sure you didn't accidentally go to a strip club?

Is it me or does it sound like he kinda liked it? And *her*.

DEAN MEYER

I think we can safely assume Dev's into hairless kitties.

HUDSON CASE

Who isn't?

[**Dean Meyer** changed the group name to **Hairless Kitty Lovers Anonymous**]

[**Darian Meyer** has left the chat]
[**Dean Meyer** has added **Darian Meyer** to the chat]

GARRETT MEYER

He is being rather quiet all of a sudden. I'm taking silence as agreement.

DEV MENON

I'm quiet because I'm regretting the day I met you idiots at Hudson's daughter's wedding. And of the eight billion people in the world, fate decided *you* were going to be my best friends.

[**Dev Menon** changed the group name to **Five Schlongs Hen Party**]

DEAN MEYER

Anyone else notice how he tried to distract us with that sappy speech and dodge admitting the truth? He totally likes this hairless chick.

[**Dev Menon** has left the chat]

# five
## dev

It's My Only Wish

I pinch the bridge of my nose in the back of my chauffeured car as the familiar streets to my parents' home float by. The morning's shareholders' meeting replays in my mind. It started off as more of a scathing critique of our disappointing quarterly earnings than a discussion in any way.

Thankfully, I managed to navigate the barrage of questions by highlighting our additional investments into research and development of driverless technology, justifying the less-than-stellar results and subsequently, easing some of the tension. Still, it wasn't the most uplifting news to deliver.

The car comes to a stop, and Ralph, our family's chauffeur of nearly twenty years, steps out to open my door, nodding as I exit. His usually stoic expression has a hint of humor in it today. "A hat today, sir?"

Suppressing my groan, I trudge toward the house, clutching the Taro milk tea with boba pearls in my grasp. "Don't ask."

Taking a moment to breathe in the warm September air, I mentally prepare myself for a conversation with my dad. He may have taken the next few months—the remaining time she has left on this earth—to spend with his terminally-ill wife of thirty-five years, but I could bet my entire savings account that he hadn't missed tuning into our shareholders' meeting. And I'd double down on that bet that I won't be getting any words of praise from him about how things unfolded, either.

But he's not the reason I'm here, nor is he the reason I feel like I'm suffocating even in the open air.

I'm here for the one woman, besides my little sister, who I love immeasurably and beyond words—my mother.

A woman I would trade places with in a heartbeat if I could.

Stepping into the spacious foyer, I find Deena walking back inside from Mom's rose garden, wearing a pair of long-sleeved pajamas adorned with a boba tea graphic. It's my ten-year-old sister's latest obsession and her most recent personality. There isn't a boba tea shop in town she hasn't visited or a flavor she hasn't tried.

Her face lights up, her long dark brown hair flying behind her as she rushes toward me. "Is that for me?"

I fake a scoff, bringing the cup closer to me. "No, it's for me, hence why I have it."

Her fists find her small hips. "You don't even like boba. You said it felt like you were drinking fish eggs. Also, no one uses 'hence' anymore."

"Firstly, I happen to love drinking fish eggs, and secondly, 'hence' is a fantastic word that deserves a comeback."

She shakes her head in exasperation, grabbing the cup and taking a long sip. "Ahh! Just what I needed this morning." Glancing over her shoulder, she eyes the backdoor. "You're not telling Mom, are you? You know how she gets about me having so much sugar."

I pretend to think about it, rubbing my chin while avoiding the way my throat constricts.

Since Mom's diagnosis a few months ago, she's begged us to all act as normal as possible. And though Deena's sugar consumption should be the least of her concerns, I wouldn't put it past Mom to lecture her about it.

"Well, since I didn't even get a hug or a 'you're the best brother in the world,' I'm sort of tempted to tell her . . ."

Deena wraps her thin arms around me, looking up with a grin, her eyes the same shade of brown as mine. "You're the best brother in the world."

"Now I just feel like you're saying it because I asked you to say it."

"Ugh, Dev!" she whines.

Grinning, I ruffle her unruly hair. "Fine. You're safe for now."

She releases me, eyeing my head. "What's with the cap? You never wear caps, but now I can see why. Your head looks like it's two sizes too big for your body."

I shoot her a mock glare, reaching for her drink. "Gimme that back."

"No!" Deena giggles, darting away from my reach and rushing up the staircase. "See ya later, Mr. Potato Head. Thanks for the boba!"

My chuckle fades as I fix my gaze on the backdoor.

Taking deliberate steps, I exit through the door to find Mom sitting on a chair, draped with a woven blanket, watching one of her hummingbird feeders in the distance. A tiny bird revs its wings, sipping nectar as it hovers in the air.

Mom's hair has started to grow back after the rounds of chemo, but it's still sparse, her eyes more sunken with each passing day.

But before I can make my way to her, the door behind me creaks open and Dad slips out, a tray in hand with two cups of steaming tea. He's taken little help from the staff during the day, insisting on being the one to take care of Mom as much as possible.

"Dad." I offer a tight smile to the man who bears a striking resemblance to me, despite our contrasting skin tones and eye color. His deep tan and onyx-colored eyes to my sun-kissed complexion and brown eyes. Neither Deena nor I inherited our mother's pale blue eyes or blonde hair.

Dad's eyes flick to the top of my head. "I see you're really set on shaking up the culture of the company I built. In just a short time as CEO, you've not only managed to reverse our profits, but decided it's no longer a priority to dress appropriately. You asked the senior leadership team to wear hats at our quarterly shareholders' meeting."

Yup, he definitely tuned in.

I hold back a bitter chuckle. How foolish of me to have expected a decent greeting for once. Perhaps a, *"Hey, son, how are you? That was a tough meeting, but you seemed prepared."* No, that would be asking too much.

Slipping my hands into my pockets, I square my shoulders. "We handed out hats with our company logo to everyone to lighten the mood."

Dad gives me a reproachful smirk. "And what did that accomplish? Empathy for our lackluster results? Did share prices soar because of it?"

My jaw clenches, a headache thrumming in my temples. I have half a mind to tell him that share prices would have plummeted if shareholders saw the CEO resembling Vanilla Ice under this hat, but I leave that bit to myself.

And speaking of headaches, my mind drifts to the woman who triggered mine this morning.

She's also the reason I hastily threw on a hat right before the meeting, given I had little time for another haircut. And since I didn't want to be the only one wearing a hat, I asked the entire leadership team to do so as well.

"You know as well as I do that you left when the economy was booming. You were part of the decision to expand into new markets and increase R&D spending. Now those costs are reflected on the earnings reports, hence the results you saw."

I stifle a smirk at my use of 'hence' again, imagining Deena's scowl if she were here.

Dad is about to respond when Mom's soft voice floats over to our ears. "What are you two whispering about over there? Come over here so I can see my son."

Dad and I exchange a silent nod, tabling this conversation for later.

"Good morning, sweetheart." Mom's frail hand reaches for mine as I approach. "Is your dad giving you a hard time about work again?"

She scowls at Dad as he places the tray of tea in front of her. She must have managed to get out of bed today, unlike last week, when she was confined to it.

For all my dad's flaws, namely his towering expectations of his children and his company, he's always been a devoted husband. If I'm honest, he's been a good father to me and Deena too, in his own way. But where Mom has always been our haven of understanding and solace, Dad's been the disciplinarian, pushing us to strive for more, to never settle.

But I've realized that achieving Deepak Menon's expectations is about as attainable as winning a staring contest with a statue. Whether I'm the youngest CEO to manage a business of this magnitude or not, expecting Dad's praise or even a pat on the back is useless.

But my grievances with my dad pale in comparison to the looming loss we'll both face in the upcoming months. The loss of the woman who binds our family with her love. The loss of someone so irreplaceable, we'll never recover. It's a thought that haunts me daily, knowing in just four to six months, based on her recent prognosis, I'll lose my safe haven, my mom.

"Hey, Mom." I clear the gravel from my voice. Leaning

down, I press a kiss to her cheek and sit next to her. "Nothing I can't handle." What I want to say is it's 'nothing out of the ordinary,' but I know how much it stresses her out when there's tension between Dad and me, and that's the last thing I want for her. "How are you feeling?"

"I'm perfectly fine," she lies.

"At least take off the hat in front of your mother," Dad requests from his seat across the table, but it sounds more like an order.

I hesitate but do so, only to see their shocked faces a second later.

"Jesus Christ, did you lose a bet?" my dad asks, astounded.

"Dev, what happened to your hair?" Mom adds, looking horrified. "Did the barber fall asleep while cutting it?!"

*Ha! Funnily enough...*

I weigh out telling them the story but decide against it. Somehow, telling my parents about the strange encounter I had with a hairdresser—who likely moonlights as an auctioneer—and her hairless felines sounds about as ridiculous in my head as it would coming from my lips.

I put my hat back on. "It's a long story."

Thankfully, my parents don't push me for answers, and a few seconds later, we're settled into a comfortable silence.

Mom shifts in her chair. "Your father helped me out into the garden this morning since I wanted to smell the roses we all planted together years ago." She presses her palm over mine. "Remember that, Dev? We put Deena in her bouncer out here, and the three of us took turns entertaining her while we gardened."

My eyes prick, remembering the times when we were all happy, healthy. "I remember."

She casts her gaze around the garden, taking in the arched trellis with the vines running around it and the lush landscape.

She truly made this little space hers—inviting, serene, and beautiful.

"I wanted the fresh air on my face and to hear the birds chirping. I was tired of being confined to my bed."

I stay silent, even as her words lodge inside my chest like jagged stones.

She draws in a ragged breath, her eyes shimmering. "I've had a fulfilling life, I really have. I've been lucky enough to have two wonderful children, to travel, and to enjoy all the luxuries of life." Her voice waivers as she swallows. "I just wish I could have seen . . ."

When she doesn't complete her thought, I turn toward her, gently squeezing her hand. "What, Mom?"

She shakes her head, a tear slipping from her eyes, betraying the mask of bravery she usually dons. "Nothing. I was being silly."

I gently grasp her face, wiping her tears. Her skin feels thin under my thumbs. "What were you going to say? What is it that you wished you could have seen? You know I'll move heaven and earth so you can see it."

Her hollowed gaze finds mine. "It's not something you can show me, sweetheart. I mean, you would, I'm sure, if I had more time, but . . ."

"But, what? What is it?" I urge, resolute in making my dying mother's wish come true, even if I have to bring the damn Taj Mahal here piece by piece and reassemble it for her myself.

"I just want to see you happy."

My throat tightens. "I am happy."

She snorts out a laugh even as her powder blue eyes brim with tears. "I may have an inoperable malignant brain tumor, son, but I haven't lost brain function yet. I can see when my children are truly happy, and I know you're not. You're running yourself thin from work, no thanks to your dad." She pauses to glare at my dad, making him shift uncomfortably in his chair. "And it's been a year and a half since Sister Camila—"

"Mom," I interrupt before we go down a path we've been down several times. "You need to stop calling her that."

"I need to stop calling her *Sister Camila*?" she argues with the little strength in her voice. "Why? She's the one who suddenly decided, after years of dangling you along, that she wanted to marry Jesus! You know I will have a discussion with Him when I get up there."

I muster up a reluctant chuckle at her attempted humor, even though it kills me inside that she's joking about her impending death.

She's still pissed on my behalf with Camila's rather spontaneous decision to *"renounce this material life and serve our Lord"*. But I'm completely over it. In all honesty, I don't think I even mourned us for a week.

Yes, Camila dropped her bombshell on what would have been our fifth anniversary—coincidentally, the same day I planned to propose. But strangely, I found a sense of relief amidst the shock.

Perhaps our fate was already sealed. Between my frequent business trips and our increasingly disconnected relationship, we'd both gotten complacent; we both stopped fighting for us. Our physical distance had only widened the emotional chasm between us. I think it was in those times of loneliness that Camila turned to her faith.

Still, that Camila would literally go and become a nun after being with me for five years? *That* I hadn't seen coming.

She was always a compassionate, service-minded person— in fact, that quality had captivated me all those years ago. Her kindness and generosity were a direct contrast to the type of people I was surrounded by daily, and I found myself drawn to her sweetness. But despite those things, there was always something missing between us, an intense magnetism that keeps two people intertwined.

Something akin to the love my parents still share.

I thought we could move past it, that maybe we didn't even need it. We were both decent people who cared for one another; what more could anyone need? But now that I've had time to reflect on our relationship, I realize how important that missing connection, that spark, was.

A spark I've never felt with anyone ... until this morning.

I brush the thought aside as soon as it surfaces, reassuring myself that the only "spark" I felt with the eccentric woman was the zing of her clippers getting a little too cozy with my scalp.

"Anyway, that wasn't the point," Mom says, shaking her head.

"Then what was the point?" I ask.

"I know you can't give it to me, Dev, and I want you to know I don't blame you. Honestly, it just slipped out and . . ."

"What is it?" I urge. "Tell me."

She takes a breath as if gathering her resolve. "I wish I could see you get married."

My heart comes to an abrupt stop.

That was definitely *not* what I was expecting her to say.

*Married? She wants to see me get married? How? When? To whom?*

I know I just told her I'd do anything to fulfill her wish, but ... get *married*?

She must see the blood drain from my face because she places a hand on my cheek. "Sweetheart, it's just a wish. People often die with unfulfilled wishes. You don't owe me anything. You already have so much on your plate, so please," her voice quivers, regret evident in her expression, "don't take this to heart, I was just—"

"Well, that's not a lot to ask." I hear myself saying, like I'm being puppeteered by someone else entirely.

*What the fuck are you even saying, Dev? Did those clippers nick your brain?*

My mom's eyes flit between mine in shock. "What?"

I swallow as my mind whirls to come up with something, *anything*. It's my dying mother's last wish. One I wouldn't forgive myself if I didn't fulfill. And I told her I would if I could, so even if I have to fly in a mail-order bride to do it, I fucking will, if only to ensure my mother attends my wedding.

"It's not a lot to ask, Mom. In fact, I've been, um, dating someone."

"What?" both my parents ask aghast at the same time.

"Yeah," I lie, torn between excitement and guilt. "We've kept things private. You remember how overwhelming it was when the media constantly followed Camila and me? Well, I've been dating this . . . woman, and we've talked about marriage."

Mom's face lights up for the first time in a long time, her hand finding her chest. "Oh, Dev! Are you serious?"

My heart hammers as I lean into the fib. "With your health and everything, I hadn't brought it up, but yeah, I've found someone I want to marry, and if your wish is to see us—"

"It is!" Tears stream down Mom's face, her shoulders trembling. "It's my only wish, Dev."

I steel my nerves, determined to do anything for the woman who's given me so much. "Then consider it done."

## six
# piper

### Try Talking Dirty to Her

I watch, mouth agape, as the finest man roaming God's green earth leaves my salon with surely the worst haircut he's ever had, sending my stomach plummeting.

The man has graced the covers of magazines over the years, often regarded for his thick, luscious locks and impeccable sense of style, among other enviable traits. The fact that I managed to butcher the very thing he's renowned for is a bitter pill to swallow. Honestly, if I'd handed my cat the clippers, she'd have at least made it look intentional.

And speaking of my cat, she's currently perched on the windowsill, one paw on the glass, longingly watching him walk to his chauffeured car like he's a can of tuna that got away. She turns her head toward me when Dev is out of sight to give me her most scathing look, letting me know this was all my fault.

I reach out to pet her. "I'm sorry, sweet thing. I didn't mean—"

But she doesn't let me finish, jumping off the ledge before putting her tail up in the air, like a one-finger salute, and walking away from me without so much as a backward glance.

I turn to find Sarina and Joshua standing behind me. Sarina's lips clamped in a way that suggests she's clearly struggling not to laugh while Joshua is wincing so hard, I'm worried his face might get stuck that way.

God, I'm never going to live this down, am I? Thank goodness we don't have clients waiting in the lobby, but I'm sure the staff has already heard about the fiasco. Around here, news travels faster than a politician's dick pic on the internet.

I fold my arms over my chest, looking at my best friend, knowing she'll have something to say that will simultaneously make me feel better and worse. It's a talent very few possess, but one Sarina excels in. "Well, go on then. Tell me how royally I fucked up."

"Oh, no." She shakes her head as Joshua runs to retrieve the phone ringing at the front desk. "I was actually thinking we could take advantage of your Edward Scissorhandsness. Make it into a lucrative new service, even. We could call it," she waves her hands out in front of her like she's gesturing to a billboard, "'Piper's Art of Surprise,' where her client doesn't know what kind of hair he'll walk out with! I think it'll do really well!"

*Smartass.*

I try to stifle my laughter, but between the events of the past half hour and the sheer exhaustion, it bursts out of me like an explosion of snorts and giggles. "You're a butthead," I say between laughs, wiping the tears from my eyes. "But seriously, of all the heads to nod off on, did I have to choose the one attached to the richest guy on earth?"

Sarina wraps me in a hug, similar to the way I've seen her hug Rome, her six-year-old son. "Look, it could have been worse. He could have been the richest and the most attractive guy on earth. Thank God, he looked like a river troll. You might have even done him a solid. With that haircut, maybe he'll finally have a shot at getting laid."

I groan, pinching her side, knowing she's being sarcastic.

You'd have to be blind, deaf, and living under a rock to not find him attractive. I know Sarina is just trying to keep me from falling into a pit of despair and self-loathing. "Pretty sure the man has never had any trouble getting laid, regardless of his wealth."

"Okay, so he's *mildly* attractive and has a wad of cash. Bid deal! That's like, our entire clientele in a nutshell."

"Yeah, but I haven't fucked up any of their hair this bad."

"True. You've earned your quota for the year. Perhaps the decade. But right now, what you need is sleep. Maybe later we can give you a crash course in hairdressing." She winks.

"I can't," I protest, even though my legs are barely holding me upright. "I have another client coming in fifteen minutes. He's the tight end for the 49ers."

"Don't you worry about him and his tight end," she declares, making me grin. "Nisha and Tatiana are covering the Hammond party for now since Tatiana's next appointment cancelled. I can take your client list for the next couple of hours. Grab an Uber and go home for a nap—no one needs you falling asleep at the wheel. I'll call you if we need anything."

I hesitate for a moment but know she's right. If I don't get some sleep, I'll be risking another disaster. And one is plenty for the day.

"Okay," I say reluctantly.

Except, little do I know at the time that disasters have a way of coming in twos, and the next one would be the reason I'd be losing sleep for the foreseeable future.

I wake up with a start to *"Despacito"*—Nisha's ringtone, set on a night she decided to show off her twerking skill atop a bar while donning a sombrero—assaulting my eardrums on full blast. Given that my friend has let loose all of four times in her life, I'd considered the night a success.

"What the hell?" I grumble, slapping my hand over my phone to stop the cacophony, but it ends up dropping off the nightstand instead. I'd forgotten to set it on silent before I fell into my slumber. "Dammit!"

The ringing finally stops, and I breathe a sigh of relief, sinking back into my pillow. But the reprieve is short-lived when the song restarts.

Cursing, I fumble out of bed, bringing the phone to my ear. "Please tell me this is an emergency and you've been kidnapped by aliens and you're calling me to negotiate your release. Although, given that you woke me up from one of the hottest dreams I've ever had, I might negotiate for them to keep you."

I don't mention that the dream happened to be about an especially irate billionaire I had the displeasure of meeting today. She'll jump to conclusions and no one needs that.

"We need you back at the salon," Nisha says, ignoring my grumbling. "There's a . . . situation here that requires your presence."

"Requires my presence?" I repeat, brows pinching. "Why are you speaking like you're a housekeeper on *Bridgerton*?"

I pull the phone off my ear to look at the time. Despite my body's reluctance to want to leave my bed, my mind feels surprisingly alert. It's a miracle what a two-hour nap can do.

"Piper," Nisha says again, a bit more urgently. "Can you head over right now?"

While my best friend isn't one to horse around like Sarina and me, generally we can at least get her to crack a smile. I'm not getting that vibe from her today.

I clamor out of bed, already heading to the bathroom to freshen up. "Yeah, I'll be there soon. What's going on?"

Of the three of us, Nisha's always been the level-headed one. Sarina and I often tease her that if we were ever in an end-of-world situation, Nisha would be calmly organizing an evacuation while we would be debating which shoes to bring. So for her to sound out of sorts is unsettling.

Did one of the other stylists go home sick? Even so, we always have on-call stylists available. Our salon's reputation depends on us keeping our wealthy clientele happy and on schedule, given most can't even spare five minutes.

"You'll see when you get here," she responds ominously. "I've gotta go, but just get here as quick as possible."

And with that, she hangs up, leaving me staring at my blank screen for clues. I don't have the time to ponder it, though. After ordering my Uber—since I'd left my car at the salon—I gather my long hair into a braid and rush over to check on Natalie Nutbottom and Kevin, my pair of rare miniature plush lop rabbits. As usual, I'm hoping to catch them in the act of fornicating, but as usual, they're on opposite ends of their palatial bunny cage.

I've seen them snuggle occasionally, but no matter how much I encourage Kevin to hump his girl, he refuses. I personally think it's because of Natalie's haughty, "I'm too good for you" attitude. It makes my sweet and sensitive Kevin feel insecure, and he just can't get it up under that kind of pressure, bless his furry little heart.

I've been trying to get them to mate for several months, ever since I paid a shitload for them off the breeder across town. They're a rare breed, and I'm hoping to sell their adorable offspring as a side-hustle. The breeder I got them from swore it would be easy, that they call it "multiplying like rabbits" for a reason, but at this point, I'm wondering if I need to take them to a vet, or couple's therapy.

I pull Kevin out of the cage, giving him the same encouragement and sage advice I always do. "It's okay, buddy. Hang in there. She'll give in one of these days. Maybe switch it up a bit today. Try talking dirty to her. Women love that."

With that, I lock up behind me and hop into the Uber.

Ten minutes later, I'm rummaging through my purse for my chapstick as I walk into the salon, but my search comes to an abrupt stop when I catch Nisha's concerned face.

"What's wrong?" I ask, watching her exchange a worried look with Joshua before glancing behind her toward the salon's private rooms.

Nisha rushes over, grasping my elbow and speaking in a hushed voice. "Dev is waiting for you in your room."

My brows pinch. "Dev? I thought he said he'd rather swim with a pool of piranhas than set foot in here again." *So maybe those weren't his exact words, but they felt just as harsh.*

Nisha pulls me down the hall. "Apparently, he changed his mind. He came by fifteen minutes ago, insisting that you fix his hair. When I told him you'd already left, he asked for your address. When I refused to give that to him, he basically implied that he could track it down himself if he needed to. And since I doubt he was bluffing, I told him I'd call you and ask you to come back. I didn't want to risk him showing up at your door."

My eyes widen. "But that doesn't make sense. Why come back hours later to the same place that botched up his hair when there are a million other salons in the city?"

Nisha shrugs outside the door to my room. "Your guess is as good as mine, but he wasn't open to a debate. I figured maybe he's offering us a chance at redemption."

I bite the inside of my cheek, giving her a nod. She's right. No use overthinking it. If he's ready to give us another shot, then who am I to argue? It also doesn't go unnoticed by me that my sweet friend used the word, "us", despite knowing I'm the one responsible for this morning's disaster.

I pull her into a quick hug. "Okay, I'll see what he wants."

Stepping into the room, I find Dev scrolling his phone. His dark and intimidating gaze lifts to meet mine, sending a current zipping down my spine.

I've never been one to be easily intimidated. Hell, it's one of the reasons Dad and I never got along. I was always too mouthy, too unruly for him. No matter how much he tried to shape and bend me to his will, I remained the outlier, the square peg in a round hole, the glitch in the matrix. To this day, I'm his biggest mistake and his worst disappointment. But that's not the point.

The point is, I don't flinch, I don't crumble or cower. I've always been comfortable being the wild card, the one who dances to her own song. But with this man—towering at six-foot-something, with his warm chocolate eyes, dark brows, and supple lips—I feel like I'm walking a tightrope, teetering between that familiar defiance and an unexpected desire. At any moment now, I could free fall. But the question is, will he be the refuge that saves me or the tempest that drowns me whole? My guess is he'll be the latter.

"Mr. Menon," I say in greeting, pushing aside the strange sensation his presence evokes. "I see you've reconsidered my offer to fix your hair."

"Imagine leading an important shareholder meeting wearing this cap," he responds irritably, ignoring my comment and pointing to the baseball cap on his head. But despite the clash with his formal attire, the cap gives him a rather laid-back vibe, annoyingly making him even more charming.

Still, a twinge of guilt tugs on my insides as my gaze flicks to his head. "Like I said, I'm really sorry. I can understand how upsetting that must have been, and I'm willing to do anything to make it up to you, starting with blending your hair so it's—"

"And that's why I'm here," Dev says, cutting me off.

I breathe in a sigh of relief at his words, glad we're finally on the same page. Perhaps Nisha was right. Perhaps this is a means of saving our reputation and redeeming ourselves in his eyes.

"Okay, great!" I respond happily, sauntering toward the shelf to grab a cape.

But just as I'm about to reach for the fabric, Dev's voice has my hand halting mid-air. "To cash in on your offer to do *anything*."

I turn to him, puzzled. "Excuse me?"

Dev folds his arms around his chest. "I'm not here for another haircut, Ms. Parker; I could get that anywhere. I'm here to collect the other part of your promise. The part where you said you'd do anything to make it up to me."

Though I said those words, a part of me wishes I could go back in time and punch myself in the face for doing so, because based on the look on Dev's face, I have a feeling I'm going to wish those words never spilled from my mouth.

"Um . . ." I stall. "What exactly is it you'd like, if not the haircut?"

Dev raises his head, his eyes piercing as he delivers the two words I never anticipated. "A bride."

## seven
# piper

Your Pussy Really Wants To

"A bride," I parrot like a malfunctioning robot, my brain trying to catch up as if I've missed the punchline to a joke.

Dev blinks, keeping his gaze steady on me. "Yes. A bride."

"Uh huh . . ." I drag out, giving him a chance to append a bit more information to his limited vocabulary, but he just stares at me. "Sorry, are we playing some form of charades here, or is 'bride' a code for something?"

With all the air and authority of a king rising from his throne, Dev pushes up to his feet, towering and self-assured. "I'm neither playing a game, nor sending hidden messages. You promised you'd do anything to make up for the disaster from this morning, and I'm here to cash in."

I reel back because I'm still unclear about what the hell this man is saying. "Yes, I said I'd do anything to make up for botching your haircut, but what the hell does a bride have to do with anything? Does this salon look like a bridal dealership to you?"

With the most nonchalant demeanor, one that belies the bombshell he's about to explode over me, Dev delivers his condition—the second disaster of my day. "I'd like you to be my bride."

I immediately squawk out a high-pitched laugh that sounds like some sort of mating call for prehistoric birds. My next breath, however, stalls inside my chest, and I stare at the man in front of me. Has he lost his goddamn mind? Maybe he inhaled too much hairspray?

But then, as the sheer absurdity of his request—or rather, his command—finally sinks in, I can't help but burst into another fit of laughter.

"I'm sorry, I thought I heard you say you'd like me to be your bride," I choke out between giggles. "Maybe we should take a closer look at your head, Mr. Menon, because I'm starting to wonder if my clippers accidentally passed through your scalp and grazed your brain."

With his hands casually nestled in his pockets, looking as stoic as the Sphinx, Dev waits for me to regain my composure.

A few more waves of laughter ripple through me before I wipe the corner of my eye, noticing Dev's not laughing at all. A second later, any trace of amusement vanishes from my face and dread trickles down to my stomach. "Oh my God, you're serious."

"I rarely joke, especially around virtual strangers." He pauses for a beat, letting me come to terms with why he's here. "My mother is sick, Ms. Parker. Terminally sick. Her doctors have given her a prognosis of four to six months—"

"Oh God, I'm so sorry," I say in a rush, my hands flying up to cover my mouth.

I don't know this man, but whether it's his stiffened stance or the way he was blinking back the sheen in his eyes, all I want to do is pull him into a hug. But given the fact that until now, all he's shown me is his unflappable, and somewhat icy, exterior, I don't completely feel comfortable crossing that line.

As for me, I've never been one to hide my feelings, or as

Mom often calls it, my 'glass house of emotions'. I wear my heart on my sleeve, and while that means I'm honest and transparent, it also leaves me vulnerable and exposed.

Dev's jaw tightens as if he's struggling to contain his emotions. "She has one wish before she—" He takes a shaky breath that has me stepping toward him unintentionally. "And it's to see me get married. Which is why I'm here."

"Wait a minute." I pinch the bridge of my nose, trying to process this absurd situation. "Let me get this straight. You're here, proposing marriage to me, because you want to fulfill your mother's last wish, even if it means marrying a stranger?"

"Yes."

I gape at him. "And you couldn't have asked anyone else on this side of the hemisphere?!"

"I could have, but I didn't. And I won't."

*This guy and his cryptic short answers!*

"Why not?" I ask incredulously.

"Because no one else owes me a debt," he states matter-of-factly.

"This is one hell of a price tag for a haircutting mistake, Mr. Menon," I scoff, but Dev continues to give me that same resolute stare. "And what if I'm with someone? What if I have a steady boyfriend? What if I can't marry you because I'm in love with the man of my dreams?"

Dev's brow lifts. "Judging by your colorful, and frankly, *unwelcome*, dating anecdotes and your habit of naming men after breakfast meats because you can't even remember their names, you're practically a walking ad against commitment. I'm pretty sure I'm safe assuming you don't have a situation you can't get out of." He pauses for a beat. "Which, by the way, would be a condition of this arrangement. I will not tolerate entanglements with anyone else."

"Firstly," I lift a finger with feigned offense, but mildly impressed he was listening to my dating anecdotes, "slightly rude, though completely accurate. I don't do attachments, commitments, or love. And secondly, what about you? If I can't be *entangled* with anyone, then neither can you."

"Agreed. That won't be an issue." His lips curl into a wry smile, as if my line of questioning was somehow my agreement to his outrageous demand.

I shake my head, wondering why I'm still in this conversation and haven't kicked this delusional man out already. "So what? You're asking for some sort of fake wife situation?"

"I would assume you'd be my fake fiancée for a few weeks before you're my fake wife, but yes."

Holy shit, he's actually thought this through.

I blink rapidly, my mind racing. And though I'm not even remotely considering this ludicrous offer, I am wondering how far he's thought this through. "And then what? As in—" I clear my throat, because even though I don't know her, it pains me to talk about someone's living, breathing mother in the past tense. "What about after she . . ."

I watch Dev's throat bob and stifle another urge to wrap my arms around his tapered waist and lay my head on his broad chest.

"We'll divorce," he states coolly. "We can cite any number of reasons or call it irreconcilable differences." He purses his lips as he lifts his head once more. "I would provide you with a hefty settlement, of course—any home or apartment in the city, cash—"

I raise my hand, stopping him. "Not to sound ungrateful, Dev, but I don't need your money or your offer for a new home. While I'm not the richest person on the planet like you, my salon is thriving, and honestly, I have everything I need."

In fact, with the success *Haircuts and Heartthrobs* has had recently, I moved out of the home I shared with Nisha, Sarina, and Rome and bought my own place—my swanky two-bedroom condo not too far from here. I make great money and live a pretty comfortable life, so while one could argue that you shouldn't look a gift horse in the mouth, money hasn't ever been a motivator for me. I value independence and respect.

Dev's shoulders roll back and I get the sense my response hasn't pleased him. "Unfortunately, your salon will not be doing so well once I put out a statement about my rather terrible experience here today."

I scoff before taking another step forward so my chest is practically plastered against his. I'm not one to get fired up quickly, but this is the last time this rich asshole threatens me with a lawsuit or public humiliation or whatever he thinks he has up his sleeve.

"If this is your way of convincing me to fake marry you, Mr. Menon, you're doing a shit job," I start, my index finger pressing into his chest. "I said I didn't have a price—not the one you'd proposed anyway, but I hadn't said no. But given that you've been a jerk since the moment you walked into my salon this morning, telling me to shut up and calling me an imbecile after I made a mistake that I wholeheartedly apologized for and promised to repair, I'm inclined not to help you. Not even in a short-term fake-relationship situation."

The truth is, Dev's sharp remark earlier had hit close to home, dredging up memories I've long fought to keep buried. I'd been thrown into a marred past formed during my most formative childhood years with my deadbeat father, who called me an idiot or "rocks for brains" any chance he got. It was his favorite ammunition against my flimsy self-esteem.

And then there was my high school boyfriend, the one I'd given my heart to and was convinced I'd marry. He'd laughed in my face when I'd said I'd wanted to go to beauty school instead of college, shattering my heart when he said he could never marry an "uneducated airhead".

To this day, Nisha believes it's because of Andrés that I

seek the company of "nameless" men, binding myself with no-strings-attached arrangements, unwilling to risk my heart with someone who could hurt me again. But the truth is never that simple, is it? We're not mere caricatures shaped by a couple of deep cuts in our past. We're complicated and messy beings, forged from the permanent scars those wounds left behind.

As convenient as it would be, I can't blame Andrés for my commitment issues. My sense of unworthiness, my belief that I don't deserve better, or that I couldn't keep an accomplished or well-read man because I'm not smart enough, is rooted far deeper than I ever gave him access to. And that's a truth and a battle that's always been mine to confront.

Dev's chest rises and falls against mine, his glare searing my skin as it travels down to my lips. Unapologetically, he holds it there, though his eyes soften ever so slightly when they drag up to meet mine. "You're right, I have been a jerk, and I'm sorry for saying something so harsh and unwarranted."

I lift my chin, slightly surprised by his quick but sincere apology. "Thank you. I appreciate that."

His voice is gruff. "Name your price?"

I bite my bottom lip, watching Dev's gaze flick down to my mouth again.

What would be a fair trade? Nothing, really, but perhaps I can think of something beneficial to the salon, while also making him uncomfortable. Why should I be the only one out of my element in this situation?

It's no secret the man is a recluse of sorts. Sure, he's been on magazine covers, leads a very well-known company, and has been invited to speak at more events than the president, the Pope, and the Dalai Lama combined. But from everything I know, he doesn't like the public eye, keeping his private life exactly that—private.

So, if I'm going to name a price—not that I have any intention of accepting—I should at least see if he's willing to meet it. The salon does have that marketing campaign to save . . .

"Become the exclusive model for our salon," I say as my eyes rake over his sharp and scruffed jaw, down his thick neck. "For the time spanning the arrangement, you'll do a couple of photoshoots, some social media teasers, celebrity endorsements, and become the face of *Haircuts and Heartthrobs*."

Dev's nostrils flare, his discomfort clear as he weighs out my lengthy request. He's thinking for so long, I'm sure he's going to reject the idea, but then he surprises me. "Fine, but—"

"Shh." I lift a finger to his lips, stopping him mid-sentence, but not before hearing a soft intake of his breath. "Yes or no, Mr. Menon?"

"Yes," he croaks under my touch, his eyes hooded as an electric current sizzles between us.

"Good." I smile, feeling victorious as I drop my hand.

"So you accept my proposal, then?"

His voice is smoky and smooth like aged whiskey, and with the way his closeness stirs something deep inside me, I want to say yes; I want to be swept up in his plans, even if they're fake and temporary. But I pull away, my body wailing at the loss of contact with his warm and solid chest.

"Listen, Dev . . . can I call you Dev?" I cock my head.

I swear his blink takes longer than a slow-motion replay of a snail's race. "You've had no qualms about it before."

"Huh. I could have sworn we were into the whole 'Mr. Menon, Ms. Piper' exchange that always makes conversations more sexually charged. Not that there's anything sexually charged between us," I assert, "because I'm more like an atom bomb in terms of the type of charge I emit, while you're clearly a double-A battery."

"Clearly," he deadpans, his lips twitching.

"Anyway, as I was saying," I press on, undeterred by the

tiny dimple I just saw make its debut on his left cheek, and getting back to the more serious issue at hand. "I can imagine how heartbroken you must be about your mother. Given the fact that you're actually considering marrying someone so your mom can be at your wedding, I can tell you really love her. And I truly am sorry that you and your family are going through this, but I can't be a part of it. Not only am I a terrible liar and could never pull off something like this, but I also don't feel right deceiving someone, even for their dying wish."

His shoulders tense again. "And you feel right about being in a position to help but won't, even when it's temporary?"

I place my hands on my hips. "Maybe I'm not the helpful type. As you rightly pointed out, we're virtual strangers. How much do you know about me, anyway? What if I'm a terrible person?"

"Your hairless cats would beg to differ. You rescued them from a pretty shitty situation."

As if summoned by the devil himself, Vajayjay saunters into the room just as Joshua swings my door open to tell me my next appointment is waiting in the lobby.

My cat meows cheerily at the sight of her favorite human —*no, not me*—zigzagging between his legs and rubbing her neck against his ankle, the little ho she is. It's as if she's eavesdropped on our entire conversation, her rounded eyes practically begging me to reconsider.

I watch Dev take her in. He sees it, too—her blatant pleading—and given that he's likely the most shrewd businessman to grace this salon, I know before he even says it that he'll sway me with his next words, even if he does give me a nickname I'm going to loathe.

"Say yes, Peter. It's clear your pussy really wants to."

## eight
# piper

A Micropenis Will Not Do

"Good God, woman, what kind of crack did you put in this?" I moan, shoveling another forkful of the risotto Sarina made into my mouth. "It's heavenly."

Sarina, Nisha, and I are cozied up on the couch in my family room, devouring our meals during our bi-weekly girl's night on Saturday. Well, I'm the only one 'devouring,' wolfing down the delicious tomato stuffed with peas and bacon risotto like I'm in a race, while my best friends nibble at it demurely like the cultured civilians they are.

Even after I moved into my own place, we wanted to keep our tradition alive. Rome, Sarina's six-year-old son and my honorary nephew, usually brightens our girl's nights with his infectious energy. However, his dad, Sarina's ex, took him to the new space museum and wanted to keep him for the weekend. So it just feels quieter tonight, given the pint-sized, space-loving genius isn't here. I swear, his encyclopedic knowledge could put even the most well-read adults to shame. God, I miss the kid.

Since my move, we've rotated hosting duties, with each of us bringing something to the table, literally. And given our one and only rule, that it has to be homemade, and my track record for burning water, I've graciously taken the role of mixologist, in charge of the cocktails while Sarina and Nisha supply dinner and dessert.

With what I need to tell them today, I may or may not have used a heavier pour of vodka.

"Thanks," Sarina says, reaching for her cocktail glass before taking a healthy sip. "And damn, you're getting really good at making these!" She turns the glass in her hand, looking at the purple liquid with renewed approval. "What is it?"

"It's called a lavender-blueberry spritzer," I answer, reaching for my glass. I shrug, keeping my frown hidden. "I figure, if this hairdressing thing doesn't work out, I might have a future as a bartender."

Sitting across from me, Nisha places her half-eaten plate on the table before folding her feet under her on the couch. "Babe, you can't beat yourself up about what happened anymore. It was a mistake—"

"Yeah, a mistake that's now costing me more than I ever bargained for," I mumble under my breath, though not low enough to go unnoticed by my friends.

"What do you mean?" Sarina asks, her brows knotting as she chews. "I thought everything got smoothed over and he forgave you."

I let out a resigned sigh, mentally preparing for the conversation I've managed to dodge all week. It's not that I was purposely avoiding it—okay, maybe just a little—but between our hectic schedules at the salon and our busy personal lives, there hasn't been a free moment to sit and chat.

I place my plate on the coffee table before rubbing my forehead with the tips of my fingers and squeezing my eyes shut, bracing for their reaction. "Yeah, so technically, it *did* get smoothed over, but he asked for a favor . . ."

"A favor," Nisha echoes. "Like free haircuts for the rest of the year, because the bastard is only a billionaire and can't afford to pay for them. That kind of favor?"

"Sort of." I chuckle awkwardly. "Actually, he asked me to marry him because it's his dying mom's last wish to see her son get married and he wants to fulfill it."

Silence follows my words for so long, I wonder if maybe I've accidentally activated a mute button. I cautiously peek through my fingers to check if my best friends are still there.

Unfortunately, they are. And while they both have completely different features and characteristics, they're currently giving me the exact same look, like I just told them I'm quitting my job to become a professional armpit smeller.

Honestly, they probably wouldn't have been as shocked if I *had* told them that, given my extreme aversion to smelly armpits—one of the reasons I had to break things off with Jimmy Dean. He would get so worked up during sex and, well, I think his glands were a bit more active than most people's.

Anyway, back to the subject at hand.

"What do you mean, he asked you to marry him?" Nisha asks incredulously, her expression a mix of horror and confusion.

"I mean, he asked me to marry him." My heart hammers as the weight of my decision sinks into my stomach.

Both my friends are now sitting at the edge of the couch, as if they physically can't be comfortable during a conversation like this.

"So, what did you say?" Sarina asks cautiously.

"He can't be serious," Nisha scoffs. "He's clearly grieving and has lost his mind."

I take a moment, tipping back my cocktail glass and downing my liquid courage, feeling the vodka blaze a trail down my esophagus. Licking my lips, I square my shoulders and face my friends again. "I said yes—"

"What?!" they both scream.

"But honestly, I got a pretty solid favor back from him too, you guys," I continue, feigning nonchalance. "He agreed to become our celebrity model in exchange for a few months of being married."

"You said yes?" Sarina's voice escalates an octave. "Are you fucking serious right now? Piper, you don't even know the guy!"

I give her a faraway look. "Do we ever really know anyone? I've known my mother my whole life, but just last week, she told me she loved gorgonzola. It truly tilted my world on its axis. So, really, can we be sure about anyone?"

"Oh my God." Sarina's eyes connect with her sister's before she searches my face. "You've officially lost it. And we were witnesses to the entire year you'd dyed your hair auburn."

"And the time you convinced us to take a Kia Rio up an iceberg in Iceland and we got stuck."

I muffle a snicker, recalling the helicopter rescue mission and being in the arms of this burly Viking-looking dude as we dangled over the ice. Nisha and Sarina shot daggers at me the entire helicopter ride back. Ah, good times. What doesn't kill us makes us stronger, right?

"And the time you got Chinese characters tattooed on your ankle, only to find out months later that they translated to 'turkey sandwich'."

"That was a failed Google search on my part, and I still stand by the fact that the letters look cool around my ankle!" I take another breath. "Look, I know this sounds crazy, even for me, but I just . . . felt bad for the guy. It would be a temporary arrangement, anyway; you guys know I can't do permanent and complicated, so this works out. Once his mom passes, we'll go back to our regular lives. It'll be like hitting rewind on the whole thing."

"*Not complicated?* Piper, this is the height of complicated!" Nisha's tone drips with disbelief. "And what do you mean, it'll be like hitting rewind? You'll be a divorced woman afterward. Marriage doesn't disappear from public record."

"Divorced-schmivorced," I pfft. "It's not like half the population doesn't have a failed marriage or two under their belt. This is an understanding, a simple marriage agreement. And it's for a good cause. You know how I love a good cause. Remember the 'Socks Without Partners' donation we started at the salon?"

"You mean the one we *still* don't know what to do with?" Sarina deadpans.

I roll my eyes. "It'll be for a good cause when we figure out what that is. Anyway, my point is, this marriage will be for a good cause—"

"Piper," Nisha pinches the bridge of her nose. "The reason this is going to get complicated is because you already like the guy."

I gasp so loud, I start coughing. "I do not! I would never like someone so cold and emotionless and demanding."

*And gorgeous, and selfless, and enigmatic. Yuck!*

"I bet he has a micropenis with how cold he runs," I continue, not admitting that I definitely felt something that was not micro in any shape or form when I went chest-to-chest with him that day for threatening the salon. "I've heard it's a real thing, actually. Men who are cold-natured tend to have small penises because their penises shrivel into their body."

"Can you stop saying penises?" Nisha drones.

"All I'm saying is, with the way I like to be fucked, a micropenis will not do."

Sarina snorts out a laugh, quickly snuffing it with her hand when Nisha shoots her a derisive look.

"I don't know, Piper," Nisha continues. "This seems like a disaster waiting to happen. You can fool anyone else, but you can't fool us. Ever since Andrés, you've been scared to commit—"

"Oh, here we go," I huff, rolling my eyes to the ceiling, as if pleading for divine intervention. "You know my feelings about commitment aren't solely based on my asshole ex-boyfriend from high school."

"Yes, but you haven't been exclusive with anyone since him, either. I don't know . . . this is new territory for you in so many ways."

"And what?" I ask, rising off the couch, partly to refill my glass from the pitcher on the kitchen counter and partly to escape Nisha's penetrating gaze. "You're afraid I'll fall in love with him?"

"Or worse." She turns on the couch to watch me walk back with a full glass, which I accidentally brimmed, so now I have to take a big swig to make sure it doesn't spill over the sides. "Hurt, heartbroken."

Nisha has had an interesting history with love and heartbreak, having married her high school sweetheart not too long after we graduated. Except after a few years of being married, they divorced when he made his pursuit of Hollywood a priority over their marriage. And though she's been single for years, I know she still pines for her ex. Hell, just yesterday I caught her watching one of his movie trailers, only for her to quickly close the tab when she saw me. She swears she's over him, but Sarina and I know the truth.

I shake my head as if the notion of being heartbroken is preposterous. Fool me once and all that. Won't be going down that path again. "You don't have to worry about that. When no hearts are involved, none can be broken. Plus, you know my rules. They're ironclad."

Nisha shakes her head with an exhausted sigh. "Dear God, not your rules."

"They're ironclad," I repeat. Because they are.

Sarina, who's downed most of her drink in the time Nisha and I have been talking, finally chimes in, "I'd like to officially register my vote that this is a monumentally bad idea."

"Noted," I reply, taking another sip.

"But seeing as you're hell-bent on forging ahead," a smile overtakes her entire face as she lifts her almost-empty cocktail glass in a toast, "let's get the party started, bitches! To micropenises!"

Nisha groans, lifting her glass as a reluctant smile forms over her face. I join next, lifting mine to clink with theirs. And right as we're settling back into the couch, my phone buzzes on the table—a FaceTime call from Mom.

I excuse myself, leaving my friends to their concerned whispers, before answering my phone. A smile spreads across my face as my mom's familiar features paint my screen.

While Rowan and I have eyes the same golden-green color as the man we unfortunately call our father, Mom's are a warm honey-brown, the same shade as her and my hair. Her shoulder-length locks look freshly trimmed, in contrast to my long and straight hair, cascading to my waist.

"Hey, Mom!" I greet her. "Love the haircut. The bangs work for you!"

"Hey, sweetheart!" she chimes, swiping a hand over said bangs. "Thanks, I just wanted a change."

"Well, it looks great!" I say, noting how the new hair seems to have taken a few years off her features.

Like Rowan, my dad was a famous hockey player at one time, but unlike my brother, he was always a shit person—a coward and a narcissist. After nearly two decades of marriage, during which Mom dedicated her life to him and to raising us so he could further his career, he left her for a woman almost half her age.

Just like that. Snap of his fingers and two decades of love evaporated into thin air.

Rowan and I watched Mom pour all of herself into that marriage—her youth, her needs, her identity. And what did Dad do? Just up and left.

For years, Dad never spared a glance for the family he abandoned. And after years of hoping and waiting for him to get his head out of his ass, Mom also gave up, settling down with her second husband—a man who treats her like the queen she is—in Tampa.

I couldn't be happier for her, really. But I also can't deny that watching her heart shatter like that, remembering the nights where she cried herself to sleep, fundamentally altered my perception of love and commitment.

So, see? It wasn't Andrés who brought on my issues. They were firmly in place prior to him.

In some ways, losing Dad brought Mom, Rowan, and me closer. While Dad was in our lives, Mom was always on edge, trying to be the perfect wife. She'd fret over every detail, from keeping a spotless house to making the most perfect meal every night, while Dad treated us all like we were a burden he had to carry. He had some respect for Rowan because of their shared interest in hockey, but me? He treated me like a disposable trinket.

And while it took Rowan years to sever those ties with Dad, I closed the door on him long ago. My life is not a rent-free apartment. If you want space in it, you have to earn your place; pay the rent. I simply have no room for people who haven't earned the right to be there, including my father.

Sure, my parents are just one example of a failed relationship. Perhaps I shouldn't be as jaded as I am, but then I saw it happen again to both Nisha and Sarina—relationships that left them broken and picking up their pieces.

I've heard words like "love" and "commitment" be exchanged, only to be disposed of when they're used up. I've held my mom and my best friends as they cried in my arms.

I've felt the sting of not being enough, not being valued. And I promised myself I'd never put myself in a position to let someone do that to me again.

Because, in the end, people leave. They decide you aren't worth it. And I'd rather live my life moving forward, unattached and uncommitted, than be saddled with a broken heart.

Mom gleams. "Now, tell me how you are. What's new with you?"

*Oh boy, where to start?*

I clear my throat. "Well, I have some news . . ."

Without further delay, I tell my mother about the recent, ahem, *changes* in my life, namely the fact that I'm now engaged to Dev Menon and that we plan to be married in a few weeks. While I do mention the urgency is due to his mother's health, I refrain from elaborating on the facade, sticking to the narrative that Dev and I met at the salon a while ago and have since gotten to know each other well. Well enough to now want to be married.

Like my best friends, my mother, and my brother are lunatics when it comes to protecting me. And while it's great to have an army like that behind you, it does take a certain amount of energy to fight them when they think you're going down the wrong path, as seen by my discussion with Sarina and Nisha.

Mom's mouth drops open for a few seconds before she registers what I've told her. "*Married?* Piper, I'm not sure what to say. This just seems so sudden."

It's not surprising that she's shocked. My mother knows I've never thought much about tying myself down with one person.

"Why didn't you tell me things had gotten so serious with someone? And Dev Menon, of all people? He's a name everyone knows nowadays."

I give her a reassuring smile. "I know it's shocking for you since I haven't mentioned him before, but Dev and I wanted to keep things between us until we knew how we felt about each other."

Mom eyes me quizzically, similar to the look Nisha and Sarina gave me earlier. "Still, this feels . . . rushed. I understand his mother's health is a factor, but sweetheart, marriage is a huge commitment. Are you sure you know what you're doing?"

*Nope, not at all.*

I gulp down a fresh set of nerves. "I know, Mom. I can understand why you're worried, but I just need you to trust me, okay?"

"And you're sure you know him well enough to spend your life with him?"

Nope again. "Yeah, I'm sure."

Thank goodness she can't hear the way my heart is hammering inside my chest.

My mom eyes me for a few seconds, looking for what, I'm not sure, but finally relents. "Well, if this is what you both want, then I'm thrilled for you. Tell me when you decide the date and when you need me there."

Relieved, I give my mom a few more details about the plan before we hang up. Which isn't much, considering Dev and I haven't spoken since he left the salon after I agreed to our arrangement.

My relief is short-lived when, not even three minutes later, my phone buzzes again and my brother's face lights up the screen. He doesn't even wait for a greeting.

"You're engaged?! I swear to God, Piper, if it's one of your sausage dudes, I will kill the motherfucker."

## nine
# piper

I Didn't Bring Extra Panties

> UNKNOWN NUMBER
>
> We need to discuss our arrangement, along with a recent amendment. When do you close up at the salon tonight?

I've just finished a rather long hair treatment for my previous client when I find the message waiting on my phone. It's clear who it's from, but I ask anyway because one can never be too sure.

Plus, one can never find too many ways to irritate their new fake fiancé.

> ME
>
> Sorry, is this arrangement in regards to the Socks Without Partners humanitarian crisis we're collecting for at the salon? Are you the hand-puppeteer I reached out to earlier to take my socks?

I can practically see him doing one of his slow blinks. The one where he simultaneously takes a long breath and likely prays that he can suppress his need to strangle me. Not going to lie, that blink might be my favorite thing about him.

I save his number into my contacts while I wait. I have a feeling it'll be a bit before he finds his composure.

> **DEV**
> This is in regards to our marital agreement and an amendment we can speak about in person.

I bite down on my bottom lip to suppress my smirk because even though no one can see it, I'm not sure I'm ready to admit how much fun I have getting under my unflappable fiancé's skin.

> **ME**
> Ah, then no. I'll be extremely busy for the next three decades. How is 2055 looking for you?

> **DEV**
> Piper.

I can almost hear the exasperation dripping from his tone without him having said my name out loud, and I can't help the giggle that escapes my lips.

It's been a week since I last spoke to my fake fiancé. A week of radio-silence after he strode out of my salon, with both my phone number and my reluctant agreement to his proposal. He'd said he'd be in touch, and I'd patiently waited. But for the last few days, I'll admit I've wondered if he'd had a change of heart. I was partly relieved—hoping that was the case—but surprisingly, I was disappointed, too.

Not enough to reach out—not that I had his number, anyway—but enough to catch myself checking for any missed calls and messages.

Perhaps somewhere between saying yes and telling my

family and friends about my engagement, I'd started to thaw on the idea. To look forward to it, even.

I leave him on Read to tidy up my workstation and disinfect my tools. The salon gets a thorough cleaning each night from a professional crew, but each stylist and masseuse is expected to keep their rooms cleaned between clients.

When I come back to my phone, another message is waiting for me.

> DEV
>
> I realize you've made it a mission in life to be as difficult as possible, but I'm running low on time and patience. Can I swing by when the salon closes?

I drum out another response he's not going to be too happy about.

> ME
>
> Oh, well since you put it that way, how can I resist? You must tell me where you acquired all that charm and charisma, Mr. Menon. I'm positively envious.

> DEV
>
> You're the most aggravating woman on the planet.

I giggle, leaning my hip against one of my cabinets.

> ME
>
> And yet, you still want to fake-marry me.

> DEV
>
> I'm reconsidering it.

> **ME**
>
> Really? Don't tease me. I have a tendency to pee when I get excited, and I didn't bring extra panties.

There's a long pause, the text bubbles jumping on the screen, only to disappear, until his next response comes through.

**DEV**

> Are you available tonight?

> **ME**
>
> You know, after not hearing from you for a week, I was secretly hoping you'd bonked into lamppost, gotten temporary amnesia, and forgotten this whole fake marriage charade.

**DEV**

> Sorry to disappoint.

I wait for him to elaborate, perhaps clue me in on his radio-silence all week, but of course, he doesn't. Why should he when this is neither a real, nor a normal relationship and he doesn't owe me an explanation of his comings and goings?

But then he surprises me with another text.

**DEV**

> I was in Germany for most of the week, and with my busy schedule and the time difference, it was hard to find a time to chat.

I'm just typing out my response, my lip tucked back under my teeth and my grin begging to be let free, when Joshua knocks on my door, letting me know my next client is here.

## Pretend For Me

> **ME**
> I do believe that text was higher than your four-word maximum. Quite the chatty Cathy today. You feeling okay? Should I fetch the smelling salts?

**DEV**
Is that a yes for meeting tonight?

I suck in my cheeks, knowing there should be no reason I should be feeling this giddy about a guy who's likely at the limit of his exasperation with me, but I can't help it. Maybe it's because I imagine that, even in his curt responses, there's a hint of a smile there.

Or maybe I want to believe there is.

> **ME**
> I suppose it is. I was planning to leave around seven-fifteen. The only plans I had were to encourage Kevin to fuck Natalie Nutbottom. Between you and me, I really think the ice is melting between them and their slow-burn is about to turn hot and steamy. After that, I was going to watch the latest episode of *Bite For My Love*. Have you seen it? It's so good. Basically, the contestants get paired up with potential love interests and make a mystery meal together. Afterward, they decide if they want to move forward together or pair up with someone else. Want to watch an episode with me?

I'm just about to head out of the room to get my next client when my phone buzzes once more and I chuckle, not at all surprised by his response.

**DEV**
No. I'll see you at seven-fifteen.

"You good with me leaving a few minutes early?" Joshua asks, stopping by my room at the salon around seven. "I was going to take Michelle out for dinner tonight. It's our six-month anniversary."

"Aww!" I grin at him. "You guys are so cute. Yes, go. Have fun. I'll close up. I'm expecting someone, anyway."

"Oh?" His brow rises. "Like a billionaire tech mogul, someone?"

Joshua, along with Nisha and Sarina, are the only ones who know the engagement isn't real, but he's the only one who believes it's not as fake as it seems. Whatever that means.

"Yes," I reply, placing the last of the used haircutting capes in the laundry bin. "We're supposed to discuss 'our arrangement,' per his text earlier. I'm assuming the terms and conditions of this whole thing and getting our story straight for his parents."

"I mean, aside from the timeline, given that you met last week, it's not a completely unbelievable story. You can always go with the truth of how you met—he was referred to the salon by your mutual friend and you fucked up his hair."

"Wow, thanks for the reminder, you big jerk," I deadpan, but relent with a smile.

Joshua shrugs. "You have to admit, it's a funny meeting. But you can embellish it a little by saying that instead of threatening you, he actually asked you out for a date after you fixed his hair, and that you've been dating ever since. Make the timeline seem longer."

I nod. "Yeah, maybe."

I'm putting the cats in the back room for the night, five minutes after Joshua leaves, when I hear the familiar sound of the salon door opening. I saunter down the hall to greet my fiancé, only to find it's not him standing there.

My brows rise at the sight of Oscar and Mayer at the door holding a bouquet of flowers. "Hey!" I manage, offering them a hesitant smile. "What are you guys doing here?"

I'd shot the brothers a text a couple of days ago, mentioning I had some news to share and agreeing to meet over the weekend. So, it's a little surprising that they're here today instead.

It's not that they've never shown up at the salon before, but we usually have an understanding to meet at their place. There's never been anything serious between us, which has suited me perfectly fine. No strings means no expectations, and no expectations means no risk of hearts getting involved and inevitably broken. But suddenly I'm feeling a little awkward with their presence here, given I'm expecting my fiancé any minute.

"We were in the area, so we decided to swing by," Oscar says. "Glad you're still here; otherwise, these would have gone to waste." He indicates the flowers in his hand, sauntering over to hand them to me.

I take the bouquet, the lilies filling my senses, before setting it down on the reception desk. "Thank you. That was really thoughtful of you."

"Any chance you'd be up for an impromptu date?" Mayer asks. "Have you eaten?"

"I know I'm starving," Oscar adds, his eyes scrolling down my body before he winks at me. "But more for dessert, if you know what I mean."

I tense.

The banter isn't uncommon between us. Hell, I participated in it the last time the three of us were together weeks ago, but now it feels . . . wrong. Undesirable and off-color.

"No. Actually, we need to talk about that—us, I mean."

Oscar's fingers graze my jaw. "We can talk at dinner or back at our place, if you want?"

"She doesn't."

All three of our heads jerk in the direction of the voice, devoid of all humor.

"Dev?" I gasp, staring in bewilderment as the most handsome man I've ever seen closes the distance between us, his hands casually tucked inside his pockets, betraying the murderous glint in his eyes. Eyes that are currently locked onto Oscar's fingers still hovering in the space between him and I. "I didn't hear you come in."

He stays silent. And whether it's the look of irritation on his face or the set of his jaw, something in me pulls me to his side. Wordlessly, I find myself sliding my hand in his, as if instinctively knowing he needs it.

Our fingers intertwine and electricity crackles through me, sending a shiver down my spine. His skin is warm and gentle against mine, kindling something I hadn't acknowledged was there before, deep in my core.

Surprise flashes across Dev's face before he swallows, making his Adam's apple bob. But when I give his hand an encouraging squeeze, some of the tension releases, and he finally takes a real breath.

"Dev," I say, looking back at the bewildered identical blond twins in front of me. "This is Oscar and Mayer—"

"Victor and Mason," Mayer interjects, but his correction evaporates from my mind as if he hasn't even spoken.

"Guys, this is my fiancé, Dev Menon," I carry on, looking at Dev's profile. He's still clenching his jaw, his dark eyes smoldering.

"Dev Menon?" Oscar asks, his gaze flicking from mine to Dev's face bewilderedly. "*The* Dev Menon? As in, the CEO of *Menon Inc.*?"

"*Fiancé*?" Mayer adds, his face contorting with disbelief. "What do you mean, your *fiancé*?"

"She means the guy she's going to marry," Dev drawls, like he's dealing with morons when he could be doing so much more with his time. His thumb caresses the back of my hand and I wonder if it's intentional. Probably not. "*Me*."

"But—"

"Listen, fellas," I jump in, wanting to get this explanation over with before my fake fiancé has a not-so-fake coronary. "I wanted to have this chat later, but honestly, I'm glad you're here now. I know this is surprising for you, but let's face it, we were never exclusive."

I clear my throat. "And then . . . well, Dev happened. So, while it was fun between us, I decided it was time for me to settle down."

A grin finds my lips, knowing I'm going to annoy my husband-to-be with the rest of my response, but also knowing it's becoming my most favorite thing to do so.

"Dev has been crazy about me for some time, hell-bent on marrying me, begging every chance he had. It was becoming quite cumbersome to keep saying no, and given the man's prospects are *clearly* limited, I took pity on him."

Dev's lips twitch, and I internally high-five myself.

"This is all just happening so fast," Mayer mumbles disheartedly, his hand brushing my bicep again. "You sure you don't want to think about it some more? Maybe we can change your mind—"

"You can't," Dev interjects sharply, his voice laced with ice, his nostrils flaring. "And if you have any intention of using that hand for the rest of your useless existence, I suggest you remove it from my fiancée."

Mayer's eyes widen before he drops his hand, but not before the three of us stare at Dev with a mirrored look of shock.

I've seen annoyance and exasperation cross his features before, but rage? That is new.

Given that the media is always regaling him as the most composed and level-headed tech genius of our time, I'm positive they haven't seen this side of him. A side that says he doesn't make empty threats.

He looks outright lethal, despite not having lifted a finger. And given Oscar and Mayer's swift departure from my salon without so much as a goodbye, I gather my fiancé isn't the type who ever needs to.

I turn to face him with a smirk, squeezing his bicep. "You know, if this whole 'broody billionaire' thing ever fizzles out, you'd have a solid career as a bouncer. What, with all that intense jaw clenching, nostril flaring, and bicep flexing, you'd be a shoo-in."

And what do I get in response?

That's right. Another one of his drawn-out blinks.

## ten
# dev

### The Yin To My Yang

We're still facing each other, her citrus scent swirling in the air between us, despite the scent of those damn lilies trying to overpower it.

An urge to grab them and shove them into the nearest bin nags at me, but I rein in the impulse, knowing I've already acted like enough of a caveman for one night.

I've never been one to resort to threats or barely held displays of . . . what would you call this? Possessiveness? A claim on something—someone—that's mine? But she's not mine.

Sure, I've had my fair share of battles with Dad to prove that I'm every bit the CEO he was for *Menon Inc*. But fighting for a person, for her attention? That's uncharted territory.

But then I saw one of the blond idiots reach for her face— touch her fucking skin—and molten lava coursed through my veins.

Honestly, I'm baffled by it all—this overwhelming protectiveness and uncontained fury. This entire arrangement is a farce, destined to dissolve with my mother's passing. So how is this blind and barely controlled rage rearing its head at the mere sight of someone touching her when she's not even mine to touch?

Her amber-flecked green gaze assesses me before my own dips to the luscious petal-colored curve of her lips. As those tantalizing lips lift upward, so do my eyes, and I clear my throat, taking a step backward.

"We should—"

A distant scratching and muffled meows halt my words, and both Piper and I turn to the sound.

Piper smiles. "Someone knows her man is here and she's anxious to see him." She turns to me, eyes hopeful. "Would you give my girl some love? I promise, she's not like this with anyone else."

I nod, following Piper down the hall. "I was actually wondering where she and the other cats stayed when the salon was closed."

She glances at me over her shoulder, that mischief I'm getting familiar with dancing in her eyes. "You were thinking about me and my pussy, were you?"

My eyes hood. "Never said anything about you. Your pussy, however . . . ?"

Piper turns to face forward again, but not before I catch the pink in her cheeks. *Yeah, sweetheart, two can play this game.*

She clears her throat. "The salon is open seven days a week, so someone is always here to take care of them, but we put them in this room at night before we leave so they don't get into trouble or get hurt." With a turn of a key, she unlocks the door to the cats' room. "They have their beds, litter box, and water in there."

Sure enough, Vajayjay slips through the crack in the door as it swings open, heading straight to me. Her large jade-colored eyes take me in before her tiny mouth pulls back for a soft meow, showing me her canines.

I've never been a cat guy, never even had an inclination

toward them. But did I maybe, possibly, perhaps watch an hour of cat videos on YouTube while I was on my way to Germany? Maybe, possibly, perhaps.

As I bend to scratch behind her gray and pink ears, Vajayjay wastes no time climbing up my arm and laying her head on my shoulder. With each stroke down her back, she rubs her chin against my ear, licking it.

"Holy shit," Piper exclaims, bewildered. "Who are you, and what have you done to my sassy, 'I will be owned by no man' cat?"

Five minutes later, we've put Vajayjay back in her room, along with the others, and Piper is turning off the computer at the reception desk.

"You never did answer the two sausages that were in here," I say, barely holding back a sneer, thinking about the assholes again. "Are you hungry?"

She nods, walking up to me. "Starving. I have a date planned with my frozen pizza. Want to join me? It's about the only thing I can make." She smirks before she winks. "I promise not to top it with sausage." At my glare, she lifts her hands up in surrender. "Too soon. Got it. So, about that pizza . . .?"

"Tempting, but no," I reply. "I hate pizza."

Piper's mouth drops open in disdain. "Who the hell hates pizza? I knew you were a robot."

Annoyed at myself for not having thought of getting reservations earlier, I pull out my phone, dialing Lenni, my admin. "Can you get me a reservation in thirty minutes at *Sakura* for two?"

Piper's widened eyes assess me before she rolls them. "Of course you'd demand a table at the most exclusive and booked-out restaurant in the city, thirty minutes before needing it."

I raise a brow, sliding my phone back into my pocket. "And I'll get it, too. You know why?" I lean in so our faces are only an inch apart, not waiting for her answer. "Because I always get what I want."

"Move in with you?!" Piper practically shrieks, and the patrons at the tables next to us turn to stare. "What do you mean, the amendment is to move in with you?"

I stay composed, having anticipated this reaction from her, given it's similar to the one when I asked her to marry me.

To be honest, I still can't believe she agreed to marry a stranger with little to gain on her part, besides using me as the face of her salon and to save its reputation. Not that I would have tarnished its image like I'd threatened.

I'll admit it was a low-handed move on my part. I wouldn't have carried through with my threat, but fuck if I didn't love seeing that fire ignite in her amber-flecked eyes. She was stunning then—all that personality and wit housed inside that petite frame of hers—and she's mesmerizing now.

Sitting to her right, my eyes travel down her torso, taking in the small breasts beneath her metallic short-sleeved shirt that's cropped and showing off a smooth, toned stomach above high-waisted black trousers. She'd pulled her hair into a long braid in the back seat of my chauffeured car, and with it out of the way, I can finally admire her slender neck. There's a line of tiny moles that travel down from it to her collarbone, and it takes everything I have to stay focused on our conversation when all I want to do is trail my tongue over them.

Jesus, she's a vision, and if I don't control the fucking boner barely hidden behind the tablecloth draped over my lap, we're going to end this conversation early.

I take in a long breath. "I need to release a statement to the press tomorrow regarding our engagement. If they think we're trying to hide it, gossip rags will have a field day. They'll do that anyway, but I've learned that getting ahead of the communication is key. But when it's all out there, do you realize what's going to happen?"

"Yes," she states adamantly. "You might not know this, but I have a pretty famous brother in the NHL. I know that our engagement will get a lot of media attention, but I don't see how living with you will change anything."

I knew she was Rowan Parker's sister—it was part of the background check I had done before asking her to marry me. Still, I pinch the bridge of my nose, no longer interested in the dragonfly noodle dish in front of me. "Let me ask you something, Peter—"

"*Piper*," she corrects, those fiery eyes narrowing in determination.

"Do you have paparazzi follow you around everywhere, camping out in front of your salon, or lurking around your condo because of your brother's fame?"

I can practically see the wheels turning in her head as she connects the dots. "Aside from your visit last week, and a few times when really high-profile clients have come in, no, we haven't had to deal with cameras. We beef up security when we know celebrities are coming to the salon."

"Right, but has any of it been for you, specifically?"

She shakes her head. "No. Most people don't know that I'm related to Rowan."

"Now imagine the frenzy when they find out you're marrying the CEO of the world's most profitable company?" I watch as understanding dawns in her eyes. "Unfortunately, I'm constantly being followed and photographed by the paps. Even more so than my parents. It's something my ex had to deal with and it made her miserable, and unfortunately, it's something you'll have to deal with, too, no matter how much I don't want that for you."

"So we'll beef up security around the salon and my condo. Why would moving in with you make this any better?" she argues.

"Because my house is practically a fortress. Not only is it tucked away from the paparazzi, but it's also highly secure. Yes, it'll increase your commute to work, but those are things we can deal with."

"But—"

I gesture for her to let me continue. "But what I can't do is take a chance on your safety and privacy, Peter."

Her shoulders slump. I know she wants to argue, but knows I'm right.

"Of course I'll increase the security around your salon. The way I was able to get inside past your doorman today? Or the way those two idiots were able to come in past salon hours?" My molars grind, remembering the way they fucking touched her. "Yeah, that shit isn't going to fly anymore. And staying with me will at least give me the peace of mind that you're in the safest place possible when you're home."

Piper shakes her head. "But it's not *my* home."

I tilt my head. "Then make it yours. You would have had to move in with me after the wedding, anyway. You know, until . . ." I look away, the words stuck in my throat. Fuck, just the thought that my mom won't be here in mere months cracks my heart open each time it enters my brain.

"I know," Piper whispers, grasping my hand in my lap, reminding me of how she did the same thing in front of those assholes who showed up at her salon. Her touch tempers the storm inside me, dulling the ache that felt unbearable only moments ago.

I look down at our connected hands, torn between wanting to pull away and needing to tighten our grasp. "It'll also reinforce the facade. No one will question our relationship if we're living together."

As if my words are a bucket of cold water to her emotions, something crosses Piper's expression. She straightens in her chair, withdrawing her hand from mine, and making me wish I could retract my words.

But I don't.

Because the more we acknowledge this charade now, the easier it will be for both of us when it inevitably ends. Because there's no denying it will.

I haven't known her long enough, but from what I see, the woman is the yin to my yang, my polar opposite in every way that matters, and that's putting it mildly.

She's spontaneous, wild, and possibly a little unhinged. She literally prattled on about her plans to breed her rabbits for ten minutes on our way here, for God's sake, telling me she plays songs like "*Lick It*" by Khia to set the mood for them!

And while she doesn't shy away from any physical connection, the woman runs for the hills at the mention of commitment. In fact, from what I can tell, she's committed to chewing the same stick of gum longer than any past relationship.

Meanwhile, I'm steadfast, reliable, and thrive on routine and order. Apart from Camila, I've had two other women in my life, both of whom I slept with after having committed to them.

So to even consider something working out between us long term is laughable, given everything—from our personalities, our worlds, and our outlooks—about us is fundamentally different in every way.

We're silent for a few moments while I dig into my noodles. We still need to discuss our story, given my parents have invited her for dinner this weekend, though I suspect we can keep the premise of how we met relatively the same.

She plays with the dumplings on her plate, still irritated about having to move in with me. I gather she's wrestling with the changes coming her way over the next few months.

Deciding to give her a few minutes, I refrain from jumping into the next order of business. But as usual, the tables turn as they often do between us, and I realize that when it comes to being a pain in the ass, Piper Parker wins the gold every time.

Her eyes sparkle. "Want me to make your home mine, huh? Fine. But I hope you know what you're in for, Mr. Menon. There's a reason my brother wrapped yellow police tape around the wing of the house I occupied when we both lived with our mom." Her smile turns as saccharine and deranged as the Joker's. "But I have a feeling you're the type who likes to learn the hard way. And you're in luck . . . you know why?" She doesn't wait for my response. "Because I'm a damn good teacher."

# eleven
## **dev**

Five Schlongs Hen Party

---

**DARIAN MEYER**

[Link to Finance Focus Weekly magazine article: Tech Titan Ties the Knot: Dev Menon, CEO of *Menon, Inc.* Engaged to Piper Parker]

I feel like I accidentally watched the last episode of The Bachelor, Season 4562, without having seen the earlier episodes. Not that I'm complaining.

@Dev Menon, what the hell is this? You're getting married?!

**DEAN MEYER**

What in the name of the father, the son, and the holy ghost of Jeff Bezos is happening here? Dev, is this for real? Was it her hairless . . . cat that convinced you?

[Family Guy's Herbert the Pervert stroking a scared-looking cat GIF]

@Darian Meyer, don't you dare exit this chat like the hairless pussy you are.

# Swati M.H.

**GARRETT MEYER**

Dev, buddy, don't you think that perhaps you've taken customer loyalty too far? Are you sure you're not suffering from Stockholm Syndrome after that haircut?

**DEV MENON**

I needed a bride and she owed me a debt.

**GARRETT MEYER**

Owed you a debt? Who are you, fucking Jaime Lannister from Game of Thrones? Who repays a debt for a bad haircut with a lifetime commitment?

**HUDSON CASE**

Wait. Is this MY Piper? The stylist I sent you to? Why the hell would she agree to something like this? Is she in some kind of financial trouble?

**DEV MENON**

Firstly, please refrain from using my fiancée's name with any sort of possession. She is not YOUR anything. Secondly, this has nothing to do with money. She didn't ask for a dime from me.

**DEAN MEYER**

Ooh <wincing emoji> did you guys hear that? You know, the sound of Hudson's balls being handed to him?

**HUDSON CASE**

What I heard was Dev acting like a caveman.

**DEV MENON**

As if you'd do anything less if I'd said the same thing about Kavi.

## Pretend For Me

**HUDSON CASE**

Nah. I'd have done a whole lot more.

**DARIAN MEYER**

So, circling back to the event that's currently on every news channel, @Dev Menon, are you saying she's marrying you out of pity? Because the last time we checked, you were just trying to grow your hair back after she hacked it off and you guys seemed to be on the outs.

**DEAN MEYER**

Oh, there was something growing alright. It just happened to be in his pants.

**GARRETT MEYER**

Clearly length isn't an issue for her, then. Good for you, man. Why should only the long and girthy guys get all the action?

**DEAN MEYER**

Don't forget pierced <winking emoji>.

But seriously, I'm happy for you and Snipperella. Your short stick deserves more action than what that sex doll in your room that looks like a nun can give you.

```
[Dev Menon has left the chat]
[Darian Meyer has left the chat]
[Dean Meyer has added Dev Menon to the chat]
[Dean Meyer has added Darian Meyer to the chat]
```

**DEAN MEYER**

What? Too soon? It's been a year and a half since Sister Camila. Felt like an appropriate amount of time had passed to be able to use that joke. No?

**DEV MENON**

@Garrett Meyer, hypothetically speaking, if one twin meets a grisly end in a tragic accident, does the other one get phantom pain?

**GARRETT MEYER**

We're fraternal so, no.

**DEAN MEYER**

[JLO crossing arms around chest, harrumphing GIF]

I know where I'm not welcome.

**GARRETT MEYER**

And yet it's never stopped you. . .

**DEAN MEYER**

@Dev Menon, is the wedding going to be as impromptu as this engagement? I'll need ample time to learn a choreographed dance routine.

**GARRETT MEYER**

Just bring a gift instead, buddy.

**DEAN MEYER**

I've been told I'm quite the dancer.

**GARRETT MEYER**

Our mother's friends telling you that is not reason enough for you to believe it. Most of them have had hip-replacement surgeries.

## Pretend For Me

DEAN MEYER

And yet they jump onto the dance floor whenever I'm doing my rendition of the sprinkler.

HUDSON CASE:

Maybe they're thinking you're having a seizure.

DEAN MEYER

Also, I'll have you know, Bertha Marie's hips moved like well-oiled machines after she got them replaced. I gave those babies a go, before Mala, of course, and they were a treat!

DARIAN MEYER

Jesus. She's more than twice your age.

DEAN MEYER

Age is just a number, little brother. You should know that better than anyone, given you're married to someone who can't vote yet. And let me tell you, Bertha's new hips had more action than a bull ride at the county fair.

GARRETT MEYER

<face-palm emoji> Please. No one encourage him any further.

DEAN MEYER

Back to the wedding. @Dev Menon, just curious, will the pussies be in attendance?

@Darian Meyer, don't you fucking dare.

[**Darian Meyer** has left the chat]
[**Dean Meyer** has added **Darian Meyer** to the chat]

**DEAN MEYER**

Goddammit, Dar! Why are you like this?

**DEV MENON**

We haven't thought that far.

**GARRETT MEYER**

Not thought that far? You proposed to a woman you've known for a week! Pretty sure time is just a suggestion to you, my friend.

**DEV MENON**

Didn't you wake up married to a passenger from your flight to Vegas?

**HUDSON CASE**

He's got you there, @Garrett Meyer.

**DEV MENON**

I heard she bawled her eyes out when she realized she was married to you. That must have pricked that little ego of yours.

**GARRETT MEYER**

She didn't bawl. And what happened with us was completely different. I'd known Bella for four years.

**DEAN MEYER**

The dude became a monk after he laid eyes on her, too, even when she flat-out showed him no interest.

**GARRETT MEYER**

Good things come to those who wait.

# Pretend For Me

**DEAN MEYER**

Mala knows it better than anyone. She played the long game and look how well it turned out for her. She got me.

**HUDSON CASE**

Agree to disagree.

**DARIAN MEYER**

@Dean Meyer, you know as well as the rest of us, you were the winner in that relationship. You still don't deserve her.

**DEAN MEYER**

She had me at my first dog treat.

**HUDSON CASE**

Are those still a staple in your daily diet?

**DEAN MEYER**

Fuck, yes! You should taste the dog treats she makes.

**HUDSON CASE**

Shame. I just recently moved on from puppy chow to adult cuisine. But I agree with Dar, you don't deserve that wife of yours.

**DEAN MEYER**

Shhh, don't tell her. She has a tendency to get a big head.

**GARRETT MEYER**

Oh, god. Brace for it . . .

**DEAN MEYER**

She also has a tendency to GIVE good head.

[**Darian Meyer** has left the chat]
[**Dev Menon** has left the chat]
[**Hudson Case** has left the chat]
[**Garrett Meyer** has left the chat]

> DEAN MEYER
>
> What's funny is you think I won't add all you fuckers back.

twelve
## dev

I Do Like To Swallow

My eyes have a hard time figuring out what to land on when I swing my door open.

They first halt on Piper, taking in her cascading brown hair that could double as a scarf over both her shoulders, before flicking to the boy of about five or six in a short-sleeve polo and shorts, who's clinging to a hardback book as though he's keeping it from flying away. But what truly captures my attention, making me wonder if I've stumbled onto the set of a low-budget reality show, is the sizeable cage she's clutching on her other side.

That's right, a cage. Complete with two very exasperated-looking rabbits.

My brows rise in question, but before I can voice my confusion, she waves her free hand, gesturing to what I think is my home. "You realize there are countries that are smaller than this house alone, right? Like Google Earth would need to zoom out a few times to capture it. And we just walked past an infinity pool in your courtyard that could double as a small lake. Should I expect a helipad too, or do you just park your flying car in the garage like the rest of us peasants?"

Suppressing my smile, I bite the inside of my cheek. "Yes,

there is a helipad on the premises, and a landing strip in the back."

A sly smile stretches across her lips. "Well, I guess I have something in common with this house, then." She leans in, whispering against the shell of my ear, sending a zap of electricity down my spine, "Except my *landing strip* is in the front."

My jaw clenches, and I swear to God if there wasn't a kid—and two caged animals—staring at us, I'd have grabbed her by the back of the neck and demanded proof.

Clearing my throat, I welcome them inside, casting a furtive glance at the portable travel zoo in her grasp. "Is this all you brought with you?"

After signing some non-disclosure paperwork, along with a prenup that my legal team required after our chat at the restaurant a few days ago, Piper mentioned that she'd be bringing along "a few essentials" for her extended stay, but she definitely hadn't prepared me for a kid and rabbits.

She waves a dismissive hand in between us. "Oh no, I have about six other suitcases, a couple boxes of shoes, and a few more full of knick-knacks that your chauffeur is bringing by later." She must see the look of shock on my face because she continues, "I didn't want to have to keep schlepping to my condo every time I needed clean underwear, you know? So, I brought a few extra things to make it feel like home around here. Just the essentials, like I said."

"Right..." I say, hesitantly. "Just the essentials."

Gently setting the cage down in my foyer, she introduces the boy beside her. "This is Rome, my best friend Sarina's son. He's off school today for one of those mystery teacher work days, and since both my besties had to be at the salon, I told them I'd watch him. But truthfully, I'll do just about anything to hang out with this kid." She looks at Rome adoringly, making him blush. "You're excited about spending the day helping your aunt move in, aren't you, Romeo?"

Rome nods enthusiastically, his eyes gleaming behind his glasses. A light blue strap secures them to his head and his frames have tiny Saturns depicted on them. Lowering his book, the kid shoves his hand out at me for a shake. "I'm Roman Kabir Arora-Weston, but you can call me Rome. I'm six years old, and my mom says I'm going to be a 'new clear' scientist because I like space stuff." He proudly displays the cover of his hardback. "See? This book is called *Cool Space Facts for Kids*."

I take his small hand in mine. "Space facts, huh? What's the coolest one you know?"

Rome thinks about it for a moment, his mouth twisting to the side. "That a million Earths could fit inside the sun!" His eyes go wide. "A million! Can you believe that?"

I shake my head. "That's pretty unbelievable. Want to know my favorite space fact?"

Rome's brows shoot up, his glasses shifting on his face as he nods.

"Did you know that the moon is actually shaped like a lemon?"

Rome's mouth hangs open. "No way! Really?"

I nod, feeling satisfied having impressed the kid. "Really." I grin. "By the way, you have a pretty impressively long name, Roman Kabir Arora-Weston."

He beams with pride before sticking out his right hand enthusiastically. "It's cuz I'm half Indian American, like my mom," he declares, before sticking out his left hand, still holding the book, as if literally showcasing his dual heritage. "And half Caucasian American, like my dad. See?"

"I see." I chuckle because the kid is cute as fuck. "Well, guess what?"

"What?" he asks, leaning against Piper's leg.

Smiling down at him, she absentmindedly brushes his hair off his forehead, and for reasons I can't quite comprehend, the gesture tightens my chest.

I clear my throat, sticking my left hand out and mirroring his enthusiasm. "I'm also half Indian American because of my dad." I throw out the other arm. "And Caucasian American because of my mom."

"Whoa!"

I raise a brow, placing my hands inside my pockets and rocking back on my heels. "Looks like we have a lot in common, kid."

Rome grins up at Piper. "Aunt Piper, can I stay here with you sometimes?"

"Um . . ." Piper hesitates, glancing from him to me. "Well, that's up to Mr. Dev—"

"You're welcome to stay here anytime you want, buddy. Maybe you could even teach me more about space."

Rome gives me a toothy grin before his gaze drifts to my living room, where something has caught his eye. "You play with Legos?"

I follow his gaze to the small shelf with some boxes neatly stored in them. "Yeah, sometimes when my ten-year-old sister, Deena, comes over." I tilt my head to the shelf. "I've got bracelet-making kits, cross-stitching kits, tons of art supplies, and Legos. Want to go check them all out?"

Before I've even finished speaking, Rome has toed off his shoes and is rushing to the living room with his book. I turn back to see an indiscernible expression on Piper's face. The rabbit cage is now next to her feet, and the rabbits themselves have huddled together in a corner, their chests quickly rising and falling with each breath.

She pulls all her hair over to one shoulder and for the first time, I notice that she's wearing some sort of off-the-shoulder faded pink shirt, revealing the strap of something black and lacy underneath along with the constellation of moles traveling down her collarbone.

And not for the first time since I've met my stunning fake fiancée, my dick hardens inside my pants at the thought of ripping that lace off her to lick and suck each one of those tiny moles down her body.

"Thanks for letting me bring him over," she says, making me rip my eyes from her smooth skin. "He's pretty easy, but I'll warn you, once he's done with that book, he'll literally repeat each fact until you have blood coming out of your ears."

I chuckle. "He seems like my kind of kid."

Piper pulls her bottom lip in between her teeth, but I see a smile lurking behind it.

I raise a brow in question, waiting for her response.

She shakes her head, her eyes tracking down my face to catch at my lips. "You're pretty damn good with him for a guy who probably barks out orders to his scared minions all day."

Smirking, I say, "I'd appreciate it if you didn't go around ruining my supervillain reputation. I need to keep those minions on their toes."

She places her index and thumb on the corner of her smiling lips and pretends to zip them. "Your secret is safe with me, Lex."

"Lex?"

Piper gives me a derisive gasp. "Yes, Lex. As in *Lex Luther*, the wealthy archenemy of Superman?" When I pretend ignorance, loving the way she gets worked up, she continues with a huff, "Jesus, Menon, I truly expected better from the future ruler of the world. You've disappointed me."

I smile. "Have I?"

"Yes." She nods, gesturing to the large modern chandelier in my foyer. "This massive house with its glass walls, decorative infinity pools, and sprawling terraces . . ." Her eyes gleam with mischief, a playful glint I've come to recognize. "The way you just interacted with my sweet Rome, and that . . ." her eyes drift toward my left cheek before coming back to my lips, "that dimple of yours you keep so well hidden . . ." Her voice drops to a whisper, sending a chill down my spine. "It's all so very disappointing."

I take a step toward her. Why? I couldn't tell you.

Hypnotism, maybe?

Magnetism, perhaps.

Optimism, altruism, botulism? Sure, add those in, too.

My voice is low, challenging, even to my own ears. "Is that so, Peter?"

"Yes," she murmurs almost inaudibly. I watch her throat work on a swallow, her eyes flaring as I close the rest of the distance between us so my face hovers inches above hers. "All so underwhelming, really."

"You've noticed my dimple, have you?"

She shakes her head, her long hair swishing over the gentle slope of her breasts. And I can bet every fucking dollar in my bank account that her nipples are stiffened peaks behind that curtain of hair. "It's certainly very unremarkable." Her eyes lock on my lips. "Unimpressive." She licks her lips. "Un . . . un—"

"Peter?" I ask, my senses filling with her citrus scent.

"Yes," she responds, her chest falling on an exhale.

"Are your rabbits fighting or fucking?"

"Yes," she croons. "Fucking."

My lips twitch, knowing she hasn't registered a thing I've said. "Piper?"

"Yes."

"I'm asking because they look like they're about to rip each other's throats out."

Her brows furrow, and for a second, it's as if she has no idea where she is. Suddenly, she pulls away with a yelp and falls to the floor in front of the cage. "Oh my God!" She looks up at me, her face pale. "Dev! Natalie Nutbottom is trying to kill Kevin!"

Not a moment later, she opens the cage and manages to pry the weaker rabbit out, cooing at him . . . or her, I can't tell. She's just about to lower the cage door when the other one hops out, and before either of us can react, it's tearing through my house with all three of us—me, Piper, and Rome—hot on its tail. Yes, pun fucking intended!

And wouldn't you know it, Piper insists I call the blasted creature by its full name, but not too loudly because it may get scared. Which is why, a few minutes later, I'm sprinting around my house, whisper-yelling, "Natalie Nutbottom," like a certified lunatic.

My fingers are pressed under my brows, my elbows digging into my thighs as I try to even out my breaths.

What a fucking disaster, and that's not counting the five-thousand-dollar table lamp shattered on my bedroom floor, the two-thousand-dollar vase that's now cracked on my kitchen countertop, or the Hermes blanket adorned with rabbit shit.

No, the disaster I'm referring to comes with the name of Piper Parker. A calamity I seem to both be drawn to and afraid I'll drown in.

She's been in my house barely an hour and already, it feels like a tornado has swept through it, leaving both destruction and a newfound dread in its wake.

I've asked myself the same question no less than a hundred times as I've crawled through every room and inspected the space under every piece of large furniture, playing hide-and-seek with the horrible creature masked as an adorable rabbit: What the fuck was I thinking when I asked her to move in?

No joke, her fucking rabbit literally hopped through every one of my downstairs rooms, and for a while, every time one of us tried to catch her, it seemed we were breaking or toppling something else in the process.

It was Rome who finally found her behind a box of blankets in the guestroom closet—the room I planned to have Piper stay in. It took a bit for Piper to catch the beast, but thankfully, she got her back inside her cage. She placed a makeshift cardboard barrier between the furry savages to keep them away from each other for the time being.

"There's no way Jackass Thumper and Asshole Roger are staying in my house," I growl from my perch on the sofa across the overturned coffee table in my previously pristine living room.

Two gasps resound inside my ears.

"Mr. Dev said bad words!" Rome says, sounding both astonished and impressed.

"Their names are Kevin and Natalie Nutbottom, and they are staying where I am staying. So unless you've changed your mind about me living with you, they're staying right here."

That from my tornado of a fiancée.

I lift my head from my hands, glaring at her across the overturned coffee table in my previously pristine living room. "Peter, I swear—"

"Remember that legal paperwork you made me sign yesterday?" she asks, interrupting me.

I slow blink, trying to stay calm. "Yes."

She examines her fingernails as if suddenly concerned with the magenta polish on them. "I might have added a little amendment in there while your lawyer was using my bathroom, indicating that my pets are allowed to live in your home as part of this arrangement." At my gaping mouth, she adds, "And I may have initialed and dated it, too, you know," she shrugs, "for consistency's sake. I'm nothing if not consistent and law-abiding."

I run my hand down my face as Piper high-fives Rome. And even in that movement, it's not my impending demise I note, but the way her pink shirt drops further down on one side, revealing more of that silky skin and the lacy strip of fabric underneath.

I place my head back inside my palms.

God, I'm so fucked.

A few seconds later, Piper's giggle has me lifting my head from my hands once again. Her hand covers her mouth as she shakes with laughter, tears running down her cheeks. Her gaze darts between me and Rome, and when he sees her laughing, the tension melts away completely. A smile stretches across his face and before he can help it, he bowls over, joining Piper in laughter.

I'm glad someone finds this funny.

Although, even as I shake my head, not wanting to acknowledge the past hour, I recall the way we were all frantically running through the house looking for her damn rabbit, and I find myself chuckling under my breath, too.

Jesus Christ, what have I gotten myself into?

Piper wipes the tears from the bottom of her lids, a smile still stretched across her face, while I struggle not to let those plush lips assuage my irritation. "I was going to ask for a house tour, but it seems we don't need one anymore."

I manage to keep my tone neutral. "How very fortunate for me."

She composes herself, her eyes narrowing. "Oh, and since I was forced to vacate my home for this dump, I think it's only fair I get to have my pick of rooms."

I take a deep breath. "Let me guess . . ."

She lifts a hand. "No need. I quite loved your spacious bazillion-dollar closet and bathroom, not to mention that enormous bed that could comfortably fit a family of elephants. So, when Ralph comes in with the rest of my stuff, I'll just ask him to leave it all in your room."

My jaw ticks. "There are eight other rooms in the house. You can't just—"

"Oh, but I can, can't I, dear husband-to-be?" she interrupts, resting her chin on her intertwined fingers. "Because what's mine is yours, and what's yours is mine. Isn't that how marriage works? But don't worry, I'm not kicking you out of your space. I'm happy to share it with you, and you'll be happy to know, I don't bite." She winks before dragging her teeth over her bottom lip with all the innuendo. "But I do like to swallow."

# thirteen
## piper

You Make My Brain Melt

> **UNKNOWN NUMBER**
>
> Well, well, my little Peppercorn. Looks like you're finally making waves and climbing those ladders. Bagging a billionaire?! Damn, girl! Finally making your old man proud. I told you your looks were the only thing that would get you anywhere, and it seems I was right.

My hand trembles, even as my fist curls around my phone at the sight of something I haven't seen in years. A message that has my eyelid twitching and my skin crawling. A reminder of the asshole whose DNA I'm cursed to share. And a realization that, even after years without his calloused words—as if I wasn't his own flesh and blood, but a burden handed to him—I'm not as far from a setback as I thought I was.

And just when I'm about to delete the message and block the number, there's a knock on my door that makes me jump.

"Coming!" I respond breathlessly, shoving my phone into my clutch and running a hand over my emerald-green, body-hugging, spaghetti-strap dress. It's the same dress I wore to

Rowan and Shay's pre-wedding cocktail party, but it also seems appropriate for meeting Dev's parents for the first time.

Slipping into my heels, I head toward my bedroom door.

Despite my request for him to share his room, Dev moved across the hall to the guest room the day I showed up here with Rome and my sweet bunnies.

Okay, so maybe that day wasn't the best example of their sweetness, but they probably felt woozy from the car ride and didn't love being in a new place. The entire experience may have triggered some kind of panic attack in Natalie and she lashed out at Kevin, but she's calm now.

Still, I have them separated for now. Thankfully, Kevin was not hurt, but I've made an appointment with the vet. I haven't taken them since I got them from the breeder so it's about time. Perhaps the vet can give Kevin rabbit Viagra or something. Maybe Natalie is sexually frustrated.

I swing my door open, coming face to face with Dev in a white button-down under a navy blazer and slacks. The top few buttons of his shirt are unbuttoned, and my breath catches when my eyes track over the scruff below his jaw and the stretch of his neck. The scent of him—a subtle and woodsy cologne—has me feeling dizzy.

Speaking of being sexually frustrated . . .

"Hey!" I croak out, clearing my throat and trying again. "I mean, hi!"

His chestnut brown eyes rake over my frame, flaring slightly when they halt on the subtle hint of my cleavage. "You look . . . nice." His gaze finds mine again. "Green is my favorite color."

I lift a brow. "Yeah? I didn't know that."

"I didn't, either . . ." his tongue slides over his bottom lip, "not until a couple of weeks ago."

Yeah, so *this*—his raspy voice, his swoon factor turned to

level one-hundred, and his delicious scent—is not helping my already charged up and dissatisfied libido.

I've been living in Dev's mansion, complete with the kind of security even Fort Knox would envy, for the past week. And while I've only seen him twice in that time—not counting this moment right now—given he's been traveling to God knows which countries or planets, every time has been like a tease to my vagina.

The first was when I'd just gotten home from the salon a couple of nights ago, chauffeured back because Dev's on a mission to ensure my safety, or maybe just to drive me crazy. The jury is still out.

I was rummaging through my purse when I was met with a hard and sweaty bare chest. *His* hard and sweaty bare chest, with the perfect smattering of hair as he exited his home gym. I tried to act nonchalant, even as my core clenched, but I'm pretty sure he watched me track a bead of sweat down from his collarbone. Judging by his smug smirk, he knew I wanted to run my tongue along the same path.

Then there was yesterday, when I saw him walk from his indoor sauna to his bedroom in nothing but a towel, his muscles flexing with each step. And I swear, like the time before, the bastard knew I was watching him. His stupid dimple, buried behind his scruff, appeared right as he was closing his door.

So, because I'm not above irritating him, I decided it was about time he got punished for being a vaginal-tease. I finished his weekly crossword puzzle—diabolical, I know.

Since his return, I've seen it lying around on the coffee table—one of those weekly crossword puzzles inside the financial magazines he probably thinks is the word of God. The couple of times I've glanced at it, a few new clues have been filled in. Interestingly, I've always had a strange knack for puzzles, crosswords or otherwise, and I was dying to finish it for him but have resisted the temptation.

But not last night. I snuck out of my room after he'd gone to bed and finished it, leaving it where it was. I mean seriously, who doesn't know that another word for "diplomacy" is "tact"?

This morning, as I was stirring creamer into my coffee, he emerged from his room, all GQ'd out from head to toe. His eyes practically popped out when he realized the puzzle was completed.

He held up the magazine from across his monstrous kitchen island, his expression a mixture of amusement and suspicion. "Did you finish this?"

"Hmm?" I'd said nonchalantly. "Finish what?"

He'd set the magazine down on the marble countertop, his gaze fixed on me. "This crossword. Did you finish it?"

I widened my eyes in mock indignation. "Why would I finish your crossword? Do I look like the type to do crosswords in my free time? Come on, Lex, you know I have more *tact* than that."

Dev's eyes had twinkled, realizing exactly what I'd said, but he didn't say anything as I sauntered by, making sure to catch another whiff of his cologne, storing it in memory to enjoy throughout my day.

The thing is, I've never been shy about my sexual desires. I'm generally upfront about my drive and make no apologies for it, but with Dev, something has held me back.

It's obvious he knows I find him attractive—my blatant drooling has made that pretty damn clear. But does he feel the same way about me? At certain times, it would seem so, but for some strange reason, my brain turns to goop around him, leaving me second-guessing myself.

Plus, the guy has been anything but predictable. If I were to make a move first, can I honestly guess how he'd react?

But there is the question of my ridiculous attraction to him, my desire to jump him at every chance, and my increasing sexual frustration that only he'll be able to cure.

And while I agreed to the terms of this fake relationship, we never discussed this aspect: what if one of us starts wanting more, even if it's just physical? Probably because at the time, I hadn't realized that my attraction to him would be such a living, breathing entity.

But it is. It so fucking is.

At the time, I thought my fingers and my toys would be enough to take us across the finish line. But they so aren't.

Because all I've done since I met my fake fiancé is imagine those enormous hands on me, those thick fingers filling me, and that ridiculously beautiful mouth on my skin. Between our charged banter and me practically salivating at the sight of the man, I'm not sure I can handle months of this.

I'm not sure I can handle another week!

Which is why I've created a new proposal for us. One that hasn't been discussed yet, but really ought to have been, and one I plan to suggest in the car tonight on the way to dinner at his parents.

Dev's hand rests on the small of my back as he opens the passenger door to his sports car—easily worth more than everything I own—and helps me inside. Just that small gesture, his hand on my back, not even touching my skin, has my heart pulsing in between my legs.

I'm just rechecking my lipstick in the mirror when he slides into the driver's seat. He waits for me to finish and I give him an inquisitive look, flipping the visor and sitting back into my seat. "What's up?"

Leaning across me, he reaches for my seatbelt and pulls it over my chest. His woodsy cologne envelops my senses, his jaw and neck so close that I'd only have to move a millimeter and I'd be able to feel his scruff across my lips.

Exasperated and needing a change of underwear, I throw my hands up and slap them down on my thighs just as he finishes buckling me in, shooting him a bewildered look.

His brows furrow. "What?"

"Are you doing this on purpose?"

He squints at me like I've lost my marbles. "Am I doing *what* on purpose? Making sure you're safe?"

My nostrils flare at that smirk, which has been finding his lips more and more recently. "No. I mean yes, but that's not all." At his continued confusion, I huff out an exasperated breath. "The sweet gestures, like buying Vajayjay a pink bow and my rabbits that expensive food, the barely arguing with me when I threw you out of your room, the looking at me like . . . like you're thinking the same things I'm thinking—"

His face stills, his voice dropping low. "And what are you thinking?"

I take a breath, wrapping my arms around my chest, flicking a glance out the window to get a hold of my thoughts. My heart hammers behind my ribs in anticipation of my next move. Not even I know what's going to come out of my mouth.

"Peter."

I turn back to face him. "Dev, I moved in with you and now we're going to meet your parents as a couple for the first time. I'm about to meet your mom, the person we're doing all this for."

His chin lowers but his eyes stay fixed on me, urging me to go on.

I lick my lips. "I just think that if we're going to be living together and in this fake relationship, we should . . . get something out of this too, you know? I feel this weird tension between us, this charge like I'm going to combust. Half the time I want to slap you, while the other half I want to climb you like the goddamn Redwood you are and rub my lady bits on you like I'm in heat—"

My eyes bounce between his. "Oh, gosh, I'm rambling again, aren't I? See this is exactly what you do to me." I glare at him. "You make my brain melt and I just start glitching like this. I don't act like this in front of anyone—"

"What do you mean get something out of it?" Dev interrupts, his voice sending goosebumps over my bare arms.

"Never mind." I shake my head, pinching the bridge of my nose. "You know what? Let's just get going. I don't want to keep your parents waiting, and honestly, I've humiliated myself enough. I don't even know what I was saying—"

"Piper, look at me." When I hesitate, I feel his warm hand around my wrist, gently guiding it down. He holds it there, waiting for me to meet his gaze. "What do you mean by, 'get something out of it'? I need you to be clear."

I'm positive he can hear the hammering of my heart resounding against the silence in the car. I swallow hard, feeling the tops of my cheeks burn. I have no idea why this is so hard when I've never had a hard time talking about it before.

"Dev, I like sex. No, I don't just like it; I love it. And while I'm committed to going through with this arrangement for as long as you need, I just . . ." God, my cheeks are on fire. "I have a new proposal for you."

"Which is?"

I lift my chin, pretending to have the balls to say this when my lady balls are actually shriveling up inside my lady crotch. I realize that's anatomically incorrect for me but it feels right at the moment. "I would like you to fuck me."

Dead silence.

Even my heart seems to have gotten the memo because it goes still while Dev's impassive face—save for the way his eyes darken—freezes in place.

"You want me to—"

The *ding* of my phone cuts him off, and I can't decide if I'm relieved or disappointed. "Sorry," I mutter. "Let me make sure this isn't important."

But the blood drains from my face when I read the message from the number I should have blocked earlier.

> UNKNOWN NUMBER
>
> What'd you do? Show off those tits? Good for you, sweetheart. Glad you're finally learning to use what your mother gave you. It's about the only thing she gave you that was worth anything. And you certainly didn't get any of my brains or talent. Now, tell me, when and where can we meet? I might just be in your neck of the woods, and it's been too long since I saw my little girl.

My lips curl into a snarl.

My dad is clearly off the wagon and off his rocker again. Probably sitting in some shithole bar, falling off the stool, drowning in his self-loathing and filth.

Good. I hope he fucking rots there.

He'd always been cruel, entitled, and selfish, but had he ever been as despicable and vile? Not from what I can remember. But time has a way of smoothing out the rough edges of our memories.

He'd apparently been harassing Rowan too, even showing up to his game to stir up unnecessary drama, but thankfully, my brother put him in his place. The only place he belongs—out of his life.

So why the hell is he trying to get back into mine?

The answer is obvious, of course, because he thinks he can get something out of this, and my response to it will be just as obvious.

My finger hovers over the button to block his number when Dev's voice stops me cold. His gaze sharpens on my face, which probably betrays my shock.

"Who is it?"

I shake my head. "Just a wrong number."

Dev's eyes narrow, as if knowing I'm lying. "Piper. Tell me who it is."

"Dev, really, it's no one—"

"It's definitely *not* no one," he cuts in. "Because if a message can wipe the smile off my fiancée's face, I'm going to need to know which motherfucker just wrote his death warrant."

# fourteen
## piper

Simmer Down, Tony Soprano

"Piper," Dev's mom, Claire, whispers my name, her frail hands clutching mine as she stares at me with the kind of adoration I feel unworthy of. Her pale blue eyes might look weary, but there's a kindness and understanding behind them that I haven't seen in anyone else's besides perhaps my own mother's.

A handkerchief adorned with red and pink roses is tied around Claire's head, concealing what I'm sure is a surgical scar and thin hair, but even so, her beauty is unmistakable.

And despite reminding myself to stay strong, to not think about the fact that this woman, my soon-to-be mother-in-law, is not going to be alive in a few short months, all I can think about is how shitty it is that the world will lose her all too soon.

I hardly know her, but within point-five seconds of meeting her, I've figured out that she's special. Some people just have that kind of pull, an aura and light that no disease, not even death itself, can diminish. And Dev's mom is amongst those beautiful souls.

Returning her smile, I linger just inside the threshold of her home, conflicted with the guilt of betraying her trust alongside her son. But the absolute joy shining in her eyes quells some of my turmoil.

*You're doing this to give her peace; to make her last wish come true. Put on your best performance and do this for not just her, but for the man beside you.*

In Claire, I catch glimpses of Dev, but it's the man standing behind her—tall, proud, with dark eyes as sharp as a hawk's—who unmistakably mirrors Dev.

He offers his large hand for a shake. "Piper. I'm Deepak, Dev's father." He glances at his son. "Dev has been quite tight-lipped about the two of you, but we're glad to finally meet you."

I take his hand in mine briefly, noting his assessing gaze sizing me up. "Thank you for inviting me to your beautiful home. It's good to meet you, too."

Hurried footsteps resound from the staircase a second later, and we all turn to look at a little girl who could only be Dev's sister, Deena, based on not only her resemblance to him but the lively personality he described her to be.

She waves, looking from Dev to me. "Hi!"

Dev places his palm at the base of my spine. "Deena, this is Piper. Piper, my pain in the neck little sister, Deena."

Deena makes a face at him. "Pain in the neck? I thought I was a pain in your butt, which is a title I worked hard for, thank you very much."

Dev scoffs. "Pretty sure you've never had to work very hard to earn that title. You were born with it."

"Whatever," Deena huffs. "Just for that, I'm not letting you have any of my new temporary tattoos."

"Oh no." Dev places a hand on his chest, feigning hurt. "How will I ever survive?"

She squints at him before turning to me. "Are you sure you want to marry my annoying brother? No one would blame you if you decided to run."

I giggle, looking from her to Dev. "Oh, I don't know. I think I'm going to stick it out for now."

Dev shrugs, holding out the drink we'd stopped by at a restaurant to buy her before heading here. "Well, I guess I'll just throw away this boba tea, then. You know, since I'm so *annoying—*"

"No!" She rushes to him, taking the cup from his hand and giving him a quick hug. "I was just kidding. What I meant to say was Piper is so lucky to be marrying you."

Dev chuckles as Claire gives the two of them an admonishing look. "Deena, didn't we talk about not having so much sugar? And you definitely can't have it before dinner."

Deena frowns down at the drink in her hand, her eyes hopeful. "But you wouldn't want me to waste this, would you? I'll wait to have it after dinner. Promise, Mom."

Claire shakes her head, taking a defeated breath. "Fine."

Wrapping her hand around the crook of my elbow, she gently leads me past the large sitting area, with Dev, Deena, and their father following behind us. We walk down a large corridor lined with their family pictures, and I smile at a particular one of a younger Dev holding his infant sister in his arms, to an equally massive kitchen where a couple of people I assume are staff bustle around, focused on their tasks.

As expected, though quite different from Dev's modern home, his parents' place is enormous, with sprawling ceilings, large staircases, and wall-to-wall windows on one side of the kitchen overlooking a beautiful rose garden.

The aromas inside the kitchen do nothing to ease the nervous energy fluttering inside me as I settle into a chair Dev pulls out for me. My mind races, rapidly answering questions his parents haven't even asked yet, while my heart pounds, hoping I don't screw up playing my part.

Dev takes his place beside me, his thigh brushing against

mine, calming some of my nerves, even while it sends a thrill down my spine.

Does he feel that, too? That jolt of electricity?

Clearing his throat, he casually picks up my hand, gently grazing his thumb over my knuckles, sending goosebumps soaring over my arms.

When I turn to meet his gaze, peering at him from under my lashes, something flickers in his eyes. Is that . . . affection?

Of course it's not.

It's pretend.

A performance and a production.

Sure, our conversation in the car—you know, the one where I asked him to fuck me—was interrupted prematurely by my dad's text message, but let's be real. My fiancé practically stopped breathing at my question, as if the thought itself was the most repulsive and scary thing he'd ever had to face.

God, this is all getting so confusing. Not because I don't know my role in this, but because somewhere over the past couple of weeks, my heart's forgotten that it was never supposed to get involved.

I'm just about to lean over to tell him to forget about my temporary bout of insanity when Dev's parents join us, sitting together on the chairs in front of me and Dev. His dad pulls a blanket over Claire's lap before placing a tender kiss on her temple, while Dev's sister settles herself on the chair at the end, eyeing her boba tea wistfully.

"Did you grow up in the Bay Area, Piper?" Claire asks, her voice sounding more tired than just five minutes ago.

I shake my head. "Actually, I grew up outside of Boston. I moved here several years ago with two of my best friends from high school."

Deepak's brow rises. "That's quite the long move. Is most of your family still back in Boston, then?"

"My brother and sister-in-law, along with my nephew, still

live there. My brother's a defenseman for the Boston Bolts NHL team, actually. And my mom now lives in Tampa with her husband."

Deepak's intense gaze stays on me. "And your dad? Where does he live?"

Reaching for my glass, I take a sip of water, hoping to give myself a moment to come up with an answer that doesn't sound like, *"I don't actually care where the fuck my dad is, but he did just try to contact me and I'm still unsettled about that."*

Placing the glass back down, I give him a placid smile and a version of the truth. "I don't know. My parents separated when my brother and I were teens, and I eventually lost touch with him."

I leave off the nitty-gritty details, like the fact that I blocked his number after he verbally berated me for being a *dumb piece of shit and a complete disappointment*, that he's a has-been NHL player himself who still thinks his children owe him for giving them life, or that he left my mother for his coach's young daughter, only to then end up alone after she left him several years later.

I'm trying to make a good impression on my future in-laws, not leave them thinking their son is marrying into a family saga fit for a reality show.

Dev and I exchange a look, and I glimpse an understanding in his eyes, even though I hadn't shared much about my parents with him. But then my mind floats back to our "conversation" in his car on our way here when my fiancé went all sexy mafia don and threatened to unalive whoever had texted me. The funny thing is, aside from my expression, I hadn't revealed anything about the text to him, but somehow he'd sensed I was anxious.

Still, I'd had to reel him in, given I wasn't ready to tell him about my lunatic dad, who was likely drunk off his ass somewhere.

*"Simmer down, Tony Soprano, it's no one you have to worry about."*

*His eyes had flicked back to the phone in my hand. "Then why do you look like your pet fish just died?"*

*I blinked at him. "Firstly, I was sad when Scarlett Johansson accidentally slipped into the garbage disposal when my brother was changing out her water. I still hold it against him, almost two decades later, because there's not a betta fish alive that could replace her. She was fast and furious, focused and fun." My throat had felt tight at the memory of poor Scarlett flapping around in the disposal. "I realize that's a lot of F-words but—"*

*"Piper."*

*"And secondly, I really don't like that idiom one bit. It's insensitive to aquarists."*

*"Okay." Dev took a breath so long, you'd think he was trying to inflate one of those tubular balloons in one shot. "Will you please just tell me if someone is bothering you? If you're in trouble in any way, I need to—"*

*"I'm not in trouble, and no one is bothering me," I said, hitting the button to block my father's number. "Now can we please just get going so that we're not making your parents wait any longer than they have already?"*

Thankfully, he hadn't pushed any further, and we moved on to align our "story" to avoid any mix-ups in front of his parents, which is why I'm well-prepared to answer the upcoming question from his mother.

"Families are complicated," Claire says with the same look of understanding as her son. "But Dev tells us you're a hairstylist. Is that how you two met?"

Nodding, I flash her a smile. "Dev came to my salon about a year ago and just loved what I could do with a pair of scissors." I suppress a giggle, knowing Dev is probably trying to hold back a groan. "He was so smitten by his new haircut, in fact, he asked me to be his girlfriend."

Claire's face lights up while Deepak eyes his son suspiciously. "Didn't you walk in here a couple of weeks ago with half your hair hacked off?"

A nervous laugh erupts from my lips because Dev and I hadn't aligned on this little tidbit, unfortunately, but I decide to take the lead on improvising an explanation.

"Oh well, you see, that was just me trying to modernize your handsome son here." I pat Dev's shoulder enthusiastically while he shoots me a mildly worried look. "You know, staying ahead of the trends, shake things up a bit. I suggested he try it for a day, but clearly, it wasn't his style and I fixed him right up." I wink at the man in question. "Didn't I, babe?"

Dev nods, his gaze unwavering from my face and his hand tightening around mine. "You sure did, *babe*. You have a knack for keeping me on my toes."

My eyes inadvertently slide down to his plush lips before I remember where we are. Shaking off my distraction, I turn back to face my to-be in-laws with a smile.

We're midway through dinner, chatting about our wedding—set to be held in Dev's mother's beloved rose garden—when Deepak wipes his mouth with his dinner napkin and fixes me with another intense stare that shifts the easy air in the room.

From the little he's spoken throughout dinner, it's clear he isn't much of a talker. Or maybe he just hasn't warmed up to me. With what I've read about him, given Dev has shared about as much about his father as I have with him about mine, Deepak raised his children much like he's run his businesses, with a firm hand.

"As you must already know, Piper," he starts, his brow rising, "our son holds several degrees from prestigious institutions, can speak several languages fluently, and has always been dedicated to learning and achieving. Our family very much values education. So, aside from cosmetology school," his voice hints at derision, though I can't be sure, "what other form of education do you have?"

"Deepak." Dev's mom shoots her husband a sharp look, clearly picking up his tone while the sound of Deena slurping the last bit of her boba tea fills the room. We all glance at her, but she's completely focused on sucking up the last tapioca ball through her straw.

I'm just about to speak when Dev interjects, intertwining our fingers again.

"Let me start by saying that Piper is a business owner, not unlike the two of us, Dad. And while we might hold business degrees, Piper has built an incredibly successful and unique business practically on her own. So, as much as you might expect that of me, I'm not looking for a trophy wife to parade around for her fancy degrees. I'm marrying Piper for a hell of a lot more."

His eyes linger on mine. "Not only is she beautiful, intelligent, charming, and hilarious, but she has a personality that could power the entire city. And beyond all that, she's authentic to a fault, and kind, even when she doesn't have to be." His voice softens. "There's no other woman I'd rather have by my side."

My heart skips a beat.

Damn, his acting skills are top-notch! Maybe he has a theater degree too, along with all his other fancy degrees, because I almost believed that!

The thing is, despite my ex making me feel like shit about not pursuing a formal education, and my father repeatedly telling me I'd never amount to anything throughout my formative years, I'm proud of how far I've come through sheer determination and hard work. But I won't deny it feels good to hear Dev's emphatic words, even if his feelings for me aren't real.

Clearing my throat, I find my voice again. "I think you

forgot the best part about being with me . . . free haircuts for life."

Dinner proves to be more activity than Claire can handle in one evening, so once the plates have been cleared, Dev and I offer to help her back to her room. Exhaustion lines her features, but a glimmer of gratitude sparkles inside her blue eyes when we settle her into her bed.

I quietly fill the empty glass on her nightstand with water while Dev fluffs the pillow behind her, his movements both careful and deliberate, as if focusing on his task is the only thing keeping him from breaking down. But despite his composed exterior, his eyes betray his inner anguish, and my chest tightens at the sight of the pain he thinks he can hide.

Claire reaches for my hand, silently tapping the spot next to her, urging me to take a seat. When I do, she takes my hand in hers, her touch tender as she brushes my empty ring finger with her thumb.

Her brows knit in confusion when her gaze wanders to the other side of her room, where Dev is drawing her curtains. "You didn't give it to her yet?"

Turning around, Dev's gaze finds our intertwined hands before he sees the puzzled look on my face. "I planned to do it today."

The corners of Claire's mouth curve upward. "Do you have it with you?"

Dev nods, pulling out a small velvet box from his pocket as he saunters toward us, his warm gaze trained on me. Even the way the man walks has my breaths unsteady. There's no way that can be healthy for me long term.

It's only when he kneels in front of me, revealing a sparkling solitaire in a vintage setting, that I realize what's happening and my hands come together in prayer at my lips. Forget the unsteady breaths from earlier, my breathing has now come to a halt.

I rise to my feet, blinking rapidly at the man before me on one knee. "Oh, my God."

"Peter," he whispers. "There hasn't been a moment since the day I met you that I haven't wanted you to have this. But since it's my mother's engagement ring, I thought I'd ask you officially while she was—" His voice falters momentarily as emotions threaten to overwhelm him before he composes himself, unwilling to vocalize the previous thought. "Will you marry me?"

Tears gather in my eyes as I look from Dev to Claire, finding love and encouragement in her nod. And while those tears shouldn't be real, and my heart shouldn't feel this heavy, everything about this moment is nothing but.

And so, without analyzing it for what it is or isn't, I slide off the bed to kneel in front of him. My chin trembles and a sense of pride and anguish collides inside me.

Wrapping my hands around his neck, I brush my thumbs over his scruffed jaw, peering into the eyes of the man I'm promising myself to—a man who'd literally do anything for the ones he loves—knowing I'll be walking away in due time.

"Are you sure?" I rasp, feeling a tear splash over.

His eyes hold mine in a moment that feels like a promise. A promise I know he has no intention of keeping. "I've never been more sure of anything in my entire life."

And before I even know how the next moment will unfold, I lean forward, doing something I haven't done in well over a decade—*kiss someone*—and murmur my answer against his lips, "Yes."

## fifteen
# piper

Live, Learn, Lasagna

"Holy shit, is that an engagement ring or an iceberg on your finger?" Sarina shrieks, poking her head out of the room just as I step into the salon early the next morning.

I rushed inside with Ralph covering me to avoid the two or three photographers we saw loitering on the street. While I've definitely seen paparazzi snapping pictures of me—along with a couple of magazine articles about me—they've mostly left me alone. Still, there's no reason to give them freebies.

While my salon has always had a decent amount of security around it—a doorman who only allows people inside if they are on an approved list—the extra security Dev has placed around the salon has helped deter any overzealous paparazzi from sneaking in. It's one less thing I need to worry about with the circus my life has become as of late.

"That thing could double as a paperweight!" she adds.

I chuckle at my best friend's ability to spot something from all the way down the hall, despite her tendency to be in her own world. Heading to the main desk, I notice Joshua glancing up from the computer to eye the ring on my finger. A smile plays on his lips, but he stays quiet as both my best friends emerge from their respective rooms to inspect my ring like certified geologists.

I'll admit, the ring is larger than I would have ever chosen for myself, but it's not the size but the sentimental value it holds that makes me love it.

*But it's not yours, Piper. It belongs to someone else . . . someone who'll wear it, not because she's Dev's fake fiancée, but because she'll truly own his heart. Something you're not trying to do. The sooner you remember that, the easier this will be when it comes to an end.*

"You could signal a damn UFO with this thing!" Sarina gasps, moving my hand this way and that to catch the light. "I love the vintage setting."

And despite just lecturing myself not to get attached to it or the sentimental value it holds, a smile tugs on my lips. "It's his mom's. He gave it to me in front of her last night."

My thoughts wander back to the image of Dev kneeling in front of me last night, hope brimming in his eyes, his hand trembling as he wiggled the ring over my finger. Like he thought I'd say anything but yes. Like I'd change my mind in front of his sick mother.

As if that was even a possibility.

I'd said yes without having met her. And now that I had, I couldn't fathom the thought. Not when I knew how much it meant to her to see her son settle down.

Not when it was her last and only wish, and I could help make it come true for her.

"So, meeting the parents went well, then?" Nisha asks, eyeing me curiously.

I chuckle softly. "Depends on which parent you're asking about."

My friends, including Joshua, who's both typing something on the computer and listening to the story, give me puzzled looks.

"His mom, Claire, is beautiful inside and out," I start, using the tips of my fingers to rub at an ache between my ribs. It's been there since last night. "I honestly don't know how Dev and Deena will cope with her loss. How does anyone, really? But to lose someone as wonderful as her?" The corners of my eyes prick and I shake my head. "You can tell she's their rock."

"It's heartbreaking," Sarina murmurs in agreement.

I smile, thinking about Claire. "She's something else. Warm and loving. It took me meeting her, seeing her light, to fully understand the depth of their family's tragedy. To realize how fleeting life can be, you know what I mean?" I ask my friends rhetorically. "Seconds after meeting her, I felt like I'd known her my whole life." I swallow. "And it sucks that I won't have more time with her."

For a moment we all fall silent, me looking down at my ring that feels heavy, not because of its size but because of the weight of her impending loss.

Nisha's eyes soften and she pulls me into a hug. "I can't imagine how hard this time must be for them. But as much shit as I gave you for doing this for their family," she pulls back to search my face, "I'm so proud of you, Piper. I don't think I tell you it enough, but there's not a person on the planet with a heart bigger than yours. A crazy, fun-loving, and free-spirited heart," she smiles, "but the biggest one of them all."

I squeeze her back. "You're right. You don't tell me that enough. Maybe, let's make it a weekly thing."

Nisha rolls her eyes. "Let's not go crazy."

"What did you mean by, it depends on which parent you ask," Sarina asks, reminding me to finish my story. "Did Dev's dad not like you?"

I snort, recalling Deepak's patronizing comment. "I don't know if it's so much about like or dislike as it is his expectations for his son. He made it clear he didn't approve of me, basically insinuating that I'm illiterate."

*"What?!"* Sarina and Nisha both gasp at the same time.

"Who the fuck does he think he is?" Sarina asks vehemently. "I don't care how many billions he has in the bank, he doesn't get to act like a self-righteous pig!"

"He's totally living up to the stereotype of an elitist and egotistical Indian dad, I guess," Nisha adds indignantly, right as the phone rings. Joshua answers it, typing something on the computer as Sarina, Nisha, and I move toward the sitting area to continue our conversation without disturbing him.

We're fifteen minutes from opening the salon and I still need to review my client list, but I also know that if I don't answer all my friends' questions now, they'll bug me the entire day.

"Our dad isn't like that, though. He's sweet and supportive," Sarina clarifies, as if I don't already know. He'd practically been like a second dad to me growing up. *More like the only dad.*

"Did Dev defend you or did you have to take his dad down a peg yourself?" Nisha asks, straightening magazines on the coffee table that don't need straightening.

I nod, recalling his words. "Yeah, he made it clear he didn't want to hear anything more about it from his dad."

"Well, that's good." Nisha nods, getting up to pull a chair so it is exactly in line with the one next to it.

She reminds me a lot of my fiancé that way—overly organized, with a penchant for cleanliness that borders on sterility.

I smile to myself, thinking about how we returned from his parents' last night. After a rather quiet drive back, Dev headed straight for his home office, where he stayed until God knows when. I was long asleep . . . but not before finishing yet another crossword puzzle he'd placed neatly on the corner of the living room table. Two clues were still unsolved. And my reasoning was that if he didn't want me to finish them, then he shouldn't be leaving them in the same spot every day.

*Sixty-one across: A vegetable in miso soup.* Enoki.

*Forty-four down: Section of Italian sonnet.* Sestet.

And just to irritate him further, I'd also *rearranged* his color-coded hardbacks on the shelves and placed his neatly stacked coffee cups in the cupboard below the coffee machine where he usually kept all the extra coffee supplies. I realized this was also going to annoy his housekeeper, Suzanna, but we'd recently become friends. When I tell her about it later, she'll likely appreciate someone loosening Dev's belt a little.

*Speaking of loosening his belt . . .*

God, I still can't believe what I asked him in his car on the way to his parents' place.

"Hello? Earth to Piper," Sarina says, jolting me out of my musings. She eyes me curiously. "Why are your cheeks all red?"

"Yeah, you look like one of those red-faced spider monkeys," Nisha adds, because of course she does.

Joshua, who has rejoined us, and Sarina chuckle as I roll my eyes at Nisha. "I swear, no one does compliments like you, Neesh. Have you considered a career in inspirational speaking?"

"But, seriously, why are you so," Joshua waves his finger in my face, moving past my question to Nisha, "pink?"

I take a long breath, knowing they won't drop it until I tell them. "I asked Dev to—" I wave my hand around, hoping one of them can fill in the rest without me having to spell it out, but clearly, my friends are playing dumb. "I asked Dev to fuck me."

*"What?!"* Nisha blurts right as Sarina lifts her hand to high-five me with a, "Yeah!" and Joshua looks like he's lost his brows somewhere inside his hair.

I shrug, feigning nonchalance. "Look, neither of us knows the exact amount of time we're in this. Yes, the doctors have given their prognosis, but God willing, Claire will live longer than their estimates, you know?" I look at my friends' faces for understanding. "And given neither Dev nor I will be with anyone else during that time, I suggested that we be with each other. Strictly physical, of course."

Sarina and Nisha exchange those sisterly looks I hate so much but can decipher now that I've known them forever.

"What did he say?" Sarina asks, her tone a mix of curiosity and concern.

I think back to our conversation in his car before my dad's text interrupted us. Deciding to omit the details of his text, knowing it will just worry my friends, I stick to the essential part of the truth. "He didn't."

"He didn't, what? He didn't say anything?" Joshua clarifies.

I nod. "Yeah, he went so silent, I thought I'd pushed an off button on him or something."

After the emotional night we had last night, I decided the ride back wasn't the time to bring it up again. Though I know I need to soon, if only to address the awkwardness. And given the man practically ran to his office to hide the second we got home, there's definitely awkwardness to be addressed.

Part of me feels a little stupid for even asking, given he looked like he'd frozen in time or something.

Maybe he's conveniently forgotten it even occurred.

*One can only hope.*

"Piper—" Nisha starts when I interrupt her.

"I know what you're going to say. That it would be a bad idea to get into a physical relationship with someone, knowing there is an end date to this. That it might complicate things further if he started developing feelings for me or something. But I'd already considered all that before I proposed it."

Nisha squints at me. "Just *him*? What if you develop feelings for him?"

"Pssh." I wave my hand dismissively. "You know that's not going to happen. My rules are clear for that exact reason. They're ironclad and—"

"Oh God, you and your stupid *ironclad* rules," she interjects with an eye roll that seems to take a full minute. "Would it be so bad if you did fall for a man for a change?"

I gasp so loud, I choke on my own spit. "Have you lost your bobby pins!? Of course it would be bad if I fell for him!" I squeak out, feeling out of breath. I won't admit that part of the shortness of breath has something to do with me envisioning what she's suggested and . . . finding it mildly appealing.

I shake my head vehemently, forcing myself out of the thought. "That wouldn't just be bad, it would be *terrible*! My rules are there for this exact reason!" I repeat. "It's why I state them upfront for all parties involved, and why I follow them to a T, so no one gets hurt."

"And what are these rules?" Joshua asks curiously.

He's been working with us for a year, but I realize I've never discussed my rules with him before. My girlfriends, however? They could probably recite them backwards and in interpretive dance form.

"They're simple," I start, lifting a finger for each rule. "No kissing, no spending the night, and absolutely no heart-shaped feelings."

I don't vocalize the other unspoken rules—to never become someone's priority or anything more than a delightful distraction. To never become someone's *anything*, really.

Why? Because life had taught me that it was best if you didn't have expectations. That the L-word was as dirty and foul as some of the worst four-letter words out there. It was both used and discarded often. So, the only L-words I care to stand by are 'live,' 'learn,' and 'lasagna.' Because let's face it, lasagna has never let anyone down.

"They've worked in favor of all parties involved so far," I assert, doubling down on my previous words. "And I'm sure they'll work for me and Dev, too . . . should he choose to accept. Though, as of now, that doesn't look likely, given his initial reaction." *Or lack thereof.*

Nisha sighs, as if she doesn't know how else to argue anymore. "So, what are you going to do?"

I shift on my feet, feeling unsettled. I've never had someone reject my proposal for no-strings attached sex, and while Dev hasn't exactly done that, my ego still feels bruised.

"I don't know," I admit. "I don't think I'll bring it up again, though. My vagina will probably prune up in the next few weeks, revirginifying herself to look like that of a mummified woman unearthed from the depths of a forgotten tomb." I shake my head, slightly panicked. "Forget getting a penis up in there; I'll barely be able to get a tampon in without it feeling like an archaeological dig."

"Wow," Joshua deadpans. "That visual was exactly what I needed this morning. Thanks for that."

Sarina tries to suppress a laugh while Nisha gives up whatever she's straightening to head back down the hall to her salon suite, murmuring, "Oh, for God's sake."

"Whatever," I grumble, heading back to the main desk to pull up my client list for today, when Vajayjay jumps up on the desk asking for attention. I pick her up, peppering her with kisses. "You understand, don't you, my sweet puss? You haven't had your lady bits loved in forever, either. Maybe never. We're like two peas in a very sad, very shriveled up pod, aren't we?"

In response, she jumps out of my hands, prowling over to the buttons, pawing at one repeatedly.

"I miss you," says the robotic voice.

Joshua, Sarina, and I exchange confused looks before realization dawns on me. "Oh my God, I think she misses Dev."

## sixteen
# **dev**

### Five Schlongs Hen Party

**HUDSON CASE**

[Image attachment: The one ring to rule them all]

**GARRETT MEYER**

Dude, did you go on a bank heist? You know the rest of us would have pooled our lunch money and bailed you out.

**HUDSON CASE**

I didn't rob a bank, dipshit. This is a picture of Piper's ring.

**GARRETT MEYER**

Is this what we do now? Share pictures of women's jewelry? Should we also discuss nail polish and the best ways to remove cuticles?

**DEAN MEYER**

That's pretty sexist, bro. I happen to have very healthy nails and cuticles.

Maybe Hudson accidentally shared this pic on this group chat instead of the one he has with the senior ladies he met at the last Bingo night. The one he has named "Hot Flashes and Adult Diapers".

GARRETT MEYER

Classic Hudson Case, boomer moment. [Old man taking selfie with backward Polaroid camera GIF]

HUDSON CASE

Why the fuck do I even associate with you idiots? This is Piper's engagement ring. As in the ring Dev gave her last night.

GARRETT MEYER

Wait, I thought Dev had already proposed. Isn't she living with him now? Why do I feel like I'm living in a weird time loop?

DEAN MEYER

Probably because you're a pilot and cross time zones for work. Maybe the things that happen in the present reset when you go back a time zone.

DARIAN MEYER

That's not how time zones work, you idiot.

DEV MENON

How the fuck do you have a picture of my fiancée's hand?

DEAN MEYER

Anyone else notice how growly he gets at the mention of Sniperella? Very jealous-possessive-alpha.

**HUDSON CASE**

@Dev Menon, easy there, lover boy. No need to get your toupee in a twist. She sent it to me.

**DEV MENON**

I find that hard to believe.

**HUDSON CASE**

In case you're having a case of amnesia, you do recall that I'm the one who introduced you to her? Piper and I are friends. She's like a daughter to me. She sent this picture to me when I messaged her to book a haircut for the next time I'm in town and told me you proposed yesterday.

**GARRETT MEYER**

This is probably not the time to remind everyone that Hudson married a woman younger than his daughter, who happened to work for him.

[GIF of Michael Scott saying, "Don't hurt me."]

**DEAN MEYER**

@Hudson Case, I thought your only friends are the pigeons you yell at in the park, and that post office clerk you rant to about stamp prices going up.

Also, @Dev Menon, I'm curious, did you have to put a ring on her hairless pussy, too?

**GARRETT MEYER**

I'd almost forgotten about the walking chicken breast with claws. Didn't she try to mate with your head last time, Dev?

DEAN MEYER

Someone is seriously *pussy*-whipped. Just curious, does this kitty have an OnlyFans?

[**Darian Meyer** has left the chat]
[**Dean Meyer** has added **Darian Meyer** to the chat]

HUDSON CASE

Christ. I think I need something stronger than a drink. A lobotomy, perhaps.

DEV MENON

For once, Hudson, I agree with you.

DEAN MEYER

Aww, look at hairless pussies bringing us all together.

@Darian Meyer, I swear to God, if you don't grow some actual balls . . .

@Dev Menon, just curious, since you've managed to shock us all the past couple of weeks, now that you've put a ring on it, can we assume Tiny Dev is getting action from more than just your hand?

DEV MENON

You can assume you're an asshole.

DEAN MEYER

Jesus. So catty.

[GIF of Two hairless cats fighting]

DARIAN MEYER

How has it been living with her?

## Swati M.H.

**DEV MENON**

You mean, her and her two fucking rabbits?

**GARRETT MEYER**

Hold up. Rabbits?! Are they hairless, too? Is this some bizarre fucking form of foreplay to jump-start your dick?

**DEV MENON**

She's trying to become a rabbit breeder. The little shits have chewed up one of my Persian rugs because my pet hoarder fiancée feels they need a "safe space" to run around free six hours a day. Not to mention, they wreaked fucking havoc in my house when she moved in.

**DARIAN MEYER:**

She's trying to become a rabbit breeder? What the hell?

**HUDSON CASE**

At least the bunnies are getting more action than Dev has in years.

**DEAN MEYER**

So, let me get this straight. You have a fiancée who scalped you, a hairless cat who wants to have your bald babies, and rabbits that are treating your multi-million-dollar minimalist manor like a fucking salad bar? And it's still unclear if you've been laid.

**GARRETT MEYER**

Your house was on Architectural Digest last year. Maybe you'll make Animal Planet this year. Your wet dreams are coming true, Tiny Dev!

## Pretend For Me

DEAN MEYER

Tiny Dev would be the animal featured on the cover of that issue. Captioned: Rare sighting of a shriveled up trouser snake in its natural habitat.

DEV MENON

I'm leaving this chat and changing my fucking number. Don't try to find me.

DEAN MEYER

Don't worry, we'll follow the trail of hair. Oh wait . . .

[**Dev Menon** has left the chat]
[**Dean Meyer** has added **Dev Menon** to the chat]

## seventeen
# dev

Lassoing A Wave

My eyes glaze over the work email on my laptop screen, unable to focus on a single word. I'd have better luck reading Martian with how little I've grasped over the past half hour.

I've been hiding in my office since I heard Ralph bring Piper home this evening. Yes, as part of the agreement to live with me, I also had her agree to let Ralph become her full-time driver because I don't trust her to watch her surroundings enough to know if someone is following her. Call me paranoid, but I've dealt with enough paparazzi to know that with our engagement now public, they'll be swarming her like squawking seagulls. It's for that same reason I have extra security around her salon.

I try to read the email again, but seconds later, I'm back to wading through my thoughts about the brunette living in my house. That smile of hers could cause a highway pile up.

I hear her chatting with my housekeeper Suzanna in the kitchen, their giggles floating through to my study. But it's her laugh—distinct, throaty, and free—that has my fist clenching on my desk.

"Fuck," I groan as an image of her in her oversized sleep

shirt flashes behind my lids. Aside from her short-shorts and cropped tank, it's the one she wears to sleep some nights. The one that practically shows her entire ass every time she so much as reaches for something.

The one that *definitely* showed the tiny lavender fabric nestled between her ass cheeks when she bent down to pick up her damn scrunchie as I walked into the kitchen this morning.

I spun around so fast, I nearly gave myself whiplash, mumbled a string of curses under my breath, and all but ran back to my room like my ass was on fire.

I'd seen her wearing it once earlier this week, and each time has been like a jolt of electricity plugged right into my stomach, bottoming it out.

What the fuck was she thinking walking around in that thing? I've been faltering between springing a boner and having a heart attack each time.

And as sexy as she looks in that T-shirt or those short-shorts, she was absolutely devastating in that emerald dress last night—something she really ought not to have worn, because I swear I found it hard to breathe, to think . . . to keep my damn hands off her.

There were a lot of things she really ought not to have done last night.

Like giggling while playing Connect4 with my sister for an hour after we put Mom to bed. I had business to discuss with Dad, but I'd barely heard a word he said as I watched my fiancée from my seat in his office, captivated by her little squeal of victory every time she won.

Like embracing my mother as if they were long-lost friends. In all the time Mom had known Camila, their connection had never sparked the way it had with Piper. Instantly. Fortuitously. And though I knew my to-be-wife was pretending, not a single person in the room could tell it was a rehearsed act.

Like the way she'd placed her soft lips on mine to seal our deal with the briefest of kisses.

*Or the way she told me she wanted me to fuck her.*

I'd practically gone catatonic.

Stopped breathing. Stopped thinking. Stopped functioning completely.

Wrapped in emerald when she'd emerged from her room earlier that evening had already made me feel concussed, but then she said the one thing I never expected, rendering me speechless. My brain had blue-screened like it was Windows 95.

Not to mention the way her citrus scent filled my car, the way her cheeks tinted pink, or the little gasp she couldn't stifle, surprised by her own audacity.

I'm not an idiot, nor am I blind. Over the past weeks, I've gathered that Piper is attracted to me, at least physically. The way she reacts to my touch—oscillating between pulling away and leaning further in. The way her eyes linger on my lips, with her wetting her own, or her nervous rambling.

I've become familiar with her tells.

Yet she still caught me off guard yesterday. One of the many things I'm realizing my fiancée is really good at, along with making me question my sanity and my ability to form coherent sentences.

Another thing my fiancée is really good at? Turning our living room into an emergency evacuation zone. She's not quite the disaster she advertised herself to be, but I suspect she holds back because of Suzanna. Our housekeeper is the real reason my bride-to-be hasn't unleashed her full chaos in my house.

Rolling my phone around in my hand a couple of times, I flip open my messages. My best friends are continuing on with their idiocy in our group chat, sending dumb GIFs and teasing each other.

As much as I pretend to be annoyed with their jokes, the Meyer brothers and Hudson have become the few people I can count on—friends who don't give a shit about my net worth or the things I could do for them, but ones who would give me the shirt off their backs if I needed it.

It's for that reason I messaged Hudson a few days ago, letting him know my reasoning for marrying Piper and this entire charade. I could have told them all in our group chat, of course, but I didn't want to bring down the mood or change the vibe for what the chat was meant for—buffoonery. I'd told them all about Mom's condition weeks ago, but I figured Hudson would update them on me and Piper. And given they haven't asked me about my reasons for so spontaneously proposing to my hairdresser again, I'm assuming he has.

Hudson understood immediately, without judgment or questions, telling me there wasn't a better person in the world than Piper in this particular case, but also warning me that her "heart isn't as solid and unbreakable" as she makes it out to be. But given my fake fiancée doesn't lead with the heart when it comes to men, I'm not too worried about heeding his warning.

My thumb hovers over Piper's name, trembling slightly as if it knows the weight of the decision I'm about to make. Her proposal in my car echoes inside my mind. The same proposal that's kept me hidden in my room for the past two nights like a monk in a self-imposed exile.

I've never been a "no-strings attached" kind of guy. Maybe I'm old-fashioned that way, but I've only slept with someone after having established a relationship. And while my fiancée and I do have a "relationship," on paper at least, I can't decide if sleeping together would complicate things more or make them simpler.

Well, let's be clear. My mind knows the correct answer—to stay the fuck away from a woman who's already dug herself past my barriers. It's screaming at me that going further would take her to a point of no return.

My dick, however? He's on a totally different page. One where he's begging to be freed and impatient to indulge the new proposal she set forth for him. To get something out of this arrangement, per her words. Something we both want. Something hedonistic, depraved, and unabashedly selfish.

Goddamn, that sounds tempting.

More tempting than any offer I've ever been given.

But as the battle between my head and . . . my other head wages on, I feel the scales tipping. The rational part of me, the one that's gotten me this far in life and my career, wins out, reminding me of the mess we could get into if we cross that line.

Because while I am a relationship guy, my fake fiancée is a self-professed commitmentphobe. She'd told me the day I'd asked her to marry me that she didn't do attachments, commitments, or love. Tying down a girl like that was akin to lassoing a wave. Not only would I never have her, but I'd probably lose a part of me forever in the process.

Before I know what I'm doing, I slip my phone into my pocket and walk out of my office with all the determination I can muster. It's been two nights of awkwardness between us, with her proposal hanging in the air like a heavy cloud, and given we have months more to spend together, I have to nip this in the bud.

I saunter through the living space between my office and the kitchen toward the sounds of Suzanna and Piper. But as I approach, my steps falter, my eyes landing on Piper, not in her work clothes or that infuriating oversized T-shirt, but in something even more aggravating. A fucking navy blue bikini.

"Fucking hell," I groan under my very shallow breath.

Despite telling myself not to, my gaze travels the length of her back—from her delicate bare shoulders to the strap of blue fabric clasped over an expanse of creamy skin, to the flare of her hips. My imagination kicks into overdrive as I picture my hands clasped around those hips as she rides my cock, her body undulating like a serpent I'd willingly let bind me in a spell. Or guiding her by them over my length as I fuck her doggy style, leaving punishing bruises on either side.

*Jesus. Get a hold of yourself, asshole. You literally decided none of that was an option two minutes ago. Get your dick out of her proverbial mouth.*

Forcing myself forward on unwilling legs, I notice Piper stiffen at my approach, as if she can feel me at her back. Apparently, the two women were engrossed in something on Suzanna's phone.

They both turn to face me, Suzanna's smile melting off while Piper's stays intact, if not becoming a touch more devilish. But it's not her smile that has my attention, it's the swells of her small breasts over her strapless bikini top. The hardness of her nipples behind it, as if waiting to be rolled between my fingers. And the miles of silky skin to the hem of her tiny bikini bottom, barely covering what I can only imagine is the most beautiful pussy to ever exist.

My mouth feels dry, even as I fucking salivate.

"Hey there, hubs!" she chimes, her voice as sweet and dangerous as poisoned honey, drawing my attention to her face.

As usual, her eyes sparkle with mischief, making me wonder if she's read every one of my filthy thoughts. I wouldn't be surprised if she has. The girl has to know the power she holds over men just by fucking breathing, existing.

Her usually long, flowing hair is in two buns on either side of her head, giving me an unobstructed view of her slender neck and those tiny moles I'm so obsessed with. A part of me wants to unravel her hair, if only to twist it around my fist as I claim her. While the other wants to have her play out my boyish fantasies with Princess Leia on her knees, gagging on my cock.

"Hey." I clear my throat, the single syllable scraping past my parched lips. I watch Suzanna excuse herself from the kitchen, clearly understanding my unspoken request for privacy. "Any chance we could chat for a few minutes?"

Piper takes a step toward me, her lashes fluttering. "I was just going to go for a swim." She throws her thumb over her shoulder, the movement causing her breasts to jiggle. "Wanna chat out there?"

Every rational thought in my mind screams for me to decline, to retreat to the safety of my study and tell her we'll just chat later. But as I watch the invitation playing inside her irises, her body a fucking siren's call in that scant bikini, I feel my resolve waffling.

Following her out to the pool is a terrible idea, one that could shatter the decision I've come to before I've even spoken it aloud. But, as if I'm being pulled by an invisible thread—one by the name of Piper Parker—I feel my head bob up and down before I hear myself say, "Lead the way."

I follow behind her, begging my eyes to turn away from the hypnotic sway of her hips, the curve of her spine, and the globes of the roundest, plumpest ass I've ever seen. An ass that begs to be palmed, spanked, and fucking bitten, if only so I can see how I've marked her skin.

I swear, the universe is testing my resolve today, asking if I'm *really* fucking sure about my decision.

Stepping outside, she sways her hips toward the cabinet with the towels, getting one out with practiced ease. The realization that she's been out here before, likely while I was out of town this week, hits me like a punch to the gut. My mind conjures up images of her lounging around the pool in the same scant attire and has a possessive anger rising inside me.

I make a mental note to tell my security team to turn off

the camera to the pool, my molars grinding at the thought of anyone else getting an eyeful of what's mine.

*She's not yours, jackass,* an internal voice reminds me, but I wave it off like a pesky fly.

I perch on the edge of a lounge chair, my body taut with anticipation as I watch her drop her towel on the chair next to mine before she heads to the edge of my pool.

With a gentle touch of her toes, she tests the water. Satisfied, she slowly descends each step, each movement illuminating the pool from within by underwater lights, glowing like liquid sapphire around her.

The water caresses the contours of her lithe body, creating ripples around her. Taking a breath, she fully submerges herself into the water before coming back up for air, propping herself up on the edge nearest me. My hands white-knuckle my lounger as I watch droplets of water roll down her face and neck, clinging to her skin, before reluctantly falling to the concrete under her folded arms.

"God, this water feels incredible," she murmurs, running her tongue over her wet lips. Her mouth curves up as she assesses me. "Want to join me?"

I shake my head, swallowing. "I'm good right here, thanks."

Piper juts out her bottom lip. "Oh come on, Lex. How often do you get to enjoy the things you've worked so hard for?"

Her words strike a nerve, conjuring up the imposter syndrome I'm constantly battling, reminding me that everything I have—this life, this wealth, my career—was given to me by my father. None of it is truly self-made, since all of it comes from a life of privilege . . . something I was born into.

And maybe it's for that same reason I never really enjoy anything I have. It's for that reason that I can't remember the last time I took a vacation, watched a movie, or hell, swam in my enormous swimming pool.

Sure, I've worked my ass off over the years, tried to move out of Dad's shadow and run things my way, but the fact remains: neither my schooling, my lifestyle, nor my position as CEO of *Menon Inc.* would be possible if he hadn't started it in the first place.

A fact he never shies away from reminding me. A fact he reminded me of multiple times last night when he tried to "knock some sense into me" during our private conversation in his office.

He'd insisted we had an image to maintain. That being with an "uneducated" spouse contradicted my own pursuit of education, and undermined what our family stood for.

What he was not saying, but I comprehended nonetheless, was that it undermined *him*. His authority, his reputation, and all that he'd given me.

Still, I *reminded* him, without losing my temper the way I wanted to, that I didn't give two shits about the kind of image he wanted me to uphold. That education wasn't measured in degrees, and that Piper's intelligence, kindness, and passion for life gave me a kind of perspective I never found in a textbook.

And while I was pretty fucking polite that time around, even my patience has a limit.

My eyes stay transfixed on the beautiful bombshell in front of me, looking at her as much as I'm looking past her.

What must it be like to just let go? To not carry the weight of anyone's expectations but your own on your shoulders? To just . . . be?

Piper pushes to her back, floating gracefully as she gazes up at the dusky sky with wide eyes. "It's beautiful out here this time of night," she muses, her arms and legs splayed out in the water as ripples trace her toned stomach. "And it's here, with my ears submerged under the water and my body above it, that I find peace."

My eyes track down her body again, my fists tightening around the edge of my seat as if it's the only thing tethering me to my spot.

"The funny thing is," she flicks a glance at me, "I've never liked the quiet. It always unnerved me, made me feel like I was stuck with my own thoughts. But things seem to be changing recently . . ." Her eyes meet mine. "I'm finding that the quiet and the controlled have a gravitational pull I can't seem to resist."

Water cascades down her body as Piper comes to a stand in the shallow end, fixing her eyes on me. There's a newfound intensity that's a departure to the mischief that's usually stirring within them.

Her chin lifts and she raises her hand, beckoning me like the siren she is. "Come on, big guy. I promise to save you if you start to go under."

And once again, like the chump I am when it comes to this woman, I throw caution to the damn wind and let her convince me.

Going under might be the only way I survive this.

# eighteen
## dev

You Should Come With A Warning Label

Piper watches me unbutton my shirt, her curious gaze taking on the color of the darkening sky. I drape the shirt over the lounger, acutely aware of her attention, before moving down to undo my belt. The metallic sounds of my buckle echo in the charged silence between us.

I can't help but meet her interested gaze as I unbutton and unzip my trousers, letting them slide down my thighs. Stepping out of the pooled pants at my feet, wearing nothing but my boxer briefs, I make my way to her.

Piper's lips part slightly, her eyes as transfixed on me as I was on her just moments ago. She licks her lips. "Christ, Lex," she breathes huskily. "You should come with a warning label, you know that?"

A smile tugs at my lips, both satisfaction and guilt battling within me. I'm flattered, triumphant, even, but that nagging voice inside my head demands I rein it in. That this can't progress past whatever this is.

Pushing the thoughts aside for now, I pad down the pool steps, sliding into the warm water beside her. Dunking myself completely under the water, I feel the air expand inside my lungs, allowing it to give me a chance to collect myself. I stay under for a few seconds longer, hoping the water will wash away my conflicting thoughts.

When I finally surface, driving my fingers through my hair to take it off my forehead, I find Piper watching me from the side. Her eyes linger on me, tracking the rivulets streaming down my chest.

Her elbows rest on the concrete ledge behind her in a casual pose that betrays the tension in the air. Her legs kick out in front of her, breaking the water's surface, bringing my attention to her feet as I make my way to her. Her toes are painted white, contrasting with the dark water around her.

White toes on slender, beautiful feet.

And despite the fact that I've never had a foot fetish—or *any* fetish, for that matter—I can envision myself becoming obsessed with those damn toes.

*I can envision myself becoming obsessed with every inch of her.*

I bury the thought inside the recesses of my mind as I close the distance between us, coming to a stand in front of her.

She lowers her legs, making ripples in the water around us.

"There. Happy?" I ask her, my gaze snagging on the way her chest rises and falls above the water.

She flashes me that grin—the one that screams trouble—like she's doing one of her damn victory squeals in her head. "Very," she says in a husky whisper.

I take another step forward, still towering over her, despite the fact that she's pulled up on her elbows and her feet no longer touch the bottom of the pool.

Her voice lowers and goosebumps smatter her chest despite the warm water. "So, what did you want to chat about?"

I inhale deeply, the scent of chlorine and citrus filling my lungs. How the fuck am I supposed to be letting her down when I'm seconds from grabbing her by her waist and tugging her to me? "I wanted to revisit the conversation from the car yesterday."

She drags a strand of wet hair out of the corner of her mouth, exhaling an exasperated sigh that stirs the water's surface. "I told you. That was nothing for you to worry about. I've got it handled."

Confusion bends my brows before realization has my hands balling into fists at my sides. The fucking text she got in my car.

I still don't know what it was about, but I'm willing to bet it would piss me off if I did.

Where I'm adept at concealing my emotions—though I'm doing a shit job when it comes to her, acting like a possessive lunatic—Piper's expressions are a mirror to her thoughts. I didn't need to know the contents of the message to know it had caught her by surprise, and not the kind followed by cake and champagne. It had shaken her. Her shoulders had sprung to her ears, her eyes had turned haunted, and an uncharacteristic frown had creased her flawless face.

But as much as I want to dig into that text, I'm also treading a fine line. She's done everything I've asked of her with little argument. If she's putting up a fight on this, I have to believe there must be a good reason she wants to keep me in the dark. And while I have the means to breach her privacy, I'm going to respect her wishes. It's the least I can do for everything she's doing for me.

So why is my gut waving a red flag, urging me to heed its warning?

The water suddenly feels a little colder, and I'm hyper aware of the little space between us—a space I want to both close and increase.

Biting my bottom lip, I reconsider even standing in here where all I can see, hear, smell, and practically taste is Piper *fucking* Parker. The bane of my existence, and the only one crazy enough to be in this situation with me.

I should go. Get out of this damn pool before its toxic water and her intoxicating scent have me saying the opposite of what I came here to say.

Instead, I find myself walking toward her, until I'm right in front of her. Lifting my hands, I grasp the ledge behind her as I lean in to speak at the shell of her ear. "I was referring to our other unfinished conversation."

Piper practically trembles before her eyes find mine. She flicks out a finger, dragging it up the inside of my bicep, all the way to my shoulder, before training it down my collarbone and around my pec. It twitches as my jaw locks.

Clearly, she's well versed in a game I've never been very good at.

"I see," she muses throatily. "You went all *Silent Patient* on me in the car yesterday. I figured you'd forgotten about it."

My eyes trail down her neck, finding those damn moles as the thought of dragging my tongue over them dances in my vision once again. "There's very little I forget when it comes to you, Peter."

"I hate that nickname, you know?"

"Somehow, I don't believe you hate it as much as you say you do." I lean in so the tip of my nose brushes her temple. "Somehow, I don't believe you hate it coming from *me*."

Her lids flutter, and I look down through the water between us, noticing her crossed legs, like she's trying to both subdue and spur on an urge between them. An urge I caused.

An urge I could feel on the tips of my fingers if I were to slide the navy fabric between her legs to the side and take a swipe.

And the satisfaction of knowing that I'm the motherfucker doing that to her does all sorts of wild things to my ego.

Her hungry gaze finds mine, her eyes no longer jade but a

color so dark, they're nearly black. "So, what did you decide? Are you taking me up on my offer?"

I'm about to answer when she adds, "There are some rules I just want to make sure you're aware of. Rules to keep this—*us*—safe."

Curiosity spurs me despite my better judgment. "Rules?"

In one fluid motion, her hands snake around my shoulders, fingers intertwining at the nape of my neck, sending shockwaves down my spine. The water splashes around us as she lifts her legs to wrap around my waist so she's suspended against me.

Her ankles lock behind me as her breasts press up against my chest, her soft curves to my hard planes maddening. And in one second flat, my cock goes from half-mast to steel pipe. The fucking devil incarnate knows exactly what she's doing when she grinds against me in a feigned innocent gesture, spurring on a low moan.

My heart pounds against my ribcage as my hands white-knuckle the ledge behind her in an attempt to thwart my desire to nail her to it with my cock.

"Piper," I growl in warning.

"Rule number one." She leans in, her tongue tracing my scruffed jawline, chasing a droplet. "No kissing."

My body stiffens impossibly, my breathing unsteady.

"Rule number two." Her fingers tangle in my hair. "No waking up together."

The water crackles with tension as Piper runs her thumb over my pebbled nipple. I quickly grasp her hand in mine, stopping her movement before I lose my resolve.

She chuckles softly. "And rule number three . . ." She slicks her lips. "Do not, under any circumstance, fall in love."

My nostrils flare, her words hanging around us like thunderclouds. My eyes dip to her lips. "Are those rules just for me, or did your previous sausage fest have to abide by them, too?"

Her lips tug up in a smile. "What would you say if I told you they were just for you?"

A surge of possessiveness battles with desire as I position her against the wall. "I'd say you sound worried. Worried enough to have rules just for me and not the others."

Her brow lifts indignantly. "The only thing I'm worried about," she clenches her thighs, grinding against me again and making me exhale, "is how I'm going to fit this cock inside me."

I brush my thumb over her bottom lip, listening to her breaths falter. But because my fiancée is nothing if not a risk-taker, an adventure-seeker, she chases my thumb with her tongue, pulling it in between her lips before sucking on it like a fucking lollipop. My eyes almost roll to the back of my head as I question my decision for the hundredth time since I made it.

Pulling my thumb out of her mouth and wrapping my hand around her delicate neck, I deliver my decision. "Then I guess you have nothing to worry about, Mrs. Menon."

"Ms. Parker," she corrects me. "I'm not Mrs. Menon yet."

"You will be soon enough. Might as well get used to hearing it now."

She ignores my statement. "Why did you say I have nothing to worry about?"

I tilt my head, looking down at her with a measured gaze. "Because my answer is no."

"No?" Piper reels back, her brows twisted in confusion. "Your answer is no?"

I give her a short nod.

"But—"

"Let's just make one thing clear," I interject before she can protest further, leaning in so my words brush against her ear. My breaths skate over her wet skin and a shiver runs through her. "The only person who needs those rules when it comes to us is *you*. Because if I were to say yes, the only person who'd break all three . . ." I lift a brow, watching realization dawn upon her before her mouth sets in a hard line, "is also you."

Setting her back on her feet, I whisper a truth I hadn't even realized until now, a truth cloaked in a language she won't understand. *"Tu hare ya na hare, jeet toh meri pakki hai, meri jaan."*[1]

---

1. Whether you lose or not, I'll still be the winner, sweetheart.

## nineteen
# piper

Take Him Salsa Dancing

"This was the bridal jewelry my mother-in-law gave to me to wear for my and Deepak's Indian wedding ceremony," Claire says, handing me a large red velvet box. "You don't have to wear it, but it's yours, nonetheless."

I hesitate taking it from her, feeling that same stirring of guilt inside my gut. "Thank you," I whisper, brushing my hand over the soft fabric and the tiny aluminum clasps on one end.

We're sitting in her beloved garden, watching some gardeners fertilize her rose bushes under the late September sun. With only two clients coming in earlier this morning, I'd decided to message Claire to see if she'd be up for visitors. I thought perhaps she would be sleeping or not in the mood for visitors, but she'd immediately responded with an emphatic, Yes! along with at least twelve emojis.

With Dev in Beijing this past week, our communication has been limited to texts. But with the wedding looming—caterers, music, cake, and a million other details demanding attention—I needed to wrangle out a firm date for our wedding. Even keeping it small enough to fit inside his mother's rose garden, we still need to send invites and prepare. Thankfully, we settled on a date at the end of October.

And because I like pushing my luck when it comes to my fiancé, I also managed to get a promise out of him to come into the salon tomorrow morning for his first photoshoot to be the face of our company.

It'll be the first time I'll see him since he left me speechless and soaked—in more ways than one—in his swimming pool. The memory of him, his eyes searing against mine, his body pinning me to the wall behind me, and his words spoken like a threat as much as an invitation sends a shiver down my spine.

But now that the wedding date is finalized, I want to make sure I include Claire in any preparations she wants to take part in. Which is the reason I'm visiting today, to get an understanding of her wishes. Well, that, and the fact that I honestly couldn't wait to see her again.

Given her deteriorating health, I know she won't have the stamina to be a part of every decision, even if we were to meet with the vendors at the house, but my hope is that the wedding is everything she hoped it would be.

I open the clasps on the box to reveal a beautiful golden ensemble that looks like it was handcrafted. The substantial choker with pearl accents would likely cover most of my neck and décolletage, a pair of dangling golden earrings gleam under the sun, and a large gold, emerald, and pearl medallion at the end of a string of pearls looks like it might be a head piece fit for a queen. A pair of golden and pearl bangles complete the set.

"This is . . ." My breath catches as I look at Claire, bundled up under a blanket, sitting beside me. "You must have looked so beautiful on your wedding day."

She smiles, her pale blue eyes looking off into the distance. "It feels both like it was yesterday and a lifetime ago." She looks at the box in my hand. "I remember I needed help getting on my *saree* and that head jewelry, but Deepak's family was there to help, accepting me with open arms."

I smile, sensing she might have more to say.

"It's a big part of Indian culture to give the new daughter-in-law jewelry as a symbol of welcome and acceptance. And while Deepak came from humble beginnings, his mother had held on to this from her own wedding to give to me."

"Wow," I breathe, looking back down at the set that's been passed on for multiple generations in my hands. "It's beautiful."

She nods. "We had two small ceremonies—one in the church my parents insisted upon and one in a Hindu temple. Neither Deepak nor I protested much about anything our parents wanted." Her smile wobbles as if she's in the throes of memories. "All we cared about was being together. He was, and still is, the love of my life."

My throat tightens, my brows coming together as I ward off the prick of tears at the corners of my eyes. "I can tell how much he loves you."

It's not an exaggeration. The man worships the ground she walks on.

Earlier when I arrived, he gave me a curt nod—not terribly unwelcome—before walking me out here to her outdoor sanctuary. He'd then settled Claire into a chair cocooned in blankets, leaving a cup of hot tea at her side. The only reason he isn't hovering out here now is because she'd shooed him away to give us time to chat alone.

"He's a complicated man, my husband," Claire muses, keeping her eyes trained on the roses. "He loves us all dearly, but he's always had sky-high expectations of our children, especially Dev."

She pauses, seeming to think for a moment. "Not that I'm making excuses for the way he's been, but Deepak had to take care of his five brothers and sisters at a very young age after his dad passed away. His mom didn't have much of an education, nor did she work, and Deepak was the oldest. I think some of the way he is with his children comes from the weight of that responsibility he never shed—always striving for more, always focused on the next thing."

I swallow, both of us silent for a beat.

"Despite his hard exterior and his impossible standards, he is proud of his children. He just has a hard time showing it, and that's created a rocky path between Dev and his father. One I've tried to pave wherever I could, but . . ."

Melancholy plays on her features as she trails off, shaking her head. "I'm sure Dev has opened up to you about him?"

I keep my expression neutral, knowing she thinks we've been together for far longer than we have before, giving her a short nod.

The truth is, beyond this arrangement and the minutiae of living together, I don't know much about my fiancé. Sure, I know trivia-level things, thanks to the media and Wikipedia, like his number of degrees, his almost permanent status as the world's most eligible bachelor, and the tabloid drama about his split with his long-term girlfriend. The speculations about that breakup ranged from reasonable to wild; a few magazines even claimed she'd become a nun because she'd found a 'higher calling'.

I'd almost choked on my coffee when I read that one morning. No offense to the Almighty—I mentally cross myself—but who in their right mind would want to leave a man like Dev for any path that wasn't leading directly to his bed? Given that *I know* the man is packing enough heat in his pants to make a firefighter blush—what with me *accidentally* grinding over him in the pool—I'm positive he could show any woman the pearly gates of heaven every time he was inside her.

Noticing Claire's tea, untouched and fairly cooled, I close the jewelry box and lift the cup, urging her to drink.

Her hand wobbles as she takes a sip before placing her hand on top of mine. "You're a sweet girl, Piper. I can see how much you love and care for my son. And while I wish we could have had more time to spend together," her eyes shimmer as she blinks back the tears, "I couldn't have picked a better person for him myself."

My heart sinks as I work to keep my expression schooled, the complexity of my strange feelings for Dev, the weight of Claire's praise, and even just her sincere approval making me feel like both a fraud and a coward.

"Thank you," I whisper hoarsely.

"I know I shouldn't ask for more . . . You both are already giving me a chance to be at your wedding well before you probably would have planned it, had it not been for this situation, but if I could—"

"Anything," I say hastily, gently tightening my hand on hers.

"Take him salsa dancing."

I sputter out a laugh, even though my heart feels like it weighs a thousand pounds. "What?"

Claire chuckles. "What I mean is, make him see that you can't live life sitting on an office chair. You can't live life flying across the world to a beautiful new city, only to come back not having seen a single thing outside of a conference room. That, no matter how much money is in your bank account, you won't care for a dollar of it if you're lying on your deathbed without having enjoyed all the moments that you let fly by."

I nod as a tear escapes through my lids unbidden.

She squeezes my hand. "Drag him out of his office and out of his shell, kicking and screaming if you have to. Take him to a concert, or salsa dancing, or hell, enter him into a karaoke contest if you have to." She chuckles softly. "Just make him live, Piper. Make him laugh. Show him there's a world beyond that damn laptop screen of his."

I nod again, surprisingly calm under the weight of her unexpected request. Perhaps it's the fact that having fun, being adventurous, and truly enjoying life has never been a chore for me. Perhaps the idea of getting Dev out of his shell doesn't feel like a hurdle, but an exciting challenge. Or perhaps a part of me just wants to hear his laughter rumble out of his chest, to see that dimple dance against his cheek, and to have those intense eyes trained on me while he does it.

"I promise," I say, surprised at how much I mean it.

twenty
# piper

## Maybe Rub Up Against His Leg

**UNKNOWN NUMBER**

Any chance you'd be up for meeting your old man tomorrow? I can be wherever you want. Or I can come to your salon.

ME

Unless you're looking for your ass to land in jail, do not show up here.

**UNKNOWN NUMBER**

Oh, well, hello there, daughter! I figured that was the only way to get you to respond to me. Fine, if I'm not allowed in your precious place of business, then tell me where and when.

ME

No. Leave me the fuck alone, Dad. I have nothing to say to you.

**UNKNOWN NUMBER**

It doesn't matter if you have anything to say to me or not, Peppercorn. I have some things to say to you. In fact, I have some things to ask of you. Where and when?

> UNKNOWN NUMBER
>
> Ignoring me again will only make me more insistent.

> UNKNOWN NUMBER
>
> Piper?

> UNKNOWN NUMBER
>
> Don't be the ungrateful bitch I expected you to be.

> UNKNOWN NUMBER
>
> Piper?

"Please tell me this photoshoot doesn't involve you getting near me with a pair of scissors," my fiancé drawls as he scrolls his phone. He's leaning against a wall nonchalantly, while photographers buzz around adjusting lights and fussing with the background.

We converted the cats' room for our photoshoot today. They're not happy about it—meowing as if we replaced their gourmet food with rotten kale—but let's not get into that.

I give him the stink eye. "Are we ever going to get past that? You know I have a list of stick-up-their-asses clientele like you, don't you? They're perfectly happy with my services."

That gets his attention.

Sliding his phone into his pocket, he gives me that intense stare that always manages to make my lady bits stand at attention like they're contestants on *The Voice*. "Your *services*?"

I cross my arms around my chest, internally high-fiving myself for drawing his gaze to my breasts. His eyes slide lower, taking in my exposed midriff. I'm in a long-sleeve white crop top and flared denims that accentuate my ass, my hair in two long braids over my breasts.

"Yes. My services. Are your ears still plugged from the flight, Menon?"

He leans in, his subtle woodsy cologne adding to all the things happening to my lady bits. "My ears are fine, but if you don't check that attitude, your ass will earn a very special kind of . . . service."

I reel back just in time for one of the photographers to yell, "We're ready for you, Mr. Menon."

Dev smirks at me, strutting over to take his position in front of the cameras like he's a peacock at a pigeon gathering. *Arrogant asshole.*

"Not going to lie, your fake fiancé is hot as fucking Hades," Sarina whispers in my ear, having materialized beside me out of thin air.

She must have slipped in a minute ago, but I hadn't noticed. Probably because I don't notice much else when a snooty billionaire is taking up all the space in the room. I turn toward her, noticing she's carrying Snatch in her arms like a newborn baby.

I snort with an eye roll, masking my agreement. "Yeah? Well, Hades just called. He says he wants his ego back. Trust me, my fiancé's hotness is directly proportional to his . . ." I purse my lips, not finishing my thought on purpose, making both Sarina and I giggle before her cat decides she's had enough and demands to leave the room.

Sarina lets Snatch out before turning to me with a huge smile stretched on her face.

"Oh my God! You fucked him, didn't you?" she whispers, placing her hand over her mouth this time as if someone could read her lips otherwise.

"No." I shake my head, but my eyes connect with the man

in question, smoldering at me like he knows the subject of our conversation. "What I meant to say is, that his hotness is directly proportional to his pain-in-the-ass factor, and they are both insufferable."

"Uh huh," she drones. "Is that why you both can't seem to stop looking at each other like neither of you has eaten a meal in months? Guarantee if no one was here right now, you would be ripping each other's clothes off."

"You forget. I *live* with the man and that has yet to occur."

*Not for the lack of trying, of course.*

Seriously, I put my best foot forward, wearing my cutest bikini and everything, but nope, the man has the restraint of a celibate monk.

I don't, though. My restraint is hanging on by a fucking thread.

"Maybe he's trying to be practical," Sarina muses. "Maybe he thinks that once you get physical, it will only become more challenging to untangle when it ends."

I scoff, plucking invisible lint off my shirt. "Then he doesn't know me at all. Entanglements aren't things I get *tangled* in."

I don't have to look at my best friend to know she's rolling her eyes. Thankfully, she's interrupted mid-eye roll when we hear desperate scratching at the door.

Sarina's just about to open it when I stop her. "It's Vajay-jay," I say with a sigh. "She's been trying to come in ever since she saw Dev walk in here. And if she's in here, she probably won't let him finish the shoot."

Sarina folds her bottom lip in a pouty face. "Aww, poor girl. She just wants a little love from her man."

"She practically licked him to death as soon as he entered," I counter. "She's gotten more action than I have. I can't even believe I'm saying this, but I might be jealous of my cat!"

Sarina giggles. "I mean, maybe you should take notes.

She's clearly doing something right." At my death stare, my asshole best friend, world renowned for her brutal honesty, continues, "Maybe rub up against his leg or purr in his ear or something."

"Wow," I say in mock indignation. "Thanks for the words of wisdom, Yoda. Also . . ." I mumble the rest of my words, hoping she doesn't hear them, "I already tried both of those things, and the asshole still didn't budge."

Sarina throws her head back, laughing, catching the attention of various people working the shoot. Despite my efforts, my face heats up, and of course, that doesn't go unmissed by the gorgeous overlord, A.K.A. my husband-to-be. His eyes hold mine before the corners of his lips turn up in a smug smile, like he thinks he's the reason for my blush.

He is, of course, but I hate how he knows it.

A second later, Sarina must decide enough is enough because she swings the door ajar, letting Vajayjay slip inside. And what does my cat do?

Yup, less than ten seconds later, she's purring in Dev's lap, climbing his shoulders while the cameras continue clicking.

"I heard you visited my mom yesterday," Dev says, looking at me through the mirror.

He's sitting on my salon chair, looking like a GQ model in a cat sanctuary, with not just my cat sprawled out on his lap, but Beaver and Snatch pawing his leg for attention. The image is both absurd and absurdly adorable. It's like I'm watching a feline version of his fan club, and to be honest, I'm not sure I'm not a member.

Dev scratches the back of Vajayjay's ear absentmindedly,

his long fingers moving in a way that has me thinking about all the things those fingers could do. My traitorous cat arches into his touch, purring even louder while making eye contact with me. I swear the little ho knows I would switch spots with her in a second and is making a show of getting what I can't have.

*See if I give you that catnip you've been jonesing for, little heathen. Momma's going to keep it all for herself because clearly, you don't know how to share.*

Dev is on a twenty-minute break, waiting for the photographers to call him again after they've changed up the set. He's also supposed to be changing into a suit once I've restyled his hair, but as it stands, I'm having a hard time recalling why we'd want to cover up what he's currently wearing.

I take a second to admire him in his polo and trousers. The fabric clings to his bulging biceps and thighs like it's painted on, reminding me of the unexpected and incredibly welcomed show I got this morning when I was on my way to work. I ogled him through the glass doors of his home gym, doing pull-ups with the focused intensity of a man scaling Everest. Each upward movement made the muscles of his back and biceps ripple under his sweat-soaked skin, and his ass was so fucking delectable and taut in his gym shorts, I practically short-circuited.

I run my fingers through his dark hair, touching it up with some gel. "Yeah. I wanted to see if she had any requests for the wedding and run some plans by her."

His expression is a mix of surprise and . . . appreciation, perhaps? "That's kind of you to include her."

I shrug. "Of course. Why wouldn't I? Isn't she the reason we're doing this?"

A strange silence passes between us, and my words settle like leaden weight amidst the tension. Do the lies we're spinning, the unexpected emotions, and the eventuality of this arrangement affect him, too? Because I can't seem to find my way through them most nights when I place my head on my pillow.

Dev drops his gaze to my cat, almost like he can't seem to hold mine anymore, but not before I see a flicker of something—longing? Anguish?—before his mask of cool composure replaces it once again.

And suddenly, I'm overly aware of all our points of contact, the air between us thickening with something I'm not ready to name. I search for a way to redirect us back into normal, less-turbulent waters where we banter without acknowledging the shifting foundation beneath our current arrangement.

Dev must sense the change too, because he takes a breath, finding my eyes in the mirror again. "Anything else you both talked about?"

Seizing the opportunity, I waggle my brows. "Oh, you know," I say, my stomach unclenching slowly, "just some girl-talk. Why? Afraid we were talking about you?" I adjust a few more strands of his hair, a mischievous grin forming across my face. "Don't worry, we have far more *interesting* things to talk about than the great Dev Menon."

Dev suppresses a smile, but I feel the tension dissipate between us. "I wouldn't doubt it."

Emboldened by our shift back to familiar territory, I decide maybe now would be a good time to drop a little bombshell. "I was telling her how my birthday was coming up," I say lightly, hoping the little tidbit of information will pique his interest. "She wanted to know my plans."

"Your birthday is coming up? When?"

*Bingo!*

"This Saturday," I say, aiming for casual, but feeling a weird flutter of anticipation inside my chest. "I'm turning the big three-oh."

He clears his throat, shoving away what I think is uncertainty. For a man who exudes confidence and self-assuredness through boardrooms and billion-dollar deals, it's both heartwarming and thrilling to see this moment of hesitation toward me. "Do you . . . do you have any plans?"

"I do, actually," I say, moving around to face him. I lean my hip against the counter, aware of how this position brings us eye to eye. "I'm taking your sister to Disneyland."

Dev's eyes widen. "You're taking Deena to *Disneyland*?"

I nod, enjoying his reaction all too much. "Yeah, we discussed it when I saw her yesterday. Your mom didn't have a problem with it. The last time I went was with Rowan years ago, and it's something I've wanted to do again. Deena said it's been a few years for her, too, so we thought we'd make a weekend of it and stay at the park on Saturday night."

"Just you and her?" Dev asks, and I can't quite decipher his tone. Is that just curiosity? Surprise? Or do I sense some disappointment, too?

"Well, no . . ." I say, studying his face. "Ralph is going to come with us, since I know you wouldn't like us going alone. I just figured you're always so busy, so I didn't ask."

I pause for effect, barely suppressing a grin and hoping he bites. I'm already looking forward to making Claire's wish come true.

"Unless . . . you want to join us?"

He ponders the question for a moment. "Yeah. I'll cancel my plans."

"*Really?*" My brows rise. Honestly, I didn't think it was going to be this easy to persuade the workaholic I'm to be marrying. "Are you serious?"

He shrugs. "Yeah. We'll take the jet. I'll also have my admin make a call to our VIP tour guide to make special arrangements so we can have privacy and security during our—"

"God," I breathe, a little overwhelmed. I knew Rowan

dealt with needing security when he went to public places, but this is on a level I hadn't considered. "Maybe Disneyland isn't the right place this year—"

"Peter," Dev says, getting my attention. "If Disneyland is where you want to go for your birthday, it's where we'll go. I just want to make sure we have the privacy we need."

"It just seems like a huge hassle now that I think about it. Maybe we can just watch a movie at home, instead."

Dev's nostrils flare. "We're *not* watching a movie at home for your thirtieth birthday, Peter. And it isn't a hassle; it's a matter of me making a single phone call."

I twist my hands together, looking down at them, feeling a tightness in my chest I hadn't expected. No matter how many times I've tried to catch him off-guard or entice him, the man knows how to turn the tables around on me.

"Thank you," I murmur softly.

"You're welcome," he replies, just as Vajayjay decides she's had enough of our tension-filled banter, getting up on her hind legs so her front paws are on Dev's chest. She stares into his eyes deeply before licking his scruff.

I giggle, shaking my head at my attention hog cat as she settles back on his lap. "I'm not sure she's going to let you even go back to work."

Dev finds my eyes, and I'm not sure he's just referring to her when he says, "Maybe I want to spend the day with her, too."

A zing of electricity courses through me before I muse, "Lucky pussy."

Dev's brow rises, a smirk playing on his lips. "You jealous, Peter?"

"No," I respond, taking a deliberate step toward him. His eyes darken, tracking my movement. I reach out, seemingly to adjust a few more strands of his already-perfect hair, letting my fingers trail down to his sideburns and his stubbled jaw. "Just waiting for my turn. But let's just say if I was on your lap, you'd be walking out of here with your pants drenched."

Dev's tongue darts out, wetting his bottom lip, seeming to consider his next words. "Is that a threat or a promise?"

In a move I wasn't anticipating myself, I scoop Vajayjay into my arms, carrying her out of the room with her siblings curiously following their sister. Placing them in the hallway, I ignore their protest as I close the door and turn the lock behind me.

When I return, Dev is still seated, studying me with a mixture of curiosity and anticipation, his hands tightening over the arms of the chair.

My voice, low and steady, despite the way my heart is hammering inside my chest, I answer his question, "Maybe we should find out."

## twenty-one
## dev

Sweet and Wild

Sometimes I wonder if I'm my own worst enemy.

The events leading up to this moment would definitely make it seem so. Of the various possibilities I could have gone with to fulfill my mother's dying desire, I chose the one guaranteed to push the bounds of my self-control. It's as if I was subconsciously hellbent on self-sabotage, knowing my chosen path would challenge not only my resolve, but my sanity as well.

Yes, my sanity. Because from the day Piper Parker walked into my life—my vibrant wild card, the match to my powder keg of repressed desires—I've realized I have little of it left.

Now, as I watch her approach, poised and determined to shatter my well-constructed walls and my diminishing willpower, I feel like I'm balancing on the edge of a cliff.

And God help me, I'm about to fall.

My body tenses with each step she takes, my senses on hyper-alert. My hands tighten around the arms of the chair as I force myself to breathe, to maintain some semblance of control. But the sway of her hips, that mischievous glint in her eyes, and her beautifully parted lips tell me I'm about to lose that as well.

And a part of me—a much bigger part than I'd suspected—is eager to do so.

Clicking some lock on the side of my chair, Piper drops its arms, straddling me as if it were perfectly natural for her to do so. As if we've done it a million times.

Her hand skates over the back of my neck as she rolls her hips over my groin, surely feeling the boner I'm hoping to force down.

"Piper . . ." I warn half-heartedly, my throat bobbing. At this point, I don't know if I'm asking her to continue or begging her to stop.

"Are you not attracted to me, Lex?" she asks breathily, dragging her hips over me again. Her hand tightens on my neck while the other squeezes her breast.

*Fuck.*

I don't respond, all the words lodged inside my throat, feeling my cock turn to stone underneath her. If that isn't enough to answer her question, I don't know what would be.

"I know you don't want to touch me," she huffs, grinding against me. "I don't know the reasons. Maybe you think it'll complicate things, or maybe it's simply that you're not attracted to—"

"Does it look like I'm not attracted to you?" I grit through my teeth, relenting as I palm the globes of her ass on my lap, even as warning bells ring somewhere in the crevices of my mind. "Does it *feel* like I'm not attracted to you?"

She hitches one shoulder up, scraping her bottom lip with her teeth. "Sometimes it feels like you can't get far enough away, even when we're under the same roof." Her body undulates over me. "Plus, you did say no to my proposal—"

"You know damn well my answer had nothing to do with attraction," I croak almost desperately.

Everything battles inside me to shove her pants off, spread her open on my lap, and show her just how attracted I am to her. Instead, I ball my hands into fists on her ass and pray I can still rein this in.

But I already know we're in too deep, without a raft or life jackets.

She fists my shirt, the engagement ring I gave her sparkling. I've noticed she never takes it off—not even when she goes into the pool—and God, there's no end to the satisfaction that brings me.

Her lips find my neck, her hot breath skating across my skin before her tongue follows the trail.

"Then touch me, Dev," she begs. "Make me come."

*Jesus.*

*This is a terrible idea. This could complicate everything. She'll leave as soon as this charade is over, and I'll be left with all the pieces.*

"Piper . . ." I try once more, leaning away to create space between us.

"Fine," she relents, her hips coming to a halt. Her forehead falls against mine as our breaths entangle between us, fast and heavy. "You're attracted to me but don't want to fuck me. Is that it?" "You know it would be a bad idea," I murmur, trying to convince myself as much as her.

She nods against my forehead, her hand still clasped around my neck. "Do you know how much you turn me on?" she asks, her words doing nothing to drown out the sizzling electricity between us. "You drive me crazy, Menon."

*The feeling is mutual, sweetheart.*

"How am I supposed to go back out feeling like a live wire?" she huffs out a labored breath as her shoulders slump.

"Maybe you don't have to."

I say the words even as I wonder how to call them back.

Her brows knit, her eyes flickering between mine. "What?"

I swallow, already knowing I'm taking us back into

dangerous territory when I'd just barely brought us to safety. "I won't fuck you, but . . ." I trail off, waiting for her to pick up where I'm leaving off.

A smile spreads across her beautiful face, a spark reigniting in her eyes as realization dawns on her. Her hips roll over me again. "But you'll watch as I fuck myself."

I manage a nod, giving her the escape clause—the fucking fine print—we both seem to be looking for.

"Don't tease me, Lex. You're always teasing me. Walking around with clothes on and then walking around with less clothes on. It's like a shock to my system every time I see you."

I bite the inside of my cheek. "It's a shock to see me with and without clothes?"

"Yes. It's frustrating," she says breathily. "Tell me this isn't like the time in the pool when you left me high and dry."

"Pretty sure there was nothing dry about you that day."

"Ugh, see?" she whines, cupping her breast and rocking over me. "This is what I'm talking about. You make me . . . you make me feel feral, Menon."

"Show me," I croak, feeling my aching hard length under her.

"You want to see what you do to me? Hear your name on my lips as I come?" She shudders, keeping her gaze on me. "Pretend it's your fingers and your cock inside me?"

I groan in response, a primal need taking over as I spread my hands over her ass again. Pushing and pulling her over me, we create a friction that's going to have us both detonating.

In one quick movement, Piper takes off her shirt, barely giving me time to catch up, before throwing her bra to the floor, too. Her perfectly round breasts spring free, her raspberry-pink nipples pebbled and so close to my face, I could pull them between my lips with the slightest movement.

God, I love the way she looks right now, her cheeks

flushed, her golden-green eyes ablaze, and her perfect breasts bouncing with each roll of her hips. And those fucking tiny moles . . .

Weeks of imagining what she looked like, and nothing I'd conjured could match the real thing—the absolute beauty she is.

I keep my focus trained on her as I wet my lips. Hell, I couldn't look away if the world depended on it. My cock throbs inside his restraint, and I lift my hips, chasing the feel of her over me, with a low groan.

Piper's eyes stay on mine as she flicks open the button to her jeans next, unzipping them. She slowly slides her hand inside them, trying to find some relief, but it's impossible, given how tight her pants are.

"Take them off."

My command reverberates inside the small room, my weakly held restraint shattering at the sight of her struggling. If relief is what she needs, then there isn't a person in the world—not even me—who could stop me from giving that to her.

Her eyes flash, a shaky breath making its way out of her lips as we both take a moment to let my words sink in.

My heart hammers as my eyes slowly peruse upward from the open hem of her jeans, with her lacy white thong peeking through, to her exposed breasts, before coming to a stop at her face. My brow rises in challenge, but I don't repeat myself.

And apparently, I don't need to, because a second later, Piper is back on my lap wearing nothing but her thong.

"Now touch yourself."

Her body shudders from my command, but she does as asked without further instruction. With one hand on my shoulder for support, she brushes her fingers around her nipple before rolling it in between her fingers on a moan.

*Christ.*

I groan my approval, wishing I could help her with it. I can practically taste her now, her citrus scent intermingling with the scent of her juices. I don't even have to touch her to know she's soaked. All because of me.

"Suck on your fingers like you'll suck on my cock, and then slide them down to fuck yourself."

Her mouth falls open at my command, but she keeps her eyes glued to mine. Lifting her fingers to her lips, she sucks two of them into her mouth, making a show of it as she moans around them. The thought of it actually being my cock has me dragging her over it again, making her whimper.

Piper traces her wet fingers down between her breasts, circling her rosy nipple, before sliding them further down. Her fingers play with her clit over the thin fabric of her thong, and I hiss, seeing how wet it is.

*Fuck! This woman is going to be the death of me.*

Pulling the fabric aside, she circles her clit, revealing herself to me. And what a breathtaking reveal it is, slick and rose-petal pink.

"Goddamn, baby," I say, practically snarling at the sight of her. "Look at that pretty pussy. Glistening and so fucking beautiful."

Piper whimpers, preening under my appraisal, rubbing her fingers over her clit. "God, Dev," she breathes, her eyes hooded as she reaches for the back of my neck again. "Do you see what you do to me?"

"Show me what I'd do to you if it were my hand."

Rubbing circles over her clit a few more times, she continues to rock over my painfully hard cock before sliding her fingers down to her opening. The sound of her slick pussy resounds louder than our breaths as she tests her two middle fingers inside, groaning at her own touch.

"Dev . . ." she whimpers, throwing her head back and dipping her fingers in further.

"Jesus, baby," I croak. "Are you always this wet for me?"

Straightening, her turbulent green stare holds mine as she widens her legs, rubbing her clit with her palm while her fingers fuck her entrance. A few seconds later, she pulls her fingers out, glistening with her juices, bringing them to my lips in response to my question.

"Always."

I don't hesitate, sucking her fingers into my mouth.

"Fuck, you taste good," I say, licking my lips. "Sweet and wild."

"You like sweet and wild?" she asks, pressing her two digits into her entrance again before taking them out and rubbing her clit a few times. Her small nub swells as she leaks over her thighs.

"It's becoming my favorite flavor."

"Yeah?" she asks, thrusting her fingers inside her with more urgency. They're inside her, past her knuckles, as she rides them and me. "You want that flavor on your lips again?"

My throaty voice, my hands gripping her ass in an almost bruising touch, and my cock screaming under her are the only evidence that I'm here. That I'm not dreaming. That this is actually happening.

"On my lips, my tongue, and my cock, *meri jaan*. I want to be drenched with you, fucking bathe in you every day."

Images of my mouth between her legs and my fingers plunging inside her practically have me seeing stars. And gone are my concerns about what this means, or how complicated we've just made things, and the million other things that take me away from this moment. Reality will strike again soon enough, but I'll deal with it when it comes.

"Dev!" Piper's hips sway harder, with less precision.

Her eyes squeeze shut, and a slight sheen of sweat covers her chest as her fingers move inside her at a frenzied pace.

Her head falls back as if she can't manage to hold it steady while she desperately chases her release. She's seconds from going up in flames.

"You're so beautiful," I praise, watching the most erotic scene unfold above me. My wildest fantasies couldn't have created this. "Your perky tits, your tight little pussy." I swat her ass, making her mewl. "You were intent on making a mess on my pants, weren't you, my little hellion?"

"Yes," she purrs, plunging in and out of herself.

Grabbing one of her braids, I pull her closer, letting my words brush against her ear.

"Spread those legs wider for me," I command, my breaths as uneven as hers. "Show me how that sweet pussy will stretch over my cock."

"Oh, God," she breathes, doing as I ask.

Widening her legs even further, she continues to work herself before dropping her other hand to rub her clit. Using both hands, she pleasures herself—rubbing her clit vigorously with one while fucking her pussy with the other like it's her only job.

I hold her steady, watching her in awe and bewilderment.

"You going to be able to take me, baby?" My words come out hoarse. "You going to be able to take my thick cock?"

And that's when euphoria takes over her entire body.

With a scream she barely contains, she bucks over me. Her eyes roll to the back of her head and her thighs quake over mine.

"Dev! I'm . . ." Piper tosses her head back, a heated moan falling from her lips as she grinds her hips, exploding like a bottle cap under pressure. "Oh, God, I'm coming!"

Her eyelids flutter and her skin is flushed and slick as her fevered eyes meet mine again. A moment later, that same up-to-no-good smile graces her lips as she releases a shaky breath.

"I knew you could show me the pearly gates of heaven, Dev Menon," she whispers breathily, her body falling limp against mine. "And you did it without even having touched me."

## twenty-two
# piper

A White Flag

"Space Mountain!" Deena shrieks, grabbing Dev's forearm and bouncing on her toes. Her Princess Elsa crown catches a glint of sunlight. We're wearing matching Elsa tiaras and gowns, actually. "Can we go to that one next?"

Her brother grimaces, his throat bobbing, before he shifts uncomfortably on his feet.

Wait, is that . . . fear I see in the unflappable and fearless Dev Menon? Surely he couldn't be afraid of a little roller coaster?

Is that why we've only been on some of the tamer rides so far? He's been clutching that park map with all his might while he skillfully steers us toward attractions like Indiana Jones' Adventure and Gadget's Go Coaster. The latter is only a roller coaster in name; it barely qualifies as a toddler ride! Hell, I think he would have taken us to an actual toddler ride if it didn't cost him his reputation.

And then, when we were just about to board Big Thunder Mountain—a rocking chair might be scarier, by the way—I looked over to see that my fiancé had conspicuously gone missing. He'd later chalked it up to needing to go to the restroom.

"Of course!" Dev responds, though I notice his voice

sounds a little higher, like he's competing with Mickey Mouse. "There's nothing I'd like to do more." He turns to me with a hopeful expression, though I'm pretty sure I know what he's hoping for. "I mean, if that's what the birthday girl wants?"

I narrow my eyes, a smirk dancing on my lips. *Nothing he'd like to do more? Really?*

Oh, this is going to be fun.

The warm California sun is finally making its way out of the clouds as we stroll down Disneyland's Main Street, USA. Though it's been overcast and chilly all morning, I'm just happy that rain is not in the forecast. At least we can enjoy the park without any weather-related interruptions.

Or any interruptions, for that matter, because even though the park is bustling with its usual magic, there's a bubble of privacy around us. Dev's security team, dressed like everyday visitors, have created a perimeter around us while giving us the room to enjoy the experience without feeling like we're being watched.

The four of us also have VIP access to all the rides, entered through private entrances, and have even taken some rides alone without the rest of the public.

I say *four* of us because Rome came with me. Sarina was supposed to have him for the whole weekend, but I begged her—manipulating her with my curled bottom lip and clasped hands, telling her it's what I wanted for my birthday—to let him come with me. Plus, I reminded her that she's been wanting him to get his nose out from reading books all day.

Thankfully, she caved. It's not that she's an overprotective mom, like my sister-in-law Shayla, but she's never allowed Rome to go to another city with someone.

And fortunately, Deena and Rome made an instant connection, despite their age difference. I was a little worried when we first boarded the jet this morning, given they'd never met. But a one-hour flight, several flavors of boba tea, and a thousand space facts later, and they'd become the best of friends.

"Yeah! Let's do Space Mountain next! Please, Aunt Piper!" Rome begs, his NASA-themed hat so low on his forehead, the bill hits his glasses. "Will it really feel like being in space?"

"I don't know, Rome," I say, lifting his hat and tucking his hair into it. "But I'm sure Uncle Dev can tell you all about it. He looks like a real roller coaster expert, wouldn't you say?"

Dev shoots me a look, and if looks could kill, the ghost of Piper Parker would be hovering over the streets of Disneyland right now. She'd also probably be stuck in a loop inside Gadget's Go Coaster in some form of hell on earth, too.

But I am glad to see my husband-to-be is finally looking at me again. If getting under his gorgeous skin is what it takes to break some of the tension that's been lingering between us ever since our "encounter" in the salon a few days ago, then so be it.

He's been attentive all day, having silenced all his work calls and making sure every detail is perfect for my birthday. It's been nice seeing him let go, even if it doesn't come in the form of raising his hands up in the air and screaming until his face is blue while plummeting a hundred feet at fifty miles-per-hour.

I'm just glad to see that rare dimple grace his beautiful face and those chestnut eyes crinkle at the corners.

I know he's been increasingly worried about his mom, still struggling to accept her situation. It's clear with the number of times he calls and visits her how terrified he is. But I also suspect he needed today, if not only to get his mind off of everything temporarily.

Still, things have been tense between us, like he's scared to get too close for fear of a repeat of what happened at the salon.

"Uncle Dev, what will Space Mountain be like?" Rome asks excitedly, and I hold back a giggle.

"It's um . . ." Dev mumbles, looking green. "Dark and fast and . . . unpredictable."

"Oooh!" Rome and Deena say together, clearly not picking up on the fact that Dev looks like he's going to be sick.

"Let's go there, then!" Rome says, heading toward the sign.

I grab his hand before he can sprint off, throwing my fiancé a bone. "I don't know, buddy. I think you might be too little for it."

"Yeah," Dev piles on quickly. "I'm pretty sure you're too little for it. Maybe in a couple of years . . . or decades."

Rome crosses his arms around his chest indignantly, bending his brows. "That's not true. I'm forty-four inches! You know I can go on all the rides as long as an adult is with me."

I give Dev an apologetic smile before turning to my godson. "I meant, you might be too young for it. It's not like the Star Tours ride we just went on, Rome. It'll be fast and scary."

I notice Dev's shudder from the corner of my eye, nervously rubbing the back of his neck.

"I won't be scared, I promise," Rome pleads. "But if you're scared, you can hold my hand, okay?"

I purse my lips, suppressing my smile. "I'm not sure I'm the one needing the hand-holding. Uncle Dev on the other hand . . .?" I waggle my brows at my fiancé. "What do you say, Lex, want to hold my hand? Let me take another *wild ride* with you?"

I take a couple steps toward him, making sure he's the only one who can hear me. "Or on you. I promise to scream your name again while I do."

Heat flashes in his eyes, and I know we're both envisioning the same thing—the way he took charge of my body without having laid a single finger on me—before he quickly masks it with a glare.

I bite my lip, fluttering my lashes and swaying from side to side innocently, making my princess gown swish.

Dev's lips twitch before he sighs, looking up to search the sky for answers. Finding my eyes again he says, "You're the devil, you know that?"

*Ha! Victory is mine!*

I adjust my tiara. "You flatter me, dear husband-to-be."

"God, look at this view," I breathe, watching bursts of color illuminate the sky and castle before stealing a glance of my fiancé from over my shoulder. And now I'm not sure which view I'm referring to.

The lights from the fireworks play across his face, casting a mesmerizing glow over his usually sharp features, and for a second, it makes me feel breathless.

He takes a step toward me so his chest is only a mere inch from my back, the heat radiating off him enveloping me against the cool breeze wafting through the balcony.

"I haven't been able to take my eyes off it," he murmurs as his eyes connect with mine and that same buzz of electricity strums between us.

It's been there all day.

There's been tension and unspoken words too, yes. But there's never been a moment without that current thrumming between us like we're two charged poles.

The hours passed in a flash after we came out of Space Mountain. I don't know who laughed more between Deena, Rome, or me, but every time we looked at the grainy, candid picture of Dev while he was on the coaster, we'd burst out into a fit of giggles. It didn't help that Dev gave us all stoney stares in response; it just made us laugh harder.

I'd made sure to purchase a copy of that picture to frame at some point because I swear, there was nothing better in the world.

I'm tempted to giggle again as I think about it because the man literally looked like the 'grimacing face' emoji, smiling through clenched teeth, with eyes as large as dinner plates. His hair was completely disheveled, probably standing on end, and I guarantee he was white-knuckling the metal safety rail even though I couldn't see it.

As discreetly as possible, I also purchased another photograph—one of me looking directly at him. Even in the dark, plunging hundreds of feet, he's all I saw.

That photograph is one I'll keep for myself . . .

A token to remember today.

A token to remember *us*.

Since he'd been such a good sport, we'd decided to give him a break from the crazy roller coasters after that, though he did join us on the Matterhorn Bobsled and came out of that looking quite pleased with himself.

We ate corn dogs and churros and Dole Whip, and we even had a private lunch with the entire Disney cast.

When we went through the shops and Dev saw me eyeing the Beauty and the Beast tea set—*seriously, I looked at it for three-point-five seconds*—he promptly purchased twelve. When I asked him why, he said he wanted a full set of *Chip* teacups so our guests wouldn't feel left out.

Because what kind of hosts would we be if not ones to serve the tea we never made in Disney-themed tea cups?

But amidst the whirlwind of today, there was one thing about my fiancé that stuck out more than ever. It's not that I'd never noticed it before; I mean, it's practically his entire personality, alongside his broodiness and quiet moments. And that's his capacity to care. His capacity to do *anything* for the people he cares for.

Whether it was rechecking Deena's safety harness on each ride, reminding Rome to stay hydrated with water instead of soda, or continuously finding ways to make sure I felt special on my birthday, the man wasn't happy unless everyone else was.

And now that the day has come to an end, we find ourselves on a private balcony, overlooking the castle with the bustling crowd nothing but a murmur below us. It's as if we're in our own little snow globe. Except, instead of the snow, there's a whole lot of electricity buzzing around us.

Deena and Rome are plastered to the railing, with Elsa and Buzz Lightyear standing on either side of them. Neither are paying attention to me or Dev, standing a little too close, feeling a little too warm. Thankfully, we're also shielded by the veil of darkness, save for the occasional dance of lights around us.

I turn around to face him, tilting my head back to meet his gaze. His usually guarded eyes reflect a kaleidoscope of colors, and I'm not sure they're only from the bursting sky.

My hands find his chest, feeling the rapid beating of his heart underneath. Slowly, as if I'm scared he'll spook—the way he did after the last time we were this close—I let them travel upward, tracing the column of his throat. I feel him swallow before the weight of his palms meet my hips. I shudder against him despite feeling the warmth from his skin seeping through my gown.

Trailing my hands up to cup his jaw, I brush my fingertips over his scruff, saying more with them than I can with words in this surreal moment.

My head is a jumble of thoughts, each one in a race with

the other, while my heart feels like it's beating steadily for the very first time in my entire life.

How is it possible for this man to make me feel like I'm flying high and sinking deep all at the same time, while also making me feel so . . . grounded? So tethered?

"Did you have fun today?" I ask him, feeling a mix of anxiety and exhilaration.

His brows bunch together. "I'm pretty sure I'm supposed to ask you that. Did you have fun on your birthday?"

"I don't think I've had this much fun in my entire life," I answer sincerely.

He smiles, and I take the moment to catalog the way his beautiful lips stretch, moving my thumb to brush that adorable dimple I'm so obsessed with.

"Your turn," I insist, feeling like a bundle of nerves.

I'd promised Claire I would pull her son out of his busy life and force him to have fun. But now, as I stand waiting for his answer, I can't help feeling worried that perhaps I didn't fulfill my promise.

Dev's eyes soften before he lifts his hand, tucking a loose strand of hair behind my ear. "I don't think I've had this much fun in my entire life, either."

A relieved smile takes over my entire face. "Really?"

"Really."

And suddenly, I feel like crying.

For reasons beyond me—and for absolutely no reason at all and for all the reasons in the world—I'm going to cry on my damn birthday, like a cliché.

Blinking rapidly, I wrap my arms around his solid frame, laying my head on his chest. "Thank you," I whisper. "For today. For everything."

Dev takes my face in his hands before looking at me with a look I can't quite decipher. I've seen a glimpse of it before but never as clearly. "Happy birthday, Peter."

I pout at the use of the nickname, making him chuckle.

He lowers his mouth, bringing it inches from mine. "Happy birthday, my beautiful Piper."

And that's when I break rule number one, lifting up on my toes and molding my lips to his in a move that can only be considered . . .

My surrender.

A white flag.

A towel I should have thrown in long ago.

*Shit. I am in so much trouble.*

For a moment we both freeze, our lips locked and our breaths colliding. For a moment, time stops and the world ceases to exist. For a moment there are no fireworks, no castles, and no one else.

Just us.

Me and him.

Then, as if a button has been pushed, everything snaps back, setting us alight.

Dev crushes me to him, one hand splaying across my back, pulling me closer, while the other travels up to tangle inside my hair. His lips move against mine, no longer frozen, deepening our connection with urgent need. They're plump and soft, completely in contrast to the rest of him, making me melt into him.

His kiss is as gentle and tender as it is brutal and demanding. Like he'd been waiting for this, yet resisting it.

My hands travel up his chest before I wrap my arms around his neck. My tiara falls somewhere as I arch my back and pull him closer.

Dev kisses me like it's all he knows before his tongue travels the seam of my lips, asking for entrance. And God, do I give it to him. Like I've been starved for it my whole life.

I don't know if it's the magic of this place or the way he

just groaned into my mouth, but I think I can safely say this kiss destroyed my rule.

This kiss *obliterated* my rule.

Because, if this is what he has to offer with kiss number one, then I can only imagine kiss number two, or kiss number four-hundred-and-sixty-three. There is no way I'll miss experiencing kiss number four-hundred-and-sixty-three!

Our tongues brush against one another as our kiss deepens, transforming into something even needier, more desperate. As if we're trying to make up for all the time we lost. All the time we could have been doing this.

Dev kisses me long and slow, the taste of him—a mix of the cotton candy we'd shared not too long ago and the beer he'd had earlier—practically causing my knees to buckle. His tongue sends currents through my spine that pools inside my feeble thong. I press my thighs together, feeling the drenched fabric between them and moan into his mouth, fisting the collar of his shirt.

*God, please don't stop. Please don't ever stop.*

When we finally part, both gasping for air, Dev's hand cradles my jaw. He thumbs my beestung lips before pressing his forehead against mine.

Our labored breaths subside as the world around us comes humming back.

The corners of his lips rise as he glances behind me. "Right on time."

I turn to follow his gaze and my mouth hits the floor. The castle dazzles with dancing stars and colorful lights, forming a message that has my breath halting inside my airways. I swing my head back to him. "You didn't!"

His smile broadens as he pulls me against him, my back to his chest, his arms encircling my waist. He brushes a kiss against my temple as we watch the words, `Happy Birthday, my beautiful Piper`, dance across the castle walls.

The crowd cheers and the final spectacle of fireworks light up the night sky.

But as the last sparks fade from the sky, a terrifying thought cuts through my intoxicating euphoria.

Rules are meant to be broken, yes. And I have a feeling I'll be breaking all of mine, courtesy of this man who is starting to burrow under my skin.

But so are hearts . . .

twenty-three
# dev

Five Schlongs Hen Party

GARRETT MEYER

[Link to Finance Focus Weekly magazine article: Billionaire Dev Menon's Magical Birthday Gesture for His Fiancée]

@Dev Menon, you romantic fuck. Not gonna lie, I'm a little offended we weren't invited.

HUDSON CASE

Dev's gone total Disney Princess. Quick, someone check his pants. His dick might've turned into a vagina.

DEAN MEYER

You think it's hairless, too? I bet it is if Sniperella has anything to say about it.

HUDSON CASE

For fuck's sake! I'm eating here.

GARRET MEYER

Dean, seriously, no one needed that mental image.

**DEAN MEYER**

You think he used his tiny "magic wand" to make all her wishes come true?

**GARRET MEYER**

Bet he took her to a "whole new world".

**DARIAN MEYER**

You guys are prepubescent.

**DEAN MEYER**

Says the guy who married a prepubescent.

**DARIAN MEYER**

You realize that joke was old the first time you made it, right?

**DEAN MEYER**

But I've found so many creative alternatives to keep us all entertained.

**GARRETT MEYER**

Can we get back to talking about Prince Charming? You know, for a fake engagement, he seems to be giving an Oscar-worthy performance, if these pictures are any indication.

**HUDSON CASE**

I spoke to him a couple of days ago, and he was still adamant this whole "charade" had an end date.

**DEAN MEYER**

The only thing that needs an end date is Dev fooling himself.

**DARIAN MEYER**

Where is he, by the way? He's been quiet lately.

## Pretend For Me

**DEAN MEYER**

Hopefully he's getting laid. It would be about time tiny Dev explored her "small world".

**DARIAN MEYER**

Dean. Dude. [GIF of Robert Downey Jr. slow sighing]

**DEAN MEYER**

Sorry, little bro. I forgot about your virginal ears.

Anyway, I have new thoughts on this so-called romantic gesture by our resident billionaire.

**HUDSON CASE**

You have new thoughts? Did you borrow them from a Magic 8-Ball?

**DEAN MEYER**

Magic 8-Ball? Is that one of those nineteen-fifties references, when you were but a young chap?

**HUDSON CASE**

Hurry up and tell us your thoughts before you lose them like usual.

**DEAN MEYER**

You're quite the funny man today, grandpa. That Viagra must have done its job last night.

As I was saying, don't you think the whole lighting up a castle with a message was a bit cliché, Dev? I mean, Danny literally proposed to Vicky that way.

HUDSON CASE

What the hell are you talking about? Are these more of your imaginary friends you try to make us jealous with?

DEAN MEYER

Only the most memorable episode of *Full House*, aside from the one where Stephanie went around imitating D.J. and it caused quite the sister fight.

HUDSON CASE

[GIF of man pinching the bridge of his nose]

DEAN MEYER

Anyway, I was expecting something, you know, a little grander. Like a message on the moon. Oooh, or maybe the sun.

HUDSON CASE

I think I lost a few brain cells from this conversation.

DARIAN MEYER

Me, too. I'm out of here.

DEAN MEYER

Off to pick up your wife from daycare already, bro?

DARIAN MEYER

`<middle finger emoji>`

[**Darian Meyer** has left the chat]

DEAN MEYER

Jesus. So sensitive.

## twenty-four
## dev

I Chose A Magic Dick

My phone buzzes inside the pocket of my jeans, my friends continuing their incessant chatter, but I still haven't responded.

I have better things to do.

Honestly, the room could fill with smoke and light itself on fire, and I'd still be rooted right here, where my fiancée has me pressed against the wall in the entryway of my house. Her mouth is completely molded to mine as her hands explore under my shirt, sending pulses of electricity through my veins.

We somehow kept it together last night at the hotel and this morning, making sure we acted casual in front of the kids, though I felt anything but.

The flight home was a blur, as was the drive back from the airport to drop off the kids. I know we exchanged small talk and pleasantries, but it went in one ear and out the other. I'm pretty sure I nodded and spoke at the right times, but I can't recall what was discussed.

Because the only thing I could recall, the only thing that played on repeat during our ride back home, was that fucking kiss.

Soft and sure and so damn perfect, it felt like a fairytale. Yeah, I get there's a pun in there somewhere.

*But fuck!* Who knew? Who knew that kissing my fake fiancée would have the power to change the way my heart beats.

She hadn't caved, hadn't broken her precious no-kissing rule, even when we'd had our "moment" in her salon. We were mere millimeters apart, and she kept a tight hold on her restraint—not that I would have stopped her if she'd let go. I mean, I'd already blurred the lines by telling her to touch herself as I watched, what was a kiss?

Until last night.

And then I knew.

Then I understood why she'd made that a rule in the first place. Because now that I've tasted her, felt her moan against my mouth, there's no way I wouldn't want to do it again. And again.

And we all know what doing something you like again and again turns into.

Attachment.

Desire and longing.

Definitely not something you can easily walk away from.

I pull her hips to mine, letting her feel my want for her—not that it would take much to feel, seeing as my dick is standing so ramrod straight, it could signal extraterrestrial life in space.

My heart thunders inside my chest as one of my hands trails down to squeeze her ass inside her fucking tiny shorts.

I almost killed our pilot when his eyes lingered longer than needed on her legs as she boarded the flight. And then I almost killed him again when he watched her take her seat. The fucker tilted his head like a fucking golden retriever as he watched her ass sway.

I run a palm over one of her ass cheeks, digging my fingertips into her flesh so hard, I'm sure they'll leave marks. *Goddamn, this ass.*

She smiles into our kiss, and I realize I might have said that last thought out loud.

A growl lodges itself inside my throat, and I almost speak out the word that keeps floating behind my eyelids. Mine.

*So fucking mine.*

I deepen the kiss, my hands skating up her bare sides. Apparently, wearing these fucking shorts that barely qualify as underwear wasn't enough; she had to wear a crop top that barely hides the bottoms of her tits, too.

Dipping below her loose top, I skirt my thumbs over her bare breasts. Breasts I've studied up close while she was writhing on my lap, with her head thrown back and her chest in my face. Breasts that have the deepest pink nipples I've ever seen, like fucking rosebuds I can practically taste on my tongue.

"No fucking bra," I growl against her lips. "Short shorts and no fucking bra. Do you realize how many people I have to kill now because they saw you like this today? Including Ralph, and I've always liked the guy."

Piper smiles into our kiss. "Caveman."

She's fucking right; I *am* a caveman when it comes to her, and I don't plan to apologize for it.

I run circles over her rosebud nipples, making her gasp into my mouth. "More, Dev. God, I want more."

And just like that, gone is the sweet and exploratory kiss from last night.

That gentle dance of lips has been replaced by something more urgent and primal. Soon, we're a mess of hungry growls, clanking teeth, and grinding bodies. Both ravenous and seeking friction, closeness, *anything* to satiate this fucking overwhelming need.

With one hand still playing with her nipple, my other finds

its way to her silky strands. I use my grip on them to change our angle, desperately plunging into her mouth like she's my only source of air.

Piper swivels her hips against me and my dick practically weeps.

My heart thunders inside my chest, and I guarantee she can feel it tapping against her own. The intensity of this moment, the weight of it as we stand on the precipice of something we're both resigned to and destined for makes my head spin. Reality blurs the edges of my focus, until all I can see is her—her taste, her scent, and the feel of her against me.

*What am I doing?*

*What in the actual fuck am I doing, helping her break her rules? Risking her getting attached*—the same as me—*when that's the last thing she wants to do.*

She clearly has her rules for a reason. They're her armor, the walls she put up to keep herself away from getting hurt, staying unattached. Just like she told me she wanted to be. So, why am I challenging her to break them like a selfish bastard?

This isn't a game.

Which is why I have to admit the truth, at least to myself.

I want her. Not temporarily, not in some sham agreement for my mother or the world. I want her in ways I've never wanted anyone. I want her more than temporarily.

Her fingernails bite down on my skin. She runs them down my abs, making them dance under her touch, before she hooks her fingers into the waistband of my jeans.

We pull out of the kiss, breathless and panting, but so fucking ready for more.

"Tell me this is actually happening, Dev," she says, shuddering against me. "Tell me this isn't just some residual magic left over from that place full of fairies, pixies, and godmothers."

I trail kisses along the moles on her neck, the way I've been wanting to do. "Pretty sure godmothers by themselves aren't magical."

She gives me an irritated squint. "Don't distract me with your sense and sensibility, Mr. Darcy—"

"Also pretty sure you've placed him in the wrong book—"

"Because I'll sue Mickey and Cinderella, and everyone else in that godforsaken place, for emotional distress."

I chuckle, lifting my palms to her face, and sliding my thumbs over the tops of her cheeks. This fucking girl, with her way of making me laugh no matter how bleak the outlook.

I know she's playing dumb about Mr. Darcy, just like I know she's the one who solves my crossword puzzles almost every night. The ones I purposely leave on the coffee table for her because I'm coming up with blanks.

She's wickedly smart, but she'd rather not show it if it means she can get a laugh from those around her, even if it's at her own expense.

It's both frustrating and endearing all at once. A part of me wants to shake her and tell her not to pretend to be ignorant when she's usually the smartest person in the room. But the other admires her for always being able to lighten the mood, for never taking herself too seriously.

But I do wonder where it comes from—her need to self-deprecate and take the attention away from herself without revealing her insecurities. Who made her feel like she needed to do that? Because whoever it is, I swear, I want to wrangle their neck.

I merge our mouths together once again, demanding more. More than I deserve. More because I don't think I'll ever get my fill.

The second our tongues touch again, I exhale against her skin, while she inhales against mine, fisting my shirt and swallowing my groan.

"Bed," I rasp against her mouth, struggling to catch my breath.

She nods. "It's honestly the most intelligent thing you've said all—"

I don't even let her finish.

Dropping down, I haul her up over my shoulder and carry her to my room.

She lets out a squeak of surprise before giggling. "Ooh, I've always wanted to get up close and personal with this ass." She demonstrates by grabbing a handful of said ass. "Maybe take an interview, go on a podcast with it . . ."

Her body sways as I continue my long strides.

"I'm quite enjoying this view, even if I am upside down," she mumbles. "Are these the babies you work on inside that gym of yours? These buns of steel." She thwacks one with an open palm. "I bet I'd chip a tooth on your ass . . . not that I'd complain. Who really needs all their teeth, anyway?"

"I do," I say, turning my head to gently bite the side of her ass, making her laugh.

Closing the door to my room behind me, I drop her onto my mattress. She bounces as she giggles, but I note the shiver of anticipation that runs the length of her, creating goosebumps over her arms.

The sight of her in her tiny shorts and that damn crop top that's now ridden up over her breasts, hair splayed out like a halo around her head, has a jolt of unneeded desire pulsing through to my cock. Unneeded, because the fucker is already painfully erect, and now I'm seconds from blowing my load when I haven't even touched her.

I suppose that's nothing new between us.

My knees press on either side of her thighs, my form large and intimidating over her much smaller one. Placing my hands on either side of her head, I hover over her, running my nose from the bottom of her earlobe down the smooth column of her throat.

I suck, lick, and bite her delicate skin. "Your obsession with these short tops and shorter bottoms is going to take years off my lifespan."

"What's a few years in the grand scheme of things?" she breathes softly as her fingers skate down to my waist, brushing my sides like she can't get enough. They continue to trail lower, until her hand cups my rigid cock over my pants, making me hiss. "Plus, it makes accessing what you need that much easier, doesn't it?"

I roll my length in her palm and she tightens her grip. "Therein lies the entire problem."

"Not if it's yours to touch."

My eyes flick to hers, searching. "Is it?"

She runs her tongue along her bottom lip, giving me a smile I can't quite decipher. "Sure seems like it to me. You've put a ring on it, haven't you?"

She leaves the question hanging between us while she works me through my pants.

"Piper," I grit, placing my hand over hers, unsure if I'm trying to stop her or help her continue.

After a few more tugs, I take her hand and place it over her head, bringing the other one up to meet it. She writhes and squirms under me, her thighs rubbing together as her scent permeates my senses, making me feel feral.

Lowering my head to her breasts, I brush my tongue over her rosy nipple, forcing a shaky breath out of her. I suck it, rolling the stiff peak around my tongue languidly before gripping it in between my teeth and tugging.

Piper bucks under me, her head falling back with a gasp. "Dev."

I do the same to the other breast, giving it my full attention, while Piper's chest heaves under my touch.

"Keep your hands above your head, baby," I say, letting go of her wrists. "Maybe hold on to something . . . You'll need it."

Piper lets out a breathless moan, reaching for a pillow to bring under her head.

I smirk, laying kisses on the ridge between her breasts while still playing with her nipples. "Good girl."

Her stomach caves as I inch my hands and lips down her smooth skin, licking and sucking as I chart my path lower. Her knees come up, her thighs pressing against my side as she wriggles under me, mumbling words I can barely make out past the blood rushing through my ears.

"Lift up," I command, hooking my fingers on the elastic of her shorts and thong. "I want to see your pussy."

"God, yes," Piper whimpers, complying to help me drag them down her legs.

My gaze halts on her ankle, and I look at her in confusion. "Why do you have 'turkey sandwich' tattooed here?"

"Because," she says, placing a hand over her ankle as if it'll disappear if she does so, "I like turkey sandwiches. Now stop showing off. Knowing multiple languages isn't going to impress me." Her brow quirks. "But your tongue might."

I grin, tossing her clothes to the floor and pulling her closer to me by her hips. I get my shoulders under her knees so her heels rest on my back. And then I take the time to feast my eyes on her.

"This beautiful pussy is all I've been able to think about lately," I murmur, running my nose up her thigh and between her slick seam.

"Oh, God," Piper gasps. "If it makes you feel better, this pussy thinks about you a lot, too. All my pussies do, actually."

"That's a relief," I muse, flattening my tongue and taking a swipe from her entrance to her clit.

"Oh God, Dev," she moans, her back arching off the bed. "Did that fairyland grant you a magic tongue?"

I smile, holding back a chuckle. "No, I could only pick one, so I chose a magic dick instead."

Her thighs clasp around my head when I run my tongue over her again. "Oh my God, this is really embarrassing, but I think I might come now."

"Don't you dare," I growl, sucking one of her plump lips into my mouth. "I have plans to eat this pussy well into the middle of the night. You're not coming until I'm good and ready."

"You're bossy and unfair, you know that?" She reaches for my hair, dropping her knees to the bed, and I gently bite the inside of her thigh in punishment. "Really living up to your Lex Luther supervillain name."

"Hands over your head, Peter."

She does as I ask once more and I get to work, sweeping my tongue over her entrance before swirling it around her clit. Over and over, I round her little nub, alternating with both the flat and tip of my tongue.

Piper writhes and moans under me, arching into my mouth. But right as I feel her clench—knowing her climax is seconds away—I pull away, licking her with longer, more languid strokes.

"No, please," she complains, her hand finding my head again, as if to urge me back. When I immediately disconnect from her, she fists her pillow, her voice whiney. "Dev, I . . . I need . . ."

Her voice trails off when I flick her clit again with the tip of my tongue, back and forth, before sucking it into my mouth. "Is this what you need?"

"Yes," she hisses, widening her thighs for me. "Just like that."

Wetting the tip of my finger with the juices at her entrance, I test one digit, teasing and toying until I plunge it deeper inside.

With her hips back up in the air, Piper's entire body comes to a halt and goosebumps scatter over her skin.

"Goddamn, that's tight," I growl, getting my finger knuckle-deep and curling it so her thighs tremble against my ears. "You think I can get another one in?"

"Yes. Yes, please." I don't need to see her to know she's nodding or that her skin is flushed.

Fucking her with my finger, I continue to work her clit, circling it first before tapping it to change up the sensation. She seems to like that based on the guttural moan that emits from her chest. I feel the vibration of it against my lips.

With my hand splayed over her belly, I sink another finger inside her while my tongue continues to focus on her clit.

"Fuck, this pussy is going to make me an addict," I murmur, licking and fucking her at a steady pace. "It's so beautiful. Just like the rest of you."

Her hips move against me, riding my face and heightening her pleasure.

"You should see the way you're swallowing my fingers. You'll look even more beautiful swallowing my cock."

Moaning, Piper rolls against me, chasing her orgasm in earnest, and I can almost feel her unravel under me as I use every trick in my arsenal to give her what she wants.

Pumping, swirling, rolling, fucking.

I curl my fingers, finding that pebbled spot deep inside her, making her suck in a breath. She's on the brink, a place that's just within reach, when I increase my pace.

"Need this pussy to flood my tongue, baby," I say against her. "Come for me."

And whether it's my words or the way I suck her clit between my teeth, pinching it before licking it, Piper's scream pierces the air. Her hands twist inside the covers as her thighs quake, and waves of euphoria roll through her body.

Goddamn, she looks so pretty.

Using one hand to press down on her belly and hip, I hold her inside my mouth, continuing to devour her pussy like I might not eat for another week. It's only when she cries out my name, riding out her last pulses, that I release her. I kiss her juicy clit once more before crawling up her body with a smug smirk.

Her chest heaves, but her glassy green eyes stay on me. I press my lips to hers, letting her taste herself on me, making us both moan.

We're lost in a dance of tongues and groans for only a few seconds when Piper reaches for my cock, grabbing and pulling it toward her.

Her eyes blaze before that wicked smile finds her lips again. "Let's take this magic dick out for a spin."

## twenty-five
# piper

You're My Favorite Overachiever

Dev smiles, eyes blazing, his chin still covered with me, before he gets off the bed.

The man is as complex as he is layered. A dirty-talking, possessive alpha under a buttoned-up guise. A thoughtful, soft-hearted human behind a cool and calculating billionaire. He's surprisingly real and refreshing. Surprisingly unexpected and so damn handsome, something stirs inside my chest every time I look at him.

"I had no idea you could do such things with your mouth." I'm raised on my elbows so I can watch the fine ass man in front of me while still trying to catch my breath. "Until last night, I thought it was only used to clip out a few words and twitch whenever you were mildly amused."

Grasping the neck of his tight T-shirt from the back with one hand, Dev pulls it off himself in one swift movement, and my mouth goes dry.

Sexy doesn't even begin to define how he looks, all rippling abs and solid pecs. It's like staring at a real-life version of Michelangelo's David, except he's got better hair, the perfect tan, and has kept up his gym routine.

Pulling his wallet from his back pocket, he takes out a condom. "And now? Has your mind been changed?"

I lick my bottom lip, watching him unbutton his jeans, letting them slide to the floor. His dick tents his boxer-briefs, and I rub my slick thighs together instinctively. God, the way I want him inside me.

"Oh, it's been thoroughly changed," I say, watching him drop his briefs to the ground. My breath hitches. "Now, I'll want that mouth on me all the time."

My eyes drag down to the V pointing to his thick cock. The one he grasps inside his massive hand, pumping it before he swipes his thumb over the pre-cum leaking from the tip.

Holy fucking hotness. The man is devastatingly beautiful, and a deadly combination of sweet, thoughtful, and considerate. The type of man who could one-hundred-percent hurtle me toward an early death.

If not death, then definitely a heart condition.

And a heart condition of that kind is so much worse than death.

He tears the packet and slides the condom over his shaft, stalking toward me again. "That's quite the change in tone, Peter . . . seeing as your first rule was no kissing."

*Yeah, well, I'm a good-old-fashioned rule breaker, Mr. Menon. Punish me and send me on my way.*

I don't respond. Honestly, I haven't quite processed our first kiss yet, despite the fact that it's all I've thought about. Despite the fact that I pinned him against the wall as soon as we got back and kissed him again.

That kiss had created an explosion inside my ribs I'd never felt before. And when our mouths had parted, a warmth had settled where the explosion had occurred. I already know that no matter how much I try to replace that warmth with the same cool disinterest and emptiness that was there before, I'll fail.

Because Dev Menon isn't content to just wreak havoc on my senses and my body. He's determined to do the same to my heart.

I reach out as soon as his knees find the mattress again, gliding my hand over his sheathed cock. The weight of him inside my palm has another pool of want dripping from me.

A huff of air passes through his clenched teeth, and his head falls back when I stroke him. "Jesus, Piper," he croaks.

"How long has it been for you?"

It's not something I'd intended on asking. It irritates me to even think about someone else touching him this way. But sometimes my mouth speaks before my brain has given it a green light.

His dark eyes meet mine. "Almost two years."

I want to ask why. Why, when I know his last relationship ended a year and a half ago? Why, when I know he could have had anyone he wanted after that? Literally, women—and men—would leave their partners for this man if that's what he wanted.

But I decide to keep those thoughts to myself for now.

I'm sure he knows I've done my research, not that anything about his life is very hard to find. It's about as private as a fish in a glass bowl. Every move and every relationship is out there for public consumption, for him to be dissected and judged by every news and gossip column alike.

"And you're choosing to break your dry spell with me?"

He reaches for my chin, grasping it gently. "There's no one else I want."

That same warmth rekindles inside my chest, threatening to consume me, so before he can do more damage, I take his hand off my chin and kiss the inside of his palm. "I want to be on top."

Dev's eyes darken and a smirk graces his lips. But he does what I ask, scooting all the way to the headboard.

Tossing my shirt on the floor, I crawl toward him, completely naked. My eyes stay on his as I make my way on all fours up over his spread legs. My hair glides over the mattress as my hands and knees sink into the fabric. I can tell he definitely likes what he sees based on the little groan that rumbles inside his chest.

With my hand on his shoulder, I straddle him, recalling the similar position we were in at the salon. A position where I'm in control.

Dev's hand spans my bare hip, while his other grabs his hard length. He glides his sheathed tip through my arousal, coating himself with me. "You want control, *meri jaan*?"

His all-too-astute gaze collides with mine, and I know there's no point in creating new walls or erecting new barriers. He can see past them, and he knows exactly what I'm doing.

He glides his crowned head through my wet seam again, making me hiss. His hand tightens on my hip, and I roll my head back, hoping he can't see my entire truth written across my face.

He slowly urges me down, and I gasp as my pussy stretches over him, taking him in a few inches. It's not entirely pleasurable, but it's not painful either, as my body tries to adjust to his size.

"Holy shit," I moan as I lift off him almost completely before I push him inside me again, a little more than before. "You feel . . . so fucking good."

Dev grabs the back of my neck, pulling my forehead toward him so our groans intermingle. "Let me ask you something, sweetheart. How much control have you had when it comes to this? To us?" He waits until my eyes slide from his lips to meet his eyes. "To me?"

I lower down his shaft, taking another inch while sucking in a breath.

"You don't have to answer because, when it comes to this

thing between us," he says, his tone unwavering. "I know as well as you do that you *can't* control it. I'm not just inside this perfect pussy of yours, Piper, I'm in your fucking bloodstream. You could work your entire life to get rid of me, but I'd still be there, lingering inside your veins."

And with that little dose of reality, he pulls me down so he's completely sheathed inside me.

"Oh, God!" I scream, feeling so full, I'm positive I'll split down the middle. I throw my head back again as my fingernails bite into his shoulder. "Oh, fuck!"

Neither of us moves for a moment, save for our chests heaving. And then I feel his lips brush against my throat—the constellation of tiny moles I have there. His tongue follows the trail with languid licks and his hand urges my hips to rock.

"Widen your legs for me."

I spread as far as I can, using my knees to pull myself up and down over him. "Are all billionaire dicks this big?" I pant as my back bows.

"Don't know and don't care," he mumbles against my neck. "Stop thinking about other billionaire dicks while mine is inside you."

I bite my bottom lip, holding back a chuckle as I rise and fall on his lap. "Sorry, I couldn't help it. I've never seen another one of this unique standing and girth. It's as stately and dignified as you are."

A chuckle rumbles through him and my core tightens around him. There's no describing how much I love the sound of his laughs. "Pretty sure 'dignified' will be the last word you'll use to describe him when you can't walk tomorrow. Now, breathe for me."

I hadn't realized I was holding my breath.

I do as he's asked, and it helps my body loosen up.

Another thing that helps my body loosen up? His mouth around my nipple.

With his fingers now tweaking my other nipple, Dev sucks my pebbled bud into his mouth, rolling it around his tongue. I feel myself getting wetter around him, sliding down his shaft more easily.

*God, this feels too good. Way better than I expected or wanted.*

Moving his hot mouth to my other nipple, he continues his ministrations while I find my rhythm fucking him. Soon my breathing becomes erratic, frantic, and I honestly have to wonder if my lungs will keep up.

Sweat beads over my brow and my skin feels hot. My fingers rise from his shoulders to tangle with the hair at the nape of his neck. His gorgeous, dark, lush hair that I still can't believe led us to this point.

The sounds of our heavy breaths and bodies colliding resonates inside the otherwise quiet room.

"I'm shocked you still remembered how to do this after all this time," I say, goading him. Even during the best sex of my life, it's what I live for. "When you said two years, I was worried I'd be giving instructions."

He huffs out an amused breath. "Well, you *are* doing most of the work."

"That's true," I say, my breaths ragged. "I suppose I deserve most of the credit. You can thank me for your orgasm later."

"How about I thank you by giving you two more?" He groans when I roll my hips one way and then the other, dragging his cock through my walls.

"It's the thing I love most about you, Mr. Luther," I say, biting my bottom lip because goddamn, the man feels so good inside me. "That go-getter attitude. You're my favorite overachiever."

Dev rewards me by slapping my ass when I lift up. With a hiss, I slam back down on him.

Soon, we find our rhythm again, though I'm riding him like he's taking me to the promise lands. And when our movements slow just a touch, Dev pulls my lips to his, kissing me with so much passion, I'm breathless by the end of it.

I've never kissed and fucked. Well, not since Andrés. But since then, the two haven't mixed, especially since kissing has always been off-limits with anyone.

But at this moment, aside from my feeble attempt to maintain some control over whatever this is between us, I honestly couldn't care what he asked me to do. I'd do it.

We detach from our kiss, and Dev brings his thumb to my clit, circling it over and over again in a way that drives me wild. Meeting me halfway, he thrusts up into me, finding that sweet spot inside me, and I feel my walls clench around him.

"You like that?" he asks, looking at where he's touching me. His heart pounds as hard as mine against me.

"Yes," I hiss, undulating over him, feeling my eyes roll backward. "Please don't stop."

"Am I hurting you?"

The gentleness in his tone has that warmth exploding inside me again.

I shake my head. "Only in the best way."

He rolls me over his cock as I slam down on him at a faster pace. I'm still feeling fuller than I ever have and there's a slight tinge of pain with the way I'm stretched around him, but I'll be damned if I ask him to stop. I never want him to stop.

He feels so fucking good—inside me, against me, around me. The delicious hints of his cologne mixed with the scent of sex surrounds my senses, and I edge closer to my impending climax.

"God, this feeling," I moan, practically sobbing. "How do you feel so good?"

"Look down, baby." He tilts his chin to where we're connected, the place where he's completely inside me. "Look how hot this is. Your needy little pussy with my cock so far inside, I'm practically touching your ribs."

"Oh, God!" I whimper, feeling the beginnings of my release.

"Fuck, you take me so well." His thumb hastens the circling over my clit, and I place my fingers over his to help him with it. "Come all over my cock, sweetheart. Fuck me like you own me."

I come with the speed and intensity of a freight train, throwing my head back and screaming into the room, only to feel Dev coming right along with me. His fingers dig into my sides, leaving more of the same fingerprints I had the last time I was on his lap.

He buries his face into my neck, groaning, but I don't miss his soft whisper, "Because you own me, Piper."

Those words . . .

Does he know what he's saying?

Is it the post-sex endorphins talking?

We're breathing in unison, descending from outer space together, when I make a move to get off his lap.

Dev's fingers tighten on me, keeping me in my place. His hooded eyes stroll over my face in adoration, appreciation. "You're so beautiful. So perfect."

I hide my smile against his neck, breathing in his scent like it's a limited edition fragrance and I'm trying to memorize it. Yeah, I have issues.

There's no denying I want to stay here. Not just a night, but for an entire lifetime. But not when this is all destined to end. Not when this was all based on my proposal to have fun while we're both in this together. Temporarily.

I lift up to find his eyes, feeling his fingers trail up and down my back. It sends renewed goosebumps flying across my skin. "Dev."

He must see it written all over my face because understanding flashes over him. "You don't want to stay the night."

I swallow, curling my fingers into his hair. "It's what's best for us."

He leans in, grasping my lips with his, and pulling me into a slow, sensual kiss.

A moment later, I shift off him, with a heart that seems tilted. Askew in a way that feels like it's ill-designed for my chest. After putting on my thong, I gather my things while Dev watches me from where he's still sitting on his bed.

I'm just reaching for his door after waving to him when he stops me. "Hey, Peter?"

I turn to see my favorite dimple cozied up inside his cheek. "Yeah?"

"You told me to thank you for the orgasm, so . . ." He gets a strangely boyish look in his eyes, despite the very adult conversation we're having. "Thank you."

"You're welcome, Lex." I raise a brow, testing out the waters. "Would you like another one tomorrow?"

He contemplates it for a moment. "I'd be an idiot to say no."

"Then I guess it's a date."

"Want to do the crossword together afterward?"

I burst out laughing. This guy. This gorgeous and adorable fucking guy.

"What am I, an animal? Of course I want to do the crossword afterward. It's the only post-orgasm activity I ever take part in, aside from watching hockey."

He chuckles. "We can do both."

I lift my brow. "I saw an entire room upstairs covered with baseball paraphernalia. Are you sure you'd want to watch hockey with me?"

Dev smirks. "I think I can make room in my life for another sport."

"Then consider it a date."

"Goodnight, Piper."

"Thank you for a great night, Mr. Menon. A great weekend, in fact."

And with that, I bolt across the living room to the safety of my own room, like I'm running from my worst fear. A fear —*a temptation*—by the name of Dev Menon. The epitome of my desire and the match ready to strike my self-control.

My rules are there for a reason, and though I've already broken the cardinal one, I'm clinging to the others like a lifeline.

A lifeline I'll need if I'm to come out the other end of this intact.

twenty-six
## piper

Might As Well Be A Different Fruit

"What the hell is this?"

My stomach curdles and my heart rate spikes seeing the picture in front of me three days later. Oscar's face is buried in my neck while Mayer is grabbing a handful of my ass as the three of us walk hand-in-hand into their apartment.

My dad—or should I say, the man I'm unfortunate enough to share DNA with—sneers at me from across our table at the coffee shop I'd specified the last time he texted.

He looks more haggard than I remember, his gut protruding so the bottom of his stomach peeks from under his stained shirt. The green in his eyes reminds me of the leaves of a diseased tree, trying but failing to hold on to some semblance of life. Some semblance of happiness.

His head tilts up arrogantly, as if he has anything to feel smug about. "This is why you'll give me what I'm asking for."

It's crazy to think this man was once a professional hockey player with a loving wife and children behind him. Now he's just a walking cautionary and bitter tale of what happens when you actively sabotage your own life.

I can't help but compare him to my brother. And though I see physical glimpses of him in my dad, Rowan couldn't be more different. With a strong sense of love and loyalty, determination both on and off the ice, and a personality capable of lighting up a sky, my brother is light years ahead of the man sitting in front of me, reeking of stale beer and shattered dreams.

Where Rowan took to Shayla's son like his own flesh and blood, our dad discarded us from his life the way one would a pair of holey socks.

That is, until he jacked up his knee, ending his professional career, and the woman he left us for packed her bags, that he suddenly remembered he had children. By then, it was too late.

Rowan tried to maintain some sort of relationship with him, but after years of more disappointment, even he reached his limit. Me, on the other hand? I slammed the door on my dad's deadbeat face the day he left. By then he'd given me years of anguish I'd likely need therapy for, anyway; why would I have wanted to prolong the trauma?

Even now, after years of proving to myself that I'm not the "brainless loser" or the "stupid shit" he often referred to me as when I was a kid, his callused words creep into my thoughts at the least expected times. Especially when I'm alone and his voice fills the void created by the silence.

As much as I pity his state, I'm all-too aware of who he is at his core—a man who's always put himself first. A man who could give two shits about anyone or anything that wasn't benefitting him directly.

I keep my expression muted, despite my face being a magnifying glass for my feelings. "What the hell are you even talking about, *Anthony*?"

He points at me menacingly. "Watch your mouth, girl. Have some respect for the man who gave you life. I'm still your dad."

I chuckle softly because laughing maniacally the way I

want to would draw attention, especially since more people seem to be recognizing me as Dev's fiancée. As it is, I had to sneak past Ralph and my security to get here.

"Oh, Anthony," I say, poisonously sweet. "You believe donating your sperm earns you respect? You're about as much a father to me as a rat snake who eats its own hatchling."

His face contorts with anger, but before he can spit vitriol, I press on, "You call yourself my dad? Since when? Definitely not since you abandoned us—"

"I fucking came back, didn't I?" His face turns bright red, like he's about to explode. "But you and your mom were always brainless, ungrateful bitches."

My cool facade falters as my hands fist inside my lap. "Say one more thing about my mother and I walk out of here," I seethe. "She's a million times the parent you ever were."

My *father* waves a dismissive hand.

"A real father wouldn't have left in the first place," I continue. "He would have guided us throughout our lives, not left us when he found something better. And a real father sure as hell wouldn't cut down his daughter at every corner—"

Anthony throws back his head, laughing disdainfully. The faint stench of his breath sours the scent of coffee that was previously lingering there.

"Cut you down?" he repeats. "Sweetheart, you were *nothing*. You had no talent, no interests, and no fucking achievements to speak of. What would I have had to cut down when there was nothing there to work with?!"

I came here determined to not let his words affect me, to steel myself to his barbs. I was going to shut him down and put an end to his constant texting. Yet here I am, fighting back those same tears I've held behind my lids since I was a kid.

I have no reason to remind him that I *did* have other interests—hair, beauty, learning to run a business—but he never cared enough to know them. I also won't remind him that, despite being a "brainless twit", I graduated at the top five percent of my high school class.

My throat burns but my resolve strengthens. Because my sorry excuse for a father will not see me break.

"Want to know what I've been most grateful for these past few years, *Dad*." I spit the word like it burns my tongue. "The blissful peace since you walked out."

My lips flatten. "I'll make it crystal clear for you. The last thirteen years without your toxic presence have been a blessing, and I'd like to keep it that way. So, whatever it is that you're here to demand—respect, a relationship, or money—you won't be getting it from me."

I shove my chair back, getting up and smoothing a hand down my flared leggings in forced calm. "Now, if you'll excuse me, I have a happy *fatherless* life to get back to—"

His hand tightens around my wrist in a death grip, eyes glinting with malice. "Walk out now and I'll make sure your billionaire fiancé and the world sees this." He taps the photo on the table. "Pretty sure the news said you two have been together for a year, didn't it? But this timestamp paints a different picture."

My breath falters when I see the date at the bottom of the picture. Two months ago. "Where did you get that?"

He gasps mockingly. "Were you cheating on the richest man in the world, Peppercorn?" he tsks, as if admonishing me. "I shouldn't be surprised. After all, the apple doesn't fall far from the tree."

My upper lip curls. "Are you referring to yourself? Because this apple is so far from that tree, it might as well be a different fruit." I lean in, voice low and deadly calm. "I'm *nothing* like you. How long have you been following me?"

He shrugs innocently. "I was just trying to get back in touch with my little girl. Figured I'd see what you were up to. I never thought you'd amount to anything, so imagine my surprise when I found out you owned a thriving salon. But then I did some digging and found out Rowan paid for your business loans—"

"I've paid him back every cent," I retort, not that I need to justify anything to him. "Unlike you, my brother, Mom, and I take care of each other."

His eyes flick to my chest. "I'm sure you paid him back. What, with all the extra income you were making with your side hustle as a slut." He scoots the photo closer to me. "Or was it after you got into bed with a billionaire?"

My entire body heats up. I'm not a proponent of hitting one's parent, but at this point . . .

"You disgust me, Anthony."

"Hey." He raises his hands like he's asking for a truce. "Don't let me stop you! You gotta do what you gotta do to survive in the world sometimes, you know? It's exactly why I'm here, actually."

My vision blurs and my stomach drops. "What do you want?"

"Nothing you can't give me. I'm in a bit of a bind with my business partner. You see, I might have used some of the funds from our business account to—"

"Spare me the details," I say, cutting him off. I have no interest in knowing more. "Get to the point."

He sighs as if he's exasperated with me, the fucking asshole.

"I need sixty grand."

"*Sixty grand?!*" I shriek, making a couple of heads in the coffee shop turn toward us. I should sit back down, but I just can't get myself to. "Are you out of your mind?"

"I went to Rowan as well, but . . ." his eyes find the fucking photo again, "I didn't have as much leverage in convincing him. Figured you would be the easiest bet. And given the very successful business you run, I had a feeling you'd have it."

"You're pathetic and a waste of space, but I'm sure you already know that, coming here asking me for money."

"I'm a *survivor*," he says plainly. "And as for you giving me money, who do you think paid for everything all those years while I was with your mother? You owe me a hell of a lot more than sixty grand, Peppercorn."

"Don't fucking call me that," I hiss, feeling a vein throb in my temple.

Silence stretches between us for a few seconds while my heart races.

If Anthony leaks this picture, not only would it bring on a media storm weeks before the wedding, but it could get back to Dev's parents. While Dev wouldn't care—given we didn't even know each other at the time—explaining this to his parents would be another thing.

What would they think of me?

His dad already thinks I'm not good enough for his son, but it's his mom's opinion that worries me most. This would shatter her heart and ruin everything Dev has wanted to do for her until now.

*Shit!*

Maybe I should tell Dev and let his team get ahead of this. But he's been worried about an issue at work the past two days—some hardware problem with their driverless cars.

That's not to say I haven't seen him.

We've slept together every night, with me showing up to his room as promised.

Last night, after he'd given me multiple orgasms to shatter all orgasms prior to them, I got down on my knees for him. When I took him to the back of my throat, he swayed like a tree during a hurricane, chanting my name with my hair in his fist while he came.

But as usual, I made sure not to stay over.

And each time after I've slipped back into my room, I've heard him head into his office to work until God knows when.

So, with everything on his plate, including his worry about his mother, the last thing he needs is my little issue. I can deal with my deadbeat dad on my own.

"Give me the money and I'll be out of your hair for good," Anthony says after taking a sip of his coffee and bringing me out of my thoughts.

"How do I know you'll keep your word?"

"I guess you don't, but you don't have another choice." He must see my thoughts flicking across my face because he adds, "Oh, and I wouldn't tell your fiancé or your brother about this, if I were you. Things might get nastier if I really did have to hand this over to my contact at ESPN. He'd find the right people to share it with. And honestly, no one benefits from that, not even me."

He rises from his seat, towering over me, thinking he's intimidating me, but I almost laugh at how small he looks. How fucking pathetic.

"I just need the money and you won't see me again, Peppercorn. God's honest truth."

I grin at the picture Shayla just sent to me of Kai and Kiara. My nephew hugs his baby sister like she's precious cargo, both wearing Rowan's team jerseys.

I'm just about to type her a message when she calls me.

"Hey!" I say, catching my wide smile in the salon mirror.

"Hey!" she greets me. "Hope I caught you at a good time. Rowan's here, too."

"Hey Pepper," my brother's deep voice resounds through her speaker, "you busy?"

I close my salon door. I have twenty minutes before my next client.

"Nope, you caught me at the right time. What's going on?" I don't let him answer, remembering I forgot to message him after his game yesterday. "Oh! Congratulations on the win yesterday!"

"Thanks!" His voice brims with pride. "It was our last preseason game. You watched it?"

I actually watched it with Dev, but I don't mention that. Instead, I huff, feigning offense. "Um, as if I'd miss it! Solid D in that last round, baby bro."

"When will you drop the 'baby bro'? I'm only a year younger."

"Never," I reply easily. "Now, speaking of babies, how is my niece? Tell her to stop growing so fast! Every time I see her, she's so much bigger."

"She's a handful, too," Shay adds. "Just like her dad."

"She's got personality and charisma like her dad, too," my brother retorts, and I don't have to see Shay to know she's rolling her eyes. "She also likes putting your boobs in her mouth like her dad."

"Ew," I say, wrinkling my nose. "Is this why you guys called me? To make me throw up my breakfast?"

"Hey, I didn't say anything!" Shay giggles. "Leave it to your brother to provide unnecessary and inappropriate details. Anyway, we were calling to check in. Do you need any help with the wedding? I know we're miles away, but if we can help with anything—"

I wave my hand in the air. "I'm okay, actually. The wedding will be really private with our closest family and friends, and the planning has been relatively easy. The venue, flowers, and caterers are all set. I just need my two dresses, we need to book a band for the music, and Dev and I need to do a cake tasting."

My mind buzzes as an idea forms. I was planning on doing the dress fitting with Sarina and Nisha, but it might be fun if I expanded the group a bit.

"Actually, I know it's short notice, but would you want to come for the dress fitting next Saturday? We can grab food and drinks afterward." Before she can answer, I add, "I'll make sure to pick a place that serves farm to table."

My sister-in-law is the biggest health nut I know. And though she's laxed her stringent green smoothie diet since she met Rowan, she's still very particular about what she eats. It's not a bad thing, but it takes some planning when we're all getting together.

"That sounds fun! Are you sure I won't be intruding?" Shay asks.

"Pfft! I would love to have all my besties there! I'll even invite Jeena and Mom. We can make it a whole girls' thing!"

Jeena is one of Shay's best friends and probably one of the most entertaining people I've ever met. We met a couple of years ago and immediately clicked. In fact, she and her husband will be coming to the wedding.

"I suppose I could come for a night. Kai is pretty independent, but I don't want to be away from Kiara for too long," she muses on the phone. I get the feeling she's thinking aloud. "She's still so young."

"Baby, I've got both of them," Rowan reassures her. "I don't fly out until Sunday evening. Plus, you've got your best friends, Dylan, Liv, and Delia, here. I'm sure they'll all be willing to help if I need anything."

"That's true. I'll make sure to have bottles of breast milk ready for her."

"And I'll make sure to assist you with expressing those if you need," Rowan adds, his voice low and . . . ew, gross!

"K, throwing up now," I say, almost gagging.

"Okay, I'm in!" Shay says cheerfully. "Can't wait to see you!"

"Me, too!"

"Hey, so I forgot to tell you," Rowan says, right as I'm about to hang up. "Dad reached out to me a couple of months ago..."

"Oh," I respond, feeling that same vein throb in my temple. It hasn't stopped since this morning when I saw the asshole. "What did he need?"

"Who the fuck knows? He asked me to meet him. Said he needed something, but I said no and that I had no reason to see him. Surprisingly, he never texted again. But one of my buddies living near San Francisco said he swears he saw him there—Dad's still recognizable to hardcore hockey fans. Have you heard from him?"

My heart hammers right when I hear a knock on my door, likely Joshua bringing in my next client.

I'm not getting Rowan involved in this. Plus, I've already given Anthony the money he demanded. It is what it is at this point and not something I want to bring others into.

"Nope. Our sperm donor knows his and my relationship is long over."

## twenty-seven
# dev

Hail Mary

My gaze scrolls down the woman standing on the other side of my bedroom's threshold. She's wearing a cropped, maroon tube top under denim overalls, showing off the sides of her smooth, toned torso. Her lashes are curled with a touch of mascara, her glossed lips are turned up in a bright smile, and her hair is set in waves down her back.

She's so beautiful, I actually wonder if she's real.

This nightly visit has become ritualistic over the past week. We've had phenomenal, earth-shattering sex where we've given each other multiple orgasms. Afterward, we either watch hockey replays of The Bolts game—where Piper watches with the enthusiasm of someone actually in the arena, yelling at the ref and cheering for her brother's team—or solving a crossword puzzle together. As the night winds down, around ten PM because the woman is regimented about her sleep schedule, she retreats to her room, only to rinse and repeat the whole thing the next day.

Why? Because we're abiding by her rules.

Rules that somehow make sense in her head but leave me wondering when she's going to figure it out. That no amount of her enforcing her damn rules will stop this train; it's already off the rails and going at the speed of infinity. I've already hopped aboard, and I'm just waiting for her to grab my hand so I can pull her in.

I work my way down her exposed arms, both extended in front of her and holding a large rabbit cage.

Wait.

*What the hell?*

*She's holding a rabbit cage again?*

Both of her rabbits side-eye me, and I swear I can hear them thinking, *"Dude, don't ask us. We're as confused as you are."*

My eyes flick back to her face, and I'm about to speak when she stops me. "Before you say anything, let me explain."

I blink at her. "Yes. That would be a good start."

"I'm taking Natalie and Kevin to the vet soon, but I figured this would be my Hail Mary," she explains, as if that should clarify everything.

"I'm sorry? *What* would be your Hail Mary?"

"Oh!" She takes a few steps forward, bypassing me and entering my room. "Us showing them how to fuck."

*The hell?*

She sets the large cage a few feet from my bed before fiddling with her phone, while I stand rooted to the same spot at my door, wondering if those brownies my housekeeper set out for dessert tonight were the *special* kind.

"I figure this might just be a case of them not having had Sex-Ed yet, you know? I mean, maybe they just need to see how it's done before they feel comfortable." Suddenly, "I'll Make Love To You" by Boyz II Men starts playing softly from her speaker. "There. I even have their Rabbit Sex Playlist going."

My brain finally reboots. "You can't be serious. You want

us to . . ." I flick a glance at the rabbits before whispering, "have sex in front of your rabbits?!" I whisper because even having this conversation feels inappropriate. "Like we're in some sort of bunny porno?"

Piper nods enthusiastically and I shake my head, looking horrified.

"No!" I exclaim incredulously, wondering if I've landed in some sort of fifth dimension. "Not only is this insane, but there's probably some animal welfare law we'd be breaking. I draw the line at animal voyeurism, Piper!"

Piper's face falls and her bottom lip juts out as she makes her way over to me. Her hands stroll up my chest before hooking together at the back of my neck. She gets up on her toes, placing her soft lips on the side of my neck, kissing and licking it softly.

"All I'm saying," she murmurs huskily against my skin, sending a tremor rolling through me and making my dick jump in response, "is to give it a chance. Who knows, maybe they'll see how hot and heavy we get and want to try it themselves. People have sex in front of their pets all the time; this is practically the same thing. And we'd be teaching them something."

She's insane. Absolutely, positively insane.

I start to protest again when she steps back. Keeping her eyes fixed on me, she unhooks the buckles of her overalls, letting them fall to her feet, and . . . fuck me, she isn't wearing any underwear.

"Piper," I rasp, taking in her smooth midriff, the belly button I've become increasingly enchanted with over the past few weeks, and her bare pussy. "Is this your way of distracting me from your strange new kink?"

A slow grin spreads over her face as she steps toward me, turning so her back is to my chest. Taking my hand in hers, she runs it over her torso before fluttering her lashes at me over her shoulder expectantly. "Is it working?"

A growl lodges inside my throat, the feel of her smooth skin sending my heart racing. "You're certifiable, you know that? Hot, but certifiable."

She clamps her bottom lip between her teeth. "So, you'll do it?"

My hand skims along her bare skin languidly, and as much as I want to keep protesting about her weird rabbits watching us, the scent of her near me and her smooth skin under my touch have me not caring as much.

"This will go down as the weirdest thing I've ever done . . ."

I dip my head to lay kisses on the side of her neck, loving the way it makes her shiver. Piper lets out a soft exhale before reaching to grasp the back of my neck with her palm.

"Nah," she says breathily. "Wait until I convince you to fuck me wearing a rabbit tail and floppy ears. Now, that's an *actual* kink of mine."

My hands freeze and my insane bride-to-be giggles. "I'm kidding, Lex. I can see you're not quite there yet."

I shake my head before my lips find her earlobe and I pull it between my teeth. My fingers trail downward, finding her lips. Dragging the tip of my middle fingers between her seam, I circle her clit, making her jolt slightly against me.

"Dev," she breathes. "More."

With my other hand, I lift the maroon fabric covering her tits and palm one, tweaking her stiff nipple. At the same time, my middle finger continues to dip lower, plunging into her entrance.

"Open wider for me," I command hoarsely against the shell of her ear. "Let me feel you."

Piper widens her stance, her hand tightening around the nape of my neck, while I shove a second finger inside her. I pull them almost all the way out before pushing them back inside, over and over until she's writhing against me. Her eyes roll to the back of her head and her juices coat my fingers, dripping down the sides of her pussy and her thighs.

I continue to pluck and tweak her nipple.

"That's it, baby. Now help me out," I urge. "Play with your clit."

Piper whimpers, doing as asked, rubbing tight circles around her clit. She turns her head, seeking my lips, and I reward her with a kiss while she moans into my mouth.

My tongue sweeps inside, exploring her taste. How did she think we could ever follow this rule of hers? Kissing her is literally all I think about, aside from eating her out and fucking her. How was she okay with depriving us of this?

The sounds of my fingers driving into her hot center are subdued by the lyrics of Marvin Gaye's "Let's Get It On" and the rabbits hopping from one side of the cage to the other.

*Jesus, how did I get roped into doing this? I swear, the woman has me fucking unhinged for her.*

I continue to focus on my task, pumping my fingers inside her, fucking her until she's breathy and wiggling against me.

"There's nothing better than this pussy, you know that?" I rasp into her ear.

She responds by rolling her body against mine. Her walls flutter around my fingers and her grip tightens on my neck. She's close.

My breaths come out just as fast as hers as I continue to thrust into her, feeling her warmth around me. She's soaked, arching and needy against me.

"It's the hottest, wettest, sweetest pussy I've ever tasted," I whisper.

Piper's body stiffens, her fingers hastening their pace and working her clit.

"Please," she begs, writhing against me, and I pump faster, nipping her shoulder.

Her fingernails dig into my skin and her pussy sucks my fingers in. Her walls tighten against them as a scream erupts from her lips.

The rabbits go into a hopping frenzy as Piper shatters against me, heaving and sweaty.

Her chest rises and falls as my fingers continue working her, though at a slower pace. "I want to bury myself inside it and never come out."

"What's stopping you?" she asks breathlessly, turning around to face me. Her skin is flushed and I'm positive, I've never seen anyone more beautiful. "There's nothing I want more."

She presses her lips to mine, kissing me slowly, as if time doesn't exist before nipping and sucking on my bottom lip.

Her fingers trail down to unfasten my belt and unzip my pants, and she dips her hand inside my briefs to grip my cock.

"*Fuck*," I groan, throwing my head back, loving the feel of her soft palm around me.

She strokes me, fisting me with just enough pressure. Her thumb rolls over my mushroom head, collecting the beads of pre-cum there.

"Want to know something crazy?" she asks, sucking a spot on my neck. "I've never wanted anyone's cock as badly as I want yours."

"I'm flattered I beat Oscar and Mayer," I say, annoyed at myself for even bringing them up.

"You know that's not their real names, right? It's just what I called them—or anyone I was with, for that matter—because I couldn't ever remember them, nor did I want to."

My eyes bore into hers as I cup my hand over hers, stopping her from working my shaft momentarily. "You remember mine."

"Of course I remember your name, *Lex*." She winks, earning herself a slap on her ass from me. I use my hand's position on her ass to bring her closer and she giggles before her smile drops and her face becomes serious. "Yours is the only name I care to remember, Dev."

A fist lodges inside my chest at the sight of her face as unguarded as mine. She feels this exactly the way I do, but I know if I say how I feel at this point, she'll bolt in the other direction.

So, instead I say, "Good. Mine is the only name that should be on your lips."

Her mouth turns up into a smile, and I can tell she's trying to cover up the little bit of her soul that peeked through.

"Though I have been trying to come up with a fitting name for this enormous sausage in your pants. I've thought about calling him Kulen, the heaviest sausage ever made." She continues to stroke me. "Did you know it weighed almost thirteen hundred pounds? Then I thought about calling him Moosewurst, which, of course, is the most expensive sausage ever made. But then I thought about how long you are and was considering calling him Cumberland, because—"

I don't let her blabber on because God knows she will for eternity if she isn't stopped. Instead, I fist her hair, tilting her head so she can look at me before slamming my mouth against hers.

Piper matches the strokes of my tongue while my dick continues to throb inside her hand.

I pull away, breathing hard, before nodding to my bed. "Get your ass on my bed. I need to be inside you."

Piper takes her tube top off over her head, throwing it to the side, before getting on all fours. Not on my bed, but in front of her rabbit cage.

Ironically, "Pony" by Ginuwine filters through her phone,

and I run a hand down my face, wondering how I stumbled into the world's most bizarre nature documentary.

Natalie, clearly not a fan of this entire spectacle, hops from one side of the cage to the other in a "Get me the fuck out of here" frenzy, while Kevin looks like he's questioning his life's choices, wondering what brought him to this point.

*Yeah, I hear you, buddy.*

As if the night wasn't weird enough, Piper reaches for a button on the side of the cage, illuminating it with pulsing disco lights, like some sort of rabbit dance club. Then, shoving her face against the walls of the cage, she speaks to Kevin in a calm and persuasive tone. "Ready, Fluff Daddy? Now, you just follow Dev's lead, okay? He's going to show you how to rock Nat's world."

I need to ask myself if I'm in a fever dream.

*Did I take fucking hallucinogens or something?*

As if she can tell I'm contemplating bailing on her—though my boner will curse at me later—Piper tosses her hair to one side, giving me a sultry look over her shoulder. She curls her index finger in my direction, beckoning me to join her.

I'm torn between hysterical laughter and genuine concern that my future wife might be a few cards short of a deck. In this case, it might be a few carrots short of a rabbit's lunch.

Is this sort of *peculiarity* genetic? What am I going to do if I have a house full of mini-Pipers as crazy as her?

*Mini-Pipers?*

Where did that thought come from when I can barely convince the woman to stay the night? And why the hell does the thought of having kids with this woman not scare the bejeezus out of me?

And then a new thought hits me out of nowhere.

I stroke my cock as the idea solidifies in my head.

Despite my sane senses, I drop to my knees behind her. It's not lost on me that she chose this position, just like she's chosen every position but missionary during our nights together. Nothing too personal, nothing that makes her feel like she's no longer in control.

And if that's what she needs for now, then that's what I'll give her. But if she thinks I won't push the envelope—make her see what's clear as daylight—then she doesn't know me at all. Little by little I'm going to chip away at that guard of hers, even if it takes me a lifetime.

Our thighs kiss as I scoot in, trying to ignore the fucking rabbit disco with the flashing lights in front of her. Dipping down, I drag the tip of my dick through her wet seam, gathering her juices.

Piper hisses from the sensation and her head falls forward. "Yes. Oh, God."

I do it again, running my round tip between her lips. This time, Piper shoves her greedy center toward me in an effort to urge my cock inside, but I grab both sides of her hips.

"You want this cock, baby?"

She nods enthusiastically. "Yes, please."

I slide my length through her folds, deliberately driving her crazy, before folding over her to speak into her ear. "How bad?"

"So bad," she groans. "Please, Dev. Fuck me. Please, please. I'll do anything."

*Those magic words.*

They're the ones I was looking for. I should feel guilty, knowing what I'm about to ask her, but then I glance back up at the rabbit dance club and that guilt flies out the window.

"Anything, huh?"

"Anything, I promise." She shoves her ass against me, trying to find the tip of my dick. "Just please, I need you inside me."

My lips lift, and I know I'm fucking evil. Evil incarnate just like this hellion under me. She's driven me to this. Night after night of her scurrying away before I can get my fill of her. Night after night of me looking at my ceiling until I fall asleep, wondering how the fuck to make her see what I do every time I look at her.

A forever.

A home worth fighting for.

A love worth risking our hearts.

So, I lean over her body, my breath fanning the shell of her ear as I throw out my own Hail Mary. "Stay the night."

# twenty-eight
## dev

What Would Jesus Do?

She goes silent at my words, her body coming to a complete halt, save for the way her back rises and falls with each labored breath.

She turns to look at me. "What?"

"Spend the night with me," I repeat, the fear in my eyes mimicking hers but for a completely different reason. Fuck, say yes.

"Dev..."

"You can be on one side of the bed, and I'll stick to the other. We can have pillows between us and I'll wear my anti-cuddling suit."

I can tell she's holding back a smile. "Anti-cuddling suit?"

I nod. "It's something I had custom-made for this very reason. It has spikes and an alarm that blares 'Unauthorized Space Violation!' so you won't be tempted to touch me. I know how you just can't help yourself."

She turns her head so it hangs between her arms again before a chuckle bursts out of her, making her body shake in a fit of laughter. "Who are you and what have you done with my stoic, unfunny fiancé?"

"I've replaced him with this incredibly attractive guy with

a big dick. The charm and humor he came with were a bonus." As she giggles, I run my dick through her seam again, punctuating my point. "Which is why you should say yes, Piper."

She looks back to catch my eyes. "Why?"

I shrug. "Sometimes you have to set yourself free, let go, in order to move forward."

I see the moment she does it, the moment she lets go. It's the same moment she nods with a "Yes," and I slam inside her, filling her in one go.

We both groan as my head falls back, eyes closed. For a second, we barely move, the sensation is so intense, I'm already seeing stars behind my lids.

Or is that the fucking pulsing disco lights?

"God," she groans. "No matter how many times you've been inside me, it always feels like you're going to break me in half."

Her eyes flick to Natalie in the cage, who's now side-eyeing Piper while nervously munching on a piece of lettuce she's holding between her paws.

"Don't worry, Nat, rabbit dicks are much smaller. You'll be fine."

"Piper?" I rasp, breathing through the sensation. She feels so good, I can barely form a sentence. "I'm going to need you to stop talking to your rabbits now."

She nods. "Okay. I just wanted to address Natalie's concerned expression. To let her know that rabbit penises probably don't come in different sizes like human ones. Not that I know much about rabbit penises—"

"Piper?"

"Yeah?"

"For God's sake, please shut up."

"Okay."

And with that, I pull back out and slam into her again, all

the way to the hilt, making us both lose our breath. My eyes drop to where we're connected, her ass against my thighs, the tips of my fingers burrowed into the sides of her hips, and the image has something wild unleashing inside me.

Pulling out halfway, I push inside her again.

"Fuck, Piper," I exhale, as if I'm pleading with her. Though, I have no idea what I'm even begging for. "Jesus, you feel so good. I'm not going to be able to hold off that long, baby."

Piper rolls her hips around me, and I use my grip on her hips to find a steady rhythm, drilling into her with so much force, you'd think I was trying to come out the other side.

My cock throbs each time it fills her. Every one of my senses feels overwhelmed. Submerged in her, in her body and in the way she makes me feel. Like I'm finally living.

"Want me to turn around so you can come all over my chest?"

Jesus Christ. Who is this girl?

I shake my head even though she can't see me, wondering how the fuck I got the hottest woman—a sex goddess—to agree to go along with my crazy ass plan.

If only I can find a way to make her go along with another crazy plan . . . the one that ends with us being together forever. Because fuck, it's the only forever I want.

"No, I need you to come first, sweetheart," I say, plowing into her. "Don't deprive me of seeing you come around my cock."

Her ass shakes each time I pound her, but damn if she doesn't jut it back against me, asking for more. My greedy little bride-to-be, giving as good as she gets, keeping in time with my rhythm.

I slap one of her cheeks hard before I pull myself out of her and sheath myself again.

"Oh, God," she gasps as I thrust into her after yet another

loud thwack against her pink ass, loving the way my handprint looks on it. "Dev, baby . . ."

Her tits swing over my rug and her hair brushes against it; the sight of her on all fours so erotic, I'm convinced I actually am filming a fucking porno.

For a second, I'm distracted by the thought of the rabbits watching us from different corners of their cage while the lights flash to the beat of "How Many Licks" by Lil' Kim and Sisqo—Jesus, how much research did she do to create this playlist?—but I shove it aside as I grab both her ass cheeks, opening them up to take in her sweet puckered hole.

Fuck. So hot, I'm about to come just from looking at it.

I curl over her again as we both charge together toward the finish line. Finding her clit, I rub circles over it with my middle two fingers while ramming into her like a man possessed. "Do you realize how perfect you are?"

A rumbled moan escapes her. "My pussy, you mean?"

I lay kisses over her back. "No, baby. You. You're perfect in every way."

She might think my words are a product of the moment. That I'm just saying them because we're fucking and it makes sense to, but she couldn't be more wrong. She's fucking perfect for me—weird rabbits, hairless cats, and all.

I finger her clit some more, picking up my pace while she pushes back against me, taking me in as far as I can go.

She moans, fisting the rug and looking up at her rabbit, who's actually facing the other way, like he's hoping we'll simply cease to exist if he doesn't look at us.

"Kevin." She tries to get his attention. "Turn around so you can watch—"

Her words are cut off when I pinch her hardened nub and slap her pussy, her cry reverberating through the room.

"Dev!" Her walls pulse around me, milking my dick, her thighs shaking. "I'm coming!"

Her orgasm crests, pulling her under, sending a flush through her body. She's so goddamn gorgeous when she comes.

I continue to pummel her, and even when her orgasm wanes, she continues to rock against me, helping me find mine. And I do, coming in long spurts inside her.

"I can feel your eyes on me. Are you imagining me naked again, Peter?"

"Yes."

Her hushed voice an nearness stirs something inside me like it always does.

I grin up at the ceiling of my darkened room. "Didn't you get an eyeful earlier, and then again inside the shower?"

She makes a humming noise. "Imagining you naked helps me sleep."

If it's even possible, my grin widens.

"I don't know if I should be flattered or insulted that images of my naked body put you to sleep," I tease, my voice low and husky in the stillness of the room.

"Definitely flattered," she assures me, shifting against the silken sheets. "The last moments inside my head before I fall asleep are precious real estate. I don't give that space away easily."

I turn to my side to face her. She's lying on the other side of my king bed, and while there are no pillows separating us, there's way more space than I prefer between our bodies. The soft lights streaming through the curtains from the backyard dance across her features, casting shadows accentuating her cheekbones and the cupid's bow above her lip.

I know her eyes are open, watching me in the darkness, but I can't make out their green color.

"And I'm the lucky bastard who gets reserved space in that beautiful head of yours?" I ask, keeping my voice barely above a whisper, as if speaking any louder would shatter this serene moment between us.

She nods, keeping our eyes locked. The air thickens between us, and I so badly want to reach across and tug her to me, to breathe in her citrus scent and feel her warm body pressed against mine.

But I won't. Not until I get a better indication of how it might be received.

After putting her rabbits back in her room, Piper and I came back here. Frankly, I'm still surprised she actually upheld her side of the bargain and agreed to stay the night. I mean, I did hold an orgasm over her head, but I was sure she was going to back out.

Before we got into bed, we took a shower together, where Piper dropped to her knees for me and I experienced the second most amazing orgasm of the night inside her mouth. I repaid her in kind once we got out of the shower, by setting her on the bathroom counter and eating her out until she was screaming my name once again.

"Do you think we traumatized them?" she asks, taking me away from the images spinning inside my head of her flushed cheeks, her hand fisted inside my hair, and the perfect "O" her lips formed when she came over my tongue.

Fuck, my dick is hard again.

"Who?" I ask, struggling to shift my thoughts.

"Natalie Nutbottom and Kevin. I feel like they might be traumatized by what they saw."

"Or they learned a thing or two. Still, probably a good idea to find them a therapist."

"Maybe the vet will tell me why they refuse to be intimate. At this point, I've tried everything."

My lips twitch. "Have you really, though? I mean, I don't think you went far enough with the sex playlist, the club lighting, or forcing them to watch our live performance."

"You're right." She nods thoughtfully, her deadpan voice matching my sarcasm. "I should have gotten some bunny lingerie for Natalie."

"God, you're weird. The weirdest, most intriguing girl I've ever met."

"You sure about that?" Piper lifts on an elbow, resting her head in her palm. "Because from what I heard, your ex was pretty intriguing, too. I don't want to believe the gossip rags, but did she actually become a nun?"

I puff out a short breath, caught off-guard by the change in topic. "What can I say? I have a type."

She smiles, waiting for me to continue. It's a topic that needs to be discussed; though, if I'm being honest, I'm surprised it took her this long to bring up. For months after Camila and I broke up, my life was plastered all over every gossip magazine in the country. I'm sure she read some version of our breakup in some magazine or online column.

"Camila and I grew apart after several years. It didn't help that I was traveling so much for work and couldn't devote the time to our relationship. In fact, we hadn't been intimate for months toward the end. Even still, I thought we were going to get married. But when I came back from one of my trips, Camila was waiting for me in my living room. Her stuff was packed and she told me she'd found a higher calling."

Piper reaches for my hand, tangling it with her own, before scooting closer to me. She places her head on my chest and drapes her leg over my thighs.

She's wearing those tiny sleep shorts I'm so fucking crazy

about, but in this position, I can finally fulfill my fantasy of palming her ass through them.

"I'm sorry. That couldn't have been easy for you."

"It's not every day your girlfriend cheats on you with Jesus."

Piper's silent for a second before her body shakes against mine with laughter. "Well, I guess this answers the age-old question of 'What would Jesus do?' Looks like he'd steal your girlfriend."

She crosses herself, looking at the ceiling and asking for forgiveness, but I can't help but laugh, pulling her closer into my arms the way I've been wanting to for so long.

We're quiet for a few moments when I decide to turn the tables on her. "What about you?"

She draws circles over my bare chest with the tip of her finger. "What about me?"

"Have you ever had a serious relationship?"

The thought of someone else holding her, touching her, kissing her the way I do bothers the fuck out of me, but I've always wanted to understand more about the way she ticks, what and who formed this version of Piper Parker in my arms.

"I had a steady boyfriend in high school. Andrés. But we broke up when I told him I wanted to go to beauty school instead of college." She's quiet for a moment, but I suspect she has more to say. "He said he couldn't see himself with an uneducated airhead long-term."

It's as if all the lightheartedness in the room fades at once. My jaw hardens and the hand I was running through her hair freezes in its spot. I lift her chin so she can meet my furious eyes. "He was a dick, Piper."

She nods, giving me one of her it's-no-big-deal smiles, but it doesn't reach her eyes. "Oh, I know. Because look at what he missed out on. I'm a fucking prize."

"Piper," I say, not liking the sarcasm in her tone. "You are a fucking prize. You're the most intelligent, incredible, and witty girl I've ever met. Surely, you wouldn't let one asshole's words fester inside your head."

A flicker of vulnerability cuts through her usually confident exterior. "No, but there was a bigger asshole who said those same things to me probably as far back as my memories go." She lays her head back on my chest. "I used to call him dad."

Jesus. What the fuck?

My anger surges, that deep protectiveness I have for this girl rising to the surface as her words sink in. I knew she wasn't close to her dad, but now I want to punch the lights out of him.

I pull her off me, laying her on the pillow so I am hovering over her. My fingers nestle in her hair while my other hand cups her face.

"Peter, listen to me," I say, my voice low and unwavering. "You are extraordinary. The kind of person people wish to be. You're so fucking talented—"

"That's not what you said after your last haircut, mister," she teases, trying to lighten the mood again because, God forbid, she just takes a compliment for once and not make a self-deprecating joke.

"—funny and sharp. But beyond all that, you're kind and thoughtful. Until you, I'd never met a single person as beautiful on the inside as they are on the outside. You're a fucking force of nature. A beautiful, and slightly insane, storm, sure," I say, making her giggle. "But there isn't a single thing I'd change about you. You're perfect."

I pause, making sure she really hears me.

"These voices inside your head telling you otherwise? They're liars and assholes. They don't have an ounce of the aptitude and charisma you hold in your pinky. They don't know you . . . not the way I do. So, believe me when I tell you, there isn't a person like you out there."

Her eyes glisten, bouncing against mine, before she reaches up and pulls my lips to hers. She kisses me with abandon, both fiercely and tenderly, like it's the only way she can express everything she feels but can't say out loud.

My heart thunders inside my chest. The words I've been holding back press against my lips, and I'm sure she can taste them on my tongue. Words I can't hold back much longer, but ones I'll keep to myself for now.

That I'm irrevocably in love with her.

## twenty-nine
# dev

Five Schlongs Hen Party

DEAN MEYER

@Dev Menon, just wondering what the groomsmen are supposed to wear. Wedding is coming up in three weeks, and I want to make sure I look <fire emoji>. Not that I need too much help in that area. Should I just wear my work uniform?

Then again, that might not be a good idea. The wedding guests might think there's a fire nearby.

GARRETT MEYER

Or a stripper.

HUDSON CASE

Wait, you're one of the groomsmen? I didn't even realize you were invited.

DEAN MEYER

Very funny, old man. You must have forgotten, given your advanced age.

## Pretend For Me

**DEV MENON**

Hold on. @Dean Meyer, did you not get the detailed email about the groomsmen attire I sent weeks ago?

**DARIAN MEYER**

I certainly did. Great choice on the tuxes, Dev. Very trendy and nontraditional.

**GARRETT MEYER**

Agreed. I'm especially excited about the hot pink bow ties. I'm so glad I turned in my measurements when I did. Apparently, there's a shortage of green velvet now.

**DEAN MEYER**

I know you guys are fucking with me.

**DARIAN MEYER**

Oh boy. If you didn't read the email, then you probably also don't know about the synchronized swim routine we're doing for him that day. I've been practicing daily.

**DEAN MEYER**

See? Now I know you guys are fucking around because that was Darian's attempt at a joke. He never jokes because, as seen in the embarrassing example above, his jokes are dumb.

**DARIAN MEYER**

Jackass.

**DEAN MEYER**

This is some fucked up shit, banding together against me. What have I ever done to you guys?

HUDSON CASE

How about making a profile for me on the SeniorSizzler dating site and then proceeding to match me with an eighty-five-year-old woman with seventeen grandchildren and six Pomeranians? Ring any bells?

DEAN MEYER

Bro. Sue-Ann was a great catch! Also, how long are you going to hold that against me? It was before you met Kavi, when you were wound up so tight you were scheduling your shits. I was just trying to loosen you up! And it clearly worked, didn't it? I'm still waiting for that 'thank you,' by the way.

[GIF of Leonardo DiCaprio lifting a glass and saying "You're Welcome"]

HUDSON CASE

You'll be waiting a long time.

DARIAN MEYER

How about slipping the DJ five hundred bucks to play nursery rhymes at my wedding and dedicating them all to my wife?

DEAN MEYER

Oh, come on, little brother! Rani loved it! I bet those songs were on her most-played list. Didn't you see how she knew all the words to them?

GARRETT MEYER

How about the time you convinced Bella that we did everything together as twins, including sharing our women? And then proceeded to tell her you'd meet her in our honeymoon suite after our wedding?

# Pretend For Me

**DEAN MEYER**

That was a joke! Are you still butt-hurt about that? She rejected me, didn't she? Even threatened to cut off the family jewels if I came within fifty feet of her. I was just testing her loyalty, bro. Again, you're welcome.

Jesus, a man can't get any gratitude around here.

**DARIAN MEYER**

Knowing Bella, she would have probably followed through with that threat, too.

**DEAN MEYER**

Alright, so I can see you guys might be airing your grievances with me, and before you pile on with the rest of them, @Dev Menon, I want to tell you that the box of custom anal wipes with your face printed on them I sent to your future wife's salon was just a gesture of my excitement in meeting her and her pussies.

**DEV MENON**

What the fuck are you talking about?

**DEAN MEYER**

Ah . . . never mind. I sense from your tone that perhaps more information might not be received well.

**HUDSON CASE**

Dev, can I please rescind his invitation to the wedding on your behalf?

**DEV MENON**

I'm definitely contemplating it. Except, for some unfathomable reason, Piper is excited about meeting the Meyer brothers.

**DARIAN MEYER**

Feel free to tell her there are only two of us.

**DEAN MEYER**

Ouch, little bro. I can see you're still salty about my jokes about you marrying a fetus, but let's not make Dev and Piper suffer. They need the best-looking and most charming Meyer brother there: me.

Speaking of your wife-to-be, @Dev Menon, how is it going with her? Are her rabbits still getting more action than you?

**HUDSON CASE**

Oh yeah, Piper was telling me she tried some new techniques to get them to breed. [GIF of Thumper and Miss Bunny kissing]

**DEV MENON**

Wait. She told you about that!?

**HUDSON CASE**

Yeah. What's the big deal? We keep up with each other's lives like any friends would. No need to get all jealous and possessive alpha, bro.

**DEV MENON**

What the fuck? She told you about what we did in front of her rabbits last night?

**GARRETT MEYER**

Uh, what?

**HUDSON CASE**

What in the . . .?

## Pretend For Me

**DARIAN MEYER**

I feel like I should exit this conversation, but I'm strangely intrigued.

**DEAN MEYER**

[GIF of Simon Cowell's "what the fuck" face being zoomed in]

Uh, Dev, buddy? Do you think you might have taken "fucking like rabbits" too literally? When Piper told you to act like an 'animal' in bed, I don't think that's what she had in mind. Or maybe she did . . . I get the feeling Sniperella is a freak.

**GARRETT MEYER**

Goes to show you, you never really know anyone . . .

**HUDSON CASE**

Jesus. I was talking about the parsley she started adding to their food. She told me it was a natural aphrodisiac. I think I need to amputate my memory after this conversation.

**DARIAN MEYER**

Me, too.

**DEAN MEYER**

On the bright side, looks like Dev's tiny carrot finally found a little rabbit hole!

```
[Darian Meyer has left the chat]
[Dean Meyer has added Darian Meyer to the
chat]
```

**DEAN MEYER**

Darian, bro, that wasn't even that bad. You know I can say way worse.

**DARIAN MEYER**

Which is why I was trying to preemptively leave.

**DEAN MEYER**

Anyway, I am so excited. I have so much fodder for the best man's speech!

Oh, Dev, I saw the news about you becoming the face of Haircuts and Heartthrobs. They went with the picture of you with one of the bare pussies around your shoulder? I will say, the messaging seems mixed. Are they selling haircuts or Brazilian waxes?

**DEV MENON**

A.) You are not the best man, and B.) There will be no best man's speech because there will be no wedding. I'm canceling it, and you are all uninvited.

**DEAN MEYER**

Aw, come on, buddy. Don't be like that. We were just trying to be *'bunny'*.

**GARRETT MEYER**

Yeah, but Dean, clearly Dev's not *hoppin'* it. Maybe we should stop. It was too *'munch'* for him.

**DEAN MEYER**

Too 'munch'! BAHAHAH!

**DEV MENON**

You guys are idiots.

DEAN MEYER

Okay, last question for research purposes for my best man's speech. Did last night's activities include you wearing a cottontail butt plug? I've always been curious about those.

[**Dev Menon** has left the chat]

DEAN MEYER

There he goes, hopping off into the horizon. Oh, look! He even remembered his cottontail butt plug.

[**Darian Meyer** has left the chat]
[**Hudson Case** has left the chat]

## thirty
# piper

Overthinking It

"Look at this kitchen!" Sarina says, scanning the length of Dev's kitchen. "It looks like Martha Stewart designed it herself."

I set Nisha's baking dish on the massive island next to the salad I made. While I'm a hopeless cook, give me store-bought ingredients—as long as it's not gorgonzola, because ew!—and dressing, and I can whip up a decent salad. Today's offering is a recreation of the Olive Garden salad to go along with the baked mac and cheese Nisha brought for our biweekly dinner because you have to be a lunatic not to love the Olive Garden salad.

"I wouldn't be surprised if she actually *did* design it," I say, walking over to the wall-to-wall fridge to pull out the pitcher of the Bloody Mary I made earlier for the three of us, along with a bottle of chocolate milk for Rome.

While my honorary nephew has seen Dev's place quite thoroughly, given the move-in fiasco of the century, this is the first time my best friends have come over.

Dev is flying back from his day trip to Seattle, but I texted him this morning to ask if I could host my friends at his place. His response?

## Pretend For Me

**DEV**

It's *our* house, Peter. You can host whoever you want.

**ME**

Well, in that case, let me send off those invites for the rager I've been thinking about hosting here.

**DEV**

Fine, but if TMZ shows up, you're on damage control. Also, no foam machines, please. The clean up is a bitch.

**ME**

Ugh, you're such a killjoy. Fine, I'll stick to just glitter bombs, then.

**DEV**

I'll let the cleanup crew know to stand-by. Try not to burn the place down, little hellion.

**ME**

No promises. Hurry back if you want to see your house in one piece.

**DEV**

I'm hurrying back, but it's not the house I want to see.

> **ME**
>
> Oh yeah? Then it must be that crossword you left for me to finish. Honestly, Menon, how do you call yourself a genius? I had to erase your answer to forty-six across. The eight-letter name for a variety of apple often used in baking wasn't Braeburn; it was Cortland. Which is why you weren't able to solve twelve-down: Constable. As in John Constable, the painter famous for his depiction of clouds.

> **DEV**
>
> Firstly, I don't call myself a genius. And secondly, no, it isn't the crossword I want to see, either. Stop being purposely obtuse.

And even if our fun banter was destined to end shortly in the future, along with our fabricated relationship, I had a smile as wide as the Mississippi River stretched across my face the rest of the day.

"So, how has it been living with him?" Nisha asks, settling into a chair after taking off her light jacket and showing off her full sleeve of tattoos.

Even with her hair pulled into a messy ponytail and literally nothing but a dab of lip gloss on her face, my best friend is the most beautiful woman I've ever seen. A warrior-goddess walking amongst us plebeians.

Beneath that tough exterior lies not only the soft soul of a fiercely loyal friend, but also a badly broken heart she guards with all her might. She often teases me for being closed off about my past, but I'm nowhere as reserved as she is.

Not that I'm reserved, per se. I don't know anyone who would use words like "shy" or "private" to describe me. I'm a ball of energy with a dab of eccentricism thrown in for balance. Okay, so maybe a little more than a dab, but who's really measuring, anyway?

As for my past? It's just not a story I like to lead with. My dad was—and still is—a toxic asshole, and my ex intensified the insecurities my dad instilled in me throughout my childhood. I've witnessed firsthand how promises turn into lies and how love morphs into hate and resentment, and I've cultivated my distrust for romantic love and my skepticism toward commitment.

You don't have to be Freud to determine I have a few underlying issues that I overcompensate with my adventurous spirit, but I'd argue that I'm not living a lie, either. I actually *am* happy. I'm proud of how far I've come.

Does that mean my insecurities and doubts don't sneak up on me? No. I'm only human; a work-in-progress. Does that also mean I'm immune to someone trying to scale my high walls? No . . . I see him, and he's succeeding.

"I feel like with how busy we've all been, we haven't properly chatted about your billionaire since you went to Disneyland," Sarina adds, grabbing two glasses of the Bloody Marys I'd set out, bringing one to her sister before settling into her chair. "Rome told me how much fun he had—"

"It was the best!" Rome yells from the family room, examining a new handmade structure of the solar system Dev got made especially for him. "You should have seen Mr. Dev's face when he was on Space Mountain. He almost peed his pants, Mom! I didn't. I was prepared for it. I knew it would be scary, but I wasn't worried."

Sarina, Nisha, and I giggle before I decide to irritate my little smart-Alec nephew with one of my dumb questions. "Rome, do you think we came out of Space Mountain younger than when we went in because we went at the speed of light?"

Rome slaps his forehead and shakes his head, making us all laugh.

"No, Aunt Piper," he groans, feeling second-hand embarrassment for me. "We can't travel at that speed yet."

"Oh." I pout. "I really thought we were going that fast."

Rome sighs. "Where's Mr. Dev? He knows so much more about space."

"He should be here soon, buddy," I answer, still giggling.

"Okay, so give us the deets before your man comes home," Sarina whispers out of earshot of Rome. "Have you guys . . . you know?" She wiggles her brows, making her meaning clear.

I can't even help the smile that spreads over my face. *God, have we ever.*

It's not like me to blush or have butterflies swoop through my stomach, but just the thought of Dev does that to me. Like, seriously, who the hell is he turning me into?

"Maybe," I respond coyly.

Sarina gasps. "You hussy! I knew it! And? How was it?"

My thoughts filter back to the past week and a half. I can no longer remember how many times we've had sex—the most incredible sex, in fact, where my lady bits sing and weep and dance and dream. Basically, my vagina feels like she's in her own little Broadway musical. But the aftermath of each night is etched into my memory with alarming clarity.

Whole.

Happy.

Like I was floating on clouds.

*Floating on clouds? Christ. Am I serious with that analogy? When did I start waxing poetic?*

But honestly, it's how I've felt, ever since the first night he asked me to stay. I was steadfast in not letting him break my rules, making it a point to sleep in my own room and away from his intoxicating pull each night. But it took one breathless moment, one plea from him to let go, and I crumbled like an over-baked soufflé on *The Great British Bake Off*.

And then his words to me after—the ones said with so

much conviction and confidence—left me feeling even more exposed than I was physically.

He was burrowing himself into the place I kept under lock and key, but could he demolish the fortress of deep-seated doubts I'd built around it?

"Alright, spill the tea," Sarina urges. "Tell us everything."

I shrug, aiming for nonchalance, but knowing my friends can see right through it. "I don't know, it just happened. One minute we were kissing under the fireworks, and the next—"

"Wait," Nisha interrupts. "You . . . kissed him?"

*Damn. I was hoping to slip that detail in without notice.*

"It was just a kiss. Don't overthink it."

*Except for the fact that it was the most life-changing, earth-altering kiss in the world.*

"Don't overthink it?!" Sarina barks, making me jump in my chair. I almost spill my Bloody Mary on my new skirt. "You haven't kissed a guy in more than a decade, and you're telling us not to overthink it? Piper. You like him!"

"I . . ."

"Don't even try to deny it," Nisha interrupts, clearly knowing what I was about to say. It's really annoying to have friends who know you better than you know yourself sometimes. "I saw the way you were looking at him when he came to the salon, and then when you dropped Rome off after Disney. I've heard you talk about him. It's unlike the way you've ever been with anyone."

I stir my cocktail with the celery stick inside it, suddenly feeling unsure about everything—my thoughts, my feelings, and the way my heart seems to have picked up its pace. "Yeah, okay. I like him. So what?"

My friends look at each other, mouths hanging open as if they can't believe what they're hearing.

"Guys, do you not remember what I told you about the

terms of this engagement?" I ask. "It ends shortly after Dev's mom passes."

"Yes, but that doesn't mean it has to," Nisha says, leaning in. "If you love each other—"

"Love?" I interrupt, my head snapping back. "Nisha, we've known each other for mere weeks, not long enough to figure out if it's love. Anyway, you know how firm I am about rule number three—no falling in love."

"Oh, Jesus," she whispers irritatedly. "Your stupid rules."

"Remind me again why rule number three is even on the list?" Sarina adds, eyes narrowing. "What's your problem with falling in love?"

I groan, taking a sip of my cocktail. I've explained this to them before, but apparently, my best friends have the memories of goldfish. "I don't have a problem with all love, just the romantic type. In my experience, romantic love is unpredictable, untrustworthy, and probably some other "un" words I can't think of right now.

"People use it too often but don't mean it enough. Love is something one person comes to rely on while the other person uses it to string them along, only to change their mind later. It's why I've chosen to stay away from it, because in the end, it breaks more people than it mends. Look at my parents. Look at you both."

I snap my mouth shut as soon as those last words are out. I wasn't trying to bring up either of their failed relationships, but honestly, can they blame me? If anything, they should be on this anti-love bandwagon with me!

I circle my finger over my glass. "I'm sorry. That was really rude of me."

Nisha's eyes soften. "Yes, but you're not completely wrong. I get that you've seen some shitty examples of love, but you've also seen some good ones. Look at Rowan and Shay. Look at how happy they are."

"Or even Dev's parents," Sarina chimes in. "Every time you visit, you tell us how much love you see between them, even if his dad is a hard-ass."

"And what about your mom and her husband? She seems to have found true love with him," Nisha adds.

*Ugh, why did I tell them about any of that? I should have known they'd conveniently bring up those examples at a time like this to make their point.*

"Look." I sigh. "Even if I have feelings for him, the last thing he needs is a complication when I promised him there wouldn't be. This was just supposed to be an arrangement between us. Plus, I haven't actually loved anyone romantically before, not even Andrés. I was too young to even know what that kind of love was at the time."

"Yeah, but now you do, don't you?" Nisha asks, and I gather she's not expecting me to answer. "You have a much better understanding of that kind of love now. You're just holding yourself back from experiencing it."

"No," I say firmly. "I'm holding us both back from inevitable heartbreak in the future."

"I might be reaching here," Sarina says, cutting into what will definitely become an argument between me and Nisha, "but maybe you're the one overthinking it, Piper."

"Overthinking what?"

We turn toward the deep voice to see Dev walking toward us.

He stalls mid-step when Rome rushes to him, and in a scene I couldn't have predicted, Dev scoops him up, placing a kiss on his cheek, before setting him back on his feet. Taking out a small object the size of a remote from his pocket, he hands it to Rome.

"Whoa!" Rome exclaims, wide-eyed. "What is it?"

"It's a new handheld projection device my company is developing. This one displays the solar system in detail."

"Are you saying I can have it?" Rome asks, oscillating between shock and awe.

"It's all yours, little man."

The expression on Rome's face is indescribable. Even behind his glasses, I can see his eyes glisten.

Dev ruffles his hair. "Go try it out, buddy. I'll meet you in a few. Let me say hi to your mom and your aunts."

Rome runs off while Sarina yells at him to say thank you before we all greet Dev. Sarina pulls him into a hug, while Nisha opts for a handshake. Both of my friends have met him during his photo shoot at the salon, but never in a casual setting like this.

After exchanging pleasantries, Dev takes a seat beside me. His warm brown eyes caress my face before he leans over, pressing a kiss on my lips.

It's brief and chaste, but it has my toes curling under the table.

"What were you overthinking?" he repeats, reaching over to take my glass from my hands before taking a long sip.

Both my friends watch with rapt attention, and I know what they're thinking—that this is real; that neither Dev nor I could be such good actors.

And perhaps that's true. But that doesn't change the fact that love—*lasting love*—is rarer than finding a four-leaf clover under twelve feet of snow.

Is there a part of me that wants to follow my heart and jump head-first into whatever is developing between us?

Yes! Abso-fucking-lutely, there is!

But there's also that other part—the rather loud and pesky one—-that screams at me to hold back, reminding me that jumping head-first will not only lead to a cracked skull, but also a cracked heart.

"She was talking about the cake," Sarina blurts. "She's overthinking the design and flavors."

Dev places his arm on the back of my chair before running his fingers through strands of my hair. "You know there's no rule saying we have to settle on one cake or flavor."

I hold back a smile. "I wasn't aware of that, actually. Are you saying if I like ten different cakes and twenty different flavors, we can get them all?"

He shrugs. "I don't see why not. How many times are we going to get married?"

His words hit me like a bucket of ice water. How many times? Once. Just *this* once. At least that is the case for me, because I wouldn't do this again unless it was for love. And since the whole love thing terrifies me, I wouldn't do it at all.

But is he implying he wouldn't do it again, either? And if so . . . *why*? In the time I've known him, he definitely doesn't seem to have the same aversion to love as I do. So, why wouldn't he do it again for real the next time?

I open my mouth, questions burning on my tongue when I meet his eyes. Soft, warm, and full of a tenderness that's become familiar lately. They urge me to lean in, to trust, to . . . hope?

But the words die on my tongue. Because at this point, I'm completely confused. Confused about what this is, what this was supposed to be, and now my own feelings about it.

Maybe Sarina is right. Maybe I am the one overthinking it.

# thirty-one
## **piper**

A Lesbunny Situation

I stare at the vet in shock.

"Ms. Parker, are you alright?"

I can feel my lips moving but no words seem to be coming out. I've become a mime. No, wait, mimes don't move their lips. I've become a ventriloquist's dummy with a mute ventriloquist.

Dev places his hand on the small of my back, asking the vet to give us a moment, and as soon as she leaves, Dev's hands find my face. His thumbs run along the tops of my cheeks, his eyes dancing with mirth.

I told him last night that I didn't need him to accompany me—I know how crazy things have been for him at work. He's also been spending a lot of his free time with his mom. But he insisted on being here, saying this was important for him too because he felt like he'd become a part of the whole rabbit breeding experience.

I can't be sure, but I swear his lips are doing that twitchy thing when he's trying to hold back a laugh. "Hey, are you okay?"

I blink out of my stupor. "They're both . . . girls?"

His cheeks puff, and now I know the bastard is trying to

hold back a grin. "It looks as though we might have been trying to create a *lesbunny* situation, yes."

"Oh, my God," I stammer, my hand finding my forehead, but I do think it's sweet he says "we," taking some of the blame off me. "How could this have happened? The breeder promised me they would mate in due time. How could he have misread their genders?!"

"Well, it's like the vet told us. Rabbit genders can be hard to determine at times. And Kevin does have a strange nodule near her . . ." He waves a hand, flicking a glance at my rabbit who just laid a string of poop in her kennel.

"After everything I've done," I complain, still feeling like I've been duped. "The Rabbit Sex Playlist, the club lights, the various diets, the number of times I played *Kama Sutra* for them on my phone . . ."

"Let's not forget our live performance for them," he adds, chuckling but quickly removes the grin off his face when he sees the murderous look on mine.

His hands tighten over my jaw, eyes softening with affection. "Hey, look. This doesn't mean you have to throw in the towel on this, okay? Now that we know Kevin and Natalie's dating preferences, we just have to find them opposite genders. Just a plot-twist in their *hare-y* rom-com." He purses his lips again to hold back another chuckle, and I pinch his side, making his shoulders shake with laughter.

"Dev, this isn't funny!" I whine. "Miniature plush lop rabbits are rare. We might not find any for a while, and—"

"Shh," he says, putting a finger over my lips that I want to bite. "Let's worry about this tomorrow. Right now, you have to get to your dress fitting. You can't be late for that since your friends will be waiting. Ralph's in the front for you."

My shoulders sink with disappointment, but I know he's right. My sister-in-law and my mom flew in this morning, and they're waiting for me along with my friends at the boutique.

And it's one of the last things I have left to do, now that Dev and I have finished cake tasting, and Dev has claimed sole responsibility for the music. We went with a classic three-tier, raspberry-filled ivory cake that will be adorned with Claire's roses.

I nod, looking up at him. "You're right."

His eyes caress my face the way I've gotten used to before he dips his face down, brushing his lips over mine. And while I know this isn't the time or place, I pull him closer, deepening the kiss for a little longer.

"Why did you bring me here, Ralph?" I ask Dev's chauffeur when he parks the car at the entrance of the Fairmont in Nob Hill. "The dress fitting is at the boutique in San Jose."

Ralph exits the driver's side and opens my door. "Mr. Menon had the entire party moved here, Mrs. Menon. He arranged transportation for everyone so your friends are all inside already."

Wait, what?

He helps me out of the back seat. "What do you mean, he moved the party here? Also, I'm not Mrs. Menon yet. Please, just call me Piper."

Ralph gives me a smile. "Apologies, Mrs. Menon, but according to the email sent to Mr. Menon's entire staff yesterday, we are to refer to you as Mrs. Menon going forward."

Oh, geez. I hold back my eye roll as I make my way toward the entrance of the hotel.

Pulling out my phone, I text the man responsible for the sudden changes.

## Pretend For Me

**ME**

> You instructed the staff to call me Mrs. Menon? <arched brow emoji>

**DEV**

> I figured your nicknames, Peter, *meri jaan*, and little hellion were reserved for me. But if you prefer they call you one of those . . .

This time I *actually* roll my eyes.

**ME**

> How about just Piper? And you've never told me what *meri jaan* means.

**DEV**

> You've never been *just* Piper, *meri jaan*. They need to get used to calling you Mrs. Menon since the wedding is less than two weeks away. Ralph just texted me to tell me you're at the hotel. How do you like it?

His first comment has me smiling as I get on the elevator, escorted by someone from the hotel staff.

**ME**

> You keeping tabs on me, Lex? This hotel is stunning. Although, you really didn't have to do this. The boutique would have been just fine for a dress fitting.

**DEV**

> I didn't want your day to be "just fine". I wanted you to remember it. Which reminds me, don't hand them your credit card. Everything, including the dresses and accessories you pick, have already been paid for.

> **ME**
> I am very much capable of paying for my wedding dresses, Mr. Moneybags.

> **DEV**
> Happy to hear that, but when it comes to you and me, I'll always be the one to pay. It's not up for debate.

> **ME**
> Maybe I like debating with you. Maybe I like getting under your skin.

> **DEV**
> I can find a few other ways for you to get under me. Have you gotten to the penthouse yet?

The doors to the elevator open and my breath halts inside my lungs as the woman from the hotel staff ushers me in. My Chuck Taylors nestle into the plush white rug as I step into the penthouse suite, taking in the views of the city and the bay from the panoramic windows. The distant hills peek out from beneath the fog as the mid-October sunlight washes over the room, making the chandeliers sparkle.

"Holy shit," I breathe. "This is . . ."

"Quite the view, right?" the lady asks with a knowing smile, but her voice is drowned out by my friends' greetings as they rush off their chairs toward me.

"Piper!" my mother says, gathering me in a hug. Her eyes are already glistening, and I haven't even tried on a dress. "Oh, sweetheart. I couldn't sleep all last night, imagining you in the dress you'll pick."

I hug her back, holding on to her a moment longer and reacquainting myself with her familiar scent. "Well, don't you go nodding off on me now. I need your opinion on what to choose."

She chuckles, taking a step back so I can hug the rest of the group.

Shayla is next, my beautiful sister-in-law, with her signature asymmetrical bob, her huge hoops, and those stars tattooed behind her ear. She's as petite as me, but where I get winded from clicking the TV remote, Shay's a yoga and Pilates fanatic. I've heard she runs six miles a day too, which, even the thought has me wanting to strap myself to the nearest comfy couch.

I give her a long hug, and when I pull back, she's dabbing the corner of her eye with a finger.

"Not you, too," I whine. "Is there something in the air inside this suite?"

Shay chuckles. "I can't help it. Weddings make me emotional. Or maybe it's the post-baby hormones." She gives me a sincere smile. "We're just so happy for you and Dev."

A twinge of guilt threatens to surface. Until recently, I'd been uneasy about my family not knowing the truth about mine and Dev's arrangement, thinking the urgency of getting married on a short timeline was due to his mother's health. But somewhere over the past couple of weeks, that guilt has faded, replaced by genuine excitement right alongside them.

Perhaps it also has to do with the fact that Dev and I got my family together on a FaceTime call last week and he met everyone, including my brother. Rowan liked him immediately, and that's saying something because even though he's my younger brother, he has protective, older brother qualities. The conversation just seemed easy, like Dev was already part of my family.

"I'm thrilled you could make it," I tell her. "I know it couldn't have been easy leaving both the kids."

She shakes her head. "They're in good hands. Although, I fully expect to come home to Kai hopped up on sugar and the baby sleeping in Rowan's arms instead of in her crib. Seriously, your brother will take any opportunity to have her nap on him. And when he's gone for games, I'm left dealing with a cranky baby who misses her human pillow."

"Why do I get the feeling you're not as upset as you're pretending to be?"

She chuckles. "Because I'm not. I know the world knows him as an NHL superstar, but that man was born to be a father."

And for reasons I can't quite understand, her comment makes me think of Dev. The way he is with Rome and his sister. His infinite patience and ability to get on their level. There's no doubt in my mind he'd make an incredible father one day.

The kind of father I never had, but the kind I'd want for my own children...

Wait. Hold the phone...

*My own children? With Dev?*

*What in the holy matrimony and something blue am I thinking?*

*This is a dress fitting for a fake marriage, Piper, not a glimpse into an alternate reality where you're not allergic to romance and happily-ever-afters. Get it together before you start thinking this is real.*

*"But it could be,"* whispers a hopeful little voice inside my head. It's been piping up a lot more as of late.

*"Oh, shut up, you idiot,"* snaps the usual skeptical part of my brain. *"Stop trying to gaslight our negative thoughts and our collection of trust issues. We're used to them!"*

But even as I turn to greet the rest of my guests—Nisha, Sarina, and Jeena—I can't shake the way my heart flips, imagining Dev waiting for me at the end of the aisle. Even if it will all be for pretend.

"Wait until you see all the wedding dresses," Sarina says, grasping my hand and ushering me toward the area where a team of stylists are waiting for me. "They even brought designer Indian *lehengas* for you to try on."

As I take in the racks of high-end garments, I notice a private chef setting up an array of pastries and delicacies on a bar adorned with huge vases of flowers and a chocolate fountain.

*Dev did all this for me?*

At some point, I'm handed a flute of champagne—the bottle on the server's tray likely costs more than my mortgage —before I'm ushered to a room in the back with my choice of dress.

I take a long breath before I exit the changing room to a pin drop silence from my friends. Their eyes are fixated on me, my mom's hands covering her mouth, while Shay visibly takes a shuddered breath.

I've already chosen a Victorian-inspired Vera Wang gown with intricate lace long sleeves and a lace and beaded bodice for our reception, and while that had everyone gasping, this designer bridal *lehenga* for our Indian nuptials has them speechless.

Standing on a pedestal, I cast my eyes down the full-length mirrors to my sides, taking in the intricate embroidery and emerald-green accents over the off-white *lehenga* skirt. It's a masterpiece of embellishments and tiny woven crystals that hug my curves and catch the light with the slightest movement.

*It's the one.*

My chest feels tight at the thought of how Dev will react when he sees me in it, knowing emerald green is his favorite.

"Piper . . ." Jeena says on a gentle exhale. "If I wasn't married to the man of my dreams and his juicy potatoes, I would marry the shit out of you right now."

My mother, God bless her, utters a confused, "Potatoes?" while Nisha and Sarina exchange perplexed glances.

Shay and I, however, just giggle softly, remembering Jeena's infamous "potatoes confession" to her husband. Interestingly, she and Wayland were also in a fake relationship situation. Theirs, however, led to a real happily-ever-after, whereas mine . . .? Yeah, we're not even going to go there right now.

"Inside joke," I say to the others. "Let's just say, Jeena has a rather peculiar fascination with *agricultural assets*."

Jeena shrugs. "If you saw my husband's A-grade *agricultural assets*, you would, too. But seriously, Piper, you look stunning."

"Thank you," I say, ecstatic about my two dresses.

I reach for my phone and text the man who made this beautiful day possible from the changing room.

ME

Lex . . . I'm speechless.

DEV

Speechless? Peter Parker Menon, is that you? The only times you're speechless is when your mouth is stuffed full of my cock.

My cheeks heat, despite the fact that innuendos and dirty talk rarely surprise me. But with Dev . . . everything surprises me. Everything affects me.

ME

Well then, I plan to be speechless several times tonight.

DEV

Fuck, I'm in the middle of a meeting with a raging boner inside my pants.

> ME
>
> <angel emoji> Hmm. Looks like you've got quite the problem there, Mr. Menon. What are you going to do about it?

> DEV
>
> I'm not going to do anything about it. *You're* the one who will spend the entire night doing something about it. When you're ready, head up to the rooftop. There might be one more surprise waiting for you.

I've just changed back into the crop top and sweats I wore earlier and am just about to respond, my mind spinning with what the hell this man thought of now, when my friends pull me into joining them for drinks and the food awaiting us.

Another bottle of something pricey is popped before we all toast and my friends cheer, congratulating me.

"So, where are you guys going for your honeymoon?" Shay asks as I dig into a few hors d'oeuvres.

I finish my bite, telling her the truth. "Honestly, with Dev's mom's situation being so fragile, we might do a long weekend in Hawaii or Mexico. Nothing too far away, if we're needed back here on quick notice..."

I don't finish the sentence because even the thought makes me feel queasy.

Shay grasps my forearm in understanding, but before the mood can dip, Jeena and Sarina come over, each holding skimpy white lingerie they must have found on the racks of clothes.

Jeena wiggles her brows. "How fast is Dev going to rip this off you on your wedding night, you think?"

Three hours and three more flutes of champagne later, I'm ushered to the rooftop by the hotel staff, and the sight nearly knocks me off my feet.

Standing in front of a sleek helicopter with its blades spinning slowly is Dev, his hands tucked inside his suit pants pockets and his smile panty-melting as he strides over to me.

I look up at him, speaking loudly against the cool breeze whipping my hair to one side. "What are you doing, Lex?"

He shrugs, his eyes locked on mine. "Picking up my fiancée."

"No." I shake my head. "I mean, what are you doing to *me*?"

His hands find my hips, his thumb brushing the exposed midriff. "I'm getting you out of your head, Mrs. Menon. Don't overthink it."

My breath hitches as the meaning of his words floats in the air between us. He overheard the conversation between my friends and me last week.

I'm just about to ask him if that's true when he interlocks our fingers and leads me to the helicopter. Helping me inside, he hands me a pair of headphones before double-checking my seatbelt. The pilot lifts us off smoothly and soon, we're flying over skyscrapers, the bay, and the Golden Gate, watching the early evening lights twinkle in the distance.

And while I've never smiled as much in my entire life, it's not the beautiful city unfurling beneath us that has my attention, it's him. The strong set of his stubbled jaw and the warm tone of his tanned skin. The way his lips move and that adorable dimple dancing inside his cheek as he points out landmarks below us.

Dev turns to catch me staring at him, a smile playing at the corners of his mouth. "See something you like, Mrs. Menon?" he asks through the microphone. His gravelly voice inside my ears rumbles inside my chest.

*Yeah. Yeah, I do. Big time.*

Heat crawls into my cheeks as I gesture to the window, lying through my teeth but knowing he can see right through me. "Just the view."

His hand reaches for a wayward strand of my hair, his eyes so intense I feel breathless.

"Thank you," I say, holding his gaze. "Today has been everything."

"It's just the beginning, *meri jaan*."

My brows fold. "What do you mean?"

His eyes flick between mine, and I swear he wants to say something but shakes his head as if thinking better of it. "Wait til we get home."

All too soon the tour ends, and the helicopter lands on the grounds of Dev's sprawling mansion. A few minutes later, we're making our way through his enormous front door and into the living room hand-in-hand when something catches my eye.

Not just something . . . *two* little somethings inside individual cages, with blue ribbons around their furry little necks. One of them is nibbling on a cucumber, while the other is sitting on hay, whiskers moving incessantly.

My mouth drops open as my shocked eyes turn to my husband-to-be. "How?"

He shrugs. "Does it matter? You wanted them, so I wanted them."

My stomach tightens, my lungs and heart feel too big, and my throat closes. And for the first time in my life, I understand the terror and agony of a heart on the verge of falling.

On the verge of shattering.

## thirty-two
## dev

Enough Is Enough

"Hey, Mom."

My mother slowly turns her head, watching me step toward her bed. Her mouth tilts up into a tired smile and she reaches out a frail hand, beckoning me to hold it. "Dev."

I take a seat on the chair next to her bed, the same way I have over the past couple of weeks when I visit her. She has a view of her rose garden from her windows in her room, but she's been enjoying sitting outside less and less lately.

A sign I don't want to consider.

I place a tender kiss on her knuckles. "How are you feeling?"

Not waiting for her answer, I quickly get up and refill her glass of water, organize her bottles of meds and the stack of books on her nightstand, and reach toward her feet to pull up the extra blanket there.

"Dev?"

"Hmm?" I notice the TV remote has fallen onto the rug under her bed, so I pick it up and nestle it near her other hand so she can reach it.

I'm just about to reach behind her to ask if I can fluff her pillows when my mother grasps my face with both hands, holding me in place. "Dev, you can't fix this."

Her words, even though I've known them since her prognosis, hit me like a hammer to hollow wood, threatening to break the last of my composure. "Maybe we still can, Mom. There are new trials coming up every—"

"No," she says simply, her eyes filling. "Please, sweetheart, don't make me beg. Let me go peacefully. On my own terms." Her thumb skates across my cheek and I realize it's to sweep away a tear.

"For twenty years, before Deena was born, you were the only true light in my life," she says, her chin trembling. "Your father was busy building the company. We rarely saw him then."

She shakes her head. "I'm not complaining, because the man never, not once, let me feel like I was secondary to his work. It's a feat few can accomplish. He always called from wherever he was, had flowers or gifts delivered almost daily to let me know I was on his mind. But you?" She wipes another tear from my face. "You were my constant. You gave me daily purpose and so much joy. Remember when you were ten and wanted the two of us to learn French? We spent six months in Paris."

"Just the two of us," I rasp, recalling our daily trips to a patisserie we'd fallen in love with, our picnics near the Eiffel Tower where we read French books, and making friends with the locals.

She nods. "It was just the two of us for a while, wasn't it?"

My voice wobbles. "I cherished every moment, Mom. Moments I'll never forget, never be able to repay you for."

Her hands drop to mine and she brings them to her lips. "That's where you have it all wrong, sweetheart. The thing is, you never have to repay me. The only thing I've ever wanted was to see you smile, to see you become the man you are today.

You've made me so proud, Dev. Both you and your sister. I've had the most fulfilling life, not because I've had the means to do anything I wanted or travel the world with the snap of my fingers, but because I was blessed with the most loving children, the most devoted husband."

I can't help the sob that escapes me, the dam that's been broken. "How am I going to live without you, Mom? Don't you see how much I still need you?"

She shakes her head, a tear escaping the corner of her eye. "I've given you everything you need, sweetheart. Everything I could have. It's something I'm most proud of—to have given the world such a beautiful, unforgettable young man." She takes a breath. "You *are* going to live, my son. You're going to flourish. And with that sweet soul as your wife standing beside you, you'll find happiness, too."

My heart lurches against my ribs as I gulp in a breath. The guilt of lying to my mother mixes with my true feelings for the woman I'm completely gone for. Not knowing if she feels the same way about me. Not knowing if she'd ever take a chance beyond the terms of this arrangement to actually make me the happiest man alive. I'd give away everything I own to make her stay.

"She's beautiful, Dev, inside and out, just like you. I can't wait to see you two on the happiest day of your lives—one of the happiest days of my own—next week."

Fuck, my heart is going to collapse.

"All I ask is that you take the example of your father and me and never stop fighting for your love. Call her from wherever you are every day, if only to tell her you love her. Those are the only words that matter. Those are the only words you'll ever find true happiness in."

My brows knit, my jaw tightening as I try to hold back another sob, but I nod. That's all I can manage.

Mom tires out a few minutes later, her eyes closing, so I

decide to let her rest. I'm just about to reach the door to her room when she speaks again.

"There's one more person who needs your love, Dev. He's a stubborn man with sky-high expectations of his children, especially you. No doubt he struggles to show you both how much he loves you, but he's not a bad man. He deserves your love."

She heaves in a breath that has my hands fisting at my side. There are no words to describe the agony of watching her slowly slip away.

"Tell him how you feel. Fight it out if you have to. But then, figure out a path forward. You both deserve it."

Part of me wants to argue that he could do the same. That he could put aside his pride and actually try to connect with his children for once. But she isn't the one I need to convince.

The man I need to confront has given me plenty of reasons throughout my life. Until now, I've tried to maintain a level of respect and subordination with him, given he's my dad and the man who's provided me with a lifestyle most can't even dream of.

But enough is enough.

If fighting it out is what I need to do to find a path forward, like Mom says, then I think it's about time I do it.

I turn my head over my shoulder to glance at the feeble figure of my mother on her deathbed. "I'll see you tomorrow, Mom."

"Let me guess," my dad says, shuffling papers on his desk and brushing past pleasantries, as I enter his home office. "You have no contingencies and no backup plans for the shitshow heard on that call today, and you're here to ask for my help."

My nostrils flare, recalling his presence on the call this morning with one of our Chinese manufacturers, stating there will be a longer-than-expected delay for a critical component for our newest fleet of cars.

Dad wasn't invited to the call, but he dialed in anyway—no doubt given information for the call by one of his loyalists on my team. It took him less than three minutes to hijack my meeting and undermine my authority in front of my team.

"We have contingencies," I respond calmly, though I'm seething inside. "But that's not why I'm here."

"How the hell did this happen?" he asks, clearly not hearing the last part of my statement. "How could there have been such an oversight? Are you so preoccupied with your new bride that you can no longer focus on work? And before you tell me that she runs a business herself, she has no idea what it takes to run one like this. Someone with as little education and the kind of background as hers—"

"Enough!"

My dad's mouth snaps shut, eyes widening at my sudden outburst. My hands fist at my sides and molten heat courses through my veins. Every protective instinct flares to life for a woman who started off as a stranger but followed me down this crazy path, putting her life on hold for me and my mother—a woman she didn't even know at the time. Why? Because of her fucking earth-sized heart.

"Before we go down a path we can never come back from, Dad, I'd like to make something clear once again. My relationship with Piper is off-limits. I will not tolerate you dragging her into any of our conversations, unless it's with the utmost respect. That woman has shown me more compassion and affection than you have in years. So, you either speak of her with respect or you don't speak of her at all." I pause, letting my words sink in. "As for your insinuation about my focus, it's both insulting and unprofessional. The manufacturing delay is affecting companies globally, not just us. Like I said, we have contingencies."

"What do you mean 'a path we can never come back from'?" he repeats my words, seeming not to have heard anything else past those.

Well, if truth bombs are what he's goading me for, then those are what he'll get. After all, I'd already decided I wasn't going to walk away from this fight.

"I mean a relationship we may not ever have, let alone mend," I say, keeping my voice steady. "The fact of the matter is, Dad, you don't trust me. You've never believed I was good enough to fill your shoes. Despite the number of times I've proven myself, you refuse to relinquish control. And this isn't just in regards to *Menon Inc.*, it applies to everything in my life, including my decision to marry Piper."

He starts to speak but I barrel forward. "For years, all I've received from you are your impossible standards and ever-changing expectations. Not love, not encouragement, not even your support. And I don't mean financially; I mean emotionally, mentally."

I clench my fists at my sides. "When you took time off to take care of Mom, I stepped in as CEO. And whether you want to admit it or not, I'm a damn good one. Except, you seem to think I still need hand-holding. You jump on calls you're not invited to, overrule my decisions, and talk on my behalf, undermining my leadership in front of my team. And now you're disrespecting my personal life and the woman I love, too?"

My jaw locks. "Let me ask you something, Dad. If anyone ever dared speak about Mom the way you just spoke about Piper, would you have stood there and listened?"

He's at least contrite enough to drop his gaze to his hands.

"You don't know Piper, and I suspect that unless you put aside your own goddamn ego and preconceived judgments, you never will. Which is really just another loss on your part because even one fucking moment with that woman would put a permanent smile on your face."

I take a shaky breath, going back to the other matter at hand. "If the company is what you want back, then take it. I'm happy to step aside, and I'm qualified enough to find something else. But know this, I won't just be moving on from *your* company, I'll be moving on for good. Without you or your expectations holding me back."

With that, I deliver the final blow before walking out of the room. "There's a woman lying on her deathbed, who has sacrificed everything to ensure there was love in this family. And while neither Deena nor I have seen much of that from you, it's time you decide what you're willing to sacrifice, too."

thirty-three
# piper

No Walls, No Rules

I've barely stepped past the threshold before his strong arms pull me forward. The door shuts behind me, and I'm pinned against the back of his bedroom door before Dev drops to his knees in front of me.

The expression on his face is haunted, forlorn and desperate, unlike I've ever seen, and the muscles of his bare shoulders and back seem coiled and tense. My brows pinch and I reach out to sweep some of the hair off his forehead, but it's as if he's somewhere else. Not entirely here.

His eyes are distant, his mouth set in a rigid line, as his hands move up my thighs and under my leather skirt. He wiggles it up my hips before he reaches for the waistband of my thong. He pulls them down, and I step out of them, only for him to bury his nose inside my seam, inhaling me lasciviously.

He pulls away, looking up at me. His burdened eyes plead with me as if he thinks I'll deny him if he doesn't beg. "I need you. Please let me taste you."

I swallow. A part of me wants him to talk to me, to tell me why he looks so burdened, while the other knows it's not the time. That right now, with whatever he's going through, this is the only way I can help him. That he needs this even more than I do. And there is no denying how much I need it, how much I want him.

I nod and it's all the invitation he needs. In what feels like a single movement, Dev lifts my leg over his shoulder, spreads my lips apart with his fingers, and buries his face inside my center.

Dear God, Almighty.

Heat unfurls inside my stomach and my hand gets lodged on the back of his head as my back arches off the door. My head falls back with a *thud* when his tongue presses against my clit. Tasting, rolling, coaxing.

With a thumb working my clit and his scruff providing the perfect friction against my thighs, he takes long, leisurely strokes, as if he doesn't want to leave a single inch of me untasted. That same thumb continues to rub circles around my sensitive bud before he stretches it out, exposing my clit, and flicks it with his tongue. Again and again.

My jaw locks and my chest heaves as I try to breathe through my nose.

Because this . . . ? This will be the way I want to die.

Under the ferocity of his tongue.

The bidding and command of his mouth.

"Oh, my God," I say through clenched teeth as the heavenly laps of his tongue wage war over my most sensitive part.

He licks me again, covering my bud with his mouth, before alternating sucking it and flicking it with the tip of his tongue, eating me out like he's getting ready to take part in the Olympics.

Meanwhile my body is preparing for a triathlon.

My short breaths, the sounds of his lips against my lower ones, and his satisfied moans have my fingers tightening in his hair. My eyes squeeze tight as I grind myself shamelessly against his mouth.

"Mmm. Yes, baby, I could do this all damn day," he mutters. "Keep fucking my tongue."

My body takes over, my mind going to the wayside as I undulate over his greedy mouth. My nipples harden and my toes curl as goosebumps erupt all over my body.

I'm on the edge, so ready to fall, when Dev places a hand on my belly. He flattens his tongue over my clit before he works two fingers inside me, working me just the way I need.

He pulses them in and out and I'm ready to free-fall, with no care in the world as to how long or how far I'll be falling. Just ready to let go.

My skin catches on fire, tension coils inside my belly, and my heart pounds out of control as Dev curls his fingers forward.

And just like that, I'm done.

Splintering from the inside out, my orgasm slams into me with the power of a storm. Every muscle contracts while I scream out my release, shoving his face into me while wordlessly begging him to keep going.

And God, does he ever.

It's astonishing how the man can look even more beautiful on his knees, with my wet and bare center inside his mouth, my leg sprawled over his back, and my toes curled.

We're a goddamn picture. An artist's muse.

Dev continues to move his tongue inside me, over me, as his warm brown gaze finds mine. It's deadly sharp now, less distant than when he started, cataloging my every move until I'm collapsing from the fury his tongue lashed inside me. He doesn't let me fall though, holding me steady as he eases his lashes and licks.

I suck in a labored breath, as if I did any of the work, and Dev presses a smiling kiss against my thigh. So proud of himself, as usual.

He lifts, keeping his hands on my hips, before standing in front of me. "Fucking delicious, every single drop of you."

He dips to take my lips in his, letting me taste myself, and I throw my arms around his neck, deepening our kiss.

"Sweet and wild," he whispers against my lips.

*Sweet and wild.*

It's the same words he whispers into my ear every night as I fall asleep in his arms. Words that send butterflies soaring inside my belly and lightning bugs floating behind my eyelids. Words I've become addicted to, much like I've become addicted to him.

I wobble a little against him before my hand drops to his erection, raging against his pants. I look up at him pleadingly, much the same way he did earlier with me. "I want you in my mouth."

He shakes his head. "I didn't do it to get something in return. I just needed to taste you."

I undo the button on his jeans, rolling down his zipper. "And now *I* need to taste *you*."

I sink down to my knees, but he quickly hauls me over his shoulder, patting my bare ass, before taking me to his bed.

"Wh-what are you doing?" I say, trying not to whine.

"You want to suck my cock? Do it from my bed. I don't want your knees on the hard floor."

A jolt of something warm and fuzzy runs through me, pricking my chest the same way it pricks the corners of my eyes. Holy shit. There is no way this man just made giving him a blow job swoony.

He gently puts me on his bed, and I take no time freeing him from his boxer-briefs. The same feeling hits me every time I see his cock—a mix of worry and excitement. It's long and girthy, with the most perfect and smooth mushroom tip.

There's a bead of pre-cum leaking from him that makes me salivate. I squeeze my thighs, feeling myself get wet again, and grip the base of his cock tight, the way I've learned he likes it.

"Fuck," Dev groans.

And just when his hand curls behind my neck and his fingers tangle into my hair, I lean over and lick the backside, along the thick vein that travels all the way to the head.

Dev moans, his head falling back as his hand tightens in my hair. "Fuck, baby . . . yes."

I do it again, running my tongue along his length before flicking my tongue on his tip. He twitches in my hand while thunderous groans rumble in his chest. His abs tense and my pussy clenches at the sight of that soft trail of hair that descends from beneath his belly button.

If it hasn't been said before, in various magazines and online columns, Dev Menon is the most beautiful man on earth. And he's even more beautiful when he's wrapped in ecstasy and halfway to coming in my mouth.

I swirl my tongue around his head a few more times before I widen my mouth and take him all the way to the back of my throat.

"Oh, God, baby," he moans, emitting a heavy breath. "Your mouth. Jesus, your mouth is . . ." I pull him out almost all the way and take him all the way to the back of my throat again. "Get on your elbows and lift your ass in the air for me."

I do as he asks, feeling the cool air in the room against my most sensitive skin only for a few seconds before feeling his fingers at my entrance again.

Dev leans over me, sliding his fingers through my wet seam as I continue to bob over his length, gagging when I take him deeper into my throat.

"That's it, baby. Suck my cock," he says, pinching my clit and making me jolt and moan around him.

I suck harder, rolling my tongue around him and keeping

my mouth wet and loose, listening to the sounds of his pleasure and feeling like a fucking queen when he praises me.

"You look so pretty with this cock in your mouth," he says, his hand guiding me up and down his erection. "The prettiest mouth I've ever felt."

That last comment unfurls a little bout of jealousy inside my stomach, but I continue to work over him, licking and sucking him off. I know he's been with others, just like I have, but did they get these words of praise? Did they do it better?

Dev's legs shake in front of me and I know he's close. I pull off him again half-way while I stroke his base with my hand, using my spit to apply the perfect amount of friction. I can feel his cock expand slightly inside me, and I'm ready for him to come when he pulls me off him completely.

I stare at him, stunned, my jaw aching from having him inside me. "Wh–"

He nods to the bed, and I see that same guarded and sullen look in his eyes. What's going on with him?

"Dev—"

"I need you, Piper. All the way. No walls, no rules."

I swallow, blinking up at him. He means my walls. My rules.

We've never had missionary sex before. Hell, I've never had it ever. Not even when I was with Andrés. It always felt too intimate for me, too raw, too exposed.

But isn't that how this man has always made me feel? Too raw, too exposed? He's never seen what I've given the rest of the world to see. He's always seen more. Always demanded more—more of me, more for himself.

And whether it's the knowledge that I've never been able to hold on to my pathetic rules with him or the vulnerability and desperation in his gaze, I nod again.

I do more than that, giving him my full confirmation by

pulling off my shirt, unclasping my bra, and throwing them both over the edge of the bed. Then I wiggle out of my skirt, throwing it over as well, before leaning back on my elbows to look at him.

And just to really hit home with my answer, I flatten my feet on the mattress and pull up my knees, opening them so he can see exactly what I'm offering.

Dev's nostrils flare as he drops his briefs, his heated gaze running rampant over me, lingering on my wet pussy. He can't tell, but I can feel my walls pulsing ever so slightly, begging for him to fill me.

More pre-cum leaks from his tip and he brushes his thumb over it before fisting and stroking himself.

We haven't been using condoms over the past weeks. At some point we'd made it clear that neither one of us wanted them, and since I've been on birth control forever, getting pregnant wasn't a concern.

Though, the thought of being knocked up with Dev Menon's baby? It's been buzzing around in my head more than I'll ever admit. Nor will I do a deep-dive into my psyche to figure out why.

The mattress sinks as Dev climbs on and I lay back. He settles in between my knees, using his forearms on either side of my head to hover over me.

Molten-brown eyes, darker and deeper than his usual chestnut color, swirl with desire. His heated body brushes against mine, sending jolts of electricity over my skin.

His large hand encompasses the back of my knee before he lifts it over his shoulder, giving himself the angle he wants, the tip of his cock nudging my entrance. His brow ascends, giving me one more chance to say no, and when I nod, he guides his length inside me.

Slowly.

Inch by beautiful inch.

And when he bottoms out, our intermingled groans and escaped breaths fill the room.

My hands find his back and my eyes collide with his, his gaze reverent as if he's seeing me for the first time. As if he's never seen anything as precious.

"Piper," he murmurs, looking down at our connection in awe. "Goddamn, baby, has it ever . . .?"

I follow his gaze, watching him slide in and out of me in a way I've never allowed a man to do, and shake my head. I know what he's asking, but I'm unable to speak. My voice feels lodged inside my throat like gravel.

No, it's never felt like this. Not with anyone.

And it never will.

Holding my hip with one hand, he pulls out and fills me to the hilt, so that he ends where I begin, begins where I end. He places kisses on my collarbone, then his favorite moles on my neck, before finding my lips.

We kiss, deep and lost in the pleasure, and his fingers find my clit as he continues to drive into me. But it's not frenzied or fast; it's perfect. Everything I could have imagined and so much more.

Taking his mouth off mine, he sucks on my nipple, making me arch off the bed. My nails dig into his back as our skin slides against each other.

We find a rhythm as Dev snaps his hips, filling me again and again. My fingertips lower, pressing into his ass as I guide him inside me, while we watch each other.

Our mouths are slack. Not a word is exchanged yet so much is spoken.

It's terrifying and freeing all at once. Like bungee jumping into a void.

But there's nowhere I'd rather be.

And when he slips his arm under me, bringing me closer, I wrap myself tighter around him. We move in tandem, slow and fast, erratic and steady. Like we've done this a million times.

But it's when we're both coming together, groaning and melting into each other, that he truly terrifies me even as he makes me see stars.

His lips move against mine, but there's no mistaking the words. At least, the ones I understand.

"I love you, my beautiful Piper. *Tujhse jeetna toh hamesha namumkin tha, meri jaan. Par tujhse harna, jannat pane ke barabar.*"[1]

---

1. Winning against you was always going to be impossible, sweetheart. But losing to you is equal to finding heaven.

# thirty-four
## piper

Am I Dying?

His words chime in the air surrounding us as moments pass with him still inside me.

My eyes draw up to the enormous chandelier in his room, its tiers of sparkling crystals cascading like winter icicles, fragile but glimmering. *Hanging by a thread*. My fingers run mindlessly over his slick back as we both gather our breaths.

God, that was . . .

Every breath and touch.

Every pulse and thrust.

He wasn't just inside me; he was coursing through my blood.

Dev shifts, trailing kisses along my neck before he removes himself from me. An emptiness takes a hold of me as I watch him walk to the bathroom. It makes my chest feel like a hollow and barren cavity.

He comes back with his briefs on, carrying a washcloth. Getting back on the mattress, he takes his time, gently wiping me down before throwing the towel into a nearby hamper.

He loves me?

Love.

Like the kind I've guarded my heart against all this time.

Like the kind that leaves you bleeding out and raw in the bowels of your own misery.

A part of me that wants to believe it, to believe him. A part of me wants to dive headfirst and leave my worries behind, letting myself get lost in the tenderness of his touch.

But the other part? That voice I'm so used to speaks up again, asking me what would happen if I said those words back, only for him to realize years later that I was never worth it.

Are you enough, Piper? Are you enough to keep a man like him?

Don't be a fool! Look at what that kind of love did to Mom. Look at what it did to Nisha and Sarina. How can you not see that you'll end up the same way?

Dev's arms gather me up as he lays down behind me, my back to his chest. His hand splays over my belly and his lips brush kisses on the shell of my ear, the nape of my neck. "You're so fucking beautiful."

I place my hand over his, hoping to wave off my growing anxiety.

"What happened today?" I ask, trying to steer my mind in another direction. "I mean, it felt like you were somewhere else at the beginning. Like you were upset, or I don't know . . . lost?"

He's quiet for so long, I wonder if he's just not going to answer. But then his fingers play with his mother's ring on my finger.

"I was lost," he murmurs. "I've been lost for a long time. But today was . . . just a lot."

I give him a confused look and watch his throat bob.

"I went to see my mom. I wanted to convince her to try a new clinical trial."

"Oh."

He shakes his head. "She's intent on giving up."

I turn around in his arms, my hands cupping his face instinctively, while our bodies stay aligned. "She's not giving up, Dev; she's letting go. She wants to live out the rest of her life with a smile on her face and seeing a smile on the faces of the ones she loves. There's a difference."

He shuts his eyes, and I know he's hoping to keep his tears at bay. "I can't sit back and just watch her go. I can't do it."

My thumbs skate over his stubble. "It's her wish. And isn't that what you've always wanted? To fulfill her wishes?"

His eyes open to lock with mine. He's quiet for a beat, perhaps accepting what I've said or filing it away to think about later.

"She also wanted me to make amends with my dad," he says, taking a long breath. "We've had a . . . complicated relationship for some time."

I huff, giving him a mirthless smile. "Believe me, I know all about complicated relationships with dads. Did you try talking to him?"

He lifts a shoulder. "I got a few things off my chest. Our relationship can't be one-sided. He has to decide he wants it, too."

"Does he have a strained relationship with Deena too, or just you?"

"Mostly me, but I wouldn't say he and Deena have an exceptional bond. He's always been hard to please." His fingers run down my back and he parts his legs so I can place mine in between them. We've woken up quite a few mornings tangled in the same way.

"What about your dad? Was he as much an asshole to Rowan as he was to you?"

I shake my head. "He was always hard on Rowan, but there was a level of respect there for him—"

"Because of hockey," he adds knowingly.

I nod. "I didn't have any such talents, nothing he could tote around like a badge of honor."

"And yet, here you are. The most talented and incredible woman I know."

I shrug, and we lay there looking at each other until I can no longer hold back what's trying to break free.

"Dev?"

"Mmm?"

"What you said earlier . . ." I clear my throat, my heart picking up its pace. "About loving me—"

"I meant it."

A heavy weight sits on my chest and I take in a short breath, pushing against it. "I'm just . . ." I pause to take a breath and try again, but the air feels thin. "I'm really—"

Dev lifts my chin with his finger so that our eyes connect. "Piper, I didn't know it at the time, but the day I walked into your salon changed my entire life. I'd gone in for a haircut but left having found the woman of my dreams." He pauses. "There isn't a person in this world I love the way I love you. This arrangement? The whole charade? It stopped being one a long time ago for me. I'm crazy about you, Peter."

I shudder on an inhale. "And our wedding this week?"

"I want it to be real, if you want it to be real. I want to spend the rest of my life with you."

My glassy eyes bounce between his as I try to find my voice. A voice that seems to be failing me in a life-changing moment like this.

He loves me?

He wants to spend the rest of his life with me?

Could he really mean it? Maybe it's because we've been living together, the close proximity between us. Or maybe it's because of how intimate we've been. Maybe it's confusing him.

Maybe it's confusing me?

Isn't this why I had all the rules?

"Did I scare you?" he asks softly, reading the turmoil on my face. "Baby, are you okay?"

I nod again, then shake my head.

It's as if something suddenly snaps inside me and every emotion comes barreling to the surface. A wail erupts from my throat, and I bury my head in his warm chest. A sob follows before Dev gently cups the back of my head. My tears stream down my face in a heavy downpour.

He loves me.

He wants our marriage to be real.

Everything inside me yearns to believe it, to say those words back and rejoice in the feeling of being loved. Of feeling whole. But that tiny voice that's been my guiding force, keeping me safe—unattached, uncommitted, and unloved—screams louder than ever.

"Hey," he murmurs reverently. "Shh, baby. Talk to me. Tell me what scares you."

God, why does he have to be so understanding? So sweet?

And gah, so fucking perfect!?

I sniffle, catching my breath, before pulling away to look into his concerned eyes.

"Everything," I murmur brokenly. "You. This. Us. I'm not right for you, Dev. I'm fucked up in the head. I want to trust what you're saying, but . . ."

I can't even finish my thought.

"Hey, listen to me." His hands grasp my face, his thumbs wiping away my tears. "You're not fucked up. You're perfect. A little diabolical," he says, trying to lighten the mood, "but so perfect. And as for trusting me? Sweetheart, trust this: I'm one hundred percent in. One hundred percent yours. There's no one else I want to spend my life with, Piper. No one I want to breed rabbits, do crosswords, or pet hairless cats with."

My stomach twists and my thoughts collide, taking me in

a million directions. My chest constricts, each breath more labored than the last, like my lungs are turning to cement.

"Piper?"

Dev's voice feels distant, muffled, like he's underwater. Or maybe I am? I sit up, gasping for air and clutching my chest. God, am I having a heart attack? Am I dying? This feels like I'm dying.

A cold sweat breaks out over my skin while my hands tremble. I think I'm going to be sick.

"Piper!"

Time slows, and the pressure in my chest builds to an unbearable level. I vaguely register the mattress shifting below me and Dev rushing out of the room.

The room spins like I'm in a goddamn Tilt-A-Whirl and I slap my hand down to the mattress, trying to steady myself, but I can't catch my breath.

God, this is it, isn't it? This is how I'm going to die.

Just when I think I'm truly on the verge of passing out, warm hands cup my face and Dev places something in my palms.

"Breathe into this!"

His booming voice cuts through the buzzing inside my brain, and I haul the paper bag to my mouth. I cover it before taking in gulps of air. My eyes squeeze tight as Dev continues to soothe me with his words, telling me I'm okay. That I'm safe. That he's right here.

He rubs my back as I continue to breathe and eventually, the vice grip inside my chest begins to loosen. My breaths slow and I finally take a few long inhales through my nose.

"That's it, baby. You're doing great." He brushes a strand of hair off my damp forehead, tucking it behind my ear. "Just breathe."

I nod, leaning into his touch.

And though the anxiety has waned, my voice still feels strained. "I'm sorry."

Dev shakes his head, kneeling in front of the bed, pulling me toward him. "No, sweetheart. Don't apologize. Never apologize." He interlocks our fingers. "Have you had a panic attack before?"

I shake my head, my mind racing to make sense of what just happened.

What does it mean that his words caused such a physical and mental response inside my body?

Is this what it feels like to come to terms with the fact that you love someone, while your body physically rejects the idea? It's a terrifying realization—that I've grown to care for and love this man, mixed with the paralyzing fear of what that means.

It took him three simple words to shake me to my core, to make cracks in the walls I'd carefully constructed around myself. I've spent so much of my adult life believing love is dangerous and that commitments lead to heartache. And now his three words are making me question it all.

But even if we love each other, even if I say those words back, can I truly believe that it'll last? What if it doesn't? Am I strong enough to face that outcome? Even the thought of opening myself up and letting someone settle into my heart, only to have it all wither away one day, is paralyzing.

If his confession had such an effect on me, what would happen if he decided he no longer loves me one day? This panic attack would be a mere twinge in comparison to the onslaught of pain that could be at the end.

"Do you want to talk about it?"

His voice pulls me out of my daze, but one look at his worried expression and I feel my heart in my throat again. "I think . . . I think I need some time, Dev. Some space."

His eyes bounce between mine, his hand loosening around mine. "Space?"

I swallow, hoping to keep a new rush of tears at bay. "I need to wrap my head around everything. My feelings, your feelings . . . they're all just a lot to process at once."

His shoulders fall and I fucking hate the way his expression does, too. Because I did that to him. I took away his smile; I put a blemish on the hope that was blooming inside him.

A pang of guilt twists my insides, but I can't take back my words. I need the space and time to figure out if I'm strong enough to face a real future with him.

Dev nods. "Whatever you need."

"It might be good for me to stay at my place this week," I say, my chest burning at the thought of being away from him, but knowing I won't be able to make sense of my feelings when I'm mere feet from him—his lips, his arms, his presence—inside this house.

He nods again, but there's no mistaking his frown. "Okay. I'll talk to Ralph about making some changes so there's more security around your condo."

I get off the mattress, in no mood to wiggle back into my own clothes. Instead, I pick up one of his button-downs from a chair and wrap it around me. I'm immediately enveloped in his scent, knowing I'll be wearing it to bed every night, like my armor and comfort all at once.

Dev helps me pick up my clothes off the floor, handing them to me. His fingers brush against mine and just that small touch sends a current through my body.

I head toward his door and am just about to step out when he stops me.

"Can I ask you something?"

His voice is soft and hesitant, making my heart clench. I turn over my shoulder, hoping to steel myself for his question, but knowing he has the power to crumble my fragile willpower. Still, I nod.

"Do you . . ." He clears his throat, standing up a little straighter. "Do you feel anything for me? Anything real?"

My chin wobbles as a pang slashes through my chest. The raw vulnerability in his eyes, the hesitant hope in his voice, it feels unbearable.

Do I feel anything real for him?

I take a shaky breath as fresh tears pool inside my lids. "The way I feel about you, Lex, is the entire reason I need to walk away right now."

# thirty-five
# **dev**

## Five Schlongs Hen Party

DEAN MEYER

[Image of new tattoo]

Mala, baby, you know how you say you never get enough time to read? Now you can multitask. Read this while you gag on my cock.

DARIAN MEYER

Dude. What the actual fuck?

DEAN MEYER

OH SHIT! That was meant for Mala. Jesus.

GARRETT MEYER

Is this for real? You got "Property of Mala Meyer" tattooed on your dick?!

DEAN MEYER

It's not on my dick, asshole. It's the area above it. My pubic region.

GARRETT MEYER

We can still see most of your dick in this, jackass!

**DEAN MEYER**

Aww bro, are you upset because my dick is bigger, even though we're twins?

**DARIAN MEYER**

Honestly, I'm scared to open these group chats anymore. This is fucking disturbing, Dean.

**HUDSON CASE**

I can't believe they make magnifying glasses that powerful. Or was this picture taken under a microscope? And now I'm wondering, what did Mala marry you for? Clearly, not for your dick or your brain.

**DEAN MEYER**

<middle finger emoji> You guys are all jackasses. Not Dev, though. He's the only one I plan to stay friends with.

**GARRETT MEYER**

Speaking of our resident billionaire groom, anyone know if he's still alive? The wedding is in four days, homies! Are we having a bachelor party or what?

**DEV MENON**

No bachelor party. No wedding. No groom because no bride.

**DEAN MEYER**

What? Dude, are you okay? Why are you talking like a machine? That's Hudson's job.

**HUDSON CASE**

Fuck, what happened? What do you mean, no wedding? Did you tattoo your dick too and now she really can't see the little that was there?

# Pretend For Me

**DEAN MEYER**

For the last time, I didn't tattoo my dick.

**DEV MENON**

I mean no wedding. She left.

**DEAN MEYER**

After you bought yourself that furry G-string and those rabbit ears to wear for your next role-play and everything?! Some women have no appreciation for men like us. Her loss, man. Her loss.

**HUDSON CASE**

Dean, seriously? Haven't we had enough nauseating visuals for one day? Dev, what led to this?

**DEV MENON**

Told her I loved her, and she made like a sock in the dryer. Poof! I made a mistake. Biggy big steak.

**DARIAN MEYER**

The hell? Guys, he doesn't sound right to me. Dev, are you drunk?

**DEAN MEYER**

I'm still stuck on the sock reference. Did she get pissed about her whites turning pink?

**GARRETT MEYER**

@Dev Menon, where are you?

**DEV MENON**

On Mars.

**DEAN MEYER**

Jesus, bro. Please tell us you're not drowning in a tub full of hundred-dollar bills. It's not a bad way to go, but a little cliché, don't you think? Unless you're also petting a hairless pussy. A wet, hairless pussy. Now that I'd get behind.

Get it? Get behind a wet hairless pussy?

[**Darian Meyer** has left the chat]
[**Dean Meyer** has added **Darian Meyer** to the chat]

**DEAN MEYER**

Darian, bro, this is no time for you to prude out. We're in a crisis here!

**HUDSON CASE**

I just messaged Piper. She hasn't responded.

**DEV MENON**

Stop messaging my wife, asshole.

**HUDSON CASE**

We've been over this, jackass. She's my friend and I'm the reason you even know her. Is it because she calls me Big Daddy? Dude, I'm sure this will all get sorted and she'll give you an appropriate nickname, too. Like Minute-Man Menon or Miniscule Menon.

**DEAN MEYER**

Is this a bad time to point out she isn't your wife, Dev?

# Pretend For Me

[GIF of Homer Simpson slowly inching backward into a bush]

DARIAN MEYER

Should one of us go to his house?

HUDSON CASE

Already on my way. Just flew into San Francisco. Be there in twenty.

DEV MENON

No. I'm not home.

HUDSON CASE

Yes, you are. I messaged your housekeeper and your chauffeur. They said you're home and you smell like rotting flesh and the porta-potty at a spicy buffalo wings contest. Their words, not mine.

DEV MENON

What the fuck? You message my staff, too?

HUDSON CASE

I like to keep tabs on my friends. Don't make this about me, Dev.

DEAN MEYER

That's not creepy or anything. I don't have staff, but I'm keeping an eye on my wax lady from now on.

HUDSON CASE

I'm ten minutes away. Dev, put some pants on. Or don't. What with your dick being so small and tattooed like Dean's, I'm sure I won't see anything.

DEAN MEYER

For the love of . . .

[**Dean Meyer** has left the chat]

## thirty-six
# dev

You Look And Smell Like A Skunk's Asshole

**[Menon-Parker Wedding]**

> **BRANDY**
>
> Hey guys! Great news! U2 is confirmed to play at your wedding! <Party Popper emoji>. Dev, Bono was touched by your call last week and happy to know that U2 is your mom's favorite band. They're looking forward to celebrating with you guys and to meeting Claire as well.

I bring my phone closer to read the text from our wedding planner before tossing it back on the nightstand. Brandy won't be getting much of a response; she hasn't with the past three messages she's sent.

My bloodshot eyes land on an unfinished crossword puzzle—one I planned to finish with Piper three nights ago, before she left and took my fucking soul with her.

Except now it's unclear if the damn puzzle will ever be solved.

Or if I'll ever get my soul back.

There's no misery worse than this. This constant reaching

for my phone every time it buzzes, hoping it's her. This sifting through her socials, hoping to get a recent glimpse of her. This endless wondering if she's thinking about me or if she'll even show up to our wedding four days from now.

I need to be admitted to a mental institution or become a case study for how your phone can become your emotional support device. Maybe they can also do a study of how confessing your feelings to the woman you love can be both the best and worst decision of your life.

My confession echoes in my mind, along with her silence. I should have read the signs then. I'd scared the lights out of her. She'd stayed for the few minutes afterward—even laid in my arms and asked me about my shitty day—but then her body had caught up to her mind and she had a fucking panic attack.

All from what I'd said to her.

And even as I watched her demons surface and her breaths shorten, making it one of the scariest moments I've experienced, I still couldn't get myself to take my words back.

I love her, and that is a truth I'll never *not* feel.

I promised myself the day she left that I'd respect her request for time and space. That I wouldn't drive by her salon or check in with her friends to see if she was okay.

But with every day that passes where I've gotten nothing but silence from her, that promise hangs precariously on a frayed line.

When she told me she needed time away, the gravity of her words didn't quite register. I'd understood that she needed space to be able to think with a clear head. What I didn't realize, until I saw her bag and her caged rabbits at the front door, was that she meant real space. Actual time apart.

The vision felt familiar, much like the way Camila had left, but the searing pain was different. A thousand times worse. The type of pain I don't see myself ever getting over—at least, not without the help of a lobotomy—unless she comes back.

## Pretend For Me

I run a hand through my hair, getting a whiff of myself and cringing at the smell of booze and perspiration. Yeah, so personal hygiene has taken a backseat to wallowing in misery over the past few days. I might have also had most of that fifty-year-old bottle of Glenfiddich. Add that to the list of my fucking problems.

Thankfully, I'd taken this and next week off work for the wedding, so my dad isn't also up my ass about missing meetings. Though, after the less-than-amenable conversation we had last time, I'm not sure he's going to be saying anything for a little while.

My doorbell rings, followed by a sharp knock, and I bring up an app on my phone to view who's at the front door.

*Hudson Fucking Case.*

A part of me thought he was joking when he said he was on his way to my house, but I should have known better. The man is as irritatingly loyal as he is grumpy. And though he lives in Portland now with his wife Kavi, he's always made time to meet up when he's in town, either for business or to check on his ranch. I take it this visit coincides with the wedding he thinks he's going to—mine.

Well, I have news for him . . .

Wait, actually, do I have news for him? I might have given him that news already in our group chat, hence the reason he's shown up.

I chuckle at my internal use of hence, knowing my sister would roll her eyes, calling me an artifact or someone from mid-century Europe.

Okay, so maybe I'm not at my Sunday best today. Specifically, I might still be slightly inebriated after a night of consuming more than I usually do. It could also explain why my head feels like it's going to explode.

Hudson rings the bell again, and I sigh with a mix of annoyance and begrudging gratitude. The man is nothing if not persistent and one of the only people, besides the Meyer brothers, who could give two shits about my wealth or name. Sure, he is plenty wealthy himself, but he'd be just as likely to show up here, ready to be annoying, if I lived in a cardboard box.

I click on a button on my phone to chat through the speaker at the front door. "Go away, Case. I'm sure there are some rowdy teens having a party you need to report or an episode of Matlock you're missing."

"Open the door, jackass. I'm only ringing the bell as a courtesy. I have a keycard to get in."

Jesus. What the hell? How does he have access to my damn house?

I blow out a resigned raspberry and unlock the door from my phone for him to come in. Not ten seconds later, he's in my room, bulky arms folded and looking at me lying on my bed like I'm the most pathetic excuse for a human.

"Jesus. You look and smell like a skunk's asshole."

I groan, shoving my head into my pillow. "Get out before I call security to take your overgrown sasquatch ass out of here."

He rolls his eyes. "Get the fuck up. I have a couple slices of pizza for you out there and my helicopter waiting. You're going to take a fucking shower, eat something, and then we're heading to my ranch."

"I hate pizza. And who the fuck eats that shit at nine AM?"

"Who hates pizza?" he asks, screwing up his face. "And who the fuck polishes off a fifty-year-old bottle of whiskey at nine AM?"

I'm sure I protest, tell him to fuck off a couple more times, and insist that I'd mostly polished off the bottle last night. Okay, so I might have used the last bit as mouthwash ten minutes ago. But the bastard digs his feet in like a bad case of syphilis.

Which is why, an hour later, I'm knee-deep in horseshit. No, not figuratively. *Literally.* Because nothing says friendship like forcing your buddy to clean out horse stalls while he's nursing a hangover that could rival a heavy metal concert.

"Fuck," I groan, taking a spot on a patch of wildflowers with my bottle of water. The fucker wouldn't give me a beer like I asked him to after making me work like a dog for the past three hours.

Since the minute we landed at his ranch, he's put me to work. From scooping out the stables—I don't think I've ever seen that much horse shit!—to patching up a few fences, I've done enough manual labor to last me a decade. I have cuts on my hands, my back is stiff, and I'm sweating out last night's whiskey through every pore.

The sounds of Hudson's boots have me turning over my shoulder to see him approaching. He throws back his head to take a long swig of his beer before he settles down next to me.

We're silent for a few moments, watching his horses graze, before I feel Hudson's eyes on me. He isn't the type to make friendship bracelets and polish your nails, but he cares . . . in his own irritable, grumpy asshole way.

"Alright, spit it out. What's going on with you and Piper? I'm in no mood to drag it out of you like I had to drag your ass here."

I sigh, thumbing the label around my bottle. "It's not much more complicated than what I told you guys in the chat. Somewhere in the middle of pretending, I fell for her. And when I told her how I felt, she freaked out. Said she needed space to figure out her feelings."

"I'm assuming you also told her you wanted to make the marriage real?"

I nod. "I do. I want her to be my wife, and not just temporarily. I love her."

"And you haven't tried to contact her since she left?"

I shrug. "I sent her a text a couple of days ago, telling her I love her and that I'd be here for as long as she needs, but no, I'm giving her the space she asked for."

Hudson nods, peering off into the distance, seeming to mull over my words.

"I met Piper a few years ago when she and her best friends had just started the salon," he says after a few moments. "She cut my hair, and since I'm a sucker for routine, I never went to anyone else. Not saying I didn't think about it though, because fuck, the woman can talk. After every haircut, I felt like I'd just gone through a stage-rendition of her entire life story, complete with a couple of musical numbers and a cast of forgettable men named after sausages."

I snort out a laugh even as something pierces my chest. What if she doesn't give me another chance to hear her endless babbling?

"But I'll tell you what," he says after taking another sip of his beer. "In the times we've texted," he side-eyes me, knowing I'll act like a possessive asshole at the mention of him talking to her, "she's never once forgotten your name."

I grunt, plucking a flower from the grass and throwing it. "Is that supposed to make me feel better?"

"No, I just mean you were different. You meant something to her from day one."

Hudson rolls his bottle around in his fingers. "But in the time that I've known her, I also found out she's had a complicated history with her dad. The way he treated her mom and both his kids, the way he walked out on them, and the marks he left on Piper's impressionable self-worth? It became the lens she used in the future to view love and marriage. Add to the fact that both her best friends have gone through messy divorces..."

He shakes his head. "Now, I'm not saying she doesn't have feelings for you or that she doesn't believe you love her. What I'm saying is, she doesn't believe she can hold on to that love. Hell, she probably doesn't even believe she deserves it! It's why she's always chosen these half-brained deli meats who've wanted nothing but a few nights in her bed. It's why she's always had her rules—"

"She told you about her rules?"

He rolls his eyes. "Anyone who's sat in her salon chair a few times knows about her rules. The girl's an open-book." He eyes me for a moment. "But I might be one of the only ones besides her closest friends to know that she broke those rules for you."

I take a wobbly breath, looking back out at the horses.

"And I thought that was interesting," he says cryptically.

I puff out a breath. "Okay, so what you're saying is she has feelings for me and knows I have feelings for her, but she doesn't know if they're enough for us to last?"

"Precisely."

I reel back, annoyed. "Well, this has been fucking enlightening. Thanks for the tarot card reading, asshole. I'd like my money back."

"Before you have a full-blown billionaire hissy fit," Hudson says, unruffled. "Let me ask you something. What's really eating at you?"

What kind of question is that? Has this guy not heard anything I've said?

Hudson must see the frustrated look on my face because he clarifies. "What I mean is, at the heart of it, is it the worry that she'll be a no-show at the wedding? Is it the promise you made your mom to fulfill her wish? Or is it something else?"

I ponder his questions for a long moment. "Look, it would suck to be left at the altar and to see my dying mom's heart break," I respond, chest tightening at the thought. "But . . . that's not really what I'm afraid of anymore. What's killing me is the thought of losing her. Of not spending the rest of my life with a woman I'm crazy about. I love her more than anyone in the world, and the idea of not being able to show her that every day. . . it's fucking crushing me."

Hudson nods. "Then, my friend, I think there's only one thing for you to do." He tips his bottle back, draining the last of his beer. "You wait."

My brows pinch. "That's your sage advice? To wait?"

"I'm not saying you twiddle your thumbs while you do it," he clarifies. "I'm saying, give her the space she needs, but show her that your love won't vanish like she expects. For as long as it takes."

"And what if she never comes around to it?"

"Then you know you did everything." He turns to me. "But given that you've been the only one to scale her high walls and break her rules, I have a feeling she knows she's fighting a losing battle. The question is, will she find the courage to surrender?"

## thirty-seven
## dev

Cue The Record Scratch

"Piper hasn't arrived yet, sweetheart. Don't you think you should call her and make sure everything is okay?"

Mom's anxious voice has my eyes flicking from the cufflinks I'm fumbling with to her. She's sitting in her wheelchair, wearing a soft pink lace dress that compliments her short and sparse silver hair. A tan-colored shawl is draped over her shoulders, hiding the frailty of her small frame.

I force a smile, even as my chest burns at the sight of hope and concern intermingling on my mother's face. "I'm sure she'll be here any minute now, Mom. Don't worry."

But the words sit heavy on my tongue because, the truth is, I don't know if she will.

It's been an entire week since I've heard from my wife-to-be. Radio silence has never been more deafening. And though I was practically crawling out of my skin, I've done my best to give her the space she needed.

But was the past week enough time for her to work through her fears? Was it enough time for her to decide she wants something real with me, too?

I suppose the next thirty minutes will be quite telling since I'll be at the end of the aisle, waiting for her there. Unfortunately, my guess is as good as anyone else's as to if she'll actually show.

Dad nods to one of the nurses on standby in the room before looking at Mom. "Sweetheart, why don't you go wait with the guests? I have a couple of things I'd like to speak to Dev about. I'll meet you out there in a few minutes."

Mom looks between the two of us before nodding, allowing the nurse to wheel her out of the room.

When the door shuts behind her, I watch as Dad closes the distance between us, taking the cufflink out of my hand and looping it through the hole at the end of my sleeve.

He keeps his head down, focused on his task, as he speaks. "I wanted to tell you . . ." He gazes up at me. "I thought about what you said to me the last time we spoke."

I stiffen, expecting a rebuke. Apart from Piper, I haven't spoken to my dad since that night, either.

"I have been rather one-dimensional—strict and calloused at times—when it came to you. And," he swallows thickly, stepping back once my cufflinks are looped, "I want to apologize for that."

I stare at him silently, because I don't think I've ever heard my father apologize to anyone but my mother.

He takes a deep breath. "I fell into a lot of responsibility early on in my life after my dad died. Responsibility for my younger siblings and my mother. I put a lot on myself to make sure no one felt the loss of our dad, at least not financially. And somehow, the continuous pursuit of success got ingrained in my personality. Somewhere between the pressure I placed on myself and the hard-fought success of the company, I lost sight of what was important."

Dad's eyes meet mine, filled with a vulnerability I haven't seen before. "I lost sight of you and Deena. I lost sight of your successes and achievements, and I became the stereotypical draconian dad from a Bollywood film."

I can't help but smile.

He places a hand on my shoulder. "I'm proud of you, son. Not only for the businessman you've become—handling our company better than I could have ever imagined, given all the pressure and responsibility on you—but also for speaking up for your beliefs, your love."

He squeezes my shoulder. "I'm sorry about the things I've said about Piper. She didn't deserve my hasty judgment, and neither did you. I can see how happy she makes you, how deeply you love her . . . similar to the way I love your mom."

Both our eyes glisten at those words, and I place a hand on his shoulder, knowing he needs it. I can imagine the pain of preparing to lose the one you've loved for over thirty-five years must be insurmountable.

His voice catches as he speaks again. "I promise to support both you and Piper from this day forward. And as far as *Menon Inc.* is concerned?" He gives me one of his intense looks. "Son, it's always been yours. I just needed to step out of your way, and I promise to do so."

"Thanks, Dad. I appreciate that," I say, my voice rough before he pulls me in for a hug, giving me a pat on the back.

He's almost at the door when I stop him. "Hey, Dad? You know that bit about you being a dad from a Bollywood movie? Can you just promise you won't break into song and dance in front of the guests?"

His lips twitch as the tension fades between us.

He feigns disappointment. "But I have five outfit changes ready for it. I even practiced my slow-motion running through Mom's roses."

At this, we both throw back our heads, laughing, and I feel years of pent-up resentment melting under a renewed relationship on the horizon. God knows, our tiny family that'll be left in Mom's wake will need each other.

A minute later, Brandy, the wedding planner, ushers Dad

out to join the guests before coming back to my room. Her heels click frantically on the hardwood floor while she clutches a walkie-talkie.

She looks like she's seconds from tears, her usually professional facade cracking under the weight of the situation. "I can't get a hold of Piper or her bridesmaids, Dev. I've tried their phones and the salon. As a last-ditch effort, I even spoke to her brother to see if he could get a hold of her. But no luck."

She bites her nails as her eyes dart around the room, searching for a solution. "Do you think you could call her again? We're literally twenty minutes away from—"

A sharp knock halts her words before the door opens and the face of the woman I've been dying to see—to talk to and hold—all fucking week appears on the other side.

The air stills and the world narrows as she steps into the room. Everything fades away—-the ornate decorations of this guest bedroom in my parents' mansion, the muffled sounds of the guests outside, and even Brandy's jittery presence. All I see is Piper and the storm of emotion in her eyes I can't quite read.

Brandy starts to speak when Piper clears her throat. "Could you give us a few minutes, Brandy?"

Our wedding planner mumbles an agreement before she rushes out of the room, holding her walkie-talkie like a lifeline. And with the *thud* of the door closing behind her, my heart lurches against my ribs.

What am I seeing here? Why does the air feel so . . . different? Why does she seem so different?

My eyes scan her briefly, looking for some sort of clue, as that same thudding heart starts to sink all the way down to my stomach when the realization hits.

She's not wearing her bridal gown.

Instead, she's here in a plain cream blouse and jeans,

dressed for a casual outing rather than the day she promised me.

The understanding of why she's here hits me like a ton of bricks. She's not here to get married; she's here to let me down gently and walk away.

It's a shock as to how I manage to stay standing.

Piper lifts her chin, reaching for my hand. Numbly, I allow her to intertwine our fingers. Her eyes glisten with emotion, determination, and something else—regret, perhaps?—and I brace myself for the words I know are coming.

Her voice cracks like the thunder inside my chest. "I can't do this, Dev."

And there it is.

My world tilts on its axis.

My heart shatters beyond repair.

Every hope, every fucking dream turning to dust with sounds of those four words. I can't do this.

I take in a shallow breath as tears gather behind my eyes, knowing I'm going to have to give the news to my mother. My sweet, kind, gentle soul of a mother who will die with a broken heart. Just like I will one day.

I struggle to stand here with my hand in Piper's, her soft touch a reminder of just one more thing I'm losing.

"I underst—"

"What I mean, Dev, is I can't do this—not the wedding, or the living together, or the sharing you with my cat, or the breeding of our rabbits that potentially leads to us breeding too, and making adorable Dev and Piper babies—if I don't get something off my chest."

Cue the record scratch.

Wait, huh?

I blink, wondering if she's said what I think she's said, or if I've somehow projected my hopes on her and dreamt it all.

"I . . . Wait . . . What?" I stammer, hoping this isn't some sort of brain malfunction. My heart, which was taking a nose-dive into the pits of my stomach, is now lodged inside my throat. "I don't . . . I don't think I heard you properly."

Her hands fall on my chest as she erases the distance between us. "I fucking love you, Dev Menon. Wholly. Truly. One hundred percent. I want to live out the rest of my life with you, have great sex with you, and be your sugar-momma, because it's clear you need one."

I stare dumbfounded at her, unable to form a response.

*She loves me?*

Piper cups my jaw, her golden-flecked green eyes gazing into mine. "I'm sorry I took off like that last week and that I gave you a heart attack today. Vajayjay was being a real bitch about getting into her carrier, but then I gave her one of your dirty socks and she seemed to get that we were coming to marry you." She waves a hand dismissively. "I have a few of your unmatched socks in our Socks Without Partners donation bin, but there was one that was dirty and—"

"Piper," I say, snapping her out of her rambling. The woman would literally keep going and we would miss our entire wedding.

"Anyway." She smiles. "What I was trying to say is, I'm sorry for the way I've been the past week. I just had to realize a few things."

As much as I want to lay my hands on her hips and pull her to me, I don't. Perhaps because I still don't believe she's here or that this is real.

"What did you have to realize?"

"That taking space and time away from you really meant nothing when all I thought about was you every waking moment. That loving you was no longer a rule I couldn't break or an option I could live without, because I couldn't see my world without you right next to me."

She swallows. "I didn't believe I deserved your love, Dev. Or any real love, for that matter. I've seen so many failed relationships that I'd convinced myself love was just a shallow word meant to be broken one day. But what I didn't focus on was the incredible and enduring love around me. The way your dad cherishes every moment with your mom, the way Shay became Rowan's entire world, the way my mother found new long-lasting love. I was so tangled in my web of fear, I wasn't ready to at the time."

She takes a shaky breath. "It took being away from you to realize those things and to recognize how deeply I'd fallen for you. I realized I had that rare, precious love all along, but instead of embracing it and pushing away my fears, I did the opposite."

Her eyes, brimming with tears, meet mine with raw vulnerability, her soul laid bare. "What I realized this week, without your touch, your words, and that dimple I'm so in love with, was that the risk of loving you pales in comparison to the misery of living without you. There's nothing I want more than to be your wife, to spend the rest of my life loving you. You're my home, my safe place, my world, Dev Menon. I don't know if I deserve your forgiveness, but I'll do anything to earn it."

My jaw clenches as I try to keep my emotions at bay.

She's here. And she's mine.

My hands work on their own accord to bring her closer to me. "Baby, there's no forgiveness to be given. You are the most precious thing in my life. Nothing is worth as much as one moment with you. You've taught me to laugh, to take life a little less seriously, and to live in complete chaos."

"Admit it, you've loved having your cabinets and bookshelves rearranged."

"Putting my shaving tools in the vegetable crisper went a little too far."

"It was because I'm still upset you haven't come into the salon for another haircut."

"I promise to, now that my face is all over the walls and commercials for it. Any chance you can lay off the sleeping pills that day?"

She pinches my side. "It was to stop an oncoming migraine, but yes, I'll be extra careful with your billion-dollar hair this time, Mr. Luther."

I smile, resting my forehead against hers. "I was fucking miserable without you, baby."

"Big Daddy Hudson told me you were bathing in alcohol."

Palm threading through her hair, I cup the back of her neck. "Is it bad that I want to murder my best friend because you call him Big Daddy?"

Her hand drops to where my dick is springing to life. "Ah, but I know who the real big daddy is."

"My dick is not sharing a name with Hudson Case, so think of something else. Now please, for the love of God, just kiss me."

She closes the distance between our lips and my world rightens.

My heart settles back into a normal rhythm, full from the emotion of having her in my arms again. A woman I truly thought I'd lost.

She fought her demons and came back stronger. To be mine.

Piper moans as our lips fuse, and I part my mouth to let our tongues touch, taking her in deeper. Her body melts against mine and I tighten my hand around her hip to bring her closer. Her taste, her arms looped around my neck, and her sweet citrus scent are the heaven I could get lost in.

We're completely immersed in the feel of one another

when there's another sharp knock on the door that forces us apart.

Piper's stunned eyes look up at me. "Shit! I need to put on my dress!"

I smile, unconcerned, because time feels irrelevant when you have forever.

"I'll let Brandy know to keep the guest entertained. Go get ready and don't rush."

Piper's brows furrow. "Don't rush?! Babe, our guests are waiting for—"

I cover her lips with my finger. "The only person you need to worry about waiting is me. And, *meri jaan*, I'll wait my whole life at the end of that aisle for you if I have to."

Except, a moment later, there's another knock on the door. It's not Brandy, but someone from my security team who opens the door.

"Don't mean to disturb, sir," he says, looking perturbed. "But you both might need to come out to address a little problem."

My hackles rise. "What is it?"

"Sir, a man who says he's your wife's father is here, threatening to go to the media with a photograph."

# thirty-eight
# piper

Rehab Isn't For Me

I was in a bubble for the past ten minutes. A serene and happy bubble with a man who will be my husband in less than an hour. For those few moments where I bared my soul to him, the world had ceased to exist. It was just Dev and me, standing on the brink of our future together.

I was miserable without him this past week. Even as I went through the motions—pretending to work, feigning smiles—I was dying inside. But that negative voice in my head that I'd coddled for far too long insisted I needed the whole week. It whispered that my agony was just a result of my "addiction" to Dev Menon and that I needed "rehabilitation" to take him out of my system.

By last night, I was jonesing so hard for him, I was ready to hook myself up to a Dev Menon IV drip and mainline him into my bloodstream. Turns out rehab isn't for me, and I'm far better off being a junkie.

But now, as Dev's hand finds the small of my back, the bubble bursts and reality comes crashing back.

My heart hammers as my brain tries to catch up with what I just heard. *My father is here?*

We hurriedly follow security out to meet the commotion

outside. My dad, drunk and combative, yells obscenities at the men restraining him while waving the photograph of me with Oscar and Mayer. It's my worst nightmare—the reason I paid him off—come to life.

Dev's dad, Rowan, and Hudson all glare at him disgustedly from a few feet away while Brandy tries to keep the guests in Claire's rose garden, instructing the staff to keep everyone entertained.

"I have proof this marriage is a sham!" my dad spits, looking from me to Dev's dad. "Look at this picture of this good-for-nothing daughter of mine. It's clear she was cheating on your son. I'll go to the press with this!"

Dev and I freeze, though I feel the heat and ire radiating off him. His body stiffens, every muscle charged to retaliate.

I step up, even as my body trembles from the shock of the scene, my eyes pooling with hurt and disbelief. Of course my useless piece of shit father would ruin the happiest day of my life. "You promised that if I paid you, I'd never have to see your loathsome face again."

Dev and Rowan speak at once. "You paid him?!"

I take a trembling breath, looking back to see the disappointment on Dev's face. "I–I thought I was doing the right thing. I wanted him gone and for none of us to have to deal with him."

"Is he the guy who texted you? The one you wouldn't tell me about?" Dev asks.

I nod, swallowing against the jagged stone lodged in my throat. "I'm sorry."

Dev's features soften as he reaches for my face, his hand cupping my jaw. "Sweetheart, you never ever have to deal with *anything* on your own, especially not a cowardly asshole like this one."

I breathe a sigh of relief but it only lasts a second when my dad sing-songs malignantly again, "Looks like you're going to have to pay up again, *sweetheart*."

Deepak's voice cuts through the rising commotion, but my heart drops when he speaks. "I'd like to see the picture."

This is it. That happy little bubble I was in not long ago has burst for good.

It's no secret Deepak never approved of me. And now, in the face of a scandal like this, he'll make his point clear. He might even threaten to take away the company from Dev if he moves forward with marrying me. Even the thought of Dev losing everything he's worked so hard for is too much for me to bear.

A moment later the picture is handed to him, but to my utter shock, he doesn't so much as glance at it. With his furious eyes pinned on my father, he rips the photograph to shreds, throwing it on the ground.

"Let's make one thing clear, Mr. Parker." Deepak's voice is cold and venomous, similar to the voice I've heard my fiancé use when he sees someone so much as look at me the wrong way. "No one threatens my daughter-in-law or my son, no one threatens my family. You think you have dirt on us?" His brow rises indignantly. "I'll have enough on you to bury you twice over, all before the cops even get here. Go ahead and go to the press, see what happens when you take on the daughter-in-law of the most influential family in the world—"

"She's no daughter-in-law. She was a useless box of rocks from the moment she was born. Hell, I don't even know if she's mine!"

"That's enough!" Rowan roars, lunging at the backs of the security team to try to get to our father. "You fucking piece of garbage!"

"And she's still nothing," my dad continues, unperturbed, his hollow, red-rimmed eyes proof of how far gone he is.

God, he looks far worse than just being drunk. He looks

unhinged, like a man lost to all the toxins he's putting into his body.

As much as his words used to stone and mar my soul, I feel nothing for them now. Nothing for him. It's not hate he's spewing for me, it's his own self-loathing that's brought him to this.

He's jealous of my successes and thinks I'm an easy target. Hasn't he always treated women in that way—people to be used and tossed away? His calloused words are no longer strong enough to pierce my resilience and self-worth. I see him for exactly what he is, trash.

"The only thing your slutty so-called daughter-in-law has," he snarls, "are the tits her mom gave—"

But he doesn't have a chance to finish.

Because before I even register he's no longer by my side, my soon-to-be husband has parted the two enormous security staff and punched my father so hard, he goes tumbling to the ground.

A second later, Dev is straddling him, his nostrils flaring and his eyes lost to his rage. My father's blood splatters over Dev's white cuffs and shirt as he continues to unleash his fury on him.

And strangely, that's not the scariest part about the situation. It's the fact that he does it without a spoken word, not even a groan. As if this isn't taking any effort on his part. As if he doesn't want to deign the moment with words, just his fists.

My father is a heaping mess of blood, and likely a broken nose and jaw, as I fly toward Dev along with my brother and Hudson, trying to peel him off my dad before he kills him.

Thankfully, we don't have to do much because Dev lifts off my dad willingly, having made his point clear.

His turbulent eyes settle at the sight of me, and I quickly gather his hands in mine.

My throat feels clogged when I see the ripped skin along

his knuckles. "Oh my God, Dev! Look at your hands." I look up into his eyes, my chin trembling. "I'm so sorry."

Dev leans down to place a kiss on my lips. "No, baby, don't be sorry." He gathers me in his arms. "Just promise me you'll never deal with something like this on your own."

I nod against his chest. "I promise."

My dad is still squirming on the ground when I walk over to him. He glowers at me, but I just stare back at him with both pity and disgust.

My jaw hardens, even as tears leak from my lids. "A father is supposed to be a protector, a champion, and an inspiration for his children. But you were none of those things for us," I say, speaking for me and my brother.

My dad tries to speak, but I bulldoze past him.

"You've never been a father to us, Anthony. Hell, you're barely even a man. And in case it's still not clear to you, let me put it in simple terms." I brush off a tear from my cheek but my voice is unwavering. "I'm no longer your daughter, and I'm *definitely* no longer your victim. You disgust me and you should disgust yourself. Do yourself a favor and get as far away from me as possible."

Dev places a protective arm around my waist, pulling me to his side. And with the calm and composure of a lion looking at his injured prey, he delivers his last words, giving me a glimpse of the mafia don I'd seen once before. "You want to dole out threats, asshole? Well, here's one I'll make sure to follow through with. Get within a hundred-mile radius of my wife from here on out, and I won't just bury you. I'll rip you to shreds and make it look like an accident. You have my fucking word."

# thirty-nine
# dev

Five Schlongs Hen Party

[**Garrett Meyer** has added **Dean Meyer** to the chat]

> GARRETT MEYER
>
> What the hell is going on in there, @Hudson Case and @Dev Menon? I can't be sure, but I thought I saw security holding someone back.

> DEAN MEYER
>
> Yoah, your event planner looks like she's going to have a stroke. This wedding is already turning out to be more dramatic than that episode of *The Boys,* where Mother's Milk gets strangled by a superhero's overextended dick.

> Also, thanks for adding me back to the chat, bro. I realize I might have overreacted to the dick tattoo comment last time. In case anyone is wondering, though, Mala was speechless. It might have been because she had my cock in her mouth but, that's neither here nor there.

**DARIAN MEYER**

Jesus. I'm literally sitting next to your wife. I can't even turn my phone because my wife is on my other side. Can you at least refrain from talking about what you guys do in your bedroom while we're at Dev's wedding?

Also, what kind of shitty programming do you watch?

**DEAN MEYER**

Firstly, how do you know I was talking about our bedroom and not ten minutes ago in Mr. and Mrs. Menon's very ornate hallway bathroom? I'd be extra careful using the luxurious Turkish cotton hand towel if I were you. Secondly, I only watch wholesome classics. I'd recommend it to you, but I'm not sure your wife is old enough to watch R-rated shows.

Anyway, Hudson, what's the deal? What are you guys doing in there for so long? And why haven't we been invited?

**GARRETT MEYER**

I honestly can't believe I shared a womb with you.

**HUDSON CASE**

Everything is fine now. I'm just heading over to Dev's room to get him a new shirt. Any chance one of you can get him an ice pack?

**DARIAN MEYER**

Uh . . . ?

DEAN MEYER

Ice pack? New shirt? What the hell happened? Did he try to pet Piper's hairless pussy and she just wasn't having it? Mala gets that way sometimes when it's the time of the month.

[**Darian Meyer** has left the chat]
[**Dean Meyer** has added **Darian Meyer** to the chat]

DARIAN MEYER

Dude! Rani is literally looking over my shoulder to see what we're chatting about. Can you chill with the cat references?

DEAN MEYER

Who says I was talking about cats? <evil smile emoji>

Anyway, Hudson, as the best man, can you give us a bit more than "everything is fine"? Because needing a new shirt and ice pack sounds about as fine as the time I tried to wax myself. I hope I never see those same nurses in the ER.

HUDSON CASE

Let's just say I saw another side of our reserved billionaire friend today. And so did Piper's asshole dad. Turns out our friend has a right hook that could lay someone out faster than your morning breath, Dean.

GARRETT MEYER

Holy shit! Dev punched his father-in-law?!

DEAN MEYER

And we missed all the action while we were out here, eating hors d'oeuvres and listening to U2 play the classics?! I mean, not that I'm complaining. The hors d'oeuvres were amazing, and I might have sprung a boner for Bono when he sang "Sunday Bloody Sunday". I kid you not, he was looking right at me.

Also, that song seems ironic now.

DARIAN MEYER

Hudson, is everything okay now? Garrett is heading inside to help get an ice pack. Do you need anything else?

HUDSON CASE

Just make sure the guests stay calm. Oh, and definitely have a stiff drink ready for our boy once he's finally hitched. Actually, make it a bottle.

## forty
# piper

A Beautiful Day

My wedding day was never my childhood dream—it wasn't even a passing thought. Not when love always felt as fragile as a sandcastle against an oncoming wave, as fleeting as a single raindrop in a barren desert.

But as I stand here, at the end of a long rose-petal-strewn aisle, my eyes affixed to the man responsible for changing my outlook, my heart, and my life, the thought of not seeing this day—not being with him—feels ludicrous.

Deena walks down the aisle, tossing flower petals in both directions, while our guests watch her with warm smiles. Thankfully, most seem to have forgiven us for starting the ceremony an hour and a half later—an overall short delay, given the events that were packed into that time.

As much as I wish I'd had a chance to talk with him after we separated, the most Dev and I were able to do after watching security haul my father away was hold each other for a few moments.

He'd cupped my face, like he always did, and asked me if I was okay before I'd grasped his hands and kissed his bloody knuckles, while teetering on the brink of tears. But there wasn't any time for a longer conversation because before we knew it, we were both being whisked off to change.

I look up to find Dev's eyes lingering at the entrance from where I'm to emerge. Though I can see him and the rest of the guests, I've managed to stay hidden.

My bridesmaids—Nisha, Sarina, Shay, and Jeena—walk down the aisle, hands tucked inside the elbows of Dev's groomsmen. Hudson, Dean, Darian, and Garrett escort my friends and sister-in-law to the end of the aisle, where they split off into their respective sides.

I look to my right and then my left, at the two men who will be giving me away—my brother and my father-in-law—and am struck with another bout of emotion. Until fifteen minutes ago, I hadn't expected Deepak in this role. But with the way he showed up for me today, with warmth and protectiveness, it felt right to ask him.

Sure, it was unconventional, but honestly, has anything between me and Dev ever followed any rules or traditions? Why should this be any different?

Deepak offers me a warm smile before he clears his throat. "I–I wanted to apologize to you, Piper. You didn't deserve my harsh critique or my cool demeanor. I've seen the light you've brought to our family, the way you've made my son smile and the comfort you've brought to my wife in her final days. I can't thank you enough. You're a gift to our family, and I want you to know how proud I am to call you my daughter."

A shaky breath runs through me, and his words are nearly my undoing. I squeeze his hand, the only response I can muster, when my brother's voice finds my other ear.

"You ready, Pepper?"

I turn to meet his eyes, the same color as mine. "I've never been more ready for anything in my whole life."

"You look beautiful, by the way."

I smile. "Thank you. I'm sorry you're missing a game for me today, baby brother."

He shakes his head, whispering softly to ensure my father-in-law doesn't hear, "You think I give two shits about a game when my sister is getting married to a man not named after a sausage? I've never been more proud."

I giggle, but even as I do, my emotions get the best of me and I take in another shuddering breath, looking from him to the guests outside.

They're all here.

The most important people in our lives. Here for us.

My eyes immediately fly to Claire, quietly taking everything in from her wheelchair in the front row. Thankfully, she'd been taken to her room to rest for a few minutes during the chaos so she's unaware of what went down. The smile on her face and the tears in her eyes are proof that today is one of the happiest moments in her life.

Her wish came true.

My wish—one I hadn't even made until very recently—came true.

My gaze finds Dev again, dipping to his dimple before dragging down his tux. Has anyone ever in the history of time had a more handsome groom?

I highly doubt it.

His smile broadens as the guests coo and giggle, and I notice someone else has stolen everyone's attention. Someone with four legs and a tail held up, right along with her chin, while wearing a custom-made Indian bridal skirt that matches mine.

Hey? Why shouldn't she get to marry her first love today, too? Neither of us imagined this for ourselves and now that it's happening, we're going to bask in the joy of it.

Our guests laugh while Vajayjay does what I'd helped her practice all week—walking down the aisle to push her button.

More laughter erupts when the electronic sound emits, speaking her words, *"I love you, Dev!"*

She pushes it a few more times—definitely not what we'd practiced, but apparently, she wants to set the record straight—making everyone laugh some more, including my groom. Then, she steps on the button she was supposed to push much later, making everyone erupt in applause.

*"I do."*

*"I do."*

*"I do."*

I shake my head, giggling as Dev drops down to pick her up. He scratches her under her head, letting her lick the side of his face, before he turns to Hudson to ask him for something. Hudson reaches into his pocket, pulling out a very blinged-out collar that Dev affixes around my cat's neck to the cheers of our guests.

Like I said, we like to keep things unconventional around here.

Once my spotlight-stealing cat is taken away to hang out with her siblings in another room, our pillow bearers, Rome, and my brother's stepson, Kai, walk down the aisle, carrying my special vows with them.

Deepak, Rowan, and I move forward to the end of the aisle and the moment our guests spot us, a ripple of hushed murmurs sweep through our guests as they take in the sight of me in my bridal attire. I catch Claire's eyes, her smile beaming as she looks at my *lehenga* and the jewels she'd passed down to me, her eyes lingering on the head ornament carefully centered in my hair.

My throat constricts, knowing she's likely recalling herself in similar garb and the same jewels when she got married.

Dev's eyes shimmer at the sight of me, his jaw visibly clenching with emotion as *U2* starts our song, *"Beautiful Day,"* right on cue.

Rome and Kai reach Dev, offering tokens of my love on velvet pillows. I watch as Dev reaches for the envelope on Kai's pillow, his usually steady hands trembling slightly as he takes out the item I'd placed inside.

Our eyes meet, recognition falling over him, as he silently reads the note I scrawled under the photograph I'd purchased in Disneyland after we exited Space Mountain. While everyone else is captured mid-scream as we hurtled down the final drop, I'm in a trance all on my own, looking directly at Dev with an expression of pure, unadulterated love.

*"The moment I knew I'd fallen, impossibly and irrevocably, in love with you."*

Dev stares at me across the aisle, his usually calm pools of brown turbulent with emotion. The photograph trembles in his hand lightly as he tucks it into his jacket pocket, right above his heart, before reaching for the item on Rome's pillow —a crossword I'd made just for us.

I watch as his eyebrows furrow. A smile erupts across his lips as he scans the clues and answers, each one a snapshot of our journey:

*Our favorite post-sex activity.* (Answer: crosswords)

*Name of the restaurant where we first ate together.* (Answer: Sakura)

*The meaning of* meri jaan *in English.* (Answer: sweetheart)

*The number of times I'll tell you I love you.* (Answer: infinite)

His smile grows with each clue and answer he reads, but it's the last one that has a tear dropping from his pooled lids.

*What you'll be to me from this day forward.* (Answer: husband)

God, my knees almost buckle at the sight of him as he looks up, eyes glistening as they connect with mine. There's so much love and adoration there. And even though my entire being begs me to run to him, to let him gather me in his arms, I stand my ground, savoring the moment.

A moment I'd never imagined, but a moment that's truly mine.

A man who's truly mine.

And as Bono's voice charges the air around us, I feel his words inside my bones.

It's a beautiful day.

# forty-one
# piper

What Heartbreak Is

**Two Months Later . . .**

My hand rises to knock on their bedroom door, currently ajar, but halts when I hear Deepak's murmured words. He's speaking to his wife as she lays on her bed, his voice a broken whisper, filled with a lifetime of love.

"Claire, my love," he whispers, his voice thick and raw. "God . . . I wish I could go with you."

A throaty sob rumbles softly through his chest. "Please, sweetheart, take me with you. I can't live without you. I can't —" His forehead drops to her shoulder, his body quaking. "I can't fathom a day without you. You're my whole life."

The teacup shakes in my hand, the tea I'd made for Claire almost spilling over the sides. The lump I usually have in my throat at the sight of my beautiful, nurturing mother-in-law doubles as I desperately hold back a sob. A curtain of hot tears blur my vision, pooling inside my lids.

I knew our time was coming to an end . . .

But I didn't think it would be here already.

Not when we should have had so many more moments to share, to live.

"Deepak," Claire says weakly, running her shaking fingers down the back of his head. "Love of my life." She pauses, taking a labored breath. "Don't make this harder for me than it already is. We'll see each other again, sweetheart. I'll be waiting for you, but I'll be patient."

"No." Deepak shakes his head, his desperate plea begging for his fate to change.

"I have loved you," Claire continues, her fingers still running through his hair, "since we met all those years ago at the museum in Santa Fe." Her chest rattles with another breath. "Remember how we marveled at that painting of roses for so long?"

"It's when I found out you loved them so much," he murmurs, a ghost of a smile in his voice.

"And you sent me a bouquet of them for months until you finally convinced me to move to California."

"Because I knew then what I knew every day with you . . ." He sniffs. "That I couldn't live without you. Not a moment and not a lifetime."

A strangled sound erupts from his throat, and I place a hand over my lips to muffle my own cry. I shouldn't be here to witness such a private moment between them, but their love and heartbreak keeps me frozen in my spot, my heart both begging me to leave while urging me to stay.

Claire sighs, and I don't have to see her face to know her cheeks are lined with tears. "I'll give you all my lifetimes, Deepak Menon. Take them all. But I need you to live, to thrive, for our children. I know Dev has found Piper, but he still needs you. He still loves you. And Deena needs you more than ever to be both her mom and her dad."

Deepak's shoulders continue to shake as he reluctantly and heartbreakingly accepts his fate.

For the past two months, Dev and I have been living here with Deepak and Claire so that we don't miss a moment with her. Because God knows, we'll miss all the moments after this . . . Every shared smile, the peaceful moments in her garden when she'd reach for my hand, and each adoring look toward her husband and children. They're all slipping away.

I lean against the wall, needing it to hold me upright. The tea grows cold, long forgotten, as tears run down my face. My heart shreds inside my chest, breaking for this family I've come to love as my own and for my proud and stoic father-in-law—a man I've come to care for as a father—crumbling and helpless at the feet of his dying wife.

"Promise me you'll be there for our kids," Claire pleads softly. "Promise to show them love daily. They need you, Deepak—"

"They need *you*," he cries, his voice cracking. A tear slips from his eye and drops to her chest when he lifts to look at her. "I need you."

Claire's shaky finger finds his chest. "You have me, right here. You will always have me, my love. Always."

There's a moment of silence, broken only by Deepak's sobs, and I realize that there have been very few moments over the past couple of weeks where Claire has been lucid enough to hold a conversation. And while I bring her tea every day, most of the time it lies untouched on her nightstand. It's both gut wrenching and relieving to see her be conscious.

But I know it won't last . . .

Suddenly, Claire's head turns gently on her pillow and her pale eyes connect with mine. And even as a tender smile turns up her lips, my heart drops to my stomach, as if knowing we're in our final moments together.

"Piper . . ." she says, reaching out her hand as I rush to her side.

Leaving the teacup on her nightstand, I tangle my fingers with hers, my tears flowing in endless streams over my face. My throat is so tight, I'm not sure I'll ever find my voice again.

It's then that I understand what heartbreak is.

It isn't just an emotion, it's a state of being and a reluctant realization that your world is about to be altered forever. It's both a deafening silence and a quiet cacophony that somehow weighs more than anything else you've had to carry.

"Call Dev and Deena, honey," she says softly, but her words thunder inside my ears, pulling a sob out of my chest. "I ... I think it's time for me to say goodbye."

# epilogue

Piper - Six Months Later

"Rome, sweetheart, look up or you'll miss most of the game," Sarina says with a mix of exasperation and affection in her voice.

Rome reluctantly lowers the hardback in his hands, *"Spacey Cadets Space Facts,"* squinting against the bright sunlight to look at the baseball pitch. He's wearing his favorite NASA hat, with its bill far too low on his forehead, and glasses that depict Mercury today, along with a Bay Area Blazers jersey Dev bought for him.

We're all wearing the team's jerseys, in fact, sitting on our plush recliners—Sarina and I flanking Rome on each side, with Dev on my other side—right behind home plate in the owner's box, courtesy of my husband, who is now a minority stakeholder for the Bay Area Blazers.

Dev's thumb caresses mine before he brings our entangled fingers to his lips and presses a soft kiss on my ring.

A ring I hold dear, not only because of the man who gave it to me, but because of the woman it originally belonged to. A woman who we'll forever miss for as long as we live.

After saying her goodbyes to her children like she'd wanted to, Claire passed peacefully with all of us at her side.

But there's not a day that goes by where we don't miss her.

For weeks after her passing, there were nights I'd cry myself to sleep on Dev's chest, and days I'd hold him while he sobbed into mine.

She'd taken a piece of our souls with her.

But she'd given a piece of hers in return.

I used that piece of her soul, and all the love she gave to me in such a short amount of time, to create my own rose garden in our backyard this spring.

In fact, just like Claire's, I can see it through our kitchen and have spent many of my mornings out there, drinking tea just like she used to, thanking her for everything she did for me.

Who knew that her one wish to see her son married would become a wish I didn't even know I had—to find the greatest love of my life? Whether intentionally or not, she willed my happily-ever-after into existence, and I'll always be grateful for that.

Deepak and Deena were wrecked after Claire's passing but have slowly found a way to move forward. And though it took Deepak a while to emerge from his grief, he never forgot the promises he made to his wife at the end—to love and be there for his children.

He's spending more time with both of them, making a conscious effort to be present. With Deena, he's learning to balance being both a mother and a father, giving her the emotional support she needs as she heads into adolescence. With Dev, he's working on mending their previous relationship and establishing new traditions, like weekly long hikes where they talk more as friends, rather than father and son.

Recently, he's taken his hands off *Menon Inc.*—working only as an advisor to Dev—and using his time to get more involved doing community projects and charity work.

We've started weekly family dinners, which have helped us

all stay connected. Deepak hasn't just made a big effort to reconnect with his kids—something I know they appreciate—he's also been incredibly caring and supportive of me, which is a far cry from what I can say about my own father. The last I heard, he ended up in jail, serving a long sentence for embezzlement and fraud.

I turn to connect my eyes with the man I love more than life itself, giving him a smile that he returns before he leans in for a kiss.

"I love you," I say, because those are three words I'll never tire of saying to him.

"I love you, too, *meri jaan*." He plants another kiss on my lips before our gazes are snagged by Rome turning another page in his book.

Now, I'm not a huge baseball enthusiast myself, but Dev's helped me learn the game better over the past few months, given he's always loved it. But more recently, he's been trying to get Rome excited about baseball as well, given Sarina has expressed her concerns that her son wants to do nothing but read all day. She's worried he doesn't get enough time in the sun and wants him to learn a sport.

Dev leans around me to grab Rome's attention. "Hey, buddy. Want me to explain what's happening? Don't hesitate to ask if you're wondering what's going on."

Rome shrugs, but I don't miss the flicker of curiosity in his eyes when he lays the book back down on his lap to watch the players take their positions.

"Is that Troy Winters pitching?" my nephew asks, pointing at the man jogging toward the pitcher's mound. "The player whose jersey I'm wearing?"

Dev beams proudly, his adorable dimple in full display. "Yep! You've been memorizing those baseball cards I got you!" He nods, looking back at Troy. "He's one of the best pitchers in the MLB."

Rome nods. "He had two-hundred-forty-one strikeouts last season and pitched one-hundred-ninety innings."

Both Dev and I exchange wide glances before I look over at Sarina with the same look of amazement.

"Holy moly, little man!" I say, poking my nephew on the side of his stomach and making him giggle. "How are you such a little encyclopedia of everything?"

He just shrugs again before we all watch Troy throw his first pitch.

One after another, Troy sends the ball flying toward the batter, only for them to strike out, making the crowd inside the stadium roar.

But the most interesting reaction to take place inside our little space in the owner's suite isn't the way Rome drops his hardback on the ground and jumps with both hands up, cheering for Troy, but the look on Sarina's face as she stares at the picture that just appeared of the Blazers' pitcher on the TV monitor. Her face is drained of color as if she's seen a ghost.

My brows draw together. "Sarina? Is everything okay? Why do you look the same way you did before I made you go skydiving with me?"

Her startled eyes collide with mine. "Is that really *Troy Winters*?"

I nod, flicking my gaze from the TV to hers. "Why?"

Her elbows find her knees before she rubs her face, but I don't miss the way her lips form the word, "Shit" so that her son doesn't hear.

"Sarina?" I say again, worried I'm missing a clue I should have seen earlier. "What's this about?"

She shakes her head just as the crowd goes wild again, along with Dev and Rome, for another play, not paying attention to us. "I'll tell you later."

The innings go on until the final out is called, with the

Blazers clinching a narrow victory. Dev and Rome exchange high-fives, and I know I definitely show my enthusiasm too, but my mind has been whirling around my best friend and what she hasn't told me. Throughout the game, she's been biting her thumbnail like it's a snack.

As we all get out of our seats, I'm hoping to ask Sarina more about why she's acting like a freak when Dev turns to Rome and says, "So, what do you think about meeting the players up close?"

Rome's eyes light up. "Really?! Even Troy Winters?"

Dev shrugs. "I mean, you are wearing his jersey, after all."

Rome starts to bounce on his feet when Sarina interrupts, "Actually, it doesn't look like we have time. I have something I need to get back for, so maybe next time."

I squint at her. Yeah, she's not telling me something, and it clearly has something to do with the pitcher for our MLB team. "What do you have to get back for?"

She swallows. "Uh, cheerleading practice."

Dev, Rome, and I all stare at her with various expressions of surprise and concern.

"Cheerleading practice," I repeat without much inflection, trying to keep myself from smiling. "Since when did you start cheerleading?"

She props her purse over her shoulder before waving her hand dismissively. "Since yesterday." She nods. "Yeah, I, um . . . wanted to get more active. You know how much I always wanted to be a cheerleader. Even in high school, I'd try to practice jumping in the air and touching both my feet. Well, I'm trying to do that now, you know . . . going after my dreams and all."

What the ever-loving fuck is she going on about?

"Anyway," she says, hiking her purse strap up even higher and taking Rome's hand. "Honey, we should get—"

"But Mom!" Rome protests. "I want to meet Troy! You're

the one who told me to get interested in a sport, and now that I am, you're making me leave early?"

I give her a look that says, "*Yeah, what's the dealio, weirdo? The kid has a point,*" to which she just glares back at me.

"Well, like I said, I'm running late for—"

"Troy!" Rome blurts out, his mouth spread in a huge smile, looking from Dev to the Blazers' pitcher, who's coming into the owner's suite with a couple more players on the team. "Dev, look! It's Troy!"

To my best friend's chagrin, my nephew's energy is palpable. Apparently, his voice loud enough to reach said pitcher's ears as well, because not even ten seconds later, Troy Winters is standing in front of us.

Interestingly, the person no longer standing in front of us? The one currently pretending to look for something underneath the chairs, her head entirely burrowed under one? Yup, my best friend, Sarina Arora.

"Hey, Dev!" Troy says, shaking hands with my husband. "How's it going?"

"Good! Congratulations! What a great game today!" Dev responds.

"Thanks!" Troy rocks back on his heels, his silvery-hazel eyes flicking from Dev to me to Rome under his baseball hat. "Is this your wife and son?"

Now, I'm not going to lie. Troy Winters is a beautiful man. He's not quite my type, since I've recently learned mine comes in the form of a six-foot-something, tanned complexion, dark eyes, a dimpled cheek, and with an ass to make angels weep, but he'd be someone's type. A lot of someones, in fact.

"This is my wife," Dev says, introducing me, to which I give Troy a quick handshake. "And this is my . . . nephew, Rome."

My heart flutters at the term my husband just used to

describe Rome. God, there is no end to the way he makes me fall in love with him every day.

"Hi!" Rome reaches out a small hand to grasp Troy's, his eyes glimmering with awe. "I'm Roman Kabir Arora-Weston, but you can call me Rome."

"Whoa!" Troy reels back, eyes wider than Rome's. "That's quite a name there, Rome! Thanks for wearing my jersey!"

Rome gleams, and I only half-listen to Dev tell Troy about how Rome's gotten into baseball recently—omitting the fact that the interest may have spurred during this game, in fact—because I'm too busy watching my best friend, who's still crouching in front of the seats, pretending to look for an item she never lost.

Seriously, what in the world is happening to her?

"Oh, and this is my mom!" Rome exclaims, pointing to the woman in question.

Sarina's head pops up and a mix of panic and embarrassment flash across her face.

"Found it!" she says, jumping with her hand in the air, pinching an imaginary item before then putting it into her mouth.

Yes . . . in her mouth.

*What. The. Hell?*

She pretends to chew it thoughtfully for an entire five seconds before jutting her hand out toward the pitcher. He's looking at her with a similar but different shocked expression than the rest of us. Honestly, I have never seen this person before—this version of my usually composed and quick-witted best friend—and I'm not sure how to feel about it.

"*Rina*?" Troy says, eyes turning to saucers as he takes her hand. "Wh–what are you doing here?"

"Hey, Troy *Trojan*." She chuckles awkwardly. "Long time, no see."

Swati M.H.

THE END!

**If you enjoyed reading Pretend For Me, please consider leaving a review. Your support means the world to me!**

**Make sure to Pre-order <u>PITCH FOR ME</u>** - Sarina and Troy's single mom, sports romcom!

**Want more of the Five Schlongs Hen Party?**
Read Darian, Garrett, Dean, and Hudson's stories next!
**Read the ELEMENTS OF RAPTURE Series!**

- Read ADRIFT—**Darian & Rani's** forbidden, single dad/nanny romance
- Jump into ASCEND—**Garrett & Bella's** marriage of convenience, single mom romance
- Don't miss ABLAZE—**Dean & Mala's** angsty brother's best friend, friends-to-lovers slowburn romance
- Download ABYSS—**Hudson & Kavi's** enemies-to-lovers, best friend's dad, office romance

**Read MOTHER PUCKER**—a single mom, hockey romance and **Rowan and Shay's** hilarious story (part of the MomComs universe)

# Pretend For Me

*Scan the code to find all my books!*

# about the author

Swati M.H. writes stories full of humor, heart, and heartbreak that always end in an HEA. She lives in the Bay Area with her incredibly patient husband, two beautiful daughters, and her pitbull, Sadie Sapphire. Her days start with caffeine and sometimes end with a glass (or three) of wine.

Swati loves staying in touch with her readers. Find her at www.swatimh.com or through Facebook and Instagram. Be sure to join her Sweeties reader group for daily fun.

# acknowledgments

In my acknowledgements for my last release, Abyss, I'd written a bittersweet farewell to the characters from the Elements of Rapture series, not having realized that they'd be showing up again in a very fun way in this book.

I have no idea what inspired me to create the Five Schlongs Hen Party text threads in this book and bring the MMCs from the Elements of Rapture back but I am so glad I did because I had a ton of fun writing them.

Will you see more of the Five Schlongs in the next book? I guess you'll have to read it to find out :)

As with all my books, I want to thank so many people for the support and encouragement.

I'll start with my husband and kids for their patience and love. They are truly my rocks. Hell, they're my boulders, my earth, the foundation that keeps me grounded.

A huge thank you to my PA, Stephanie Rash for being such an incredible friend, support, a badass and chaos coordinator. You're always willing to step up to any challenge I throw at you, and I so appreciate you for that.

A sincere thanks to my editor, Silvia Curry for being so phenomenal in what you do. I'm lucky to have found you.

Thank you to my friend and alpha reader Rachel C. for inspiring me to write Vajayjay and sending me cat videos on Instagram. I can't tell you how much your support, friendship, and your stamp of approval on a manuscript mean to me. Thank you also for coming up with the name for the Five Schlongs Hen Party! It was flipping perfect!

Thank you also to my friend and alpha reader, Sarah Beth. Sarah with an "h", I had so much fun giggling and chatting about Dev and Piper's story on our long voice memos and coming up with more and more ridiculous things. I can't even think about the rabbit voyeurism scene without thinking about how much MORE outlandish it was in our conversations. :)

Thank you to my lovely friend and alpha reader, Namita. I have no words to thank you for your daily/weekly encouragement and support. You're the ultimate cheerleader and I am so grateful for our chats, and for having found you as both a reader and friend.

Thank you also to Michelle M. for always jumping into the manuscript even when I know how tiring your day job is, and giving me your inputs after the chapters. Your comments and feedback have always helped to make my stories stronger.

Thank you Amarilys for being such a wonderful cheerleader and alpha reader. So glad Dev and Piper made you giggle. I am so grateful for your support and friendship.

A huge thank you to Sierra Sisler for your incredible insight, detailed feedback, and support for Pretend For Me. You're amazing!

Thank you also to my beta readers, Daisy Pham, Morgan Evans, Charity Johnson, and Kayla Pocernich for being so wonderful about jumping in and beta-reading this baby for me. I appreciate you all so much.

P.S. Daisy, your creativity on the swag still amaze me; thank you for the detailed texts as you read the manuscript. I LOVED hearing your thoughts on each chapter!

A special thank you to an author I admire, Pippa Grant. You gave authors some sage advice about unleashing our inner creative lunatics (I'm paraphrasing but you get the gist), especially when writing a romcom. I took your words to heart as clearly seen in this work of unhingement and ridiculousness :)

So, Pippa, I owe it to you for encouraging me to color outside the lines.

A huge thank you to my wonderful author friends (you know who you are!), my street team, and my ARC readers. I am so lucky to have you on my side. Thank you for your continuous support!

And to my readers—I love you! Thank you from the bottom of my heart for reading this book and probably side-eyeing me in a few scenes. I hope Dev and Piper made you chuckle and lightened your day!

Made in the USA
Coppell, TX
27 January 2026

69217240R10203